MASTER SWITCH

MASTER SWITCH

A NOVEL OF ESPIONAGE

William Stender

PEACHTREE

ATLANTA

Published by
PEACHTREE PUBLISHERS, LTD.
494 Armour Circle NE
Atlanta, Georgia 30324

Jacket illustration by John Christopher
Composition by Dana Celentano

Manufactured in the United States of America

10 9 8 7 6 5 4 3 2 1
First Edition

Library of Congress Cataloging-in-Publication Data

Stender, William H.
          Master Switch / William H. Stender.
                    p. cm.
          ISBN 1-56145-132-0 (hc)
          I. Title.
PS3569.T3816M37   1996
813'.54—dc20   96-14679
                                                                CIP

Dedicated to memories of my father,
The Reverend William H. Stender

FROM THE CONGRESSIONAL RECORD
JANUARY 15TH, 1992

Honorable James J. Jordan
House Committee on Government Activities

These hearings were convened in order to determine the
cause of irregularities in performance of the PATRIOT
surface-to-air missile system during the recent war in the
Persian Gulf known as Desert Storm. We have heard the
testimony of recognized experts from the United States
Army, the Raytheon Company, other countries and various
technical organizations, but this testimony has varied
widely and often conflicted on key points. All of our
allocated resources have been expended, yet this committee
has not been able to reach any definitive conclusion about
these peculiar events of the conflict except that there was
a dramatic difference between the performance of PATRIOT in
Israel and Saudi Arabia and the underlying reasons may
never be known. Why any system should do nearly twice as
well in one country than another is beyond me, but I find
it hard to believe it is a coincidence or just the luck of
the draw. The Army either doesn't know or isn't telling,
and this Committee, after six months of exhaustive work,
doesn't seem to have the capability to find out.

PROLOGUE

JANUARY 1991

He was lying on the beach sand soaking up the sun's heat, and then he was floating lazily in the swells. Slowly the water pulled him out to sea. As the current pushed him toward high cliffs, a mournful cry rose up from the rocks ahead. He was approaching the ragged shoreline and he struggled to reach the sandy floor, but the foothold he gained was barely enough to keep his face above the water and breathe. The cry from the cliff top became a scream and grew louder until he felt his eardrums would rupture. Then water turned to fire. He opened his mouth in a silent scream and breathed in the flames. In desperation, he gulped the deepest breath possible and prepared for fire to consume him. Just as the flames engulfed him, he bolted upright on the Army cot, realized he was having a nightmare, and recognized the air raid alert siren all in an instant.

People were shouting and running in all directions. Over the noise, he recognized Sergeant Johnson's voice calling his name. Soaked with nightmare sweat and not fully coherent, Captain Jerry Maxwell, Commander of Bravo Battery, 4th Battalion, 43rd Artillery (PATRIOT), United States Army, heard his voice crack as he answered the call. His wet body shivered as the memory of fire forced its way to his consciousness.

Reaching for his equipment beside the cot, he slipped into his flak jacket, grabbed his helmet and boots, and started to ready himself for combat. In the few moments it took to tie his boots, the bulky figure of Sergeant Johnson was hovering over him.

"How much time have we got?" He had to shout to be heard above the noise of the siren and the activity around him.

"No idea, sir, but the siren's been going for several minutes. Are you ready?" Johnson seemed ready to pick him up and carry him if he wasn't.

"I am now. Let's go."

The hefty sergeant and lanky captain sprinted through the crowd on a dead run. A guard at the hastily arranged security post surrounding the PATRIOT radar and fire control equipment watched them approaching and pulled away the crude barbed wire gate so they could pass through. They reached the PATRIOT Engagement Control Station and leapt up the few stairs to the landing. As Jerry came through the van door and headed for the console, an engagement was already in progress.

"What have we got?" Jerry pulled on a radio headset and leaned over the lieutenant who sat in the tactical control officer's chair on the right side of the van.

"Incoming, Captain, but they're not in our missile's range." The answer came from the young operator seated next to the lieutenant.

"What about the Israelis?" Jerry asked.

"They're close, but we can't tell for sure," the lieutenant said.

The U.S. PATRIOTs were not tied into the Israeli systems through a radio data link, so the U.S. soldiers only had a good guess as to where their systems were located and which way their radars were directed. On the display, Jerry could see the computer-generated symbols for the enemy missiles moving steadily west.

"Were we able to get an idea of the launch location?"

"No, sir, but somebody did. The radio's been overloaded with directions to the fly-boys already in the air."

"PATRIOT's away! The Israelis are firing." Johnson leaned over the operator's shoulder watching the display. His experienced eye tracked the symbols on the radar screen as they left the Israeli sites.

"New targets!" announced the operator while he moved the computer cursor over the targets that appeared on the edge of the display at the maximum range of the radar system. In a few moments, the target symbol changed to the small triangle that was used exclusively for incoming missiles, and a small, square display appeared on the screen giving the detailed data on the new targets. The predicted ground impact point of the incoming SCUDs began flashing. No one said a word as the flashing indicator danced on the screen, and then stabilized on a position well inside their assigned sector.

"How many targets?"

"I can't tell for sure yet, Captain, but there's more than one."

Jerry's eyes went to the firing platoon status panel that showed four launchers were up and ready—sixteen PATRIOT missiles set for firing. The panel of lights indicated that two more launchers were down for maintenance. Two more were on stand-by and would be operational as soon as the crews could get them ready. The siren and all of the activity surely meant they were already at it, but Jerry decided it would be better to check anyway. He looked to Sergeant Johnson, who nodded and moved toward the van door. Jerry knew he was thinking the same thing and was on his way to check with the launcher crews.

"Four targets. Time to first launch ninety seconds." The tactical control assistant sounded as though he had done this for years, but this was his first combat experience. It was, in fact, a first for all of them.

The target symbol on the radar display changed again, this time to indicate that Bravo Battery had been recognized by the Battalion Information Coordination Central as the PATRIOT system that would intercept the SCUDs.

"Well," Jerry said. "It looks like we're going to make history tonight."

"That must make about the fourth time since we got the call to come here."

"Yeah," Jerry said. "But this time it's history with a capital H. Looks like this time we're going to shoot."

"I heard that," the operator said and smiled broadly.

Everybody watched the radar screen targets move steadily to the west.

"Time to first launch seventy seconds." The operator moved the cursor on the screen again. "There are now six targets."

"Shit," Jerry let out under his breath.

"Where in hell did more targets come from?" the lieutenant asked, showing signs of nervousness.

"Don't know," Jerry said, "but it doesn't look good. It could be decoys or electronic countermeasures."

"I thought Saddam wasn't supposed to have anything that sophisticated," added Sergeant Johnson as he stepped back into the van and moved to Captain Maxwell's right side.

"He isn't," Jerry agreed. "The target could be dropping a booster or breaking up, but I don't remember anything from Intelligence that said these SCUDs break up in flight."

"We don't know for sure those sons of bitches are SCUDS," the operator was getting more excited.

"Yeah," Sergeant Johnson chuckled. "But I'll bet my month's paycheck that they're Saddam's prima donna SCUDs, all the way."

"What's our PATRIOT gonna do if the target breaks up before we get there?" the operator asked.

"I don't know for sure," Jerry said. "But I do know there's nothing we can do about it now."

"Still six targets," the operator said, bending low over the display. "Time to first launch thirty seconds."

Jerry studied the radar screen. He could now see the SCUDs were really farther apart than they first appeared. From the small display, it was impossible to tell whether they were aimed for different points on the ground, or if the intelligence reports were right and the SCUDs were just uncontrollable.

"Does anybody remember what's on the ground at those splashdowns?" Jerry asked.

No one answered.

"Six targets, time to first launch ten seconds."

Everybody in the van began a silent countdown. There was nothing else to do. The system was fully automatic at this point, and their role was to observe and be ready to insert themselves into the process only when they judged the system's computer wasn't doing what was best.

"Fire command." The operator paused melodramatically. "Fire two." Another pause. "Fire three."

The boom and roar of the first missile launch sounded from the launching area, and a slight tremor from the pressure of the rocket shook the van. The other missiles could be heard in a steady rhythm along with the sergeant's continuing monotone count of the launches.

"God, we're putting out a lot of missiles," Jerry said, as much to himself as to anyone in the van.

"Fire nine." The operator's continued count echoed Jerry's concern. He felt a shiver run through his whole body.

"You okay?" Sergeant Johnson asked.

"I'm okay, thanks. I was having a dream when you woke me. It was probably just the screaming of the siren that got to me, but I can still feel the sweat on my tee shirt."

"Yeah, I know what you mean. One of those splashdown points is going to be pretty close."

"MISSILE FOUR PREMATURE DESTRUCT!" the Lieutenant blurted. Suddenly the operator's calm was changed to raw excitement. Jerry strained to interpret the data on the screen to see if he could tell which splashdown point missile four was protecting, but he couldn't.

"Override the engagement evaluation and re-engage the target. Now!" Jerry made the command as though he had practiced this maneuver when in fact, it wasn't clear if it could even be done. When engaging airplanes, there was plenty of time to re-evaluate the target if a PATRIOT missile failed for some reason. This allowed the system to confirm that the aircraft was still threatening and then make a new decision to engage. But these weren't airplanes. These were SCUD missiles, and, while the crew had no battle experience, they knew they didn't have extra time. This was the first missile-against-missile war in history, an unprecedented scenario.

The operator's fingers clicked feverishly at the keyboard, punctuating the silence.

"We can't, sir," said the tactical control officer. "It's too late. We can't get there in time."

"New targets." Sergeant Johnson announced, still standing beside Jerry. As Jerry was adjusting his eyes to the new targets, an urgent voice called out from his radio headset.

"Bravo Six, this is Hotel Six. What happened to that missile?" Jerry recognized the voice of Lieutenant Colonel Hamilton, his Battalion Commander.

"I don't know, sir. It just blew up. It might've been some kind of malfunction on the missile, but the track looked good from here. We've got new targets."

Over the headset, Jerry heard an explosion in the background at Colonel Hamilton's location. There was an anxious pause while he waited to see if there was still someone on the other end of the line. Then he felt the pressure from the explosion and the accompanying "crump" that came with the SCUD detonation, and he remembered from his missile training course in El Paso that several sounds would be immediately recognizable the first time they are heard—incoming hostile fire in combat was one of them.

"Yeah, I see 'em on my screen, too." Colonel Hamilton's voice on the radio brought him back from his thoughts. "They're closer to you, but I'm going to have these guys give them to Alpha, just in case."

"Roger." Jerry exhaled, relieved that Hamilton hadn't been hit by the SCUD, but his face showed his resentment at the implication that something was wrong with their PATRIOT.

"Well, you'd do the same if it was you," said Sergeant Johnson as he removed his headset.

"Yeah, you're right. I reckon it's just too damn important. But I'd sure like to be able to show our system's okay."

"Somehow, I have a feeling our time will come again soon enough."

The crew watched the radar display screen as though hypnotized while the high technology battle raged on in the skies overhead. Machine against machine. Missile against missile. Bullet against bullet. The data flowing from the computer of their PATRIOT system showed that all other intercepts had been probable kills. The symbols for the PATRIOT missiles from Alpha

Battery appeared as the new targets were engaged. Some of the splashdown points were close to those engaged by Bravo Battery. The movement of the symbols on the radar screen indicated that Alpha Battery might have had a missile failure, too. When the battle was finally over and the screen showed no missiles from either side in the area, Jerry turned away from the console.

"Well," he announced, the dejection clear in his voice, "we can look forward to a full investigation of maintenance procedures and missile record checks. Our battery never had one fail during peacetime tests, and now we've had a failure on our first combat mission."

"I wonder if it had something to do with how fast we had to go just to get here?" the operator asked.

"Hell," Sergeant Johnson said. "What makes you think that was fast? Just because last Tuesday you were sitting in Germany, drinking beer, playing with your kids and watching the war on television?"

"Yeah, and now it's Friday and we're firing live missiles at real Iraqi SCUDS over Israel. I call that fast, whatever name you give it."

"Well," Jerry said, "you can be sure we'll be given plenty of opportunity to figure out what happened—the Army way."

Jerry looked back at the radar screen.

"I counted twenty-six PATRIOTs fired by both batteries," he said.

"Yeah, me too," said Johnson. "We lost one, and Alpha Battery might have lost one too, but I couldn't tell for sure."

"I could call Sam Martinez over in Alpha and ask him, but that's probably bad form while we're still under alert."

"Plenty of time to ask later."

"Maybe there'll be more firings," the operator said. "Then they'll have to let us show what we can really do."

"If we go through many more engagements like the one we just had, we'll be out of missiles pretty quick," said Sergeant Johnson.

"We can all be comforted," Jerry said as they heard the all clear wail of the siren, "by the thought that the President of the United States and the Chairman of the Joint Chiefs of Staff have probably watched the engagements and have already been advised on the steps to resupply our missiles."

"Yeah," Johnson agreed. They were both heading toward the door of the van. "It's going to be that kind of war all right."

❑❑❑❑❑

January 18, 1991
Office of the U.S. Ambassador
Tel Aviv, Israel
9:15 AM

"Yes, Mr. Secretary, I know the damage that was done this morning, and I know Israeli lives were lost. I've been asked by President Bush to convey his sincerest sympathies to the families of those who died. I've also been asked to give you the President's personal assurance that everything in his power is being done to ensure the safety of Israel from attack by SCUD missiles. We believe that seven Iraqi SCUD missiles were launched at Israel last night, and our PATRIOT interceptors got all but two of them." Lynn Boyer, career U.S. diplomat, consciously loosened his grip on the receiver and switched it to his other hand. Flexing his fingers to relieve the tension, he held the receiver several inches from his ear as the shouts came back at him over the wire.

"If the sorry bastard had only launched two, and both of them had landed, we would all agree that would be unacceptable!" the Israeli shouted back at him over the phone.

Lynn held his hand over the phone and looked across the room at the ambassador.

"This sonofabitch tries to keep his Brooklyn accent secret. When he gets mad like this, he really lets it go."

"You're the one the President sent to handle him," came the answer from the easy chair along with a shrug. The voice on the phone brought Lynn back to the continuing tirade.

"...so why do you morons think because you shot down five we are going to just sit here and take it and be happy it was only two that got through? We have, and you know we have, the capability to make him

12

wish he had never fired the first SCUD at this group of Jew boys, and for my money, I'm ready to use it—now!"

"Yes, sir, we do know, but that wouldn't be in keeping with the firm agreements between the people you work for and the people I work for," Lynn said. "And it wouldn't be in the best interest of the policies we've all agreed to pursue." Lynn pulled at his shirt to loosen its sticky hold on his flesh and paced nervously as he talked.

"You're damned right it wouldn't be! The only thing it would be in the best interest of is saving Israeli lives. Where does that stand on your President's fucking list of grand priorities?" the Secretary shouted into the phone.

"Your Prime Minister made a firm commitment to President Bush that he would not enter Israel into the conflict, and the President is counting on you to keep your word." Lynn's calm, soothing tone belied his nervousness, which was evident as he paced faster.

"The commitment our Prime Minister made was to restrain from directly engaging Iraq and in return, the United States was going to give us reasonable protection from attack. I don't consider a hospital and an apartment building lost in one night reasonable. And I don't consider some mumbo jumbo about malfunctions in a PATRIOT missile to be any answer. We want to know what your official position is. Can you can protect our country from these attacks or are we going to have to do it ourselves?"

"Mr. Secretary, Israel is being provided the same protection as U.S. troops in Saudi Arabia. It is the best that the United States has to offer." Lynn loosened his collar, sat on the side of the desk, then stood immediately and resumed his pacing.

"Bullshit! No U.S. troops have been hit by SCUDs in Saudi Arabia. No people of any nationality have been killed by SCUDs in Saudi Arabia. This now makes the third time we have been hit and, in my book, that isn't the same protection."

"Mr. Secretary, you know as well as I that the first two attacks on Israel were before the U.S. PATRIOTs arrived, before the Israeli PATRIOTs were active and before our leaders made their agreements. Under those agreements, the United States has now moved PATRIOT systems with the latest anti-missile capabilities into Israel from Germany, and we are in the process of moving more. We have an aggressive campaign to find and destroy all of the SCUD launchers. We *will* stop the damage from the SCUD attacks, but during these first few days, we can't expect perfection, and we may see a few bugs that have to be worked out."

"That's simply not good enough! Your 'few bugs' are costing the lives of Israeli citizens. If your troops and systems couldn't handle this move, your President had no right to commit to my Prime Minister to protect Israel. Don't you people even know what your equipment can and can't do?"

"Yes, we do, Mr. Secretary. But these systems have come a long way in a short time and the soldiers manning the sites have been under immense pressure. The failures last night were of a completely unforeseen type. We've never experienced these failures during tests, and in fact, we're not sure exactly what happened."

Lynn looked across the room and saw the visual reprimand on the face of the Ambassador sitting in the easy chair. He placed his hand over the phone again and held it toward the Ambassador.

"Don't criticize from that easy chair," he whispered with a caustic smile. "Why don't you come over here and talk to this self-proclaimed savior of the Hebrew race yourself, and see if you can do any better." The Ambassador smiled in return and slowly shook his head as the voice from the phone brought Lynn back to the conversation yet again.

"...my opinion you know a lot more than you're telling me!" the Israeli was shouting. "Can you explain, for example, why the failures came on PATRIOTs that were engaging SCUDs landing on Israelis, and all of the PATRIOTs engaging SCUDs landing on Americans worked perfectly?"

"No, I can't." Lynn's voice remained as calm as it had been, but his face told the Ambassador that a bomb had just landed. "At this point, we have to believe that was pure chance."

"So Americans live and Israelis die and you want me to believe it's the luck of the draw. Is that it?"

"Yes, Mr. Secretary, I do." Lynn looked to the Ambassador again who spread both of his hands in a gesture to ask if Lynn was being believed. Lynn gave a tentative nod, but held up his hand asking for more time as he waited for the rest of the response.

14

"So what plan does the mighty United States have now? Tell me so that I can report to my superiors."

Lynn relaxed and nodded affirmatively to the Ambassador, who immediately reached for the phone by his chair. Cupping his hand over the receiver, Lynn prevented the Israeli from hearing the new conversation begin.

"Get me the White House," the Ambassador said into his phone. "I'd like to speak to Mr. Scowcroft, please."

ㅁㅁㅁㅁㅁ

January 18, 1991
Central Tel Aviv
3:30 PM

Captain Jerry Maxwell could still see the smoke rising from the debris left by the SCUD attack as he walked through the streets of Tel Aviv. He heard his name called and looked up to see Sergeant Johnson coming behind him.

"Are we ready for another night?"

"Was that just this morning?" Jerry asked. "It seems like a lifetime ago."

"Yeah, time's fun when you're having flies."

"It was more than a lifetime for the people at the bottom of those flames. Last night, I dreamt of rocks and a cliff and a sensation of being consumed by flames. I can't get it out of my head, and it still seems as real as it was then, especially when I look at the fires around here."

"Well, my view is that it's just what's in the cards. When your number's up, it's up and that's it. They drew a bad missile, that's all."

"It's hard to believe it's that simple," Jerry said.

"Well, it is to me. I just know our job's to be as ready as we can be when the time comes."

"Looking at the damage those babies can do, we better be. Did you see how big the hole in that hospital was?"

"Yes, sir," Johnson said, "but we've got the answer to that problem, don't we?"

"I thought so before last night," Jerry said. "I wonder what went wrong."

"Who knows? A transistor somewhere. A missed solder joint. A thousand things could go wrong. A million."

"And you believe the story that it was just a coincidence that the only missile to fail was going for the SCUD targeted on Israeli facilities?"

"Yep. Gotta be. This system is so complex and controlled, what else could it be?"

"I don't know," Jerry said. "Something doesn't smell right. I believe it was something else."

"You really mean that?" Sergeant Johnson asked him.

"Yeah, I do," Jerry said, "I did some checking with Sergeant Masters this morning after we sent in all of the reports, and something doesn't ring true."

"I thought I saw you two in the data room with some printouts. What'd you find out?"

"From my look at the data," Jerry said, "the problem wasn't on the missile at all, but on the ground. The printouts indicate that there may have been a command sent from the ground to blow the missile prematurely. I know that doesn't make much sense, but that's what I think happened."

"Sergeant Masters said that sounded pretty far-fetched to him."

"Yeah, well, it seemed pretty unlikely to me, too, at first. But I'm going to follow up and get some help from Battalion, just to see where it leads."

"He said you probably would."

Sergeant Johnson turned right as they came to a corner, and Jerry followed along as they talked. About half a block down the street, there was a small alley and the sergeant turned again. The alley was narrow and dark, but Jerry didn't show any concern as they continued to walk. Sergeant Johnson walked as though he seemed to know where he was going. They were heading in the general direction of their PATRIOT site. Jerry heard footsteps behind him. Then he sensed rather than felt something close. It was the last conscious thought he would ever have as the three-pound steel rod hit the back of his head and caved in the rear half of his skull.

16

JANUARY
1990

weapons systems--pentagon adv 11 1-90
US Army's PATRIOT blasts "enemy" missile
USWNS Military News
adv jan 11 1990 or thereafter

By GEORGE GROWSON

WASHINGTON—The Army announced today that a modified PATRIOT anti-aircraft missile successfully intercepted a Lance surface-to-surface missile at White Sands Missile Range. This was the fifth test in the series to demonstrate the capability of PATRIOT to engage short-range tactical ballistic missiles. It was also the first test of a tactically deployable Army system in an environment designed to closely represent the combat environment. The intercept occurred miles above the famed White Sands National Monument in the New Mexico desert. An Army official, on condition of anonymity, said, "This is like hitting a bullet which was fired in Baltimore with another bullet fired from the capitol steps. A lot of people inside and outside the military said this was impossible, but the Army showed them today what can really be done." Publicly, officials for the Army stated that all conditions of the test were perfect, and that the PATRIOT had performed flawlessly. The PATRIOT was originally developed by the Raytheon Company of Bedford, Massachusetts for the United States Army to be deployed in defense against manned aircraft. It was first fielded in 1985 and is currently in the United States, Europe and Asia as the field Army's main line of defense against attacking enemy aircraft. The modifications to add the capability to engage missiles have been in development since just after the initial PATRIOT fielding, and the upgraded system envisioned will be used to engage short-range tactical ballistic missiles like the Soviet SCUD, the Argentinean Condor and the Pakistani Hatf.

ONE

Show the bastards!

Jeff Weyland leaned forward and looked over the shoulder of the young Army sergeant who was intently studying the radar display. The illuminated symbols of the screen glowed with remarkable detail, showing all the major features in the radar's field of view. The digital data on the display looked more like a computer terminal than a radar screen. In a sense, that's just what it was: a big computer with a rocket motor and a warhead at the other end of a lot of extremely complex software.

"THIS IS TARGET SITE 21. THE TARGET IS READY FOR LAUNCH."

The scratchy words came from a speaker in the corner of the small van that was crammed with electronic equipment, controls and displays, all mounted in light green cabinets. Except for the Army desert camouflage uniforms, the operators could be manning a console for a futuristic space craft. There was barely enough room for the operators, and observers like Jeff crowded the situation even more.

Nothing in the van overtly indicated the destructive capabilities of the switches and controls. The racks holding the electronic component boards that comprised the computer and communications equipment were enclosed in commercial cabinets. Only a close inspection of the labels and instructions would reveal that the hardware's purpose was to attack and destroy weapons threatening the security of the United States.

The radar display didn't have the typical rotating line civilians were used to seeing on the weather radar, but showed only computer-generated symbols of the ground features and airborne traffic in the area. The new technology used in this radar had prompted a series of jokes among the technical designers in the early days. It couldn't be a real radar anyway, the reasoning went, because it didn't go 'round and 'round like every radar always had.

"THIS IS RANGE CONTROL. THE TARGET IS CLEARED FOR LAUNCH."

Jeff had visited the target launch site earlier in the morning to make sure everything was in order and the crews were ready. The target crew at the launch site had no idea of the importance of this mission and what it could mean to their country. For them, it was just another day to "Be All They Could Be." Jeff looked back to the eerie green glow of the radar screen and clenched his teeth in anxious anticipation.

Show the bastards.

Jeff and his team had been working for five years to convince the Defense Department brass that this concept could really work. They had spent five years fighting for budget allocations and technical approvals to keep the program funded and on some sort of reasonable schedule. Those five years of work had all come down to this moment, and Jeff knew he wouldn't be let down. The "hostile target" for the test mission was a Lance missile, the U.S. Army's front line surface-to-surface attack missile. It was a big test, but Jeff knew in his gut she was ready to go.

"THIS IS TARGET SITE 21, TARGET AWAY."

Jeff shifted uncomfortably on his feet as the knot in his chest tightened. A few seconds passed and the target symbol appeared on the radar display, indicating that the radar had found the Lance missile portraying the hostile target and placed it under track. When the symbol appeared on the screen, the soldier at the console moved his hand to the toggle stick that controlled the cross-hairs on the display. He quickly moved the cross around the display until it was directly over the target and then clicked a control button located beside the toggle.

The operator pressed another button, and a small outlined box appeared on the radar display showing tabulated data of the target's position, speed, identification, and other pertinent information. Inside the computer, programmed subroutines began to churn away at the data, examining the characteristics of the target to see if it matched any of the potential targets in the computer's massive database.

"TARGET ACQUIRED AND TRACKED," the soldier at the console announced.

His collar insignia and name tag identified the young man as Staff Sergeant Johnson. A prime example of the volunteer soldiers who had joined the U.S. Army in the eighties, Jim Johnson was in his early thirties, clean cut, and confident.

After a short delay, the target identification label on the radar display changed. The target had been identified as a ballistic missile, and the target symbol became a small inverted triangle. The track amplification data flicked again. The data change indicated hostile missile targets. The estimated ground impact point of the incoming missile flashed, displaying an impact in "friendly" territory. The small triangle on the radar display screen representing the target also began to flash.

Jeff watched the tabulated readout as the target altitude and speed increased.

"TARGET IS DECLARED A HOSTILE BALLISTIC MISSILE."

The announcement came from the Tactical Control Officer, a young lieutenant sitting next to Sergeant Johnson. Both soldiers were now leaning over the console to get the best possible view of the display. The cluster of men resembled a crowd gathering to watch Johnson play Super Nintendo.

Every man in the van watched the target on the radar display move steadily in their direction.

"TARGET ALTITUDE IS 50,000 METERS."

Jeff's eyes were drawn from the monitor to the keyboard by the rapid movement of Johnson's hands as his trained fingers made a quick entry. That's an odd action, thought Jeff, since he didn't remember any entries that were required during this portion of the intercept sequence. He leaned forward to ask about it, but he drew back, deciding that the crew should not be distracted at this critical point. In his rapid movement, he brushed against the backs of the soldiers at the console, and he felt Johnson recoil from him and throw a quick glance in his direction.

"TARGET ENGAGEABLE."

Sergeant Johnson's deep voice broke the tense silence. The indicator on the display flicked. For safety reasons, the automatic mode of the PATRIOT system was disabled for the test so that a manual command was required to launch the missile. The use of the manual launch mode meant that the system would automatically bring itself to the point of missile launch and then wait for an input from the operator before proceeding to fire.

Jeff glanced up from the display. The banks of glowing green lights were bright in the dark van. All of the fault indicators from the various parts of the system were dark. The light above the missile launcher indicator was a bright green, indicating it was on line and ready to fire.

She's ready.

Outside the control van, there was no activity except for the gentle breeze that played with the desert sand. A few lizards scurried around a sand dune to find cover as a chaparral moved into the area searching for some lunch. Some distance away, there was an odd vehicle looking more like the back of a tractor trailer rig than a vehicle housing the latest in the state of the art for speed and destruction. One end was raised by large hydraulic pistons. Clustered on its bed were four PATRIOT missiles, lying like trained birds of prey waiting for instructions from their master. Until each missile was selected just before launch, it was completely dormant, hermetically snug in its container that had been sealed at the Martin Marietta factory in Orlando, Florida.

Back in the control van, Jeff was watching the radar display and had to lean forward to search the screen for any airborne traffic in the area or any other indications of a safety problem. The screen was clear except for the trail of the hostile target making its eerie green trace.

It's time.

"THIS IS RANGE CONTROL. ALL SYSTEMS ARE GO. YOU ARE RELEASED TO ENGAGE."

Sergeant Johnson glanced over his shoulder and met Jeff's eyes. Jeff nodded and looked away from the Sergeant, fixing his gaze on the button on the console. One little button among many on the panel, but this one was special. It had a red cover that had already been lifted in preparation for this moment. Sergeant Johnson's hand seemed to move in slow motion as his desert camouflaged sleeve rose above the button, and the hand came down. There was a breathless moment for all of the people in the van as they watched in silence.

Jeff stepped outside the van and stood on the steel mesh of the back platform to watch the rocket motor blast from the launcher and start the missile on its path downrange. The boom and the roar of the launch signaled that the missile was on its way. Moments later, Jeff saw the rocket plume in the air and he was buffeted by the pressure of the blast that had reached the van.

Go, babe.

The sound and the blast garishly displayed the brute force and power that was controlled with such precision. Jeff watched the missile snake through the air as it gained altitude, following its predetermined path toward the point of intercept as predicted by the computer.

Show the bastards.

A slight smile lingered as he slipped back into the van.

"MISSILE AWAY." Johnson's announcement came as Jeff returned to his place behind the soldiers at the console.

As the roar faded, the radar screen displayed the symbol that the PATRIOT missile had been launched. Jeff quickly scanned the console. All indicators showed a clean missile launch.

Next was the acquisition of the PATRIOT missile by the radar. This was critical for the flight to continue, since the missile was now flying on its own and couldn't do that for long. The radar would have to search for it in the sky and bring it under track just as though it was a target, except in this case, the computer knew exactly where to direct the radar to look. When the missile received the coded message from the radar in this search process, an on-board radio transmitter was activated that sent a coded response to the radar on the ground. Once established, this communication process was repeated multiple times every second during the entire flight and was the means by which the ground computer system and the airborne missile exchanged information. Initiating this process was a complicated sequence executed and controlled by the computer without intervention from the operators.

Again there was silence in the van as Jeff and the soldiers leaned forward to watch the display. A light flickered on the console and simultaneously a few lines of print appeared on the screen.

"MISSILE TRACK," Johnson announced, a little more loudly than his previous announcements.

Jeff released the breath he hadn't realized he was holding.

The lieutenant leaned back in his chair and glanced over his shoulder again at Jeff. He flexed his shoulders to release some of the tightness in his neck and back and a glimmer of relief began to show in his eyes. No one in the van spoke as all eyes watched the lights and readouts on the console, looking for any indications of problems. As the missile gained velocity and altitude on its way to the target, it was now under full and automatic control of the ground computer. The radar maintained track of the hostile target and the PATRIOT missile, their flight paths, and their velocities, continually sending updated commands to the missile, guiding it toward its intercept with the target.

The computer sent steering commands to a small radar antenna mounted in the front of the missile, directing it toward the incoming target. Everyone in the van was watching the display for the next significant step in the engagement sequence—the lock-on of the target by this small radar antenna in the missile. This was a technological feat that required timing between the ground and the missile measured in millionths of a second. It only took a few tenths of a second to accomplish the lock-on if everything was calculated and executed correctly, but many things happened during that brief instant.

"TVM," Sergeant Johnson announced.

Go.

The tension in the van melted into confidence. The crew heard the announcement that the system had successfully gone into the Track-Via-Missile or TVM mode, the final phase of the engagement. This mode was the unique technical achievement that made PATRIOT the most lethal interceptor in history. The target's radar reflection received by the missile was relayed to the ground so that the ground computer had two sources of information about the target—where it was as seen by the radar, and where it was as seen by the missile.

During the last few seconds of the flight, the system would receive thousands of these pulses of radar energy reflected from the target and it would make millions of calculations based on this data to guide the missile accurately to the intercept. If all of this worked right, the engagement was a guaranteed success. The PATRIOT missile would pass close enough to the target for the fuze on the missile to sense the target and explode. All of the information available to the computer—missile, target, and TVM data, catalogue data on the target, information on the warhead and the fuze, and everything known about the engagement—was combined to compute the precise steering command to the missile and guide it accurately to the intercept.

"INTERCEPT—ALL INDICATIONS POSITIVE."

Jeff watched the target symbol become erratic on the display as the computer raced to examine the data to determine if a kill was achieved. Using nothing but radar information to gauge the success of a missile kill was an extremely difficult task. Assessing an airplane kill was tricky enough, but radar-guided anti-aircraft missile systems had been doing that for more than twenty-five years, and the techniques had been refined to the point that a reasonably accurate determination could be made. But missiles aren't as easy to track as airplanes—they don't have wings, engines or pilots. A major part of this test was to see if the PATRIOT system could sense her own kill and to get a first-hand look at the radar data of the Lance after intercept.

"THIS IS RANGE CONTROL. THE TARGET IS TUMBLING AND IN PIECES. CAMERA CREWS INDICATE THERE WAS A DIRECT IMPACT."

The van erupted in cheers. This was a scene Jeff had witnessed with each PATRIOT success against airplanes. The multiple simultaneous engagements. The engagements in heavy and sophisticated radar-jamming, of highly maneuverable combat fighters, and of closely spaced formations. All the tricks the U.S. Air Force had used to defeat guided missiles in Vietnam—and then some—had been dealt with as if they were a first-grade cakewalk, and now PATRIOT had done it again. PATRIOT was the first fielded United States weapon system to engage a missile with a missile in a tactical combat environment. That day, PATRIOT showed the world what the rendezvous of two bodies in space is all about.

As Jeff watched the celebration of the crew in the van, he couldn't restrain his own smile.

You showed the bastards, old girl.

❑❑❑❑❑

Sergeant Johnson turned off U.S. Highway 54 at Newman, New Mexico, into the parking lot of Club 54, a combination country store, gas station and watering hole. The GIs and civilians leaving White Sands Missile Range found relief here after a day in the heat and sand. This club and another called the Last Roundup were the only two places to relax during the long drive from White Sands to El Paso, Texas, where most of the crews lived. He parked his car by the public telephone, got out, and walked to the booth. He pulled his wallet from his pocket, took out a card, and studied it for a second while the simple code came back to him, then he lifted the phone's handset and dialed the number and the long distance charge number translating the code sequence in his head.

After two rings, he hung up the receiver and went inside and sat on a stool at the bar. He ordered a Lone Star longneck and drank it quickly in several heavy pulls. He ordered another and took it with him as he went back to the phone and dialed the same set of numbers from memory. This time after the first ring, a woman's voice answered.

"Hello." He remembered the voice.

"It's done," he said.

"You made the entry?" The voice brought a flood of memories.

"Yes."

"At the proper time?"

"Yes," he answered, trying to show a little impatience. The voice was sexy. He thought about the body that went with that voice and could feel himself becoming aroused.

"Any problems?"

"No."

"And the flight went well?"

28

"Yes."

"And no one saw you make the entry?"

"I said there were no problems," he said, making sure she could sense his irritation at her repeated questions.

"You have received your payment?"

"Yes."

"Have you arranged your move to the next position?"

"Yes. Next week."

"Good. Do you have anything else to report?"

"No."

"You will receive further instructions," she said, and she hung up.

"OK, bitch," he said to the dead phone. He didn't tell her a brigadier general had been looking over his shoulder when he made the entry. He didn't want to lose the money, and he might if something went wrong. Good money, too, and he needed it bad. Anyway, he didn't think the person behind him in the van had even seen what he did or knew enough to recognize the difference anyway.

He walked back into the bar and wondered what would happen if he demanded to see her again. He would make her do the things for him she had done the night he met her. He had been with prostitutes in El Paso and across the Mexican border in Juarez several times since and paid for those things, but it wasn't the same. He decided there would never be another time like that, but at least he had the money. He smiled as he thought about that money in the Mexican bank and he sat back down on the stool and ordered another beer.

January 11, 1990
Huntsville, Alabama
2:15 PM

"Ladies and gentlemen, please fasten your seat belts for our descent into Huntsville International Airport." While the flight attendant busied herself picking up the last few trays from the in-flight snack, Jeff looked out the window at the lush Tennessee Valley. The Tennessee River wound its way between the hydro-electric power dams of the Tennessee Valley Authority, creating a series of lakes and making the Huntsville area a virtual paradise for anyone who liked to hunt, fish, or spend a day near the water. The giant Apollo Spacecraft pointing skyward from its exhibition stand at the Space Museum on the city's west side came into view before the screech of the tires on pavement and a heavier than usual bump on the runway.

"Welcome to Huntsville, ladies and gentlemen, the home of NASA's Marshall Space Flight Center and America's Space Camp. The local time is 2:30 PM, Central Standard Time. The weather in Huntsville is a chilly 41 degrees."

Jeff grimaced at the announcement, noticing that once again the flight attendant had failed to mention that Huntsville was also the home of the U.S. Army Missile Command, the U.S. Army Missile Munitions School, the U.S. Army Missiles and Space Intelligence Center and the U.S. Army Strategic Defense Command. Even though the Army was by far the largest employer in the region, Huntsville was still known almost exclusively for NASA.

Coming down the airport corridor, Jeff saw Jimmy waiting for him.

"Afternoon, General. Nice flight?"

"Hello, Jimmy. OK, except for a little bump on the landing. I guess it's something about our thick Southern air."

"Yes, sir. I guess." Jimmy Arnold was the driver for Brigadier General Jeffrey F. Weyland, Project Manager for the PATRIOT Surface-to-Air Missile System.

"Did Laura say if the meeting is set for this afternoon?" Jeff asked.

"Yes, sir. And there are several messages in the car. I left it unlocked, and I'll be there as soon as I pick up your bags."

"OK, see you there."

"Oh, sir..." Jimmy said, stopping at the top of the stairs.

Jeff stopped and looked around, waiting for whatever was coming next.

"Nice mission."

"Thanks, Jimmy."

You damn betcha, nice mission.

The messages in the car were all routine except for the one from Senator Hastings' office. Senator Graham T. Hastings was Alabama's senior senator, the Chairman of the Senate Armed Services Committee and PATRIOT's strongest supporter on the Hill. Jeff hit the hands-free button on the mobile phone and used the auto code to dial the Senator's office. A few short rings, and a familiar voice answered.

"Senator Hastings' office."

Honey and spice.

"Hello, Suzy."

"Well, the conquering hero," Suzy Morris said with obvious recognition and enthusiasm. "Congratulations!"

"Thanks."

"The Senator had a message for you."

"Good. I was told he had called for me." He could hear the rustling of papers while Suzy looked through her notes.

"Here it is," she said. "You're to be in Washington next Tuesday for a meeting with the staffers from Armed Services to review yesterday's test."

"Got it," he said. "I'll have Laura make some reservations and get back to you with my schedule."

"Beat you to it," she said. "I talked to Laura this morning. You're booked on the 6:45 AM flight into Washington National and staying at that little place you like in Alexandria. The meeting's at 1:00 in the Armed Services staff room. They'll expect a full dog-and-pony show. The Senator wanted me to be sure to tell you to be prepared to convince them that the test was realistic and not just an easy setup to grab attention."

"They know as well as I do there is no set-up when you try to hit a bullet with a bullet," Jeff said, a little more harshly than he intended.

"Whoa, this is me, remember?"

"Sorry, I didn't mean to overreact. At least I have the ammunition I need so I won't have to play games. Tell the Senator that I have hard data, and by Tuesday, I'll have the videotapes of a direct hit that we can play for the doubters. I wouldn't expect any problem."

"The Senator is confident you won't disappoint them," she said.

"You bet I won't," he said. "Not this time. This time the dog and the pony will put on their full act, and all the gawkers can watch in amazement."

"Great," she said. "I'll make sure all the arrangements are made."

"Thanks," he said, "I owe you one."

"You owe me three hundred and forty-six, to be exact."

"So who's counting?" He chuckled.

"I am," she said, "and don't you forget it."

He chuckled again as he reset the phone and punched the auto-dial button for his own office. The phone was answered on the first ring.

"PATRIOT Project, General Weyland's office, this is Laura."

"Hi, Laura. I'm back on the ground and should be there in about thirty minutes. Anything new?"

"Nothing more than the messages I gave to Jimmy," she said. "The meeting in your office with the senior staff from the technical division is set for 4:00 this afternoon. Did Mr. Harkness make it back with you?" Brian Harkness was the chief of the test division of the PATRIOT Project Office.

"No. He stayed in El Paso so he could go over the detailed computer printouts as soon as they're ready. He'll be bringing back the videos with him over the weekend. Has Johnny faxed the quick-look results from the flight yet?" Johnny Madkin was the chief of the Project Office's team at White Sands Missile Range. The range name had been abbreviated to its initials WSMR and the soldiers gave it the easy pronunciation of "Whizzmrr."

"Yes, he did, and I've had copies made and distributed to everyone who will be at this afternoon's meeting. Anything else?"

"Nope. I'm on my way."

Brigadier General Jeffrey F. Weyland hadn't intended to make the Army a career, but now he had been in the Army for twenty-three years. After his first tour on a Nike Hercules guided missile site, he had stayed on for one more round, and by then he was hooked. He was forty-seven years old, tall, and ramrod straight with a forward-thrust square jaw. His thick, shockingly silver, close-cut hair gave an impressive military bearing.

Jimmy came with the bags and drove Jeff to the PATRIOT Project Office located in the large complex housing the U.S. Army Strategic Defense Command. The facility was located just off Redstone Arsenal in Cummings

Research Park in western Huntsville. As Jeff walked into his office, the small crowd that had gathered applauded the success of the flight. A banner was strung over his doorway that said "We Showed The Bastards," and a small cardboard mockup of a Lance Missile, bent and twisted, dangled from a string.

The staff meeting with the technical division was well prepared and went smoothly. Steve Smith, the chief of the technical division, was a very competent engineer and a good manager. Jeff's technical background helped him as a general to develop a rapport with the civilian work force, and gave them the confidence to be open and honest with him. That had been especially helpful during some dark days of the program when everyone had to have all of the right information to make the best decisions.

Jeff could not conceal his pride as he started the meeting. He looked around the room at the familiar faces with whom he had worked so closely for so many years.

"Let me tell you," Jeff began. "Each of you should feel a tremendous amount of satisfaction in what's been accomplished. Without a lot of support from anybody else in this man's army, we've done what they said we couldn't. Yesterday, we showed the world the beginning of what will likely be a change in the way countries think about war. The nations of the world that now possess tactical ballistic missiles, and those nations thinking of acquiring them, will have to look differently at what they can expect to accomplish with that capability.

"No longer can they think that our country or our allies will be vulnerable to any missile they throw at us. With the capability this new PATRIOT now puts in our country's hands, our enemies will be more than reluctant to initiate hostilities against our forces anywhere in the world. This *single step* will eventually do more to further our mission to deter war than anything we have accomplished before. We can now see the end of the road we started together some five years ago, and each of you has done your part well. I congratulate you."

There were a lot of smiles around the room and knowing nods between friends. This group had been a dedicated force in the evolution of PATRIOT to its current form, and they were a proud team.

The rest of the meeting was dedicated to developing plans and strategies for the upcoming Washington activities. As the group filed out of the conference room at the conclusion of the session, Jeff motioned for Steve Smith to stay behind.

"What's up?" his chief engineer asked.

"Nothing major, but I saw something I didn't understand during the flight test. Just before the target was engaged, the console operator made an entry into the keyboard. I hadn't noticed that before, and wondered what it might be."

"Did you ask the operator?" Steve asked.

"I know that would've been the easiest thing to do, but things were tense in the van, and I didn't want to interrupt. Afterwards, he got away so quickly I didn't see him. Do you have any idea what that entry could have been?"

"Not off the top of my head," Steve said. "But I would assume he was calling up some special data on the target or something. Did you see any displays or anything else come up on the screen after he made the entry?"

"No, and I was looking, especially after I saw him make the input. To be honest, I didn't want to show my ignorance. After all, I'm the PATRIOT Project Manager, and I'd hate to seem like an intruder."

"Jeff, you know as much about how PATRIOT operates as anybody, and we appreciate your input. Do you want me to look into it?" Steve asked.

"No, I'm sure it wasn't important. I just thought you might have a quick and easy answer. Getting that Armed Services presentation ready should be the top item on your list. I suppose we'll also have to give the same briefing to General Grant's staff early that morning and then to General Grant himself before we go to the Hill." Lieutenant General Wesley F. Grant was the Military Deputy to the presidentially appointed Army Acquisition Executive and as such, the senior military person in the Army weapon's acquisition business. In that position, he was also Jeff's boss.

"I'll call one of the members of his staff and set up a review with them. When would you like to see the final material?"

"I planned on coming by the office on Sunday," Jeff said. "So why don't we sit down late that afternoon and see where we are?"

"Great. I look forward to it," Steve said.

"OK . . . oh, and Steve, I don't tell you this enough, but good job. I'm glad we had you along on this one."

"I bet you say that to all the techies," Steve said, but he knew this general didn't, and he felt a true pride. He and Jeff Weyland had a common bond in their devotion to PATRIOT.

❑❑❑❑❑

That evening, when Jeff arrived at his General Officer Quarters on Redstone Arsenal, he followed his long-time habit and walked straight to the stereo. One of his few indulgences, the machine was a real display of modern technology, with 135 watts per channel and all of the accessories, including ten-pack cartridge compact disc, wireless speakers in every room, and the latest in digital signal processing. Immediately, from the nearest speakers came the sounds of Waylon Jennings, and Jeff smiled down at the machine.

The high-tech redneck man.

He chuckled to himself with the thought and began to sort through the mail. He threw the junk mail in the trash and the rest on his desk. He turned on the TV to CNN with the sound muted and sat down to his evening's work, still listening to the compact disc that had switched to Willie Nelson. The papers he had on his lap were the budget and schedule material for the presentation to the Armed Services staff. The ringing of the phone interrupted his thoughts.

"Is Doctor Weyland there?" the caller asked.

"No," he answered.

"Is General Weyland there?" came the next question.

"Speaking," Jeff said, smiling.

"Hi, Daddy."

"Hi, Dollface," he said, enjoying the little game they always played. She thought he should be more proud to be a Ph.D. in aeronautical engineering than he was to be a general. He wasn't, but he also knew that being a "Doctor General" meant his Army career was limited. While the

Army embraced their technical weaponry with a maternal ferocity, they tended to look at officer technocrats as a breed apart from real soldiers. They preferred to buy their technical expertise from the civilian ranks and weren't yet sure what to do with career military officers who were also members of the technical and academic environment.

"Good to hear your voice. What's up?"

"Oh, nothing much. I saw something about you and thought I'd call," she said. "I read in the paper that our great army has successfully demonstrated another of its weapons of war which will allow us to make one more step toward the goal of killing for peace."

This was a game he didn't like. Cindy had some deep-seated resentment toward what he did for a living. He didn't know where she got these inclinations, but he was confident it wasn't from their home life. Probably from that expensive school she had attended.

"Do I need to go into my speech about the fact that what we're doing here is building defensive weapons that are only used when the bad guys have already launched things at you that will do serious harm to that pretty face of yours unless we do something to defend you?"

"Not this time," she said with more than a little sarcasm. "But thanks anyway for the compliment."

Cindy Weyland was every parent's dream. Sometimes it really didn't seem possible to him that he could have raised such a perfect kid. Sometimes, it didn't seem possible that he could have raised anything. Cindy was 23, a magna cum laude graduate of fine arts from the University of Virginia. She worked in the research section of the High Museum of Art in Atlanta, and was a promising young artist herself. She lived alone in a small apartment with a cat she had named Mouse. She was completely independent and he was proud of her.

"You're welcome," Jeff said. "It's important to me that you understand what I'm trying to do here. PATRIOT has the potential of providing protection to a large segment of U.S. soldiers and other assets that are important to our country."

"I know, Daddy," she said. "I just hate the whole idea of war."

"I know that, and you know I do too, more than most. You also know that my job here is to build weapon systems that are so good that wars won't happen."

"I know that, too, and in spite of my needling you, it makes me feel good to know that's what you're doing."

"You know, Dollface, the facts of life are that there are guys in the world who wear black hats, and then there are guys who wear white hats. I hope you know, really know in your heart of hearts, that your country is one of the true white hats in this world."

"Uh oh, the white hats and heart of hearts speech."

"I just want to make sure you understand what the world is all about."

"Yes," she said, "I do. And I love you for helping to keep our country wearing a white hat."

"I love you, too, Dollface."

"G'night, Daddy."

"Goodnight, Sweetheart."

weapons systems--pentagon adv16 1-90
Hussein says Iraqi troop maneuvers not significant
USWNS Military News
adv jan 16 1990 or thereafter

By GEORGE GROWSON

   WASHINGTON—A statement released today by the official
Iraqi news agency quoted Saddam Hussein as saying there was
no military significance to the movement of Iraqi troops
through the country southward toward Kuwait. Elite
Republican Guards have been sighted as far south as the
town of Basra in the southeastern portion of Iraq as
disputes continue to erupt between Iraq and Kuwait over
boundary lines and oil rights. There is a vast amount of
oil-rich areas between the two countries which has been the
subject of political controversy and territorial claims for
many years. Iraq has repeatedly accused Kuwait of illegally
drilling for oil on land which rightfully belongs to Iraq.
In Washington, the Department of Defense stated today that
Naval Task Forces consisting of aircraft carriers and
supporting elements of the fleet headed for the region are
not being moved because of the Iraqi troop activity, but
are on routine maneuvers.

TWO

January 16, 1990

Washington, DC

10:15 AM

"Ladies and gentlemen, the Captain has illuminated the fasten seat belt sign indicating our final approach to Washington National Airport. Please fasten your seatbelts and return all seats and tray tables to their upright and locked positions."

Home.

The plane banked and the Capitol came into view—its dome holding court over the Mall and the surrounding national monuments and museums. Now the White House appeared, and then the monuments for Washington, Jefferson and Lincoln. There is something special about landing in the nation's center that feels like coming home every time.

Jeff leaned forward in his seat a little and tried to get a view of the Vietnam Memorial, but he couldn't pick it out because of the thick growth of trees. He made it a habit to stop by the memorial frequently to keep one thing clear in his mind—it wasn't numbers being analyzed in war scenarios, but the lives of well-meaning young American men and women, most of them just teenagers. The knowledge of how many of those lives PATRIOT would save today if the United States were forced into a conflict gave him the boost he needed to continue his efforts to get the system to the field commanders.

The plane touched down at Washington National Airport with a smoother than usual landing, and the flight attendant was immediately on her feet and reaching for the public address microphone.

"Ladies and gentlemen, welcome to Washington, our nation's capital. The local time is 10:22 AM, Eastern Standard Time. Washington today is overcast, and the temperature is 42 degrees...."

Jeff went through the process of collecting his luggage. He rented a Tempo and drove through the glittering towers of Crystal City. He turned north onto U.S. Highway One and then west a few blocks toward the Pentagon. He maneuvered his way into the visitors' parking lot, went in the River entrance and followed the hallway past the new Pentagon Child Care Center.

A new Army.

Turning left in the corridor of the first ring, he went up one level of stairs and moved toward the center of the building. He turned left at the first ring into the Hall of Presidents, and continued on a route that took him past the Medal of Honor Corridor and the Secretaries of War.

As Jeff made his way toward General Grant's office, the flow of traffic was unusually heavy for a Tuesday morning. Occasionally, he spoke to people he recognized as he neared the group of offices allotted to Army Acquisition, and he kept an eye out for Steve Smith and the members of his staff who had arrived the night before. They were scheduled to brief General Grant before the formal presentation to the Armed Services staffers in the afternoon.

If we ever fight a presentation war, we'll win that one for sure.

As he made the final turn and entered the large suite, Jeff spotted Steve and two engineers from the Huntsville office.

"How did the morning's session go?" he asked Steve after the round of hellos and handshakes.

"Overall, I'd say pretty well. But we got enough of a feel to know that General Grant is still not the president of the PATRIOT fan club."

"How's that?"

"You could sort of sense from some of their negative comments that they thought they were on solid ground with their boss. They're in with him now and I would expect you're in for a few tough rounds with The Man when you get your turn."

"What seemed to be their major problem?" Jeff asked.

"I'm not sure you could point to one specific issue and say they had a problem. It just seemed to be a generic sort of thing. It's clear they don't

42

have the same devotion we do to seeing the lady's name in lights."

"Anything special?"

"No," Steve said. "A lot of nit-picking and then some comments about the uncertainty of the payload kill, that sort of thing. Several areas were obviously held in abeyance until you meet with the General. They suggested you make sure the General is up to speed before you address the specific issues at hand with Armed Services. I've pulled together some extra material with detail on her background for you."

"Thanks," Jeff said.

"What do you think his problem with PATRIOT really is?" Steve asked.

"He's Infantry," Jeff answered, as if that was all the explanation Steve needed.

"That's it?" Steve asked.

"Yep. U.S. Army infantrymen are the best field fighters in the world, and they don't lose any of that capability nor their loyalty to the Fort Benning Infantry Center when it comes to competing for money in the halls of the Pentagon. General Grant has earned his spurs in combat, and to show he's still the boss, he doesn't mind jabbing them into the sides of any planner who would take money he feels the Army could better use for advanced infantry, armor, artillery and other weapons used by the combat soldier."

"Somehow it seems that General Grant's problems with PATRIOT go beyond that."

"Yeah, I know what you mean," Jeff said. "I've gotten that feeling myself on occasion. More than once it's seemed that Grant was after me personally and not PATRIOT."

"Well, I'm glad to know you feel that way, too. At least I know I'm not getting paranoid."

"Right," Jeff said.

Lieutenant Colonel Garnett, the General's aide, came into the reception area of the suite and signaled to Jeff that Grant was ready to see him. Jeff started to follow him into the office, paused and turned back over his shoulder to Steve.

"But remember, just because you aren't paranoid doesn't mean they aren't out to get you."

As Jeff walked into the office, General Grant wasted no time on pleasantries, and immediately showed his irritation.

"Let me make sure I understand this, General Weyland. First, we spend twelve billion dollars on this system which is now going to be used to protect Air Force resources, and here you tell me that it is such a valuable asset that we are spending another bucket of money just so it can protect itself."

"No, sir," Jeff responded as he moved to the formal spot in front of Grant's desk. "The PATRIOT Anti-tactical missile Capability's Phase One program, which we called PAC I, was designed for self-defense. That was a directive of the Secretary of the Army after the number of tactical ballistic missiles in the inventory of the Warsaw Pact became known."

"Don't patronize me, Weyland," General Grant said, showing both impatience and irritation. "I'm well aware of the directions of the Secretary."

"The particular upgrade we're talking about today, PAC II, is to give PATRIOT the capability to protect assets other than herself."

"If the region on the ground that PATRIOT can protect is limited to a small area around the radar, then how can you claim to protect Army assets when all the radars are deployed around air bases?" General Grant had found his rope to pull, and in true bulldog style, he wasn't going to let go without a fight.

"Sir, our analysis has shown time and again that the best way to protect Army assets in the field is to ensure that the Air Force bases survive. In the long haul, the Army makes out better that way."

"That depends, General, on what your *analysis* plugs into those computer war games you run down there." His emphasis on the word analysis came with a sneer to make it clear to Jeff just exactly what he thought about computer war games.

"In order to get our program recommendations through the Defense Department process," Jeff responded, "we are required by regulatory guidance to use simulations and analysis to support the performance projections for the systems."

"Can you, in fact, project the intentions of the enemy?"

"No, sir."

"Then can you, in fact, project the real outcome of a real battle?"

"No, sir."

"Then how the hell can you claim that you can make performance projections?"

"We can accurately project the technical performance of a PATRIOT missile against a wide class of attack missiles from potentially hostile countries. Specifically, we can calculate the numerical probability that PATRIOT can successfully intercept and destroy a specific missile in a specific environment. Then we collect all of the probabilities over an attack and see what the results are."

"And what about enemy intentions? Enemy tactics?"

"Those are all theoretical, of course. But what we do is hypothesize a wide variety of enemy scenarios and then determine what PATRIOT's performance would be in each environment. It's sort of an 'if this, then that' process. The computer analysis is a real aid since there are so many different environments to evaluate. We also..."

"The Army's mission is to conduct the ground war," General Grant continued his assault, "not to protect air bases. If the Air Force wants their air bases protected, then by God, let them pay for it. Now you come along and want to use Army money to build an anti-missile system that can't reach enemy missiles aimed at the Army, and that's bullshit."

"It's true, sir, that the deployment of PATRIOT systems during peacetime in Europe has concentrated on the critically reinforcing air bases. However, with the current move to push PATRIOT into the Corps and to the Army National Guard, this capability will be available to Army commanders anywhere the system is placed in the world. If the Army's required to move into hostile underdeveloped countries, our soldiers will be vulnerable to attack by the significant threat that exists from tactical ballistic missiles. Without this upgrade to PATRIOT, there's no capability in the Army to ensure survival in those areas of the world."

"And once you're finished with PAC II, I assume you'll be back here for more money for PAC III?" General Grant asked, giving the appearance that he already knew the answer.

"The plans for PAC III are being developed now. This will give

PATRIOT higher kill probability and longer range against the larger group of new missiles that are coming into the hands of Third World countries."

"This is beginning to sound more and more like a Raytheon sales pitch. And then it will be PAC IV, and then PAC V, and pretty soon you'll be doing the job the President has assigned to the Strategic Defense Initiative. Where do you feel the Army's financial obligation on these missions stops and SDI's begins?" he asked.

"Sir, my mission is to develop the systems for which I have responsibility," Jeff responded.

"Are you passing the buck, General?" General Grant still hadn't looked up.

"No, sir. I didn't intend to."

"Well, since it's clear from the earlier part of this conversation that you haven't been given a charter by the Army for this development, why don't you just answer my question?"

"The charter was given to the Army by the Assistant Secretary of Defense in a Decision Memorandum which stated that the Army was to exploit the capabilities of existing systems to counter the threat to U.S. forces by tactical ballistic missiles. PATRIOT was..."

"Goddammit, General, you're answering a question I didn't ask," General Grant interrupted, slamming his hand on his desk, "and not answering the one I did. PATRIOT is a deployed Army tactical missile system, not somebody's sandbox for a technology demonstration for strategic security."

"Yes, sir. The mission of the Strategic Defense Initiative is to develop technology which can provide a defense for the United States and her allies against attack by strategic missiles. The mission of the Army Air Defense is to provide the Army in the field with a capability to defeat enemy forces attacking by air and thus provide the field commander the freedom of maneuver."

"Be more specific," General Grant said. "Exactly where will you stop in this evolutionary process of improvement? Is there a limit where the Army says 'This isn't my job, SDI, it's yours'?"

"It is my personal opinion that the Army in the field cannot depend on

46

the products of the Strategic Defense Initiative as it is currently structured to produce systems that will be of use to the tactical forces."

"At least we agree on one thing. We've got about as much chance of Star Wars helping us as we do that Luke Skyfucker will crash through that door and come in here waving his laser sword! Nothing of any benefit for the Army has ever come from those people, and nothing ever will. Now tell me straight, goddammit, where does the Army's responsibility stop?"

"The Army should continue to develop defenses against tactical missiles until we have a sufficient capability to protect Army assets in the field. We must continue to improve and upgrade our capabilities when faced with a growing and changing threat. If we don't, the Army will not be able to fight its battles using existing doctrine."

"Apparently, General, the Congress of the United States agrees with you. The funding for this program has been specifically designated by them and can't be used for anything else. But I suppose you know all about that, don't you?"

"I'm aware of the language used in the Appropriations Bill of the 1990 budget," Jeff said, seeing a glimmer of hope and pushing ahead, "and I believe the Army should embrace this opportunity to achieve some goals that could benefit our service for a long time into the future. If the Army can provide its own defense against tactical missiles, then we won't be dependent on anyone else when hostilities start."

"Yes, and if we had some ham, we could have some ham and eggs—if we had some eggs. It seems to me that unless *our friends* on the Hill were prompted by somebody, they wouldn't restrict that money from being used for other purposes." The statement was made facetiously and required no response.

It was General Grant's way of remaining in charge as he ended the conversation, and he stood and turned toward his window as he said it.

"I completely disagree with them," General Grant continued. "It is my personal opinion that your pipe dream would only create a giant hole into which the Army would pour tanks, artillery and helicopters that are sorely needed to prosecute the land battle."

He paused and looked over his shoulder directly at Jeff.

"Now I wouldn't want to hear," he continued, "that anyone wearing an Army uniform was encouraging certain Senators and Congressmen to partition that money. Am I making myself clear, General?"

"Completely, sir," Jeff responded, and the meeting was over.

⬚⬚⬚⬚⬚

At the Hart Senate Office building, Jeff walked past the outer staff in Senator Hastings' office and went directly to Suzy's small office, which was part of the senator's private suite.

"Well, how was your morning at the Battle with Running Bull?" Suzy asked as she put some papers down and came around her desk.

"Fair to middlin'," he said with a chuckle. "Kinda leaning toward middlin', though."

"That good, huh."

"Well, it seemed to end with a bitter taste in everybody's mouth. Steve thinks there is a hidden agenda in there that has to do with an unspoken rivalry between General Grant and me. I really don't understand that, but I do agree with him on one thing. I think it goes far deeper than General Grant is letting on."

"Are we getting paranoid?"

Jeff laughed.

"Steve and I already had that discussion this morning, and we decided that since the two of us feel that way, then we're only patriotic and not yet paranoid."

"What do you think he's going to do?"

"At this point, there's not much he can do because of PATRIOT's strong backing from Congress. If the Army doesn't budget the money to PATRIOT, then Congress won't give the money to the Army."

"So what does all of that mean about this afternoon's session?" she asked.

"I assume the bottom line is that I'm to take the presentation to the congressional group pretty much as I've got it laid out."

"So you're ready for the battle?"

"I've been ready for this battle for several years, and now I have all of the silver bullets I need. Last week's flight was a success that can't be denied, and I don't really expect any serious problem from these guys this afternoon."

"Don't be so sure," she said. "I heard some talk that there's going to be some real opposition. They still aren't convinced the Army needs an anti-missile program."

"Aren't convinced?"

"The conventional wisdom says that the programs in the Strategic Defense Initiative should be enough to satisfy the problem. And if they aren't exactly, then they probably can be altered to fit."

"In the immortal words of Yogi Berra, 'Déjà vu all over again,'" he said. "These people must all be in cahoots."

"Just don't expect to face an audience who'll accept what you have to say just because you've had a few good flight tests."

"Good points all," he said. "I owe you another one. How about letting me buy some of those back with lunch?"

"I'd like to, but I just can't. We're too busy here, and I'd planned to just have a quick lunch with Celia."

"Ah, the Ice Lady," Jeff said. Her friend Celia Mitchell was a strange one at best. She worked for Senator Strong down the hall.

"But you can buy back a whole dozen with dinner," she said. "You're still staying the night, aren't you?" she asked with enough of a smile to let him know she knew he was.

"A whole dozen is the best offer I've gotten all day. A man in my position would be foolish to pass that up. How about 7:30 at the Cantina?"

"Date," she said. "The meeting with the Armed Services staffers is just down the hall in the conference room by Senator Hinds's office. Senator Hastings sends his regards and wishes you good luck. Fred Finley will be there from our office."

"Do you know who else?"

"The Senator made sure that George Clark, the legislative assistant for military affairs from Senator Strong's office, will also be there since he's a PATRIOT fan. The rest, I don't know for sure, but you can bet Hensley from Senator Hinds's office will be there. He won't miss an opportunity for a piece of your flesh."

"Thanks. Any other bright news?"

"There is a message for you to call a Mr. Johnny Madkin at White Sands. He left a number, and if you want me to track him down, you can use the Senator's study phone."

"Thanks." Jeff said. "Tell me a little about Senator Strong."

"Celia's boss? How do you mean?"

"Well, he seems to be sort of an enigma. A blessing for sure, but still hard to figure. His state is Illinois, which has almost no business from PATRIOT. He's a solid, vote-down-the-line liberal Democrat, and yet he's an avid supporter of PATRIOT."

"Maybe he saw it once, and it grabbed him the way it did you."

"Maybe, but he doesn't strike me as the type. He rails at every opportunity about the wasteful programs in the Department of Defense, and he's the type my father would have called something stronger than liberal."

"Such as?"

"OK, but remember, you asked. In his milder moments, Dad would have called him a 'pinko bedwetting communist asshole.'"

"That sounds more like Mike Hensley than Senator Strong."

"Dad divided liberals into two camps. The first he called the 'credibles.' These were the people who seemed really dedicated to their cause and prepared to make sacrifices and stay the course for the long haul. The others just used the liberal line when it came time to gather votes in liberal sections of their constituency."

"And what did he call them?" Suzy asked, smiling at the description.

"The aforementioned PBCA," Jeff said, laughing. "In truth, I have a lot of respect for Mike Hensley, even though he's fighting the programs in which I believe most strongly."

"And even if you don't understand it, don't you need support from Senator Strong?"

"I need it and welcome it with open arms," Jeff said as he moved toward the Senator's study. "I just wonder what motivates him."

Jeff went into the Senator's study and sat on the couch. He removed his notes from the morning session and began to read. Suzy's voice on the intercom interrupted his thoughts.

"Johnny Madkin is out of the building. He'll call you back in a few minutes."

"Thanks," he said back to the machine, not really knowing if she could hear him.

He finished his final review and started out of the office. When he came to Suzy's desk, she signaled the phone was for him.

"General Weyland speaking."

"Hello, sir. Johnny Madkin here. I had a call from Steve Smith over the weekend about your question regarding the console entry during the test. I went over all of the printouts we have, but there's no record of any entry being made from target detection through intercept. The only actions the operator had to make were the designation of the target and the permission to launch. Both of those were done on controls separate from the alpha numeric keyboard. The system keeps a record of all entries made on the keyboard, and it shows nothing."

"Well," Jeff said, "that makes it stranger, but probably no more important. It was dark in the van, and I was pretty worked up—still I felt sure I saw him make an entry. Thanks for checking it out, though."

"Do you want me to find the operator and ask him?"

"No. I really just wanted to know if there was something about the engagement sequence that I didn't already know."

"Steve told me you would say that, and he told me why. Don't worry, I'll tell him it was the operator sitting by him that asked me about it."

"Well, OK." Jeff laughed, remembering his conversation about being embarrassed. "But don't make a special case out of it. Just mention it the next time you happen to see him."

"OK, sir," Johnny said. "I also called to the software lab at the Missile Command in your town and talked to a buddy of mine there who works in PATRIOT software. He's already called me back and said that he might be onto something and he'd get back to me if he found anything definite. Do you want his name so you can look him up when you get back to Huntsville?"

"OK," Jeff said, getting out a pencil, "but I still think we're making too much out of this thing. I really didn't intend for it to get this far."

"No sweat, sir. His name is Ben Peeples. That's with a double 'e.'"

"Peeples with a double 'e.' Got it. Anything else?"

"Not from me. Good luck on your meeting. Do you have everything you need from here?"

"Yes," Jeff said. "You people did a great job over the weekend working with Steve. Thanks for the effort."

"We're here to please, sir. Anything else?"

"No, except that I hope we'll have time for a few beers and some good country music next time I'm in town."

"Of both of those, sir, El Paso has an ample supply."

"Alright, Madkin. Then expect to drastically step up your consumption of Lone Star at my expense when I get to El Paso."

"Very well, sir." They were both laughing as they said goodbye.

"What was that problem you were talking about?" Suzy asked as he hung up the phone.

"Nothing really," he replied. "During the flight last week, I thought I saw the operator make an entry into the system at a time that didn't seem to fit. My chief engineer checked into it and passed it on to our people at the range. Johnny Madkin is our lead man there so he checked the records, and the report is that no such entry was made."

"Could you have been mistaken?" she asked.

"Possibly, and it's not really important anyway. Just another of those little unsolved mysteries of life. I'd ask the operator about it myself, but I don't have plans to be back there for some time."

"Well, good luck," she said, "I'll see you at seven-thirty. Stand me up and you not only don't get the dozen back, but it'll cost you plenty."

"Have I ever stood you up?" he asked.

"Let me think," she said with a smile.

"Let me leave," he said and made an exaggerated move for the door.

He knew he had, and more than once. But that was not a one-sided story. They were both in jobs where they weren't always the masters of their own destiny.

Oh, well, if you can't stand the heat, don't go in the kitchen.
God, I hate clichés.
God, I hate cynics.
God, I love my job.
OK, baby, let's go show the bastards!

❑❑❑❑❑

"What do you think we're going to run into here?" Steve asked Jeff as they walked toward the conference room on the back side of the building.

"Some serious opposition, if Suzy's right."

"I was kinda hoping for an easy afternoon."

"What I really think is that we should've brought a video tape of the last meeting with this group and played it for them instead of bothering with another meeting. All of the military types and staffers will play their roles like they're following a script."

"Things don't seem to change much, do they?" Steve chuckled at the thought. "Maybe we could play it in fast forward, and we could get through earlier and all go have a beer."

"No such luck, cowboy. They're all determined to be able to note in their reports to their bosses that they had spent the entire afternoon in conference on PATRIOT."

"Yeah, and from what I read in the papers, PATRIOT bashing is as popular in Congress as it is in the Pentagon."

"Always has been, and probably always will be."

"Until we have a war," Steve said.

"You're right. But the biggest part of our job is to prevent that very war from ever happening."

They had arrived at the conference room and found most of the participants were already there as they came in. By the time greetings were exchanged, the full list of attendees was assembled. Steve began the presentation without delay. Jeff leaned back in his chair and doodled on his pad while each listener took his turn with Steve.

After Steve had progressed well into the heart of the PATRIOT's history,

Mike Hensley leaned back in his chair and looked at Jeff.

"I really only have one question about all of this," he said. "How do we know that the eventual cost in dollars of a PATRIOT anti-missile capability is worth the limited effectiveness it will provide for the Army?"

"Based upon a similar question raised the last time we were here," Jeff said, "Steve has prepared a detailed analysis of a typical array of Army assets which could survive an attack by tactical missiles with and without the PAC II upgrade. This should make it clear that the investment is sound—sound in dollars even if the savings in lives are not considered. I think Steve has done his homework exceptionally well in this area, and the material is a little later in his charts."

"I want to ask a question about the warhead," Mike said without acknowledging the answer.

"Go right ahead, Mike," Steve said.

"Can this thing neutralize a chemical payload?" Mike asked.

"Honestly, Mike, I can't talk in too much detail about that in this room. I can say that we don't have a lot of information about the chemical payloads coming out of the Soviet Bloc. We do know that this new PATRIOT warhead is a damn sight better against missile targets and their payloads than the previous one we had, which was just for airplanes. As I said on the last chart, we've changed to heavier pellets and a forward-looking fuze. But what we can guarantee about a kill of that payload is a whole different discussion. Biological, by the way, falls into the same category."

"So why go ahead now?" Mike asked. Jeff was impressed that Mike seemed sincerely interested in finding out the truth rather than just poking for soft spots.

"Because we take a quantum leap forward with this warhead, and other technologies coming along are still a good while off. If we don't do this now, we won't have anything better for several years, at least. And remember, I didn't say we can't—I said we can't discuss it here. I can say this warhead gives us the best possibility currently available. I have some additional material in my briefcase on the technology in this area which tells what our warhead can and can't do, which future technologies hold the most promise against which types of payloads and when they might be available. The material is classified at a level higher than we can discuss in this conference room, but if you like, I can arrange for a briefing of that material later this afternoon in the Pentagon."

"No, that isn't necessary," Mike said, seemingly satisfied with Steve's response.

Steve continued with his presentation without receiving additional questions until he was finished.

"If there are no further questions, then," Steve said, "General Weyland will present the current program status and plans for the future."

Jeff got out of his seat and went to the front of the room. Steve moved to a seat by the overhead projector to handle the charts Jeff would present.

"I'm sure," Jeff began, "that each of you knows there is a separate program for PATRIOT growth termed the Pre-Planned Product Improvement."

Several of the staffers looked through their notes to find Jeff's first chart.

"This program is intended to use the PATRIOT technology we have in the field and produce an improved Air Defense capability against manned aircraft. It responds to deficiencies found in PATRIOT or to unexpected developments in enemy capability.

"The effort for PAC II is similar to, but is not a part of, that program, and it is funded under a separate budget line."

"Could you explain that?"

"Certainly, Mike. The programs are similar in the sense that PAC II is an improvement to the basic system, but different in that it is a totally new mission and capability. These charts illustrate the surface-to-surface missile capabilities of the potentially hostile nations. The data is shown before and after the Intermediate Nuclear Forces Treaty. The trend tells the real story.

"Many adversarial nations now have a missile capability. The United States has a treaty with only one, the Soviet Union, and what that treaty means anymore is anybody's guess. That treaty covered countries where Soviet missile systems were manned by Soviet personnel, but there are still many nations with their own missiles which are not under the Soviet umbrella. Many of these missiles were bought from the Soviet Union, and others were either bought from various weapons-manufacturing countries or made by those nations themselves.

"In this environment of easily available hardware, any country with the desire to project power beyond its own borders can buy or make missiles. This process is significantly cheaper than owning and operating a large navy or air force, the historical means of projecting power. For the price of owning one or two high-performance fighter aircraft, for example, a country could buy 15 tactical ballistic missiles complete with mobile launchers. In today's environment, it's as simple as this: if you can be seen, you can be hit, and if you can be hit, you will be killed.

"This chart shows where tactical ballistic missiles are in place around the world and where they can be targeted. Take special note that this data specifically refers to the situation after the Intermediate Nuclear Forces Treaty. This overlay shows our estimates of where those same hostile nations can deliver their chemical and biological payloads. Note that I said our estimates. Developing nations are very protective of their capability in this area, and the data is very sketchy."

"Why do they keep their stuff so secretive, while we broadcast ours to anybody who will listen?" asked the legislative assistant to the senior senator from Wyoming.

"The projection of force worldwide by the United States is intended to be a deterrent to war," Jeff said. "The more massive and destructive that force is perceived to be, the more effective the deterrent. Most of these countries don't have sufficient power to convey a peace-preserving message, so they believe that maintaining a veil over their capability gives them an edge. First as a deterrent, since their enemy doesn't really know what they have, and then as an element of surprise if and when hostilities start."

"General, may I interrupt and ask a question at this point?" The question was raised by the legislative assistant to the junior senator from California.

"Certainly, James," Jeff said.

"Wasn't PATRIOT originally designed to be an anti-missile system, but that requirement changed when the Army found out it was too expensive?"

"In a sense, yes," Jeff answered. "The original concept for PATRIOT had a nuclear warhead which could engage incoming nuclear missiles. It was a sign of the times during the sixties and seventies that the country was trying hard to reduce the defense budget and also to avoid the proliferation of nuclear missiles, so that option was dropped."

"I understand that, but if it was too expensive then, why isn't it too expensive now?"

"First, because the missiles attacking our forces in the field today are a different class, and, second, we are accomplishing the task without a nuclear warhead. It was the cost of the nuclear option that was expensive, not the fact that we were engaging missiles."

"Oh," said the assistant, and went back to some personal notes he was reviewing.

"The data on this next series of charts illustrates the cost of the PAC II program," Jeff continued. "All of the PATRIOT missiles haven't been produced, and those already in the field will be retained to be used against aircraft. Those remaining to come off the production line next year can be built in the new configuration and the first deliveries can be available in May of 1991. Aside from the missile, most of the changes are in the software.

"As Steve noted earlier, there is considerable change in the operating configuration of the system. The software intensive system turns out to be a blessing in this case. The software change that adds this new capability will be the third major update to the PATRIOT software since the system was fielded."

"Let's talk about those numbers for a moment, General," Mike Hensley said. "I saw the data Steve presented earlier, but how can we be sure that spending this money on PATRIOT is the best way to go?"

"That's an awfully broad question," Jeff said. "I can only show you the estimated savings in lives and assets if we have this capability and if we don't."

"But there must be other places an amount of money that large could be used which would also save lives," Mike said.

"I'm sure there is," Jeff said. "But it won't help us prevent wars or win them if they start."

"So you think we should measure everything we do in terms of whether it will help us win a war?" Mike asked.

"No," Jeff said. "But it is our constitutional responsibility to make sure we can win any war we have to fight."

"Any war at any time in any place against any enemy?" Mike asked.

"Yes," Jeff answered.

"Why?" Mike persisted.

"First, because as I said, it's constitutional. Second, and maybe more importantly, as soon as we aren't prepared to win a war, we will surely be provoked into one."

"Why? Pick any other country around. Mexico can't meet that criteria, but they don't have any wars."

"Would you fight a war to take over Mexico?" Jeff asked.

"Obviously not," Mike said.

"Neither would I nor any country, and that's why Mexico and others like Mexico are safe. The United States, on the other hand, is envied by many nations of the world, and there are many of those who would like to see us taken down a notch or two. In addition, there are many nations whose alliance with the United States, both formal and implied, protects them from domination by larger and stronger countries. We may not like this role which comes with being as successful as we are as a country, but we can't deny it."

"Suppose it were possible," Mike asked, "to save more lives through medical research than you estimate this capability will save in combat. What then?"

"The issue involved is not just saving lives, but, as the Constitution requires, providing for the common defense. That's what this is all about. I could easily ask, how many lives is it worth to protect our country? A seemingly impossible question to answer, but we have answered it many times in the past, and those answers have cost many lives. These tactical ballistic missiles are a new development by an old enemy and for many potential new enemies. They must be countered, or the Army can't be effective in the field. It's that simple."

"So no matter who suffers, our priority should be to build you a better missile, is that it?" Mike asked.

"It's not my missile," Jeff said.

"OK, build the Army a better missile."

"We should put priority on maintaining our commitment as instituted by the Constitution, and defense is not the only obligation on that list. Once those commitments are met, the Congress has the responsibility to determine what other programs should be mandated in the best interest of the country."

"What do you believe the American people want?" Mike asked.

"I don't think many American people have ever heard of PAC II."

"Yes, but if they were asked if they wanted to spend their money this way, what do you think would be their reaction?"

"I don't believe that would be a fair question to ask the American people. Did we ask the American people whether or not we wanted new sights for the M-16 rifle? Did we ask if they wanted flat windshields for the Apache helicopter?"

"It's not the same thing," Mike said. "We're talking here about a new mission for the Army, aren't we?"

"Yes, but in a survey of those Americans you're going to ask, sixty-five percent of them thought we could defend Washington if it were attacked by missiles where in fact, we can't. So I ask you, is that a fair question to ask the American public?"

"Let's look at the problem from a different point of view. When was PATRIOT first designed?"

"The original submission from Raytheon was in 1969." Jeff left the front of the room and moved to a chair by the table and sat.

"But the original concept was earlier than that, wasn't it?"

"Yes. The concept dates from the mid-sixties."

"So we're talking about technology which is twenty-five years old?"

"No. The program was tasked in 1972 by the Secretary of Defense to temporarily stop the development program, demonstrate the feasibility of the complex guidance system and then upgrade the technology to the latest available. In addition, there have been major upgrades to the program under the Pre-Planned Product Improvement program I mentioned earlier to maintain the technology of the system with current state of the art."

"But sooner or later, a program runs out of its ability to upgrade and has to be replaced."

"Inevitably." Jeff shrugged his shoulders.

"How do we know we're not at that point now with PATRIOT, a system which came to us twenty-five years ago?"

"Because the system did not come to us twenty-five years ago, only the concept. PATRIOT is current technology which is still able to meet the current threat. That's the yardstick we have to use. When we can't counter the threat with existing systems, we have to look to new concepts."

"Isn't it true that the Army is already looking at new systems which will replace PATRIOT?"

"There is always research ongoing, but there are no current plans to replace PATRIOT."

"But eventually we will?"

"Yes."

"And that replacement system will likely counter missiles as well as aircraft?"

"Presumably."

"Then why don't we just wait on that new system, or even hurry it along a little? Why waste money on this upgrade to PATRIOT which is going to be replaced?"

"Because the threat to our country is now. The replacement for PATRIOT, if one ever comes, will not be here before the next century. Our country has soldiers in the field now who are vulnerable to attack by short range ballistic missiles. Without protection for those soldiers from these missiles, we cannot win a serious conflict."

"At least we agree on one thing, General," Mike said.

"And that is?" Jeff asked.

"That the decision is to be made by the people I work for, not the people you work for," Mike said.

Definitely a credible, Dad, but you're right, he's still an asshole.

"I think we have gotten all of the information from General Weyland and his staff that we need." It was George Clark from Senator Strong's office. "And personally, I believe that the General has cleared up a lot of loose ends. It's clear to me that we have a situation here which was not perceived when PATRIOT was built, and we need to fix that problem. Relative to the cost of the system, the funds needed are small. And I also agree with the General, Mike, that subjects like the medical research debate need a different forum than this."

Jeff sensed the hostility between these two young men. That hostility seemed odd since they were both cut from the same political cloth.

"I would like to second what George has said," said Fred Finley. "This has been most informative. I will act as the point of contact if any of you need any further information. General Weyland, we thank you for coming."

□□□□□

Jeff was slumped back against the bench seat as he rode the Metro headed toward the Pentagon. It was getting late, but if he changed clothes in the Pentagon, he could still be on time to meet Suzy at the Cantina.

He leaned back in the seat and let his mind drift over the day. How many more days like this he had left in him, he didn't know. Each one took its toll. He had a theory that each person had only so much of what he called "plasma." It was a combination of creativity, initiative, self-discipline, motivation and the other factors required to achieve significant accomplishments. You could use it any way you wanted, but there was a limited amount each person or each organization had, and when it was gone, there was no more. Whatever it was, he had shot a wad of it this day.

As Jeff's mind drifted, he thought about Cindy, the early days with Beth, the times when they were a family and the times when they weren't.

Good thoughts, Weyland. Think good thoughts.

Doesn't always work, does it?

61

MARCH
1967

chemical weapons--pentagon adv20 3-67
Defoliant Agent Orange intended to blow cover of Viet Cong
USWNS Military News
adv mar 20 1967 or thereafter

By GEORGE GROWSON

WASHINGTON—The Air Force announced today that major
efforts were being taken to deny the Viet Cong hiding
places in the jungles along the Ho Chi Minh Trail. Plant
defoliant is being used in massive air drops in North and
South Vietnam. Despite claims from several organizations
that the primary defoliant, Agent Orange, may have serious
side effects on animal life, including humans, the
Department of Defense spokesman, Hugh McDermott, stated
that the defoliation program would continue. "The issue
here is winning wars and saving the lives of U.S.
soldiers," McDermott stated. "This program has been
demonstrated as the only viable way to deny the enemy the
cover he needs for secrecy of his movements."

THREE

March 20, 1967

Alwan Delta Village

Republic of Vietnam

12:30 AM

It was quiet.

There were no birds, cars, or city noises. Not even a rustle of wind in the trees.

It was dark.

No moon, stars, or even lights from houses could be seen. Arnie couldn't see his own hand when he reached for the radio microphone.

"Marshy Outlaw Two-Two, this is Sparky One-Six, over." The whisper over the radio was the only link to life.

The young soldier stationed further up the river reached down and picked up the handset.

"Sparky One-Six, this is Outlaw Two-Two, go." Like the call that summoned, the whispered answer was barely enough to be heard but Arnie recognized Fish's voice.

"Outlaw, this is Sparky. Something's coming down the river, over." Fish stared down where he knew the river was, even though it was hopelessly invisible in the dark. He couldn't see anything. From where he was sitting, he couldn't even see the riverbank, much less something floating on the water.

"How far out?" he asked, stirring around in his cramped quarters.

"Can't tell. It's right at max range of my light, so it must be nearly a half mile." Arnie was still whispering into the microphone, but that didn't hide the excitement in his voice.

"Can you tell what it is?"

"Not yet. But I can tell there's a lot of it. Covers about half the river. Just a minute."

Fish slid himself a little to his right and pushed his elbow into the side of the sleeping form with him in the gun turret.

"What's up?" Ronnie asked sleepily.

"Something's coming down the river. A lot of it. Arnie doesn't know what it is yet, but it's about a half mile away."

"Aw, shit, man. What do you want me to do? Arnie sees stuff on the river in his sleep."

"Just wake up. I want some company."

"Outlaw Two-Two, this is Sparky One-Six, over."

"Go ahead, Sparky."

"Fish, if I'm facing you, which way does this river flow?" Arnie's voice sounded funny.

"Your right to your left," Fish whispered into the radio.

"Then somebody better go wake up the Old Man, 'cause this trash is coming up river." Arnie's voice was openly excited now.

"Oh, shit," Fish said as he sat up higher in the seat. "I hope this isn't like the last time."

"Yeah," came the reply from the other side of the turret with a sleepy laugh. "I bet you do."

During the last attack, Fish had been so scared he had lost control of his bodily functions, and then when the firefight was over and he realized what he had done, he had thrown up right in the turret. He had been the brunt of many jokes since that night. He poked Ronnie again.

"I done told you, stay off that shit, man," Fish said. "And go wake up the Cap'n. This trash is coming upriver, and there's lots of it."

"I've never done that before. You go."

"Bullshit. I've got to stay here with the radio. Go!" Fish began cranking the handles to rotate the guns to point downriver in the direction of the water flow.

Ronnie slipped over the edge of the turret and went to the command bunker a few yards behind the big steel vehicle. The captain had made the rounds to each of the gun sections, and he was spending the night with Section Two-Two tonight. That had happened before, but this was the first time on Ronnie's watch that they had any action. He reached down and shook the sleeping captain's shoulder.

"Captain Weyland, wake up. There's something coming down the river, but it's coming *up* the river."

"I'm on the way," Jeff said. He was into his boots before his feet hit the dirt floor. "Can the light make it out?"

"No, sir," Ronnie said, "but it's coming against the current, and there's a lot of it."

When Jeff got to the gun, Ronnie had returned from waking the rest of the crew and was climbing over the edge of the steel shroud and back into his seat beside Fish. Jeff reached over the side of the vehicle into the driver's hatch, found the infrared binoculars, and used them to look down the river.

"Fish, I can see 'em pretty good now," Arnie's voice came over the radio. "You ain't gonna believe this shit—there's more of them than you wanna know."

"I can see 'em, too," Jeff said in the same whisper everyone else was using. He reached over the edge of the vehicle into the driver's hatch again and grabbed the second radio mike.

"Marshy Outlaw Five, this is Marshy Outlaw Six, over."

"Outlaw Six, this is Outlaw Two-Two-Six, stand by, over." Jeff was calling Billy Walker, the Battery Executive Officer. Billy was on the other side of the bridge with the second gun section.

"Outlaw Six, this is Outlaw Five, over."

"Outlaw Five, Sparky has action on the river. Floats with a large number of personnel coming up the river against the current. We're going to turn the lights on in about two minutes. Over."

"Roger, Outlaw Six. We'll be ready."

Jeff reached down and put his hand on another soldier just now approaching the vehicle. "Set the Battery radio to 45.60." Jeff waited while the soldier crawled through the small hatch of the steel vehicle and set the radio to the new frequency. He stopped another soldier just arriving.

"Keep the noise low and start uncanning ammo—lots of it."

The guns fired forty-millimeter shells which came packed in heavy steel cans. Each shell was about two inches in diameter and eighteen inches long. They were packed in five round clips.

"Yes, sir," the soldier said.

Even in the dark, the familiar look was recognizable in the soldier's eyes. Every soldier had that look just before a fight. A look filled with questions, anticipation and fear. The full set of standard emotions going into a fire fight.

"All set, Cap'n," the soldier said as he crawled out of the hatch. "45.60."

"Spooky, Spooky, this is Marshy Outlaw Six, over." Jeff held his breath. All of the soldiers momentarily stopped what they were doing to listen for the response.

It was quiet again.

"Spooky, Spooky, this is Marshy Outlaw Six, over." Jeff's voice showed just a hint of strain and hope.

"Marshy Outlaw Six, this is Spooky Three-Five, over."

Thank you, God.

The soldiers all went back to their preparations.

Spooky was an airborne AC-130 aircraft loaded to the rooftops with guns and ammunition, flying overhead to support their operation and others north and south of Saigon on Highway Four.

"Spooky Three-Five, this is Marshy Outlaw Six." Jeff spoke softly and slowly into the mike. "I have a target. On the water. Approximately one thousand meters south-southeast of my location. I repeat, on the water, one thousand meters south-southeast of my location. Can't judge number of hostiles, but a large group of floating something's moving upriver toward my location. Do you copy, over?"

"Outlaw Six, this is Spooky Three-Five. Copy. I have four-two-kay rounds of two-zero mike-mike. Echo-tango-alpha your location in one-five, over."

"This is Outlaw Six. Sooner's better if you can make it. I can't tell yet how fast they're moving, and if they get too close to me, then I can't use you."

"Roger, Outlaw. My rubber band's wound as tight as it'll go. I'm en route. Do you have flares, over?"

"Yes, but I don't want to use them until we fire. I have infrared on the target, and I can see them." Sparky was the radio call sign for a jeep-mounted, twenty-three-inch xenon searchlight which could shine with either regular white light, or infrared, which turned the night into a hazy red daylight when used with special glasses. He switched the radio back to his own frequency and keyed the mike again.

"Outlaw Five, this is Outlaw Six, over."

"Five, go."

"Spooky Three-Five is en route with 42,000 rounds of twenty millimeter on board and he'll be here in fifteen minutes. I'm going to have him fire the twenty millimeter from over our shoulder, over."

"I copy Spooky. I hope he knows where my shoulder is. I can't see anything with my glasses. Tell Sparky to hold the light still."

"Wilco." He leaned over and tapped Fish on the shoulder.

"Tell the light to move slower," he whispered. "They're having trouble following it on the other side."

"He's just a little excited, Cap'n," Fish said. "I'll calm him down."

"You do that."

Jeff looked through his glasses trying to make out the people on the floating hunks in the river. He was sure he could see movement, but couldn't make out any people yet. He climbed onto the front fender of the tracked vehicle which housed the twin forty-millimeter guns originally built in the 1930s for shooting down low, slow-moving airplanes.

The open gun turret was about six feet across and had two seats, one on either side of the guns, with a crank handle for the gunner in each seat. One gunner's crank steered the gun left or right and the other crank steered up or down. The gun was the old reliable "pom-pom" gun used by the Navy on ships, except it used air for cooling instead of water. In full automatic, the two guns could fire 240 rounds of forty-millimeter projectiles a minute, each with an explosive warhead. When it fired that rapidly, the guns produced so much smoke, noise and flying dirt, it had been given the nickname "Duster."

The vehicle was a modified chassis of the famous M-48 Walker "Bulldog" tank which had been a workhorse for the Army for many years.

It was powered by a huge six-cylinder gasoline engine, and was a good vehicle for its purpose, but maintaining the old gas engines in the Mekong Delta had proven to be a real problem.

Jeff was still on the front fender when he heard the buzz of the radio again.

"Outlaw Six, this is Spooky Three-Five. I have your India-Romeo in sight. I will be in position in zero-five. Which is the best direction to fire, over?"

"From the west. That'll put you firing directly over me and down the light beam. After you see my four-zero mike-mike, pop the flares, over."

"I'm out of flares here. We'll have to go with yours. With what I can see from here, it might be better if you fire first, and when the group breaks up, I'll move in."

"Sounds good to me, Spooky, let me know when you're ready."

"Roger." Jeff switched the radio again.

"Outlaw Five, Outlaw Six, over."

"Five, go."

"Zero five minutes on Spooky. We'll fire first when Sparky turns white, then fire flares from both sides of the river. Then Spooky opens fire. They'll probably hear the Spooky engines before we open fire, but I doubt they'll know who he is or what he's doing."

"Roger. We're ready this side."

Jeff leaned over to Fish. "We're going to fire first. You and Arnie get your shit together. Five minutes."

"Yes, sir." Jeff heard Fish say something under his breath.

"You OK, Fish?" Jeff asked.

"Yes, sir, I was just thinking that my mama was right. I should've kept my black ass in school."

"Remember that when you get back to the States."

The ammunition was moving up onto the back deck of the vehicle and being spread out over the engine covers. When the guns were firing, it took four soldiers to keep up with the steady flow of ammunition. Two additional soldiers got in the turret with the gunners and fed the five-round clips into each of the guns. Two more soldiers stood on the outside of the turret and handed ammunition to the ones on the inside. A practiced crew could keep the gun firing for extended periods of time this way.

"Sparky One-Six, this is Outlaw Two-Two, over."

"This is Sparky. Jesus, Fish, I can see the people now. They're all over the place out there. Those floats are crawling with 'em."

"I just hope they're only on the river and not coming up the banks, too. Those Ruff Puffs didn't impress me too much." The riverbanks around the bridge were protected by Regional and Provincial Forces of the South Vietnamese Army that were abbreviated RF/PF, called "Ruff Puffs" by the U.S. GIs. "Get ready. There's a Spooky overhead, but we're going to fire first. Less than five minutes. Do you think they know we've spotted them?"

"Can't tell, but they haven't done anything different," Arnie said. "Just slowly coming up the middle of the river. There's about twenty things floating, covering a space about fifty meters wide. There's more behind, but I can't tell how much yet. Did the Old Man call the Artillery?"

"Yeah, they're standing by, but it's too close to us for that unless we get in real trouble. I wouldn't trust those guys to hit a tank if they fired from the inside. Besides, once they fire their smoke rounds and do all of their adjustments, this fight's gonna be over."

"You hope."

"You're goddamn right I hope. I think we're nearly ready."

"Hey, black boy," Arnie said.

"Yeah."

"Shoot that thing good, OK?"

"You just keep that light working, honkey, and this gunner is going to eat me some VC." Fish switched off his radio and hunched lower in the turret with his hands gripping the cranking mechanism. "God, don't let me die," he mumbled as he slid a little further down inside the steel cocoon. "God, don't let me shit my pants again. Please, God, don't let me die. Not here."

"Outlaw Six, this is Spooky Three-Five. I am on station and ready, over."

"Roger, Spooky. Wait one. Flares not ready."

"Roger, Outlaw. Don't wait too long or I'll have to make another turn."

"Outlaw Six, this is Outlaw Five, over."

"Six, go."

"What's the holdup? I can see lots of slanty-eyed little people getting very close to my location. We're getting very nervous on this side."

"Waiting on flares. Have you heard anything on the riverbank?"

"Affirmative. I can't wait much longer. I hear the Ruff Puffs stirring around. They're going to open up soon if we don't."

"Roger. We're ready."

Fish squirmed around in the seat a little and made sure his foot was squarely on the fire pedal. Once, in training at Fort Bliss, Texas, he had his foot off to the side so the pedal didn't go down and he had missed his shot at his target. He didn't see why they made him learn to shoot at airplanes anyway. The VC sure didn't have any. At least he had learned to keep his foot on the pedal. "Shit," he mumbled, "why didn't I stay in school? I love you, Mama, and I promise I'm gonna go back to school when I get home. God, don't let me die."

"OK, Fish, your turn," Jeff whispered over the edge of the turret. "Don't shoot wild. Single fire, both barrels. Pick your targets. Whenever you and the light are ready. Do good, buddy, and I'll owe you a six-pack." Jeff rapped Fish on the helmet as he moved away from the turret and to the back of the vehicle. The gun had the capability to shoot single fire or automatic. In single fire, both guns fired one round every time the gunner pushed the pedal. This conserved ammunition and gave better results against ground targets. Full automatic firing at low angles often created so much smoke that the reflecting light from the searchlight could cut off vision of the targets.

Fish keyed his radio mike.

"Target line?" Fish asked Arnie for the exact direction to the targets as best as he could describe. Arnie's jeep with the searchlight was up on the bridge.

"Center of the river. About 800 meters," Arnie said.

"Ready?" Fish asked.

"I ain't ready to die, motherfucker, so stick it to 'em."

Fish tensed, his foot on the pedal.

"Ready...ready...FLICK!"

Arnie switched the light from infrared to white light, and the river was suddenly bathed with light and alive with people.

74

It took Fish and Ronnie less than a heartbeat to make the slight correction from where the gun was pointing when the white light came on. In that brief moment of bright light, bodies were visible jumping off the floats into the river. About the time the first round left the forty-millimeter gun, the rhythmic thump of the flares could be heard as they were being fired from behind the battle positions. In a few seconds the flares popped high overhead, and as they lit up the sky, the searchlight went off.

Arnie jumped into the driver's seat of the jeep and moved the light system since the enemy on the river now knew where he was on the bridge. He set up again a hundred feet down the bridge and started to work the light with infrared trying to pick up whatever targets he could find near the bank.

With the help of the light from the flares, Fish worked the center of the river. He picked his targets one at a time and continued firing. He had to talk to Ronnie in the next seat to make sure they aimed at the same target. Several of the floats were hit, but most of the people on them had long since gone in the water. The crude floats, more like rafts than boats, came apart easily. The fifth float that Fish hit with the forty millimeter erupted in a huge explosion of fire and water, making such a fountain of vapor and debris in the air that nothing was visible for several seconds.

More flares popped.

As the water settled, more floats became visible farther down the river. Fish started firing again, and then the sounds of the Spooky gunship dominated the area.

The Gatlin gun on the airplane sounded more like a huge electric generator than a machine gun. The rounds were fired so rapidly, no individual shot could be heard, just a deafening hum which lasted a few seconds on each burst. Fish stopped a moment to watch the action on the river. He heard the Captain on the radio.

"Spooky, this is Outlaw Six. I'm taking fire. The tracers are coming off the floats farther down the river."

"Taking fire," Fish said to Ronnie. "What the fuck's he mean taking fire? We ain't taking fire."

An explosion which seemed to Fish must have been big enough to take down the Empire State Building hit about fifty meters behind them. Simultaneously, several rounds ricocheted off the front of the armor on his vehicle.

"Holy shit!" Fish shouted and slapped at Ronnie. "We're taking fire!" He had jumped so hard he had knocked his steel helmet off. He reached for it and heard the Captain yell from behind the turret.

"Shoot the gun, Fisher! NOW!"

The tracers were brilliant streaks of green coming from the river and they could hear the familiar sound of the Soviet AK-47 rifles and the "pomp" of the mortars being launched. Fish turned the gun toward the source of the tracers first. Mortar rounds were landing wildly all around the vehicle and they could hear pieces of shrapnel pinging on the steel sides of the Duster.

"Who the fuck ever heard of firing a mortar from a raft anyway?" Fish shouted.

"I see the mortar." It was Arnie on the radio. "On the bank about 1,500 meters down."

"Spooky, this is Outlaw Six. Can you see mortar flashes from the river bank?"

"Negative, Outlaw. I have plenty of targets on the river. We might need more help."

"What about some artillery, Cap'n?" Fish shouted.

"Not until we have to," Jeff shouted back. Another mortar round landed behind them, this one closer than the rest.

"When do you figure that will be?" Fish yelled.

Jeff felt the debris fall on him from the last near miss.

"Now," Jeff said as he keyed the mike on the second radio. "Heavy Labor Three-One, this is Marshy Outlaw Six, over,"

"Outlaw Six, this is Heavy Labor Three One, over." Heavy Labor was a battery of eight-inch Howitzers which could throw a 200-pound projectile more than ten miles. The first few rounds had to be adjusted, however, and U.S. policy was that the first round would have to be an airborne burst of a smoke marker round. This prevented injury to friendly troops if the first round was off target due to some human error. The guns had been registered earlier during daylight, but Jeff was still wary.

"Heavy Labor, I am in contact with an unknown sized force on the river south southeast of my position. Would you start your fire about two klicks down river from me at Romeo Papa Four-Two and work your way up?" Jeff figured that far would be safe. A klick was GI slang for a kilometer, and two klicks was about a mile and a half. Romeo Papa Four-Two was Registration Point forty-two, a preselected position the artillery had on their plotting boards.

"I see the mortar!" Fish yelled as he turned the gun toward the river bank.

"Don't you worry about the mortar!" Jeff shouted. "I've got artillery coming for that. Stay on the river." Small arms rounds were pinging all around now, and Jeff had laid flat and snuggled himself safely behind the turret.

Safe is a relative term.

I wish I'd stayed in school, too.

He felt the turret turn as Fish moved back to the river and started firing again.

He reached over the turret, got Fish's handset and yelled, "Sparky, come up on the Artillery frequency and adjust their fire onto the mortar." There was no verbal answer, but the radio squawked once. No fire from the enemy on the river was going on the bridge, so Jeff assumed Arnie should be able to work easily. The infrared glasses Arnie had would easily pick up the muzzle flashes from the mortar, and from his height on the bridge, Arnie was the best to adjust the fire.

There was a major explosion on the far side of the bridge.

"Outlaw Six, this is Outlaw Five, over."

"Six. Go."

"I'd like to report that the enemy has violated the Geneva Convention and has started to use nuclear weapons, and if he does that again, I'm really going to be pissed."

"Are you still intact?"

"Safe and mostly sound, but I'm going to look at that hole in the morning. If I didn't know better, I would think that was an eight-inch Howitzer."

"No chance, buddy. Heavy Labor hasn't even started firing yet. They're going to work the banks down river and the Sparky's going to adjust them to try to hit the mortar."

"Good idea, but what just landed here was no mortar."

"Roger. It had to be a rocket, but I never saw it or heard it. That means it came from a good distance away. I'll tell Arnie to keep a lookout from the top of the bridge."

"Shot, over," he heard from the radio on the artillery frequency. That meant the artillery had fired their first rounds. He then heard Arnie's voice on the radio and put the mortar problem out of his head for the moment. Fish and the gunship were working the river over well. The second pair of Dusters on the far side of the river had opened up, and Jeff knew they were probably taking small arms and mortar fire as well. Trying to look from his awkward position behind the guns, he couldn't tell the difference between floating debris and people in the river. There was so much debris the river looked like a logjam. He heard the flare launches continue to pop behind him. The enemy mortar rounds continued to land, but were still scattered.

The smoke round from the eight-inch gun lit up in the air about two miles down river.

"Well, there's our artillery, the Queen of Battle," Fish said. "Christ, nobody could live through that."

"I hope they have some real bullets left!" Ronnie shouted at Jeff.

They could hear Arnie on the radio patiently trying to explain to the artillery Fire Direction Center how to adjust the big guns.

The first impact of a big eight-inch shell landed well inland from the bank and down the river from the mortar position. Arnie was on the radio immediately, and soon another round landed in the water about one hundred meters short of the mortar. Arnie called again to give more directions. The next rounds that hit were a barrage all around the mortar, and then the mortar stopped firing. A temporary lull came right after the barrage and he could hear Arnie plainly now on the radio.

"Hit 'em one more time. Same place."

Jeff chuckled at how the artillerymen must feel taking directions from an untrained observer. To those guys, violating their fire adjustment radio protocol was right up there with forgetting to salute a five-star general.

"Why has Spooky quit firing, Cap'n?" Fish shouted.

"They're making a turn to get the aircraft into firing position again," Jeff said. "If they fire back this way, the rounds might ricochet off the water and into us."

"I hope they understand that concept as well as you do."

"Just fire the gun, Fish."

Fish was firing slowly now, but was still at it. The incoming rounds had slowed, too, and Jeff decided to venture a full, but quick look. He got up on his knees behind the turret. The river was still well lit from the flares. Debris was everywhere. Four or five of the floats were still on the water. Some small arms fire was coming from one of the rafts farther down the river, but it stopped when Fish let fly a near miss, spraying water which probably got the shooters wet. There was a mumbled curse from inside the turret, and then Fish fired again and this one was a hit.

"Adios, motherfucker," Fish shouted and continued firing until he had hit all of the floats. He stopped firing and there was another lull.

They waited.

"Outlaw Six, this is Spooky. Whataya think?"

"Spooky, this is Outlaw Six. I think the Northern Pass is safe for the Great White Settler once again, but I think I'll prop one eye open for the rest of the night just the same."

"Roger that. Our replacement is getting airborne now. If you need anything else, we're always ready to oblige."

"Thanks, Spooky, I owe you a beer. If I happen to get by your nice air-conditioned Officer's Club with the soft bar stools and good-looking women anytime soon, I'll buy you one."

"Hey, Outlaw, it's rougher than you think. Last week the ice machine broke down and we had to cool the beer in a meat locker. I've still got a good load of ammo, so I'll work the river banks on both sides until I'm empty in case any of the bad guys made it to shore."

"Roger that," Jeff answered. "Thanks again."

"Any time, Outlaw. Spooky out."

Jeff switched the radio back to his internal frequency.

79

"Outlaw Five, this is Outlaw Six, over."

"This is five. All quiet here. I have two wounded, none serious."

Jeff stood up on the back of the vehicle. It was over. The troops were already out of their firing positions policing up the brass casings from the forty millimeter rounds. He walked over to his jeep, turned on the big AM radio which occupied most of the back seat, and picked up the handset.

"Roving House Three-One, this is Marshy Outlaw Six, over." Roving House was the radio call sign for his parent organization.

"Marshy Outlaw Six, this is Roving House Three-One, over."

"This is Outlaw Six, I have an after-action report, over."

"Roger, Outlaw Six, send your message, over."

"Roger. Time: Zero-One-One-Five, Two-Two March. Encountered Victor Charley of unknown strength on Alpha Delta river. Detected by Sparky One-Six using India-Romeo. Engaged with four-zero mike-mike from Outlaw Two-One and Two-Two, two-zero mike-mike from Spooky Three-Five and eight-inch from Heavy Labor. All enemy engaged, enemy losses unknown. Two Uniform Sierra wounded, minor and treated on site, over." Jeff could see the jeep coming off the bridge with Billy in the passenger's side.

"What is estimate of enemy killed, over?"

"No estimate. Hostiles were in the river. I can't tell the difference between dead people and floating debris, and it's moving away from me pretty fast, over." The jeep pulled to a stop, and Billy walked over to him.

"Marshy Outlaw Six, this is Roving House Three-One. I need your best guess on the enemy killed from your observation of the battle, over."

Billy rolled his eyes and sat on the running board of the jeep pulling out a pack of cigarettes.

Roving House Three-One was Major Simpson, the Battalion Operations Officer. It was his job to maintain control and knowledge of all battalion activities, which included reporting enemy kills.

"Staying up until 1:30 in the morning in the command bunker must be his way of participating in the hardships of war," Billy said.

The U.S. high command in Vietnam was obsessed with reporting body count. In a war like this one, there was no other way to measure success.

Capturing ground didn't matter, because you would abandon it and move on in a few days, anyway. All the normal accomplishments didn't matter here except the body count, and it was worshipped.

"Give 'em what they want," Billy said as he stood up and stretched. "Tell 'em 500. I counted nearly that many we got on our side alone, and surely you guys got a few over here."

Jeff gave Billy his best commander's disapproving look as he keyed the mike.

"I estimate five-zero enemy KIA. Maybe in the morning we can get some kind of real count when we do a sweep, but my guess is that a lot of them will float down the river or get carried off by their buddies, so we'll never really know for sure."

"Your battle estimate is sufficient. Anything else to report?"

"We received one hit from something big. I don't know what it was, but it was no mortar. We didn't see any rocket traces, and it was too noisy to have heard it, but I believe it had to be something like that."

"Roger, Outlaw. Anything else?"

"Shit," Billy said. "They don't even care if the bridge is intact."

"Negative, Roving House. The action seems to be over. Spooky worked the banks for a while and has left. We'll put out a good guard for the rest of the night. I'm going to need about seven-five-zero rounds of four-zero mike-mike here tomorrow."

"Roger, Outlaw Six. This is Roving House Three-One, out."

Jeff and Billy walked back over to the Duster. Fish had a big smile on his face and was obviously proud.

"Good shooting, Fish," Jeff said. "I owe you that six-pack. What say you change the shift and let's get some sleep?"

"Yes, sir," Fish said, hardly able to contain his own pride. "Anybody smell something funny here?"

Ronnie was just climbing out of the turret. He turned his back to them and jumped down to the ground and ran off toward the makeshift latrine. Fish had a big smile.

"I did it. I don't know how many VC I killed, but by God, I didn't shit in my pants."

"Just remember what you promised your mama, soldier."

"You bet, Cap'n. And you can put that in the bank."

Billy and Jeff walked back to the bunker where Jeff had his cot rigged.

"I'll stay over here with you," Billy said. "I don't think any more of them will come tonight."

"OK," Jeff said.

Though vastly different from so many wars before it, Vietnam still brought men incredibly close together in a short time. Jeff and Billy were no exception. Their faith in one another had become complete—it had to be.

They both knew that they were feeling the same emotions that the troops outside and all of the soldiers before them felt after a battle. Coming down off the adrenaline high was sometimes as difficult as the battle itself. They felt relief that they were still alive, and they wondered when the next battle would be and what their luck would be that time. They sat cross-legged on the mattresses in the bunker, smoking.

"So?" Billy said.

"So what?" Jeff asked.

"So what, my ass," Billy said. "Where's my goddamned dollar?"

"You call that saving my life? All I heard was some whiney-assed crying about being attacked with nuclear bombs, for christ sake."

"I paid you last week."

"That was different."

"This is just like last month in Saigon. You wouldn't pay then either."

"That wasn't even a firefight. Besides, we agreed we weren't ever going to talk about that night."

"What the hell you mean it wasn't a firefight. I got shot at. Just because it was a girl doesn't matter to the bet. I should have let the goddamned Vietnamese police take you. But no, I helped. And then there wasn't so much as even 'Thanks, Billy' or 'Attaboy, Billy.' Nothing. And I didn't even get my goddamned dollar. I should'a just let 'em take you."

"I said I don't want to talk about that any more, and I mean it. You bring that up again and I'm going to get into when you ran us out of ammo shooting at ducks. And there's no dollar for tonight. Go to sleep."

"Gimme another cigarette."

They both lit up another and then another after that as they sat in the dark bunker, each with his own thoughts.

Goddamned war.

◻◻◻◻◻

Rolling into the base camp, the Dusters turned right to follow the road assigned to tracked vehicles while the two jeeps stayed on the main road and continued toward the battery's headquarters building. The dust inside the base camp was stifling. The entire camp was a fine powdery silt which instantly turned into dust if it wasn't kept damp. The buildings were a ragtag collection of odd-looking structures, and bunkers made from sandbags and steel planking were everywhere. Buildings were made from whatever materials were available, and combat damage was evident in most of them. Elderly Vietnamese men and women, their backs bent from their labor, trudged along on both sides of the roads as they went about their daily duties in support of their American visitors: doing laundry, filling sandbags, doing small carpentry jobs, cleaning latrines and carrying out other jobs the GIs paid them to do.

As Jeff's jeep rumbled into the compound under a wooden archway emblazoned with their motto, the First Sergeant of the battery was waiting for him at the door to the headquarters building. The Dusters had the best-looking and best-equipped compound on the entire base because all of the support units wanted their protection. The VC were so afraid of the Dusters that they wouldn't attack any convoy they were escorting. In a combat version of "you scratch my back and I'll scratch yours" which has been in existence since the first soldier carried a weapon, Jeff would shuffle the schedules and protect supply convoys back and forth to the depots north of Saigon in return for the first pick of the supplies. Jeff also had to admit that their good fortune was due to Billy Walker's natural ability to steal anything of use which wasn't firmly attached to something that couldn't be carried by a couple of GIs, another combat custom dating from the first armies.

"I hear you got a little taste of the fuzzy last night," the First Sergeant said as Jeff and Billy got out of their jeeps. "How'd it go?"

"Piece of cake," Billy said. "If all of our crews were like those, Uncle Ho would surrender overnight. Tell me it's the weekend or at least the afternoon so I can have a cold beer."

"Cold beer coming up." He smiled. "But there's an urgent message for the Cap'n to call the Head Duster as soon as he gets in." The Head Duster was their Battalion Commander.

"He's probably upset by your low estimate of body count last night," Billy said. "Only fifty. Shit, he probably could have gotten that many from his command helicopter." Billy laughed out loud even though Jeff gave him a hard look for making a public joke of the Battalion Commander in front of the First Sergeant and several troops standing around.

Jeff went inside the building constructed of board and sandbags up to about chest height. Above that was screen wire and a tin roof. He went into his office, picked up the combat field telephone and turned the crank. He shut the door to the office and sat down at his desk.

When Jeff came out a few minutes later, Billy could tell something was very wrong. This was not a discussion over body count.

Jeff leaned against the wall, looking at the floor. Billy said nothing. After a few moments, Jeff looked up directly into Billy's eyes. He tried to speak but couldn't. He went back into his office. When Billy came to the door, Jeff was in the chair behind the field desk with his head buried in his arms on top of the desk. Billy waited. In a few minutes, Jeff raised his head.

"Last night, my wife died during childbirth," he said. "The baby died, too."

❑❑❑❑❑

As the Boeing 707 lifted off from San Francisco International Airport bound for Boston, the flight attendant came down the aisle serving drinks.

"Jack Daniels and water," Jeff said. The flight attendant smiled at him. He wanted to sleep and hoped the whiskey would help. The flight

84

from Saigon had been long and full of soldiers going home from the war, and sleep had been impossible.

The flight attendant returned with the drink. Jeff stared at the ice cubes and tried to picture Beth in his mind. He took out his wallet and looked at the photo of her he carried. He knew there had been some complications early in the pregnancy, but had no idea she was in danger.

I'm sorry I wasn't there, baby.

I should've been, but I wasn't.

It isn't my war, but I'm still sorry.

Whenever he thought of Beth, he always remembered their first meeting. He was a freshman engineering student at Brown University, and she was a sophomore in the art department. They were at a classic college fraternity mixer where the alcohol and discussion flowed freely. Jeff had drifted to a small group engaged in a discussion which was coming down pretty heavily on the U.S. government in general and the military in particular. He normally didn't like to get involved in these debates, but these students seemed friendly and genuine in their discussion, and there were several pretty co-eds among the group.

"The U.S. has no right to interfere in the internal workings of other nations," a young boy with pimples was saying, "and any president who sends troops into foreign countries should be held accountable for his actions."

Several other comments of a similar nature finally prompted Jeff to put his opinion on the table.

"But if the United States is asked by those countries to help them defend a constitutional government against attack by an enemy which is also an enemy of the United States, why shouldn't we help?" he asked, thinking the comment would get a dignified reaction and response from the group.

Four people spoke at once, and the onslaught was so rabid, Jeff felt like he had just accused each one of their mothers of following after troop ships. Instantly, the whole group had identified him as the enemy and was attacking him without mercy—all except the girl with the long dark hair who was the reason he had been attracted to this group in the first place. He looked at her pleadingly.

85

God, she has pretty eyes.

As he was still being verbally assaulted, she moved to him, put her arm through his, leaned close and whispered, "I need a drink. Will you take me to the bar?"

He held her arm tight and whirled toward the bar, leaving the group talking to themselves. They didn't even seem to notice he had left.

"Thanks," he said, "you've rescued me from the jaws of the liberals."

"Don't you like liberal ideas?" she asked with a smile Jeff thought was the most gorgeous he had ever seen.

"I like a lot of liberal ideas," he said. "It's the liberals I seem to have problems with."

"Some of them are a pain in the ass until they grow up." She felt him physically flinch when she used the swear word.

They drank, talked, and danced, and when the evening was over, he asked if he could see her again. She looked up at him and said yes, and their eyes met and lingered there for a moment.

They dated on weekends at first and met for lunch occasionally. The lunches and dates became more frequent, and they drifted into meetings every day. As they went through the school year, she thought it was strange that he had not made a more vigorous sexual advance toward her. They kissed frequently, but seldom passionately. She wondered if he was afraid of sex or afraid of her. She finally decided that he was just responding to his upstate Massachusetts fundamental conservativism, and that he had been raised to treat a lady as a lady during casual relationships. Summer vacation came and they held hands and kissed and promised they would write while they were home.

Jeff's homecoming from his first year at college was as perfect as the rest of his life had been. Raised in a small town in rural Massachusetts, he was the ideal All-American boy. A good scholar who was captivated early by the technical sciences, he had nothing but good memories of his childhood. His home was a timber farm, and he had spent his time in the woods horseback riding in the hills, camping, and fishing. His father was the doctor for the community, and he knew that secretly his father wanted Jeff to become a doctor and continue his practice. But Jeff was bitten by another bug, and from his earliest memories, he intended to be an engineer. His heroes were Einstein, Von Braun, Fermi, and the other great minds emerging from the postwar technical revolution.

He was a tall, well-developed young man and had done well at athletics in school. His senior year, he lettered in three sports and took the high school to the state championships in baseball and football. He received an ROTC scholarship from the Army and chose Brown University for its technical reputation. His parents' home was maintained by the Thomases, a middle-aged couple who lived in a spare bedroom at the Weylands'. Mrs. Thomas had been his nanny and Mr. Thomas had loved to take him outdoors. While he loved his parents, he also had very deep feelings for the Thomases, and thought of them as part of his family.

He worked the summer after that first year at Brown at the sawmill which made rough lumber from the timber harvested on his family farm and other timber farms in the area. He enjoyed being home, but it didn't take much time for him to recognize that something he wanted very much was missing. He wrote to Beth every night, and mailed his letters faithfully every week. At first he thought she would get tired of reading so much of his writing, but her letters to him were regular, also. By the end of the summer, he knew that when they were back together this fall, he wanted never to be separated from her again.

Fall came, and when they met at their favorite spot on the bench outside the Administration Building, he told her how he felt. She cried and they held each other close. He got on his knees right there and asked her to marry him, and she said yes. They didn't bother to talk about a date, because that wasn't important. They would be together forever. Soon after, they made love for the first time. She knew it was obvious to him that he wasn't the first for her, but he never mentioned it.

At Christmas, she went with him to Massachusetts to visit his family, and at Easter, they went to Virginia to visit hers. Both sets of parents approved, and it was agreed they would wait until Beth graduated to get married. School was easier than usual for Jeff after that, and he continued as a standout scholar. They spent the summer after his sophomore year together at his home, and he showed her the places where he grew up.

They spent days in the woods, and she began to share his love for the outdoors. After his junior year, they married and moved into a small apartment near the University. Beth worked in the Art Department of the school and he went to Fort Sill, Oklahoma, for his summer camp required by ROTC. Beth got pregnant that spring and Cindy was a welcome, but late, Christmas present.

Graduation brought the Army obligation from the ROTC scholarship. Jeff was commissioned as a Second Lieutenant in the Air Defense Artillery and sent to Fort Bliss, Texas, for basic officer's training using the Nike Hercules Surface-to-Air guided missile. Their first duty station was in Germany on a Nike Hercules missile site, and, while she was happy with her family, Beth was concerned about how much Jeff seemed to like the Army. She hadn't bargained for a life as an Army wife, and even though Jeff hadn't discussed anything else, she assumed he would leave the Army when his four-year obligation was over.

Jeff did like the Army. The men he was associated with seemed to be true professionals. The officers and the enlisted men alike were all top-notch, the cream of the Army's crop—well-educated, intelligent, and dedicated to defending the United States and her interests. He went about his work in the same manner he had approached his whole life and developed an instant relationship with the men working for him. He was a respected officer with a promising career. He didn't think often about the decisions of the future, and Vietnam was an unheard of place halfway around the world.

Vietnam. He heard of it soon enough. As an Air Defense Officer, Jeff initially had little chance of being sent since there were not too many missile sites in Vietnam. There were a few HAWK sites around Saigon, but not enough to create a large demand for officers. Then he heard about the Dusters. He sat nights in the lonely duty chair on the missile site and thought about his friends who were already in combat, not sitting in an air-conditioned van in Saigon, but in real combat. When the time came, he never had the nerve to tell Beth that he had volunteered to go, and when he told her he was leaving, she told him she was pregnant with their second child.

Jeff could feel Cindy's tight squeeze as he held her tiny hand. He thought that if this was tough on him, only God knew what this child must feel. When he had first arrived, it was apparent that she recognized him mostly from the pictures in the room she and Beth had shared while he was gone. He had been gone eight months, and she had just turned four years old. That meant he had been away for a large part of her life. He wondered if she knew him well enough to love him. Did she even really know him at all? Her mommy dies and now comes this man who, for the most part, is only a face in a picture. The squeeze on his fingers reminded him he was all she had.

Don't worry, little girl with the baby-doll face.
I'm your daddy, and together, we are going to make it through this thing.
Somehow.

He could hear her sniffles, and he reached down and picked her up and held her close to him. She put her arms around his neck and hugged him tight and her tears flowed.

"I love you, Dollface," he whispered in her ear.

"I love you, too, Daddy," she said softly.

The preacher was finished and Jeff knelt down beside the grave and helped Cindy's little hand pick up some of the loose dirt and throw it on the casket. As Cindy took one long last look into the dark hole in the earth, she held tightly to her daddy's hand, and they walked toward the car.

Back at the house, Cindy sat in his lap while he rocked her in the chair that had been her mother's favorite. She had not let go of him since they had returned from the cemetery, and he wondered if she would be able to handle it when he left.

Several days later he packed up his camping gear, and he and Cindy left on horseback for the woods. Her grandpa had gotten her a small pony, but she rode on Jeff's lap on the stallion which had been his lifelong friend. They spent three days in the woods, and even though she was only four, she adjusted well to life outdoors. The days were spent fishing, catching bugs, walking, and talking. They set some snare traps, but when they caught a fox, Jeff could tell Cindy's concern for it, and together they bandaged it and turned it loose. Nights were spent at the campfire and they became best friends, a friendship that would last them all of their lives. She slept inside his sleeping bag with him, and her mother wasn't mentioned.

On the last day, Jeff felt he had to tell her. He knew it wouldn't be easy, and he didn't know if he had the words to help her understand.

"Dollface, we have to go back to Grandpa's today."

"I know, Daddy."

"You know, every little girl has a mommy and a daddy," he said as he watched her closely. "Your mommy's not going to be with us any more, and it will just be you and me."

"I know, Daddy." She reached out and grabbed the fingers of his hand and squeezed them hard.

"Someplace in this world there are people trying to take other mommies and daddies away from their little girls."

"Why?" she asked, looking at him with her big eyes.

"Well, I don't really know," he said. "I guess some people just don't know how much little girls love their mommies and daddies. I have to go for a little while and help them. Do you understand?"

"I think so. Will you come back?"

"Yes, Dollface, I will come back."

"OK, Daddy."

If he never knew before, Jeff knew then what total trust and faith was, and what the Bible meant when it said "Come to me as a little child." He picked her up and held her to him and told her how much he loved her. "You will stay here with Gramma and Grandpa, and Mr. and Mrs. Thomas will take care of you, and soon, I will come back for you, and then we will be together forever."

"OK, Daddy," she said.

The ride off the mountain was quiet. Neither of them spoke as Jeff guided the horse on the trails toward the house. At the house, she helped him put the stallion's tack away and then they held hands as they went indoors. She hugged her Gramma and Grandpa and was full of stories of adventures in the woods.

Surely she wants to tell those stories to her mother, but she's a real little trooper.

"Daddy is going away," she told her Gramma. "To help other little girls. He will be back soon."

"I know," said his mother. Jeff could see the tears in his mother's eyes. His mother had been against his going into the Army and was angry about his going to Vietnam. He had never talked to her about it, but his father had confided that she had been distressed ever since she had heard he was going.

"Yes, Cindy," his mother said, "your daddy will be back." She turned from the child and walked from the room.

"Why is Gramma crying?" Cindy asked Jeff.

"Because she misses your mommy, too, Dollface."

⊔⊔⊔⊔⊔

Soldiers were still being carried into Vietnam on chartered airliners, and it was impossible for Jeff to conceive that when he got off this plane, he was going to be in Saigon. He thought probably the strangest feeling in the world must be to travel on a civilian airliner and be able to look out of the window and see a firefight on the ground. It wasn't real. Life wasn't real.

Bullshit, Weyland. It is real.

Most of the soldiers on the plane were going to Vietnam for the first time. A few were like Jeff, returning from emergency leave or going in for their second tour. The faces on the plane showed what was in the minds of the soldiers. Though Jeff was a young man, some of these troops looked like boys to him. At Saigon, they would be herded into buses which would take them to the replacement depot at Long Binh Post. He hoped he could avoid that circus since he already had a unit.

As the troops filed into the terminal, Jeff heard a familiar voice.

"Hey, Cap'n Weyland, over here."

It was Fish. He was in well-worn combat fatigues and a jungle hat with that special crushed look of the boonies. His M-16 was slung over his shoulder with an inserted double magazine of live rounds prominently displayed, taped end-to-end in the popular Vietnam style. Most of the soldiers on the plane had never been near live ammo except on training ranges under strict supervision, and to them, Fish looked more like some grizzly war fanatic than the respectably seasoned veteran that he was.

"What are you doing here, Fish?" Jeff asked, although he was genuinely happy to see the Duster gunner. Fish was visibly concerned that he was in trouble.

"We heard you were coming, and since we were sort of in town anyway on kind of an escort mission, we thought we'd sort of come by and make sure you got a proper escort outta this place." Fish was obviously proud of himself.

"Sort of."

"Yes, sir, sort of."

"How'd you get here?" Jeff asked, afraid he already knew the answer and letting the beginnings of a smile show on his face.

Fish's face broke into a broad grin as he realized he wasn't in real trouble after all.

"Drove that fuckin' Duster right up to the front door, and your chariot awaits outside, sir." Fish swept off his jungle hat, making an exaggerated bow and sweep of his hand.

"You must have seen that in the movies," Jeff said.

"We told them guards at the gate we had been assigned to guard the perimeter because there was intelligence information that there was going to be a big VC attack tonight. Told them we had been fighting 'em all the way up the highway, and they were just down the road."

"So I'm just supposed to walk out of here and climb on that Duster, and we'll ride away into the sunset." Jeff was laughing now.

"That's the plan, sir," Fish said, "but we better make it fast. That big fucker is double parked."

Outside the terminal, Fish was true to his word. There sat two Dusters with their engines running as though ready for a fast getaway. Then Jeff saw the true architect of this mission. Sitting on the passenger side fender of the front Duster was Billy Walker, smiling down at Jeff like a carnival barker.

Jeff smiled as he saw the chess knight stenciled on the front door of each Duster with the words "Have Guns" above and "Will Travel" below. That had been the Battery's motto ever since they started running the highways every night. All of the troops had rallied behind the motto and considered themselves to be modern-day Paladins.

He threw up his gear and climbed to his favorite spot to ride—outside the turret up front beside the guns. Somebody threw him a flak jacket and sixty tons of steel jerked forward as the two behemoths started off. They were stopped immediately by an air policeman major who insisted that they couldn't go straight ahead. Billy jumped down from the front track and told him they were on a combat mission. The AP insisted that they would have to turn around right where they were and go back the way they came. Track vehicles were prohibited on the roads, he said, because they did so much damage. Billy looked back at Jeff. Jeff shrugged. Billy smiled, turned back to the AP major and saluted, then turned to both Dusters and shouted.

"OK, let's turn 'em around and go out the way we came in."

Fish, who was driving the second track, showed some doubt.

Jeff leaned over to him and smiled and said, "You heard the man, Fish."

Fish grinned and picked up the radio handset to talk to the other Duster.

"Listen up, assholes, neutral steer left, and let's go home," he said into the mike.

Jeff reached for the gun tube and got a firm grip. In neutral steer, the left track was in reverse and the right track was in forward so that the vehicle would literally turn on its own axis. A by-product of this maneuver was that as it made the turn, the thirty tons of steel corkscrewed itself through almost any surface except reinforced concrete. As they completed the turn and drove away, Jeff looked over his shoulder at the air policeman staring at the expansive crater where the road used to be. Billy was standing at attention on the deck of the rear Duster rendering a perfect and very formal military salute.

"How sweet it is," Fish sang as they made their way through the gate of Tan Son Nut Airport and started their long trip south.

He was back to the war. Ninety-six days to survive. From the turret,

Fish had the radio going full volume, tuned to Armed Forces Radio, Vietnam.

The Animals blasted the GI's anthem of the Vietnam War.

"We gotta get out of this place
If it's the last thing we ever do.
We gotta get outta this place.
Girl, there's a better life for me and you."

Ninety-six days. Survive, hell.
Just stay alive.
Yes, Cindy, I'll be back.
Count on it.

JANUARY
1990

weapons systems--pentagon adv 16 1-90
Underdeveloped countries stock up on tactical missiles
USWNS Military News
adv jan 16 1990 or thereafter

By GEORGE GROWSON

WASHINGTON—In a press release today, the Pentagon stated
that the number of tactical surface-to-surface missiles
deployed in the third world countries has increased
dramatically in the last several years. "The proliferation
of short-range, surface-to-surface ballistic missiles has
produced a revolutionary new concept of warfare in Third
World countries," the statement noted. "Countries
possessing missiles with more than 200 kilometers' range
include Turkey, Bolivia, Argentina, Pakistan, Libya, Iraq
and many others. The Soviet SCUD, the Argentinean Condor
and the Pakistani Hatf are all available on the open market
for sale to the highest bidder, and have ranges from a few
hundred kilometers to over a thousand kilometers."
    With these missiles available to commanders in Third
World countries, high-value targets like command
facilities, airfields and population centers could be
attacked deep within territory of friendly nations occupied
by U.S. forces. Every hostile country which possesses these
missiles is now a potential aggressor and can project power
over a large region without the fear of starting a nuclear
conflict. The Army declined to comment on the ability of
U.S. forces to destroy these missiles in flight once they
have been launched.

FOUR

The Cantina, with its Tex-Mex atmosphere and spicy Mexican food, was a hangout for the Hill regulars, mostly congressional staffers. The occasional house member or two and sometimes a senator gave the establishment its reputation as a place where power lunches were held and major political deals were made.

Jeff came in the door, went straight to the bar, and ordered his high-tech redneck drink, a Jack and water. The Cantina was decorated as a genuine Texas honky tonk and always had a band that played country music, but Jeff thought most of its patrons were playing the role of the urban cowboy rather than really enjoying the down-home country. Turning from the bar, Jeff scanned the room looking for Suzy. As the small band in the corner started into "Friends in Low Places," he spotted her, dressed for the western atmosphere of the club, sitting at a small round table near the dance floor. He stood and watched her for a few moments as she sipped from her margarita and ran a hand through her streaked blond hair. A glance around the room as he walked toward her told him that most of the men present were very aware of her.

"See, I'm not only here, but I'm on time," he said as he arrived at the table.

"That's your second great accomplishment of the day," she said, close between a smile and laughter.

"OK, I give up. What was the first?"

"Your great debate with Mr. PBCA," she said, now softly laughing under her breath.

"So, you heard?" he said, obviously not amused.

She was laughing aloud now, and didn't answer, but nodded her head.

"I don't think it's that funny," he said. "Maybe it would be if the consequences weren't so important."

"I know," she said, putting her hand over her mouth trying to keep some semblance of composure. "And I know it's important to you. But just the idea of him trying to convince you to give up PATRIOT so we can fund medical research is almost impossible to picture."

"In your presence, I'll pass on the proper term for him."

"Another of your father's descriptions?"

"Yes, and since this one's a little rougher than the first, I'll let it pass for now."

"Probably for the best."

"PATRIOT's not only important to me, but it's important to our country. These are serious issues we're talking about and real lives we're trying to save."

"I know," she said. "I'm a friend, remember?"

"How did you hear so quickly?"

"Fred came by the office and told me. At first he was as mad as you, but when I started laughing, he started too. I guess that's why it still seems so funny now, because once we started, we both couldn't stop laughing."

"Well, it did have its moments," he was smiling himself now.

Their waitress wore a short cowgirl skirt and a low-cut, off-the-shoulder blouse which revealed a lot of cleavage. Jeff did not look directly at her as he gave their order.

"We'll have an order of nachos and cheese dip with a side order of jalapeños and another round of drinks. For dinner, I'll have a combination fajita plate and she'll have a taco salad supreme." The waitress wrote down their order and left with an extra wiggle.

Another lonely Tuesday night.

"You remembered what I like," Suzy said. "I'm impressed."

"You're supposed to be," he said. "I checked in my little book before I came."

"So what else do you have on me in your little book?" she asked.

"Lots," he said. "I keep tabs on you through secret agents planted in the halls of Congress. You look very western and very nice."

"I'm flattered," she said. "But to be honest, I like you in your uniform better."

"Yeah, the uniform gets 'em all. It's really the reason I stayed in the Army." Jeff glanced down at his slacks and knit shirt. "Not too western, but what the heck, neither am I. I just happen to like country music. Strange taste for a guy from upstate Massachusetts, but you like what you like, I guess."

"You look fine. Most cowboys would like to look so good."

"Thanks. Now it's my turn to be flattered. I'm glad you and Fred got such a kick out of my afternoon."

"Don't say I didn't warn you. I told you they weren't convinced."

"You did indeed. But not being convinced is a long way from what I ran into in that meeting. I'm not real sure exactly what to make of all that."

"Don't be too concerned. A lot of that is political posturing. I think you can count on Senator Hind's vote when the time comes. They're just making sure that everybody knows who owes who and for what."

"Sure?"

"Sure."

"Good, then let's talk about something else and enjoy dinner."

"Now that's a fantastic idea. I'm glad I thought of it."

The waitress brought the chips and Jeff busied himself mixing the hot peppers into the dip. He took the cheese bowl, poured half over the peppers and stirred. He tried the first one, coughed and immediately took a hard pull at his drink.

"Perfect," he announced, although his voice showed more than a little strain. He held the bowl toward her. "Try some."

"No thanks," she said. "I'll stick to the mild," reaching to pull the cheese bowl toward her. As the band switched to Alabama and began singing "The Closer You Get," her blue eyes met Jeff's for a quick second. She looked down at her drink and slowly rubbed one finger over the salt around the rim of the glass.

"I'm glad we were able to do this tonight," she said. "I haven't been out for a long time. It feels good. Just don't let me have too many margaritas. The last time I went to Margaritaville, I almost didn't get home."

"How do I know when you've had too many?" he asked.

"Do you remember the song 'Jose Cuervo'?" she asked.

"Yep," he said. "A favorite party song from days gone by."

"Well, if you see me with somebody else's shirt on, it's time to go." She was laughing.

God, what a beautiful smile.

"Waitress, another margarita for the lady," he said, holding up his hand in mock request. Now she was laughing hard.

"I'm serious," she said. "Margaritas go straight to my head."

"I thought they went to your shirt," he said, laughing. It felt good. He hadn't laughed out loud in a long time.

Dinner came, and they shared each other's food and talked some more, but no more office or business. After the food they had coffee. The band had been on a break, but the piano player had returned early and started a solo rendition of Floyd Cramer's "Last Date."

"Would you like to dance?" he asked.

"I know this sounds like a line from a B movie, but I thought you'd never ask," she said softly.

They moved to the floor, and as he put his arms around her, she felt like fine silk. The top of her head came just to his shoulder, and he breathed in her scent, a clean smell like the woods being roasted by the first warm sun of spring. They moved slowly around the floor with several other couples. By the end of the song, the rest of the band was back and they immediately broke into their opening of Alabama's "Mountain Music." He started to move back to the table, but she stood her ground and held his hand. He looked back at her with the best little lost boy look he could muster.

"You promised," she said with a dainty mock stamp of her foot. "The last time you were in Washington, you promised you would do the Texas two-step with me."

"You are exactly right," he said. He felt awkward because he knew he wasn't a very good dancer, but he didn't want her to feel he wasn't enjoying himself.

He put his arm to her shoulder and they took off across the dance floor at a fast clip. Another six or so couples came to the floor, and before the midpoint of the dance, they were all together in a rousing round of western line dance. By the time the dance was over, they were both out of breath and laughing when they got to their seats.

"That was great," he said, on the way back to their table. "You really are good. Where did you learn that?"

"My sister made me take lessons. She said it would help my social life in Washington."

"Your sister is a smart woman," Jeff said.

❑❑❑❑❑

Jeff sat in the living room of the nicely appointed townhouse in the Old Town portion of Alexandria overlooking the Potomac River. His papers were spread in front of him on the coffee table, and from a back room floated a mournful tune about old black and white photos. A hefty shot of Gentleman Jack Daniels on ice sat beside a bowl of mixed nuts. Jeff put his papers on the table and leaned back into the couch.

I couldn't ask the Lord for much more than this.

In spite of all the bashing, he felt that the day had gone well. It appeared that he was going to get the funding needed to carry the program through the next year, and that should put the second phase of PATRIOT Anti-Missile Capability in the field. There was still the problem of General Grant, and he didn't know what that future held. Regardless of the outward appearances to the contrary, general officers were still pretty much an old boys' club, and once you were on the outside of the club with your nose pressed up against the window, it was hard to get back in.

Well, we showed the bastards, and now they're going to show us. Go into the bullring often enough and eventually you'll get the horns.

He picked up his drink, went to the bedroom, slipped off his shoes, and lay down on the bed. The room was dark, and he could feel the Jack starting to work on him.

Too many peanuts.

"Too many peanuts spoil the Jack?" he heard in reply, and realized he must have been thinking out loud.

He looked toward the door and saw her standing with the faint light from the hall behind her showing through a pale blue silk, lacy negligee.

Yes, Lord, and if a man were to ask for a little more, that would be it.

❑❑❑❑❑

The radio woke Jeff with the sounds of soft country, and he reached across the bed, but Suzy was gone. He sat up, fully awake.

If I felt any better than this, I'd have to become a Democrat.

The rich smell of coffee was coming from the kitchen. He slipped into his pants and found her busy at the counter with breakfast.

"You're becoming a regular little domestic," he said as he came up behind her, wrapping his arms around her waist and holding her tight.

"My mama always told me if I was going to love a man, I should make sure I fed him breakfast so he would remember me all day." Then she added, "Of, course, you won't forget me in the first place if you know what's good for you."

"No, ma'am, I won't," Jeff said with a grin, holding his hands up to show his innocence. "Your mama was a smart woman," Jeff said and reached out for a piece of bacon. "Between your mama and your sister, you got a lot of good advice."

"What's on your schedule for today?" she asked, turning to face him.

"Why is it that I suspect you already know my only plan is to catch the 9:30 back to Huntsville?" he asked, and slapped her on her buttocks as he started from the room.

"Well, I just needed to know for sure before I called the office and let them know I'll be a few minutes late."

"Now there's a good plan."

"Maybe today you'll have an easier time than you did yesterday."

"I will by definition. Today I don't have to see General Grant or Mike Hensley, and any day without them is a better day."

When he looked at her, she had an impish smile on her face, and she said, "I know a secret about your General."

"And?" he said, obviously curious.

"Well, you have to promise not to ever tell."

"I will only tell in the rare instance that it would set that pompous ass back in his chair one small notch. He is the most difficult senior officer I've ever had to deal with."

"Down, boy."

"Sorry. So what's your secret?"

"You've got to promise first."

"What if I promise that if you don't tell me, I will tear off all of your clothes, cover you with those eggs, and really have breakfast?"

"Then I would consider that the high point of my month."

"OK. I promise."

"He's having a fling with Celia Mitchell," Suzy said.

"That's the most improbable thing I've ever heard."

"Don't forget you promised."

"Who'd you hear that from?"

"I didn't hear it from anyone. I was in Senator Strong's office one day, and she got a call from him and was very irritated about it and told him not to call her there any more. I didn't know who it was when she was talking to him, but when she transferred the call to the Senator, I heard her say it was General Grant. She didn't know I was there, and when she noticed me she thought I had just come into the room, and I didn't let on that I'd heard. I'm sure she didn't think I did."

"Well, just because he said something cute to her when he was calling Senator Strong doesn't mean they're having a fling."

"Oh, it was more than just saying something cute. It was clear from even the one side of the conversation I heard that there was a real thing going. They talked about meetings and things they did."

"Well, well. There's some flesh and blood behind all that Infantry steel after all. I'm surprised that a man in his position would allow himself the luxury of an affair."

"You're one to talk," she said.

"He has a wife and two kids still in college. There's a little difference as far as the Army is concerned."

"You mean the Army would have something to say if a married officer had an affair?"

"More than something. In today's Army, that's considered a real no-no along with daytime drinking and a long list of other sins," he said. "I still can't picture General Steelface and the Ice Lady having at it. It just doesn't seem to fit."

"Well, I think you're too rough on her. She's really a nice person who just has a difficult time communicating with people and with men especially."

"'Difficult time' is an understatement, but you're right. That's a good secret, and I don't think I'll tell it. Ever. No one would believe me anyway. I'm going to take a shower."

"Why don't you wait until after?" she asked.

"After what?"

"If you have to ask that, I'm not going to give you this breakfast," she said, and turned her back to him to finish cooking. "Breakfast is in five minutes."

As he went to the bedroom with the paper, Lee Greenwood was singing "I'm Going To Take My Baby On a Morning Ride."

Yes, I am. Yes I am, indeed.

Iraqi military maneuvers--pentagon adv14 3-90
Iraqi forces continue to build along border of oil-rich
Kuwait
USWNS Military News
adv mar 14 1990 or thereafter
By GEORGE GROWSON

   WASHINGTON—A U.S. Army spokesman said today that
intelligence sources indicate that Iraqi forces continue to
build steadily in the southern half of the country. The
forces appear to be coming from the border with Iran to the
east and moving south toward Kuwait. The forces of Iraq and
Iran have not exchanged direct gunfire in some time, and
Iraq has had long-standing disputes with Kuwait over the
exact lines of the border between the two countries and the
rights to several oil-rich locations. After repeated
attempts to obtain a statement from the Iraqi Embassy on
the troop movements, a spokesperson finally said, "It is
not Iraq's policy to discuss the location or movement of
any military forces with anyone outside of the Iraqi
government." He added that Iraq was a "peace-loving country
who only wanted to get along with her neighbors."

FIVE

Jeff had just finished packing his traveling bag when the phone rang.

"Is Doctor Weyland there?" Cindy asked.

"Speaking. The doctor is in but is only accepting calls from special patients."

"Do daughters qualify as special patients?" Cindy asked.

"Daughters are at the top of the list. Hi, Dollface. What did you have on your mind so early in the morning?"

"You always forget that I'm an hour ahead of you," she said.

"You're right," he said. Even when she had gone away to college, Jeff couldn't get used to the fact that she wasn't at home. He was sure every time she called, it was to ask him to bring home some food for her rabbit or to say that some dastardly little boy had done some dastardly little deed to her at school that day.

"Besides, when do I need a reason to call my father?"

"You don't, and it's great to hear from you. I heard from Suzy that some of your pieces are going to be displayed in a Washington exhibit, and the two of you are going to get together while you're in town."

"Yep. I'm going to make one last attempt to convince her you're really an evil warmonger disguising himself as a considerate gentleman, and the truth is you hate house pets, and you don't even brush your teeth up and down."

"I don't hate house pets, and I'm practicing my brushing technique," he said.

"You made me keep Carrots outside," she teased. Carrots had been a cute little Easter bunny she had gotten from her Aunt Betsy which had grown up to be a seventeen-pound house destroyer.

"Carrots ate the lamp cords," he said, remembering how she had cried the first night Carrots spent outside in the rabbit house they had built together. It was an elaborate structure with two rooms and a separate area for feeding. He had wanted to make it so nice that Cindy wouldn't feel bad when the rabbit went outside. It didn't work.

"Not to mention your slippers," Cindy reminded him.

"So tell me about your exhibit."

"I thought you'd never ask. It's in a little gallery in Georgetown that has a lot of big-name artists on consignment, and they're having a special showing for several of them and two of my pieces will be featured as a 'rising young artist.' What do you think about that?"

"Are your pieces going to be for sale?" he asked.

"Why are you only interested in whether I get money for my paintings? I have a good job and make a good living, and I don't create my art for the money."

Damn.

"Sweetheart, you know that I really don't care if you sell your paintings or not if you're happy. It just seems to me that it's something artists do."

"Some artists are interested in values besides money."

"Enough, enough." He laughed, wanting to change the subject. He and Cindy were as close as a father and daughter could be, but occasionally they seemed to get into these petty little discussions. It was as though she wanted to establish for sure that there was some ideological difference between them. He didn't believe there was, but somehow she seemed determined to make it appear that way.

"So what do you and Suzy have planned?" He was obviously pleased that Cindy and Suzy had become friends even though they had only met a few times. He and Suzy had gone to Atlanta for a weekend just so the two women could have some time together, and they had discovered they were kindred spirits.

"She's going to come by the gallery tonight to see my great works and the stuff from the other lesser knowns there, and then we're going to walk around the other shops in Georgetown and have dinner at whatever place strikes our fancy. I called to see if there's any chance you might be able to be there, too?"

"No chance, Dollface," he said. "I'm on a train moving so fast that it doesn't even come to a full stop at the stations. I'm packing now for Boston and then El Paso for a few days. We have another big test at White Sands, and this might be the last one I see for a while. The crews have done an unbelievable job keeping up with the program, and I have some awards to pass out to some of the troops. I'll be in the Atlanta airport this evening, but long after you've left."

"OK, then," she said. "But once we girls get out on the town, you're taking a big risk that we'll find ourselves a couple of cowboys and hoot 'n holler till dawn."

"Well, somebody better tell the cowboys to look out. You girls have a good time and tell Suzy I'll call her from Boston."

"We will and I will. Bye, Dad. I love you."

"I love you, too, Dollface," he said and hung up.

That is one little girl who will never know how good it makes her daddy feel to hear her say I love you.

Fathers who don't feel that way are missing out on a big piece of life.

Back on your feet, Weyland.

□□□□□

As the group of PATRIOT government personnel filed out of Jeff's office later in the morning, Steve Smith stayed behind with Bill Sadler, the resident software manager within the PATRIOT project.

"What's up?" Jeff asked.

"Well, it's about that little quirk you saw the last time you were at the test firing against the Lance. Remember?" Steve asked.

"I do now."

"Something made me remember it when I was talking with Bill the other day, and I asked him what he thought it might be. His first reaction was like mine, that it could be any number of things, until I said that Johnny reported the stored record showed no entry. That led us down several other trails, and all of them were dead ends."

"I'd convinced myself that I must've been mistaken," Jeff said, "and I'd just put it away on a back shelf. What makes you bring it up now?"

"Well, Bill thinks that if it really did happen, it might have been some type of background software. I don't know much about that area, but he says that some special programs can run in the background of a computer and not be detected during operations. An example is the virus epidemic we had a year or so ago. Programs were running wild on machines and even being transferred from machine to machine without anybody ever knowing about them. We had to get special virus-removing software for our machines in the office.

"When they ran the bug-finder on my machine, we found twenty-three viruses on it. I even found some on my machine at home. Of course, PATRIOT's computer doesn't have the amount of public software or public use our personal computers do, and I doubt we have any viruses in her, but the thought is still there. Maybe there was some type of special background software running on her that day. Maybe a test or something Raytheon put in. I don't really know, but it was just a thought."

"How would a software program like that get on the system, Bill?" Jeff asked. "I thought all of the software was now under configuration control by the government."

"It is, in principle," Bill said. "But the tests going on now are for checking out new software developed by the contractor for testing the anti-missile capability, and Raytheon has closely monitored the computer throughout the entire development cycle."

"So what would be the purpose of having some unknown piece of software lurking around hidden in the computer?" Jeff asked.

"I don't know, General," Bill said. "And it gets over my head pretty quick. I thought since you were going to Raytheon this week, you could ask around up there and see if anybody could give you more information."

"Maybe I will, but we're probably making much ado about nothing. Thanks for the input."

As Bill and Steve left his office, Jeff made a mental note to talk to an old friend in Boston.

What the hell. I had been meaning to make that visit for some time, so it isn't really going out of the way.

⬜⬜⬜⬜⬜

"Ladies and gentlemen, please fasten your seatbelts for our descent into Boston."

Jeff was glad it was night and a dark one at that. He really didn't have a fear of flying, but something about coming into Boston always made him remember the airliner that crashed into the bank at the edge of the water while entering Logan International. When he flew in during the day and looked out the window at the water, the plane always seemed too low. In the dark, all he could see was the Boston skyline, and he could reasonably assure himself he wasn't going to crash into that.

He folded his briefcase, which he had dutifully opened on leaving Atlanta only to promptly fall asleep. He was happy he could sleep easily on airplanes. This was going to be a short night and the next few days were full. He smiled at the thought of some of that fullness, since Suzy was to meet him here for the weekend. That would make the next few days of meetings much more pleasant. He thought of how their first few moments together would be and started making another mental list of the things they could do in their two days. The little fish place down on the waterfront for sure. Some fresh lobster and a good bottle of wine would go great after her flight. He settled back in his chair, dozed off again, and slept until the slight bump of the landing woke him.

"Ladies and gentlemen, welcome to Boston, home of the Boston Tea Party. The time is 11:05 PM and the weather in Boston is clear, but a chilly 19 degrees."

He drove through the tunnel and up onto Interstate 93 North and settled in for the drive to Bedford, some 35 miles north and west of Boston. Coming to Boston made him feel good because it meant that for a little while, he would be close to home. He could see the Bunker Hill monument on the

113

right standing tall in its image of the Washington monument. While he liked seeing the town by driving up old Route One, the interstate drive was a relief when it was late at night and he was tired.

He checked into the motel and immediately picked up the phone to dial Suzy. No answer. He smiled to himself.

Maybe my two girls decided to have a night on the town after all.

He lay on the bed, turned the TV to CNN, and started recapping all of his mental notes from the day. He was anxious to hear from Raytheon and the other contractors on their progress. It was going to be mostly formality, but it would be good to see the entire program reviewed at one time, and it would give him a comfortable feeling to know that they were so close to completion.

□□□□□

The first day's events were more like theater than weapons development. The government presented first, and then the contractors were on the hook for their review of the program. They covered all of the concerns raised by the government, and went through the basic program status of systems delivered, production problems and solutions, cost incurred and projected, and any items or concerns they might have.

When the series of briefings had ended and the meeting crowd was breaking up for the day, Jeff turned to Richard Teacher, a Raytheon vice president who had been beside him all day.

"Max Fisher works here in the PATRIOT software laboratory," Jeff said. "He's an old friend, and if you have a few minutes, Dick, I'd like to drop by his office."

"Certainly, General Weyland," Dick said. "I know Max well. Let's cut through to the back corridor here, and we'll be right there."

"Thanks," Jeff said as they started through the building.

"How do you know Max?" Dick asked as they worked their way through the large facility.

"We served together in Vietnam. When he came to work for Raytheon a few years after finishing his hitch, we were able to get in touch again. I'd like to have a private conversation with him for a few minutes, if that's OK."

"Certainly. Here we are," Dick said as they approached a small cubicle formed by chest-high metal partitions. As Jeff walked in, he saw Fish sitting at his desk.

A little heavier maybe, a little balder, but that's my Fish.

"Well, I'll be goddamned!" Fish said as Jeff came into the office. He stood up and came around from behind his desk. The two men shook hands, clapped each other on the shoulder several times and then finally surrendered to their impulse and wrapped each other in a bear hug. "Why didn't you let me know you were coming to see the Fish-man?"

"I didn't know if I was going to get time for a visit. As it turns out, there's something I'd like to talk to you about, but this doesn't seem like the place to do it. Could you get free for a little while and let's go somewhere?"

"Sure. It's past time to quit anyway. I was just cleaning up a few things before I left."

"How about something to drink?" Jeff asked.

"How 'bout you follow me to the house and have some of Sarah's soul food and see your godchild and let the others crawl on your lap?"

"You're sure Sarah won't mind?"

"Mind? Are you kidding? She thinks you were sent straight from heaven to make me whole. Besides, she always cooks enough for an army," Fish said, smiling and patting his waistline, which was showing more than a little growth. "Home's my favorite place to eat and always will be."

"It looks like it," Jeff said, laughing. "Okay, I'll see you in the parking lot in thirty minutes."

ᑐᑐᑐᑐᑐ

It took the better part of an hour to catch up on old times and family status and to retell all of the old tales about the Paladins. Finally, after dinner, when the kids were put to bed and they were together in the living room, Jeff got to his question.

"Fish, you're still familiar with the detailed workings of PATRIOT's software, aren't you?" he asked.

"Every bit and byte and one and zero," Fish said. "I can tell you anything you need to know."

"Well, this is strange and probably way out in left field, so I didn't want to involve any of the Raytheon brass. If I'd asked the question in the meeting today, half of Raytheon would be turned over by now, and it's all probably for nothing."

"Shoot," Fish said, leaning back in his chair.

"I was at the first full-scale flight test against the Lance missile. You know the one I'm talking about?"

"Who can forget that. I saw the photographs of those two missiles touching nose cone to nose cone. Pretty impressive."

"During the engagement sequence, I saw the operator make an entry into the console. It didn't seem to make any sense to me at that point in the process. I asked Steve Smith about it, and he couldn't come up with anything. Later, when they checked the tape of the flight at WSMR, there was no record of any entry being made."

"Specifically, at what point in the sequence did he make the entry?" Fish asked.

"Just after target track, but before missile launch."

"Well, I agree with Steve. No reason for any entry then. Unless he was calling for some additional data on the target."

"The target data was already on the screen. Anyway, the record should show any legitimate entry."

"Yeah, that's a puzzle, all right. What do you want me to do?"

"Actually, I had forgotten about the whole thing. Steve came to see me this morning with an idea, and I thought I'd run it by you since I was going to be here. Anyway, I haven't seen you for a while, and this seemed like a good excuse to get together."

"Like we've ever needed an excuse."

"Steve said if the software didn't register the entry, then it probably wasn't part of her normal operating software set. Some additional software might've been added by Raytheon for a special purpose. It could've been running in the background or something. What do you think?"

"Possible, but not probable. I know all the sets of software for each flight, and any changes to the standard set go through me. As a general rule, Raytheon wouldn't put any non-functional software in the system on a flight day. Too big a risk, and if something goes wrong, then Raytheon's on the hook. Besides, that system belongs to the government, and we aren't supposed to tamper with it."

"OK, then you give me a better answer."

"Don't have one. Don't have any answer. Maybe you were mistaken, or maybe the entry just didn't get on the record. Did you ask the operator?"

"No, Johnny Madkin was going to, but I told him not to make a big deal out of it. At any rate, he never got back to me, and then I forgot about it until yesterday. They're going to check at the range, but the chances are that the operator isn't there anymore. At the time, and even now, it just didn't seem important enough."

"Probably isn't, but it does seem strange," Fish said. "You want me to look into it?"

"No, not really. I just thought something might occur to you off the top of your head, and just wanted your opinion on the background software, and you've given me that. But if you have a day when you just don't have anything else to do, it would be interesting to know just what did happen, if anything. I'm going back to El Paso from here for the maximum range test, and I'll be in the van again. If the same operator does happen to be there, I'll ask him if he remembers."

"Ask him after the flight. That way if he does it again, you'll be sure. In the morning, I'll check out our hardware here to see if there's any unauthorized code lurking around. We keep the master set of software on my machine, and we cut the tapes we send to WSMR and to the systems in the field."

"How difficult is it?"

"Can't say for sure until I get into it. Some of this stuff is hard to find. I don't have any experience with it on her computer, because it's never come up before. I'll have to write up some special code to do the check. I can run a simple check first thing in the morning, but a really good one will take some time and thought."

"It's probably not worth that much effort," Jeff said.

"Nah, no big deal. I should've done it before, anyway. Now that you bring this possibility up, it's a precaution that needs to be taken. We don't want any bugs in your girl. Not healthy."

"OK. As long as it needs to be done anyway."

"That it on that subject?" Fish asked.

"Yeah, I guess so. Why?"

"Well, I wondered that since you were here and all and you've asked me your question, could I ask you one?"

"Sure. Shoot."

"Why are we doing the satellite thing?"

"Did your bosses ask you to ask me that?" Jeff chuckled.

"No way. They don't know we get along at that level, and if they did ask me to take advantage, I think they know what I'd tell'em. It's just something that doesn't seem to make any sense to me, so I thought I'd ask."

"You want the short answer or the long answer?"

"Why don't we try the short one first, and maybe that'll be enough. If the short answer is 'shut-up and leave it alone,' I'll understand that."

"No," Jeff said smiling. "Nothing that over-protective. But the government is determined to get into the software business and PATRIOT's the most software-intense system in the Army."

"But giving the government total control of PATRIOT software and then sending updates out by satellite is an unbelievably complex task. I'm not sure the government is up to it yet."

"Well, you see buddy, our first concern is what you just said, and that is that Raytheon believes they are 'giving' the software to the government. That's the wrong view for a contractor to take. The software belongs to the government and it's the government's responsibility to maintain it and update the systems in the field. That's a type of control over the system, and for political as well as military reasons, that control should reside within the government."

"But sending out software over a satellite net is a high security risk."

"That risk is known and understood, but it's smaller than the current risk. With the manual process now in use, a magnetic tape has a good chance of either falling into enemy hands or being sent to the wrong site and causing major technical problems."

"But the program is so far behind schedule and over cost, it's likely to hold up the PAC II delivery."

"I can see I should have started with the long answer from the beginning."

"I'm sorry, sir. I don't mean to sound like a Raytheon puppet, but when we're trying so hard to get this new PAC II capability wrapped up for fielding and we are saddled with something like this, it just doesn't make sense."

"Well, since you've taken us this far, let me just be blunt. Yes, there are a lot of problems with the satellite program. Now while I don't think this is a sinister plot by Raytheon to manipulate the government, I do believe that Raytheon sees that it is in their best financial interest if this concept is not implemented, but I intend to see that it is. Raytheon is going to have to make a choice. Either they recognize that this program will be completed by them for the agreed price and get on with doing it in an aggressive manner, or the government will take over the entire process altogether."

"That's pretty clear. Do you want me to pass that message on up the line?"

"No. I think I made the message pretty clear today."

They finished their coffee, Jeff said good-bye to Sarah, and he and Fish parted at the door with promises to stay in touch more often.

□□□□□

As the Executive Session wound down late the next morning, the Raytheon program manager received a note from his secretary and came over to Jeff.

"Max Fisher says he needs to talk to you before you leave," the program manager told Jeff. "He said on the phone would be OK. There's a phone you can use in the office next door."

"Thanks," Jeff said, and took the slip with the number on it. Fish answered on the first ring.

"Just thought I'd give you an update, sir," he said.

"Fish, it's been twenty years. When are you going to quit calling me 'sir'? Hell, I'm the godfather for your oldest child."

"Old habits die hard, General," Fish said. "In my mind, you're still my Cap'n. Do you want to hear what I found or not?"

"Shoot," Jeff said.

"I ran a quick test on the master software set on the PATRIOT computer here in the lab. Nothing. That means that either nothing's there or whoever put it there is pretty clever. I'll have to do some more homework to develop a full set of checkout software, and it may take some time. Between the changes to the software for PAC II and that stupid satellite thing, I'm pretty snowed under."

"The satellite thing isn't stupid, Fish."

"If you say so, sir."

"I say so."

"Yes, sir."

"Tell me about this someone clever," Jeff said.

"Well, what I mean is that if something's really there and it didn't show on the tests I did, then it couldn't be there by accident. And whoever put it there is a real expert on mainframe operating systems and also has a knowledge of PATRIOT software nearly equivalent to mine."

"Is that possible?" Jeff asked.

"Possible, but highly improbable. My educated guess is that there's nothing there."

"Something happened. I saw it. If what you're telling me means what I think it means, it may be more important than you think."

"Do I translate that to mean I should raise this in the priority of my daily schedule?"

"Maybe you should put it on your evening schedule. Try to make sure you're discreet."

"Yes, sir. By the way, there's another fellow working on this in Huntsville."

"Really. Who?"

"Name's Ben Peeples. I forgot when we were talking last night, but when I came in this morning and started digging around, I remembered it. Works over at the software lab at the Missile Command. Know him?"

"No. But now that you mention the name, I remember Johnny Madkin saying Peeples was a friend and he was going to give him a call about the entry. Do you think he found anything?"

"In fact, I know he didn't. I talk to him a lot. A while back when all this came up he told me that he was looking for something in this area, but I didn't know it was for you. He ran into the same front end blocks I did this morning and let it drop since it wasn't a high priority. He had some good ideas on what to do next, though."

"Why don't we let him follow through on those and we'll see what he finds?"

"Sounds like a good plan to me. I'm really snowed here. You want me to call him?"

"I'll get Steve to touch base with him when I get back to town."

"OK."

"Good. Keep me posted, Fish."

"Yes, sir."

□□□□□

The slightly balding man pulled the car into the parking lot of the White Horse Tavern and parked beside the public phone in the parking lot. He looked around nervously as he walked to the phone. Some men he knew were coming in and called to him. He passed the phone booth without stopping and went into the tavern. At the bar, he ordered a scotch on the rocks and gulped it down. He looked around the room until he was sure no one was watching and went back outside to the phone booth. He took the receiver from the hook, dialed a set of numbers and a charge number from memory, waited for the first ring and then hung up the phone. He went back into the bar, ordered another drink, and waited a few minutes before going back to the phone booth and dialing the numbers again.

"Hello." He flinched a little, startled by the sharpness of the voice on the other end of the phone.

"Hello. It's me. I've got something to report."

"What?"

"I heard my boss on the phone today."

"Have you been drinking?"

"No." He turned his back to some other people going into the tavern and hunched into the corner of the booth.

"I told you not to call me when you'd been drinking."

"I haven't, I swear."

"So what did you hear?"

"He was talking to someone about the code."

"Are you sure he was talking about your code?"

"Yes."

"Who was he talking to?"

"I don't know. I saw him on the phone, so I went into my office which is next to his so I could hear. I didn't hear the whole conversation, but there's no doubt he was talking about the code."

"You mean he found it."

"It doesn't sound like it, but just the fact that he's looking makes me nervous. If they do find it, there's going to be a big investigation and I'm going to be on a very short list of names. There's not that many people who could write that code."

"Don't panic. Did they seem to know what it was?"

"No."

"Is he going to look some more?"

"Yes, but I didn't get the impression it was a very high priority."

"Then they don't know anything. Quit worrying."

"That's easy for you to say. They're going to get someone in Huntsville to look for it."

"How do you know that?"

"I heard them talking about it."

"Do you have a name?"

"It was Peeples. A guy named Ben Peeples. He works for the government laboratory there in Huntsville."

"Could he be a problem?"

"What do you mean?"

"I mean, can he find the code?"

"Yes. I know him and he's very sharp. Given a priority and some time, he could find it."

"OK. I'll take care of it. Now quit worrying."

"What do you mean, 'You'll take care of it'?"

"Just what I said. It won't be a problem. Now go back to your whiskey."

"Can you come to Boston?"

"No, and I told you not to use locations on the phone."

"I want to see you."

"Not now. Call me if you hear anything else."

"Sure. I will. You know I will." He started to say good-bye, but heard the phone disconnect on the other end.

weapons systems--pentagon adv15 3-90
Congress holds hearings on Iraqi military maneuvers
USWNS Military News
adv mar 15 1990 or thereafter

By GEORGE GROWSON

WASHINGTON—Congressional hearings convened today on the military situation in the Middle East. The Senate Armed Services Committee and the House Committee on Government Operations both initiated questionings on topics relating to the security of United States' interest in the region. The primary concern seemed to be the continued southern movement of troops within Iraq. Republican members played down the movement, saying it was the internal business of Iraq, while Democratic members seemed to be attempting to make some connection between these movements and secret agreements between the Bush administration and Saddam Hussein, the President of Iraq. The session was eventually adjourned by Chairman Fredric McGee (D-MN).

SIX

March 15, 1990

Washington, DC

11:30 AM

Celia Mitchell left the Hart Senate Office Building by the door on C Street and walked at a brisk pace in the general direction of Union Station. Every male in the vicinity paid full attention to her. Looking neither left nor right, she made her way through the crowds on the sidewalk, seemingly oblivious to the stares. Strikingly attractive, she had a disarming kind of confidence which somehow conveyed an unmistakable sexual presence and a tactical aloofness all at once. Her favors were reserved for the select few men powerful enough to pave the road to her future. Tall and elegant, she had a mane of jet black hair which flew wildly below her shoulders.

One or two lowbrow catcalls came from the opposite side of the street, but the only sign of Celia's having heard them was a slightly tightened grip on her purse. There were no returned smiles, nor any girlish display of pride.

Striding briskly, she turned left on Second Street and made her way toward a small area of private homes and a few exclusive apartments. She rounded another corner, and the walkway narrowed to an alley which led to a small complex of several bungalow apartments arranged around a courtyard. As she passed through the courtyard, Celia did not slow her pace or move her gaze to admire the lush tropical beauty of the garden. A few quick steps took her across the courtyard and directly to bungalow 3, where a key from her purse opened the door.

Inside, the living room was elegantly furnished with period art and furniture which came with the four thousand dollar per month rent. Celia thoroughly checked the bedroom and bath, and then went to the bar to make sure the maid had the right liquors and ice ready. She entered the small walk-in closet in the bedroom. After selecting another key from the ring, she unlocked a door in the side wall of the closet, hidden by several pieces of hanging clothing. She carried a large black valise to the bed and, with another key from the ring, opened it and removed several of the articles. The first sign of a smile came as she put them in a neat row just under the edge of the bed.

Behind the open closet door, there was a small walkway which turned to a narrow corridor ending behind the head of the bed. Celia had to turn sideways to squeeze herself through to the end of the corridor, where a video recorder looked through a mirror into the bedroom. Inserting a new long play tape, she checked the rest of the equipment and activated the recorder. A quick glance through the mirror and into the bedroom brought another smile.

She went back to the bar in the living room, poured a stiff glass of whiskey and turned on the television. A small control on the rear of the set had a selector switch. Celia flipped the switch until she saw the view of the bedroom, then set the switch back to its original position and turned the set off. The first small sip of her drink caused a slight movement of her head as though it burned her throat. She leaned against the bar as the heat from the alcohol spread through her body and settled. The rest of the drink followed in one hard swallow. The whiskey slowly made its way into her, preparing her for the job ahead. She refilled the glass and carried it with her to the bedroom. She slowly undressed, carefully hung her clothes in the closet, and placed all her personal items in a small drawstring bag. The shower, turned to full force and hot to the touch, filled the bathroom with steam.

The combination of the steamy shower and the whiskey left her visibly relaxed. In the bedroom, a long look at her body in the full length mirror produced another slight smile. All she wore was a small silver locket on a silver chain around her neck. Her hands moved from the locket and caressed her body and finally settled on the beginnings of a small plumpness in her lower belly which brought a frown to her face in the mirror.

Finished with her self-adulation and criticism, Celia opened the small bag she had brought and took out a strapless lace bra and matching black bikini. A long black silk gown from the closet completed the outfit, and another look in the mirror ensured that the appearance was right. The combination of the sheer black silk and her dark complexion created the perfect image. Black was the color she wore most often in this apartment, and the expensive gown was standard equipment for these interludes.

She checked her watch and relaxed since there were a few more minutes to wait. She sat on the couch and thought about what would happen next. Her mind drifted to a faraway place and a special man. He demanded her services, and she would obey as she had all of her life. This was the most important mission he had given her after a long succession of smaller jobs. It had taken years to get herself to the position she had obtained—years of being in small jobs, using both men and women as stepping stones. This project would be the culmination of all that effort. It was the last mission that would require her to stay in this country. When this endeavor was successfully completed, her reward was to return to her homeland and to him.

As she sat there, she thought for the first time that she might not succeed in what lay ahead. Never before had she failed, but this time was different. This would require a total command and control of a spirit not easily governed.

She heard steps on the walk, and then a key in the door. She relaxed into the corner of the couch, draping the gown so it exposed most of her leg and gave a hint of the black lace beneath. As he drew closer, she saw that there was no love for her in his eyes. There was only a lust which seemed so strong it might consume him.

Standing, she smiled broadly and put her arms around his neck. She kissed him roughly, pressing her body against his. His arousal was obvious, and she ground her body against his. For a moment they stood in a firm embrace, and he could hear her deep breathing. He groped her buttocks and pulled her to him even harder. Pulling away, she went to the bar and began to fix them both a drink.

Lieutenant General Wesley F. Grant sat on the couch and watched Celia. He could see the skimpy lingerie through the sheer gown. His desire for

129

her was obvious in his nervous movements and darting eyes. He waited and watched as she brought him the drink.

He took a swig of the whisky, then set his drink down and reached for her. She came to him willingly. He kissed her roughly on her mouth and groped her breast. She returned the pressure of his hands with her body and moaned, urging him on, pressing, moving into him.

Slowly and without taking her eyes from his, she eased away from him and handed him his drink. He finished it quickly and watched as she sipped hers. She stood and the tie of her gown loosened. It hung open as she took his hand and led him to the bedroom. She pulled him to her on the bed and he tore open the gown, ripping the delicate fabric. He buried his face in her breasts and roughly sucked her nipple. She raked her nails down his back and he groaned in ecstasy. His total absorption in her body seemed to signal her control of his spirit and it convinced her that she would succeed.

She pushed him down on the bed and removed his clothes, then, sitting astride him, she removed her bra as he watched. She reached over the side of the bed for one of the items she had so carefully selected for the general's pleasure. She stood with her legs on either side of him and drew the belt along his chest. The general grasped her ankles with both hands and moaned as he watched her move above him. Celia smiled into the mirror and her face reflected an unmistakable expression of triumph.

ロロロロロ

She finished tidying up the bedroom while General Grant was using the shower. She was visibly pleased with her performance and moved quickly and purposefully around the room. He came from the bath, one towel wrapped around his waist while with another he still rubbed his head.

"Celia," he said, "that was terrific. I have never had such a rush, not even in combat."

She came to him, leaning into his wet body and removing the towel around his waist. Her lips were so close to his ear he could feel them move as she whispered and he could feel her hands moving on his buttocks and groin.

"It just comes naturally with a lover as sensitive as you." He could feel the moisture of her breath in his ear. "It makes me feel good too," she added.

"Each time it seems to get better," he said. "What goes on in that pretty little head of yours to be able to think up these things?"

She walked back to the bed.

"Most of my little toys and tricks, as you call them, were things you told me about, remember?"

"Yeah, I remember. Do you remember all of the other things I said, too?"

"Have I ever forgotten?" Her smile was a promise to him.

"No, you haven't, baby, and you'll never know what these afternoons mean to me."

"By the way," she said, "did you have your meeting with General Weyland the other day? Someone from our office went to a meeting with him that afternoon, but I don't know what it was about."

"Yes, I'd met with him that morning. He's a good officer, but with a one track mind." General Grant seemed to feel self-conscious about his nudity now that the conversation had turned to business, and he started getting dressed.

"How do you mean?" she asked.

"He only cares about PATRIOT, regardless of the priorities of the rest of the Army," he said. "I had a hard time convincing him that it's my job and my bosses' job to help your side of the business decide how to spend Army money, and not his."

"But it's important that PATRIOT funding be kept intact if our little plan is going to work."

"Don't worry," he said. "The funding's secure. The people on your side made sure of that. But if we can't get them to untie the money when this is over so we can spend it on other things, then our plan won't come to anything. I think I need to talk to Senator Strong to make sure he understands."

"Senator Strong understands everything," she said. "He wants to keep all of the communication through me so that no one suspects what's going on. When the time is right, he will make sure that the proper arrangements have been made. He has many favors due him from the other Armed Services members."

"When is he going to let me in on the whole plan?" General Grant had finished dressing now, and had made the transition back to his command voice. "I feel a little left out in the cold not knowing what's going to happen next. Why shouldn't I support PATRIOT just like he is?"

"We've been through all of this before, Wessy. It's important that you have your position established. That way, when the time comes, it won't appear out of character for you to come down hard."

"I know we've been through it all before, and I understand why my role has to be like it is. On the other hand, I'm a three-star general and not used to being kept in the dark or given directions from a messenger, even if it's someone as special as you."

"I can only do what the Senator tells me."

"I understand that, but in the back of my mind, there's just the beginnings of a worry that I may not be getting the whole story."

"How do you mean?" she asked with the sign of an authoritative edge to her voice.

"I mean there are certain aspects of this which just don't make a whole lot of sense."

"It makes perfectly good sense to the Senator."

"That's why I think I should talk to Senator Strong," he said. It came out like a little boy trying to convince his mother a second piece of dessert was good for him.

"No," she said. "Not now."

"When?" he asked.

"When I tell you," she said, and her voice didn't sound anything like a mother. It was the first time he had heard that tone.

"I think that I should decide that," he said, standing a little taller and looking down at her.

"If you do, I can assure you that you will regret it," she said with a look and a voice that was as cold as ice. She turned from him to move into the living room and left him standing there alone.

He stood as though he were made of stone for a long time looking at his reflection in the mirror. He finally turned and followed after her.

As he came into the living room, she came to him, put her arms around his neck and pulled him to her. Her kiss was hard and sensual, and she pulled him close, pushing her breasts into his chest. He stiffened momentarily and then kissed her back hard. His hands reached for her buttocks and he squeezed until he knew he was hurting her. Memories of the last two hours came flooding back into his head, and he started to become aroused again.

"Celia," he said, "you're a hard case to figure out."

Her hands went to his crotch and unzipped his pants.

"Don't try," she said.

⌑⌑⌑⌑⌑

General Grant left the bungalow and walked toward the taxi stand on Fifteenth Street. His head was full of thoughts, mostly about the quick remark Celia had made that "he would regret it." He tried to think of what she meant. Did it mean the Senator would be irritated? Did it mean she would not be so aggressive with him in bed? Did it mean she might not have sex with him at all? Or worse yet, did it mean she might tell someone else about their games and toys? None of those alternatives sounded very attractive. He had only two choices. Play it her way or get out, and he knew for sure he would regret it if he just quit. In the end, he decided not to find out.

When she first told him about the plan, she made it clear that she had other options with other high ranking military personnel in key places. And he didn't want to lose his contact with her. Not now. God almighty in heaven, not now. He had never even allowed himself to dream about the things he had just done. A few times during their marriage, his wife performed oral sex for him, and that was the wildest his sex life had ever been. And she had been quick to remind him of her distaste for the act. Many was the night when he had lain awake on the bed and dreamed of sexual activities that he was sure he would never experience.

But these fantasies paled in comparison to Celia's seemingly insatiable

133

desire for him and her total lack of inhibition in bed. It had all happened so fast. The call from her telling him that she had something the Senator wanted her to discuss with him. The lunch. The dinner. Their first meeting at the apartment when she explained the basics of the Senator's plan to him. She had been sort of cute when she abruptly told him that he had better go. She had seemed almost embarrassed. He pushed her a little about why, and she finally admitted that she felt attracted to him and the few glasses of wine she drank with dinner were affecting her. If he didn't leave, she might embarrass herself.

It took him aback so that he actually did leave. But he thought of nothing else for several days. Each time he remembered her, he would become aroused. When he found it strange that she was attracted to him and no other woman had ever been, he told himself that it was probably the first time she had been around a real combat soldier. When he thought of her, he was also reminded of the Senator's plan and his thoughts became clouded. A strange plan, and one which worried him. He didn't understand enough of it to be able to judge its full merit. It was far afield of what he expected from politics, but this was his first assignment with a direct interface to politicians at that level. This must be the way the game is played, he thought. Hardball.

❑❑❑❑❑

Celia sat on the couch watching the video. She always watched after the sessions were over to make sure the necessary elements had been captured on the video. It was also enjoyable because it helped her understand even better what really pleased and what didn't. Thinking about General Grant brought a chuckle. Anything pleased him. Anything and everything. Some thought was going to have to be given to preparations for the next time. Experience had taught her that as long as each time was better for the man than the last, they would come back again and again, no matter the potential consequences.

Today had been a success. Their first battle of wills, and she had won decisively. It was now clear to both of them that he realized there was more

134

to their relationship than physical attraction. She had seen men come to that realization before. Oddly, they became more demanding sexually. She assumed it was because they knew they were paying dearly for the service they were getting. They were paying by allowing themselves to be used, and generous customers deserved to be treated well. They also became more acquiescent to her requests. When they reached that stage, the game was over. For General Grant, it was definitely over. All that was required now was make sure he received the proper directions. There wasn't even a need to worry about pushing too hard anymore. As long as the sex was available to him, plenty of it, and the way he wanted it, she would be in complete control.

Her thoughts went back to the man who had sent her on this mission. He was a man and not some puffed-up weakling who couldn't resist being trapped by sexual favors. He couldn't be dominated by her or any other woman. She dwelt for a moment on their last time together and the things he had taught her. He had explained how this mission would get her established, then had told her to wait for further instructions. How long ago had that been? Years. And never any personal contact since.

The details of the current plan came through a courier. She didn't understand the plan completely, but she knew her role and what was expected of her. And she had been successful. First the man in Boston. Then the one in El Paso. Then General Grant. All of that had been easy.

Senator Strong had been the easiest. It didn't even require sex, although that didn't matter to her. Using sex of any type to accomplish her mission was just part of her job. It didn't take her long to know that sex wasn't going to work with the Senator. Her first small discreet moves to him were met with rigid rebuffs. Just a little investigation from one of the residents from her country verified what she suspected. The Senator was a closet homosexual. She decided not to try to use that information in her approach to the Senator. She was convinced that his commitment to his country was stronger than his fear of being revealed. He was a purist and an intellectual, so she had approached him from that viewpoint. It wasn't as firm a control as she had over General Grant and the others, but the Senator's role didn't require that. Soon, his part would be over, and she would be done with him.

Celia arrived at work promptly as usual the next morning, well before the rest of the staff began to arrive. She always had the office ready when the key people came in, and her presence made certain they knew who was responsible. She was a respected member of the staff, not only because of her contribution, but because everyone knew the Senator considered her his confidante and entrusted her with many responsibilities. She was able to get any information from any member of the staff because they always assumed she needed it for something she was doing for the Senator. She had the full run of the office and access to even the Senator's private files.

When the Senator arrived, he immediately summoned her to his office.

"Did you meet with General Grant?" he asked.

"Yes," she said. "We met at my apartment for several hours."

"Isn't that risky for a man in his position?" the Senator asked.

"I don't think so. It's a rather thinly populated neighborhood. Besides, he always brings his aide with him so there are never any questions."

"He talks about this business in front of his aide?"

"Oh, yes. And the inference I get is that there are others in the Pentagon who have concurred with his plan. It seems to be rather a routine part of their operation."

"So how did he say things were progressing?"

"He said things were going well. The tests this spring and summer at White Sands have convinced the Army that PATRIOT can shoot down missiles. He greatly appreciates the role you have played in helping him get the system to this point. He believes that in another few months, the truth about the system's performance will come out, and then we can set in motion the rest of the plan."

"Strange fellow, that one," the Senator said. "I never thought I'd be plotting with the likes of him. I also never thought I'd be supporting the development of a system as expensive and wasteful as PATRIOT. I hope we're doing the right thing."

"So do I, but I believe we can trust General Grant. He's got more to lose here than you do. If his plan backfires, it could cost him the appointment as Chief of Staff."

"I never knew that the Army could have such devious schemes within its own walls. The plan makes sense, but something just doesn't seem to fit."

"General Grant and the other people he says he represents are very concerned that Congress is choosing which weapon systems the Army must develop. The PATRIOT upgrade is an example of what he thinks must be stopped. He feels the Army must be given a budget for weapon system development and acquisition to be spent at its discretion."

"I know, I know," the Senator said. "You've explained all of that to me before."

"All he wants is for the tags to be removed from the allocation of the funds. Let the Army decide how to allocate the money. Once the real truth about PATRIOT's performance comes out, he'll be in a position to demonstrate to Congress how the Army could've made the situation better if only they had been able to make the choices."

"Since the testing has gone so well, how can he be confident the system will perform poorly in the future?"

"I don't know, but I think he may have a few tricks up his sleeve."

"You mean he's going to somehow derail the system?"

"No, I don't think that. I just think he knows something nobody else knows. Or at least only a few people know. I'm betting that there's a problem with the testing and the PATRIOT project is covering up for some reason."

"Hmm. That sounds plausible. You can never trust those people to tell you the truth. The one thing you can always count on is that they'll stick together and try to cover it up if there is some kind of a problem."

"In the meantime, General Grant says that it's imperative that you continue your support for the program. It has to be funded through this next year if all of the plan is going to work, and the Army must dedicate all of its anti-missile resources to the PATRIOT."

"What about the SDI?" the Senator asked.

"That's not a factor, he says. The SDI is still concentrating on space-based solutions to the problem and is still a long way from any contribution."

The Senator came on strong. This was a rallying point with which he was well familiar, and by reflex, he went into an oration.

"And a long time from now, they will still be a long way from a contribution. The worst thing Ronald Reagan did during his presidency was to convince the American public that there was an affordable defense against strategic nuclear missiles. There isn't now, and there never will be. We continue to throw billions away on wasted research of hoards of engineers with fancy degrees in how to design totally useless concepts and never build anything."

"General Grant shares your beliefs on that," she said. "He says that if we succeed on this plan, he has support within the Army to work the SDI funding. He believes the Army can accomplish a lot more in the missile defense area than SDI and with a lot less funding. That way everybody wins. But when the time comes, we'll have to attack the SDI credibility just like we're going to attack PATRIOT."

"That's a goal worth pursuing," the Senator said. "Maybe the Army people aren't quite as stupid as I had thought they were."

"General Grant seems very sincere," Celia said. "And I think he'd like to work with you on other things as well."

"Well, he'll have to do that through you," he said. "I don't want other senators to know we have anything going. It would hurt too many of my other projects."

"Yes, Senator," she said with an understanding smile, "I'll tell him."

March 17, 1990
Huntsville, Alabama
9:30 AM

"You kids go on back in the house and help your mama," Ben Peeples said to his two children.

"OK, Dad," they both said, happy to be finished with the weekly chores. The two kids scrambled to the porch and into the house.

Ben picked up the last plastic bags and carried them to the street in front of the house. He looked back with pride at his lawn and the trim two-story house on its spacious corner lot. He saw a car pass and then turn at the corner. As he gathered the garbage cans and lids from the morning's pick-up, he kept his eye on the car and driver as it stopped and the driver went to the back side of their house. That was normal since the house was situated on the corner and the back door really served as the main entrance for most visitors. He had seen the same car slowly pass by thirty minutes or so earlier like the man driving was looking for an address. He finished up with the cans and was about to put away the rakes in the garage when he saw Deb standing in the front door.

"Benjamin, could you come in, please?"

He was instantly on alert. Benjamin was his full name, and when she called him that instead of Ben it was their private signal that something was wrong. When he called her Deborah instead of Deb, it meant the trouble was from his side. She sounded strange and frightened for a routine Saturday morning. Ben looked at the car parked on the street by his drive.

"Let me put these rakes in the garage," he said with his eye directly on her. She knew Ben kept his shotgun and deer rifle locked in a gun vault against the back wall of the garage attached to the house, but he couldn't see her face behind the screen door to read her reaction. She turned away from him and then turned back to face him again.

"No," she said. "You better come now. The children need some help quickly."

He dropped the rakes and started walking toward the porch and his wife. He instinctively walked faster and then ran up the stairs to the door. As he opened the door, Deb seemed suddenly pulled backward, and he saw the masked face. Then he saw the gun.

"Over there," the mask said, pushing Deb to him.

"Where are the kids?" Ben asked his wife. She was trembling, and he held her close to him.

"Shut up," the mask barked. "Any more comments and this won't be as pleasant as I'm going to try to make it."

"In the bedroom," Deborah blurted to Ben. She had started to cry and Ben held her tighter.

The pistol spit and Ben could feel the impact of the silenced round near his foot.

"That was the only warning. The next one will find one of you. Do you both understand?"

"Yes," Ben said. "What do you want?"

"Well, now just what do you think I want, Mr. Suburban Homeowner." The eyes of the mask roamed over Deb, and Ben felt her stiffen.

"We don't have much money here, but you can have it all," Ben said. "There's some jewelry in the box on the bedroom dresser. And some bearer bonds and gold coins in the safe. You can have it all."

"Yeah. I just bet I can. Why don't we just go through the house and you can round it all up for me."

Ben started to the back of the house with his arm around Deb.

"She comes with me," the mask said as he reached for her.

"No," Deb said and pulled tighter into Ben. The gun moved like a lightning flash and struck Ben just below his temple. Ben fell to one knee and Deb went with him, trying to keep him from collapsing. Blood ran across his cheek and dripped onto the new beige carpet.

"Help him up."

Ben was wobbly, but Deb got his arm around her shoulder, and he was able to regain his footing.

"Now, I'm going to say it again. She fucking comes with me!" The mask reached across and pulled Deb by her arm to his side. He pushed Ben with the silencer on the end of the pistol.

"Now let's go find that stash you mentioned."

They walked through the house as Ben collected all of the valuables he could remember and put them into a pillow case as he was told by the mask. The last stop was in the bedroom.

"Now shut yourself in the closet," the mask said to Ben. The lips were tight behind the mask as the man looked at Deb, still held to him by her arm.

Ben reached for Deb.

"Not her."

Ben didn't move and the man brought the gun up to Deb's head.

"After her, it'll be the kids. Your choice."

"Go on," Deb said, her head hanging, refusing to look at him. "I can do it."

"That's a good girl. I just bet you can."

Ben still didn't move. The silencer of the gun pressed against her cheek.

"Go!" Deb screamed, and as she did her knees buckled and she fell to the floor. The mask moved to grab her with the hand holding the gun. Ben moved quickly, but the gun hand moved faster and the metal of the heavy automatic caught him full force on his chin. He reeled back from the blow and fell on the bed.

Making a spitting sound, the silenced gun fired, and his body jerked. The gun spit again. Deb lay sobbing on the floor, and when she heard the sound of the gun fire the second shot, started crawling to the bed. As she got to Ben's feet, the mask reached out and pulled her away by her hair. He lifted her head until her face was grotesque in its position and agony and moved her toward Ben as he lifted the gun toward her face.

"Pity," he said. "But it wouldn't be any fun unless you wanted it."

He fired one last time, and she fell on top of her husband.

"And I can tell you don't."

Staff Sergeant James E. Johnson pulled the mask over his head and pushed it into the pocket of his jeans. He lifted his sweatshirt and put the pistol between the jeans and his belt and covered it again with the sweatshirt. A slow smile covered his face as he looked down at the couple on the bed. In his groin he could feel the heat of the pistol barrel and silencer through his jeans. He folded up the pillow case and casually carried it with him as he walked to the stolen car. He drove back to the shopping mall, circled twice to make sure everything was calm, and parked the car beside his rented Lincoln. He was careful to put it in the space just the way he had seen the department store employee park when she had arrived at work that morning. He reached under the dash, removed the wiring harness he had installed, opened and then locked the door, and left in his rental for the airport.

"Well, who'd have ever thought it?" Mike Hensley asked as he sat on the couch with his drink, dressed only in his boxer shorts.

"What do you find so strange?" Celia asked. Her thin robe was draped from her shoulders so that most of her breasts were exposed. The sheer robe made it clear she had nothing on underneath.

"Me and you. Here. Like this."

"Why is that so strange?" she asked as she sat down beside him.

"You know what I mean, Celia."

"You mean because I'm an 'older woman'?"

"No. Gosh no. Not that."

"Don't you like me?" she asked as she moved her lips close to his ear. She let the tip of her tongue trace down his neck, then buried her face in the corner of his shoulder. "Didn't you enjoy it?" she whispered.

"Like you? You're fantastic! It was great. In fact, it may be the best sex I ever had. It's just that we're such an unlikely pair. Besides, you're not that much older than me, and you're prettier than any woman I know, younger or older."

The robe disclosed more as she pulled herself up onto him, forcing him to lay back on the couch.

"I heard about your meeting with General Weyland the other day. I also heard you gave him a pretty hard time."

"Well, you know how these Pentagon big dogs are," Mike said. If you don't push them down every now and then, they just get carried away. Sometimes I think they must feel they have the right to tell us what to do."

"Boy, do I know what you mean. I have to work a lot with them for Senator Strong. He won't even talk to them so I have to do it. I mostly work with General Grant."

"Now there's a whole series of case studies, all in one uniform."

"Yeah," Celia chuckled. "Sometimes I have a tough time with him."

142

"How so?"

"Well, you know. He really thinks of himself as Mr. Macho Man. He only thinks of me as some little girl. It's hard for me to stand up to him sometimes."

"You need some help?"

"No. Not help really. Maybe just some reinforcement every now and then. I tell him what Senator Strong wants, but I'm not sure he always believes me. But Senator Strong won't talk to him. Sometimes it would help if someone else could pitch in."

"You just let me know when and what to say, and I'll take care of that bucket of lard. He doesn't come on to you, does he?"

"Oh, gosh no," she laughed. "He knows better than that."

"Well, whenever I can help, you just let me know."

"I will, Mike. And thanks." She slid closer and as she moved over him, her hands found the elastic band of his boxer shorts. Mike could feel her breasts pushing into his face, and he sought her nipple with his mouth. He found one and felt the other brush near his eye. His eyes flicked open at the light touch and his heart stopped completely as he found himself looking directly into the eyes of another man standing over them. Mike scrambled back from Celia. She looked puzzled and then afraid when she saw the terror in Mike's eyes as he looked over her shoulder. She jumped from the couch and pulled her robe around herself.

"What the hell are you doing here?" she shouted at Johnson.

"Just came by to let you know I had finished that little job for you in Alabama. Thought there might be a reward in it for me." Sergeant Johnson stood back from her, smiling. "But it seems I've come at a bad time since you already appear to be handing out rewards. Or maybe it isn't bad after all. Maybe I'm in line for a little commendation myself." He reached out for her robe and she jerked away from him.

"I've asked you not to come here. How did you get in?"

"With this," he said, holding up a key. "You don't give me enough credit." He walked around the room a little. "You've spruced the place up a bit. What did he do to earn this kind of treatment? Or are you just priming him up a little? I bet he didn't do for you what I just did."

Celia looked to Mike, who was cowering in the corner of the couch and back to Johnson, who was obviously very drunk.

"Don't say any more," she hissed at Johnson. "Go to the other room."

"Well, maybe I'd rather stay right here and watch the two of you finish what you were starting since it was just about to get interesting. Are you going to do all of the things for him you do for me?"

"Get out! Now!"

"In a word, lover lady, no. I ain't going anywhere. Why don't you tell college boy here to leave. Or aren't the little jobs I do for you more important than that teen-aged hard-on he's losing real fast?"

"Shut your mouth. You're saying too much." She turned back to Mike and softened, sitting on the couch beside him. "I'm sorry, Mike. This is an old friend who has apparently had too much to drink. Maybe we ought to call it a night, and then I'll try to get him a cab."

Johnson slurred a loud laugh.

"Yeah, I'm an ol' friend, all right. But ain't no cabs run all the way to White Sands, missy. No ma'am. Can't get no cabs to that missile site where you sent me."

"Shut up, I said. You're going to say too much."

"Maybe I'll do some talking with this," Johnson said as he pulled the pistol out and waved it in her face. She stood and reached for the gun, but his hand moved fast as he slapped her face, and she fell backwards onto the couch. He pointed the gun at Mike.

"She's really something, ain't she? You know, when she first come to me, she told me I was the only one. I believed her, too. That's how good she is. Then I found out different. But some of them aren't with us anymore, are they, Celia?"

"I'm telling you, shut your big mouth. He's a Senate staffer and can cause lots of trouble."

"Well, Celia baby, I didn't figure you would have anybody in here who wasn't important. Like them others I watched you with, and the ones I did for you. How many others you got coming in here, huh?"

"None," she said, softening and looking up at him. "Jimmy, Mike was just coming by to do some work, and we got a little carried away.

144

Isn't that right, Mike?"

Mike started to stand, but Johnson pushed him back onto the couch with the point of the gun.

"You just stay put, college boy. You think you're pretty hot, don't you? Riding high on a woman like this. Make any man feel good." Johnson was getting himself worked up now. He was almost bouncing from one foot to the other.

"Take it easy, Jimmy," Celia said.

"Is that what you told college boy here? Take it easy. I bet you told him he could take it any way he wanted it. That right, college boy? Well, your feel good time is over. Say goodbye to the lady, lover-boy." He raised the pistol directly into Mike's face and pulled the trigger twice.

Celia flinched as she felt the blood and brains splat on her face and body. She didn't look at Mike, but stood and faced Johnson who turned to look at her. His breath was fast and he was licking his lips rapidly, still bouncing from one foot to the other. His lip was curled to one side in a sort of lopsided smile as his eyes fell to her breast. She opened her robe to give him a full view, moved to him and put her arms around his neck. As she pulled his head to her chest, she could feel the slimy residue of Mike's face slick between her smooth skin and Johnson's unshaven face, and she smiled as she heard the gun drop to the floor.

MARCH
1962

Israeli land disputes--pentagon adv22 3-62
PLO, Israel continue violent territorial disputes
USWNS Military News
adv mar 22 1962 or thereafter

By GEORGE GROWSON

WASHINGTON—Gunfire was exchanged on several fronts in
disputed Palestinian territories yesterday and early this
morning as Israeli warplanes strafed and bombed several
suspected Arab terrorist camps. Diplomats from the United
States, Great Britain, Israel, and Arab nations including
Saudi Arabia, Libya, Iran, and Syria met to discuss
territorial claims and conditions for a cease fire. A
spokesperson for the Palestinian Liberation Organization
stated that the PLO would not participate in the talks, and
would refuse to recognize any agreements which resulted
from the talks. While none of the meeting participants
would comment directly, it was clear that hopes for real
progress in the talks any time soon were very remote.
Robert H. Forester, the U.S. representative to the
conference, said, "We're trying desperately to stop the
current flow of blood in the Middle East on a day-to-day
basis. Beyond that, we haven't even thought."

SEVEN

Sharifa's small legs stretched as far as they would go as she tried to take bigger steps to match the tracks of the men who had traveled on the dusty trail early that morning, but she couldn't quite reach. Her grandfather made this walk every day as he went to and from the garden upon which their family depended. Sharifa carried the small pail containing her grandfather's lunch and the goatskin water flask she took to him each day as he worked the patches of vegetables and grain in the small plot. As she stepped sideways to avoid a large rock on the trail, she held her shoulders back in pride that she was now old enough to perform this duty. Her older brother Saad had to move on to more important tasks.

As the path got steeper on the slopes of the mountain, she stopped to rest at a small clearing where the midday sun was shaded by a large rock overhang. The rocks on these hills were as much a part of her as her own body. Rocks, dust, sand and water were what made up her understanding of nature. Water was drawn from the village well and treated as though it was sacred. Sharifa remembered hearing the old people talk of the well in their previous village which had gone dry and forced the small group to pack their belongings and go in search of a new site for their homes. That move had brought them to this place Sharifa loved. It was the only home she had ever known. The surrounding hills acted as a natural funnel to collect the rainfall from the storms that moved through the desert. Centuries of erosion had created a small natural valley hidden in the mountain where the soil was much richer than the sand of the desert. It was here that the village elders chose to maintain the garden plots for the families of their tribe, while the buildings and livestock were kept in the central area in the floor of the desert so they could not be trapped by their enemies.

From her vantage point on the side of the hill, Sharifa looked across the desert and saw mountains in every direction. The wind blew her long black hair across her face, and she took both of her hands and pulled her hair back over her shoulders. Her eyes followed the path as it ran to the foot of the hill and into the rows of buildings in her small village. She walked the streets with her eyes until she found her family home. It was made of mud brick with a tin roof, and on one end of the building there was a chimney, but no smoke was coming from it. Cooking was reserved for the evening when the fire's heat was needed to help ward off the desert chill.

She could see some of the other children and some of the older men making their way up the trail to the valley where she was going to take her grandfather his lunch. Across the desert floor, she could see the peaks of the mountains. She shuddered as she remembered the tales she had heard of men who went hunting in those mountains and never returned. She was six now, and was only occasionally allowed to stay awake into the evening and listen to the adults' discussion, but she was fascinated by the stories which had been handed down from generation to generation.

Beyond the village, she could see the small herd of horses and camels used for work and transportation. Only last week she had taken her first ride on a horse. Her brother put her on the back of a pretty mare and walked her from the corral onto the main road leading through their village. She held her back straight and sat proudly as the horse walked through the main street, Saad holding a strap tied to the bridle. The other children had stopped their play and watched as she rode the horse past them. That night, she had imagined she was a beautiful queen from a foreign land being led on a black stallion to a new home.

As she sat on the side of the hill, she yearned to be older. She wasn't sure what young women did to contribute to the family as they matured, because she had only her brother's role as a model. Her picture of perfect womanhood was her mother, but her mother had a family to care for. In addition to her brother, who was fourteen, she had a three-year-old sister

152

named Mafta who was her responsibility. Her brother worked alongside her father to provide the cash income that supported the family's needs. She wanted to play a more important and responsible role in family activities, but knew she would have to be older for that to happen. For now, she would have to be content with helping her grandfather in the garden, looking after baby Mafta, and starting school next year in the village.

Her world was almost ideal, except that she was worried for her father. She wasn't sure what the problem was, but she had heard the heated discussions some nights after she was sent to bed. Her uncle Sakhar, her father's brother, was a frequent visitor to their home in the evening. He and other men would often talk late into the evening, and the talk scared her. Most of it she didn't understand, but they talked of people dying and of having to leave their village. The talk was mostly about people they called the Zionists and the Americans. She had heard of America from the other children who were already in school. Her father would become angry and shout that he would never leave his home, regardless of the consequences, and Uncle Sakhar would try to talk her father into taking the women and children to another place so the men could stay and fight without fear for their families. But her father would insist that this was their home, and this is where they would stay. It made her happy to know that she would not have to leave this place she loved so much, but the talk from Uncle Sakhar frightened her.

Once, she almost asked her mother about it, but she didn't because she was afraid that she might be judged harshly for eavesdropping. She felt frustrated that she was old enough to understand most of the words the adults used, but she was often unable to grasp their meaning or the thoughts they were trying to express.

Last night, there had been strangers in the group gathered for the evening's discussion. They had come to the village in trucks just as dusk was settling on the desert. They carried guns and they were dirty, but the villagers had treated them with respect. A large man whom Sharifa thought must be their leader had eaten at their table and then spent the night in Sharifa's home. The meal prepared for the stranger had been the best their family had to offer. At her mother's direction, Sharifa made a special trip back to the garden in the hills to bring home additional fresh food for the meal. The importance of the occasion was noted by the presence of glasses on the table for water. Sharifa could only remember seeing real glasses on the table a few times before, such as her parents' wedding anniversary.

The stranger was a gentle man who was treated with a great amount of respect by the village. He was very complimentary of her mother's dinner and had made a comment to her father about his beautiful daughter. Her father had been proud, but it had embarrassed Sharifa. She had blushed and looked down and couldn't take her eyes from her lap for a long while. When she finally looked up, the handsome stranger was talking excitedly to her father, and she could see the brightness in his eyes and feel his genuine concern for her family.

After dinner, other men from the village arrived at their house, each bringing with him one of the strangers who had arrived on the trucks. Sharifa and her mother left the men in the room at the front of the house and went to the back room to clean the remains of the dinner dishes. She was jealous that her brother was able to stay in the room with the men and with the intriguing stranger.

Later, as she and her mother lay down to sleep, she could still faintly hear the men's conversation. She waited until her mother was breathing deeply, slid out of her small bed and moved to the door connecting the front and rear of the house. She leaned her back against the wall, pulled her knees under her chin, and sat in the position she had many times before while listening to her father and uncle and the other adults. She strained to hear the voice of the gentle stranger who had spent the evening in their home, hoping that he would agree with her father that they should never leave this village.

Suddenly, the room was quiet, and she realized the stranger was going to speak. She had noticed at the dinner table that everyone fell into a respectful silence whenever the man spoke. Hearing his gentle voice, she instantly felt a comfort in his words. He seemed to say exactly what she was feeling as he spoke of their love for their land and of the generations who had struggled to survive and provide for their families from this harsh country. He spoke of the majesty of the mountains and the beauty of the desert in the spring and of the peace which had been theirs for centuries before the return of the Zionists. He spoke of great battles which had taken place so they could live on this land. And then he spoke of great battles yet to come. He said that he would be with them as they fought these battles and that one day, the land would be theirs alone, and their enemies would no longer be a threat to them. His voice was like fine music to Sharifa, and it softly lulled her to sleep.

By the time Sharifa came from the house the next morning, the strangers were already loaded in their trucks and leaving the village. She was disappointed that she would not get to see their visitor again as she ran from the house to watch the trucks make their way down the main road and away from the village. As she went back into the house for breakfast, her mother smiled at her and stooped to put her arms around Sharifa and held her tight. Her mother said that her father had told the stranger of finding Sharifa asleep by the door, obviously from listening to the men's discussions. For a moment, Sharifa had been frightened that she was going to be punished, but then the gentleness of her mother's voice told her that was not the case. Her mother said the stranger had been so touched by Sharifa's beauty and by what her father had said to him about her love of the land and her heritage, that he had left her a gift. Her mother handed her a small pouch which was pulled together at the top by a silk cord.

Opening the pouch, Sharifa removed a small silver locket. The locket opened to her touch, and on one side, there was a small figure. On the other was an engraving in Arabic letters which Sharifa was not old enough to read. She recognized the figure as that of the gentle stranger, and she asked her mother about the writing. Her mother said it was an Arabic saying which meant that the land was their life, that all life was dependent on the land, and the land must be loved as they loved their father and mother.

As she sat on the side of the hill, Sharifa took the small pouch from her pocket and held it in her hands. Her mother had made her leave the locket beside her bed and take only the pouch, but she already knew the appearance of the figure and the words so well that she could visualize them in her mind without having the locket in her hands. Her father had promised to fashion her a necklace so she could wear the locket around her

155

neck, and she had vowed never to remove it. She tried to remember the look in the visitor's eyes as he spoke to them at the dinner table the evening before. She found she couldn't remember the eyes exactly, but she could remember the feeling of complete peace it gave her when she looked into them and listened to his voice. She pictured him giving the locket to her father and swelled with pride as she thought of the words the two men had exchanged.

A rumble in the desert brought her back from her daydreams, and she thought a storm must be approaching. She enjoyed watching the storms in the desert and seeing them come toward her village. Although she could see for many miles from her position on the side of the hill, she could not see any storms in the area. Still the rumbling continued. Across the desert at the foot of the big mountain, she could see large dust clouds building and growing. Suddenly, truck horns started a frenzy of sounds in the village, and she could see people running between the buildings. Then she saw the airplanes. They were coming from the direction of the clouds by the far mountain and were headed directly toward her village. There were many planes, and as they approached her village, they separated and began to dive on the small group of buildings, firing guns as they approached. Sharifa was more frightened than she had ever been, and she buried her head in her lap, and held her hands tightly over her ears and fought the urge to watch and listen. The noise of the attack was so loud and the pressure from the explosions was so great, she thought surely she was going to die. When there was a moment's lull in the tremendous noise, Sharifa looked up and saw her village completely in flames. On the far side, there was a plane passing low over the village, firing machine guns into the smoke. The plane was headed directly for her little spot on the side of the mountain, and as it came closer, she could see the helmet of the pilot turning one way and then the other as he surveyed the area. The plane came so close, Sharifa could see the face of the man behind the glass shield. From the movement of his head, she could tell that the pilot saw her and the plane turned in her direction. For a moment, their faces were locked, and then the plane abruptly turned away from her and headed over the mountain in the direction of her grandfather. Sharifa could hear the explosions of the bombs all around her, and again she covered her ears and buried her head in her lap.

She had no idea how long the attack lasted or when the planes left, but when she awoke and lifted her head, her village was gone. All that was left was rubble and huge black billows of smoke. Eventually, she stood and began the descent to the village. There was no sound except the barking of a dog somewhere among the destroyed homes. She stepped carefully over the debris trying to find her house until she came to the location she knew must be theirs and started to look carefully through the remains of her house. Her father was there, with the family rifle clutched in his hand. Her brother was beside him, buried under the collapsed tin roof of their small porch. Her mother looked as though she was trying to get into the house through the back door. She still held baby Mafta in her arms, but no sounds or movement came from either of them. Sharifa found her bed and retrieved the locket from the crushed drawer of what used to be the small bedside table. She took the small pouch from her pocket, placed the locket inside and secured the silk cord. She moved some of the debris from the remains of her small bed and pulled the torn mattress to a point between her mother and her father. She lay on her side with her knees pulled tightly upward to her chest. In both hands, she held the locket tightly.

"There is only one survivor, sir, a small girl."

"Bring her to me, Ahmad." The tall man spoke with authority as he directed the soldiers around him.

The small convoy of trucks had found their way back to the village the day after the attack. They had lain in hiding for the entire day when the rumblings had first been heard since these were men who were experienced enough to know the difference between thunder and bombs. The trucks, camouflaged and hidden well, had stayed put throughout the day and night. After a full day of waiting, they began the move back through the destroyed villages. The men had searched the entire group of buildings in this village looking for signs of life, but found nothing except Sharifa on her mattress, clutching the small pouch. When they brought her to the leader, he could tell that she was not conscious.

"She will not wake, Al Hamie," the soldier, who was named Ahmad, said. The soldier was an extraordinarily large man, and held the small girl tenderly in the crook of his arm. His free hand was held tenderly beside her face to protect it from the harsh desert sun. He handed the tiny body over to the tall stranger gently.

"Other than some minor scratches, she does not appear to be wounded."

The man took the girl from the soldier and looked into her face. He recognized Sharifa as the daughter of his host during his visit to the village. He saw her hands clutched the small pouch he had presented to her father as a gift for his daughter. He spoke to her softly of her parents and his love for them. He looked away at the smoke from the village, and then looked to the heavens and prayed aloud as the tears made dirty streaks in the dust on his face. When he looked down at her again, her eyes had opened, and she was looking at him. He kept his voice gentle as he directed the soldiers in the burial of the dead and the search of the village for weapons and valuables which he would leave in one of the surviving villages. He carried Sharifa with him as he returned to his vehicle for the journey ahead. As the column of trucks pulled away from the village, Sharifa did not raise her head to see. She stayed on the lap of the visitor with her face resting against his uniform and closed her eyes again, the locket still clutched in her hands.

Sharifa awoke from a deep sleep and was immediately frightened. Apart from being in a comfortable bed with many pillows and covers, she had no idea where she was, and the visions of the bombing were still in her head. She felt the small pouch in her hand and clutched it tightly to her chest. She rubbed her eyes with her other hand, and then noticed the mark on her palm. It was blue and looked like a drawing of a star with six points, and the pain she felt was immediate as she recognized the star. She tried to rub it away, but it wouldn't come off by her touch, even when she pressed hard. She looked down at herself to see that she was wearing a sleeping

158

gown which was made of fine material, long and white and held around her neck with a silk cord similar to the one which held her locket pouch closed.

Slowly, she sat upright in the bed and looked around the room, which was more glorious than anything she had ever seen before. The walls were smooth and such a bright white they nearly gave out their own light, and the doors were trimmed in gold, as was the single window in the room. Beautiful curtains hung about the window from the high ceiling to the floor, pulled back at the center with a golden sash. The floor of the room was something Sharifa had never seen before, ceramic tile, and was so immaculately clean that it shined. Near one corner was a small table and a chair. The chair was covered in what appeared to be the same material as her locket pouch, but it was a deep purple instead of the blue of her pouch. On the wall across from her bed, there was a large wooden wardrobe. The doors were carved with very complicated patterns, and Sharifa studied the patterns for a long while trying to make out what they were. It was apparently some very dangerous looking animal, but she could not tell what the carved scene depicted. In the corner opposite the small table was a large tub which sat on legs made from brass.

Sharifa cautiously moved to the side of the bed and slipped over the edge until she could feel the toes of one foot touch the tile of the floor. She stayed still for a moment. Her mind was a jumble of thoughts, mostly fear of what lay ahead, and she held her breath and stayed in the same position for as long as she could. She then slipped herself completely over the edge of the bed until she was standing on the cool tile floor. She moved cautiously to the window and then heard voices, which she soon realized were coming from the direction of the door. On her tiptoes, she ran over to the door and put her ear to the seam around its edge to listen. As she did, she felt the door move just a fraction. In panic, she ran and leaped on the bed and pulled the covers over her head just as she heard the door opening. The language was definitely Arabic, but with an accent different from that she was used to in her home. The manner of speech was familiar to her, though, since it was the same as the strangers who had visited her home yesterday.

Or was it really yesterday? She realized she had no idea of how many days had passed since she was on the mountain going to visit her grandfather. She remembered a dream of being in the arms of the tall stranger, and he was comforting her with his gentle voice as he carried her away from the ruins of her village and the family that had been taken from her. It must have been a dream, but it seemed so real. She didn't remember anything from the time that she last covered her head and ears so that she couldn't see the terrible planes. She remembered how clearly she saw the face of the pilot in the plane that came so close to her, and the blue star on the tail of the plane which was the same as the blue star she now had on her hand.

Sharifa heard the voices of the women in the room with her. They were talking about her, and from the conversation, Sharifa judged them to be friendly. They laughed a lot and called her by name and talked about how pretty she was and wondered when she might wake up. Slowly, she pulled the covers down from her head and peered out at the room.

"Well, see, she is awake," said the woman nearest her. "Hello, Sharifa dear, I am Sawsan and this is Nofa. She and I have been taking care of you. I hope you are comfortable."

"Yes," Sharifa said, still not too anxious to come out from under the covers.

"Well, now," Nofa said, "it's time to get up and take a bath and have something to eat. He wants to see you as soon as you are ready, and he is very busy."

"I'm hungry." Sharifa could hardly believe she had said it even as she heard her own voice. It was the first time she realized that she was, indeed, very hungry.

"Of course you are, dear," Sawsan said. "It's been a long time since you ate."

The last meal Sharifa remembered was breakfast the day the strangers had left their village. Thinking about that meal reminded her of her mother's cooking in the kitchen, and that reminded her of the last grotesque scene she had seen . She turned her face into the pillows and began to cry softly. Sawsan came to her immediately and sat on the bed, pulling Sharifa to her. Sharifa let the covers fall from her hands and leaned into Sawsan, who was now holding her in both arms.

160

"I know how it must hurt, sweet little flower of the desert. He told me what happened, and there is no tragedy which can hurt a little girl more. We can only hope that soon he will be able to stop the fighting, and all of this will be over. We all pray to Allah every day that he will run the Zionists and the Americans from all of these lands so that we can all return to our homes."

Sharifa looked into Sawsan's eyes, and she saw a kindness and understanding that reminded her of her mother. She pulled herself a little closer into Sawsan's arms.

"Sawsan," Nofa said, sitting on the other side of the bed, "we have to get this little flower fed, bathed, and dressed because Al Hamie wishes to see her before his late evening meetings begin. It is clear already that he has taken quite an interest in you, Sharifa. He called you the most beautiful flower of the desert."

Sharifa knew she should blush and be embarrassed by this compliment, but she didn't know who had made it.

"Who is this person?" she asked.

"Why, I thought you knew. It was he who brought you here. He said he had spent the night in your home the night before the planes came to your village, and the locket you have in your hand is his personal gift to those who are special to him. There are no other lockets like that one except for the ones he has presented to those he favors."

Sharifa remembered the tall stranger with the gentle voice and the eyes so dark and deep they looked like you could walk right into them.

"I remember him," she said. "He was very kind to my family."

"Al Hamie is a very kind man," Sawsan said. "Not just to you and me, but to all Arabs."

Sawsan busied herself around the room while Nofa fixed a plate of food and took it to the small table.

"Come and eat, little desert flower," Nofa said.

Sharifa jumped from the bed and went to the table and sat down to eat. She had never seen so many types of food before. Some she recognized, but most she didn't, and she wanted to ask what each was, but she was embarrassed and remained silent. The food was delicious, and as she ate the first bites slowly, the food going to her stomach made her realize just how hungry she was, and she began to eat faster. Nofa stood beside her and smiled as she ate.

Sawsan went to the door, opened it and said something to someone outside. Several men came in carrying large jugs of water which they poured into the tub. The water was hot, and Sharifa could see the steam coming from the tub. Several more jugs of water came, and Sawsan tested the water to make sure it was comfortable.

"I think that will be just right," she said as she opened the doors to the wardrobe. From an inside drawer, she took a small bottle and poured some liquid into the tub. Sharifa could immediately smell the scent of the perfume as its aroma filled the room. Returning the bottle to the drawer, Sawsan took several towels from a shelf above the drawer and placed them on a small stand at the end of the tub.

Sharifa was taken with a sudden feeling of embarrassment when it occurred to her that the two women were going to give her a bath. Indeed, she was anxious to feel the heat and the scent of the perfumed hot water around her, but she had never been undressed in front of anyone but her mother. Modesty by the women was a strict rule in their house. She looked nervously from the tub to Sawsan to Nofa and back to the tub. For just a moment she stopped eating and looked at her plate as the thought of her mother bathing her filled her again with sadness.

"Oh, she's growing sad again," Sawsan said as she looked at Sharifa. Both women knelt beside her to put their arms around her.

"We understand how you must feel, little one," Nofa said. "We were both specially chosen to look after you because we have lost our loved ones also. My little Neefa would be one year older than you if she had not been killed by the war. Sawsan lost her husband and two sons. Now neither of us has any family but you. I know that our loss can't take away your hurt, but at least you can know that we understand how you feel and that we love you."

Tears were on Sharifa's cheeks, and Nofa took the sleeve of her dress and wiped them away. Then she leaned over and kissed Sharifa where the tears had been.

162

Sawsan reached down to the plate and picked up a small piece of meat. Sharifa had already tried the meat and knew it was delicious. Sawsan placed the morsel into Sharifa's mouth and then reached for another. The two women continued to feed the small girl until the plate was empty.

"Now, for the bath," Sawsan exclaimed. Sharifa was reminded of her embarrassment as Sawsan and Nofa rose from around her, and she lowered her head and again looked at her plate.

"No reason to be shy, little flower," Sawsan said. "We've bathed many little children before you came along. Why, my own little Neefa and I used to bathe together in the river every day."

"Besides," Nofa said, "who do you think took your desert clothes from you and dressed you in these?"

The two women led her to the tub as Nofa stood behind her and untied the silk sash around her neck, letting the gown fall to the floor. They held her hand as Sharifa stepped into the tub and sank into the hot water. She soon forgot her embarrassment as Sawsan and Nofa fussed over bathing her. They washed her hair and then dried her with large soft towels. Sawsan went to the wardrobe, took out a lacy white dress, and brought it to Sharifa while Nofa brushed her long hair dry.

"I think this will fit just fine," she said, pulling the dress over Sharifa's head.

"And I think the white will be just perfect against your dark skin," Nofa said. Sandals were added, and a ribbon in her hair which matched the lace trim of the silk dress. Nofa took the pouch and locket from her hand and placed it in a pocket of the dress.

Sharifa looked at her reflection in the mirror on the back of the door to the wardrobe and blushed. She had never thought of herself as pretty, but with this beautiful white dress and the white lace ribbon in her black, shiny hair, she looked like the princess she had dreamed about so many times. She allowed herself a small smile in the mirror, and then she blushed again.

"You are a beautiful flower indeed," she said. "Time to go now."

Nofa reached and grasped Sharifa's hand.

"We don't want to keep him waiting," Sawsan said as she moved to the other side, and the three of them went hand in hand.

Outside the room where Sharifa had slept, they entered a maze of hallways with many people going in every direction. Most of the men had on uniforms and many were carrying weapons. It was unusual for Sharifa to see so many women without their faces covered; she had also never seen so many uniforms. Sawsan and Nofa kept her between them as they navigated purposefully left and right through the hallways of the building. It was the first time Sharifa had seen a building so large. Sharifa remembered the conversations of her father and her uncle about the many soldiers who could help them fight the battles, but she never pictured that women could help, too. In her mind, she began to try to think of herself as one of these women who could help the soldiers fight to save her homeland.

The three women were approaching a door being guarded by four soldiers.

"This is Sharifa," Sawsan said to the guards as they approached the door. "He wanted to see her before the late meetings began."

The soldier who was the largest and appeared to be in charge looked at Sharifa and smiled.

"Hello, little one. I am Ahmad. You are indeed as beautiful as I have heard," he said. "He has asked about you several times, and I have told him that I checked and you were being well taken care of, but he is very anxious to see you."

Sharifa blushed at all of this attention and held her hands together in front of her dress and looked at the floor. The guard opened the door and led the two women and the girl into a small room. There, four more soldiers stood guarding a pair of large wooden doors which had elaborate carvings similar to the doors on the wardrobe in her room. In the bigger scene on this door, she could see a man with a sword fighting a fire-breathing monster.

Ahmad knocked on the door and opened it without waiting for an answer. He went inside and closed the door behind him, leaving Sharifa standing between the remaining guards. Sharifa looked at Sawsan and Nofa, but they were silent and not looking at her.

After just a moment, the door opened and Ahmad held his hand toward Sharifa.

"Come, little one, he will see you now." Sharifa looked apprehensively toward Sawsan and Nofa, but Sawsan smiled and nodded her head and gave her a little push from behind. Sharifa reached for the hand of the soldier as he led her into the room. She looked behind her expecting to see Sawsan and Nofa following, but they were waiting outside, and Sharifa saw the smiles on their faces as one of the outside guards closed the door.

When she turned to face the front again, she gasped involuntarily and stopped to gape at the wonder she saw. The room was so large that she couldn't take it all in. It was filled with furniture and hangings on the walls the likes of which Sharifa had never seen even in pictures. Tapestries, paintings and carvings of every type decorated every available spot in the room. Huge carved or ceramic elephants stood beside every place for sitting. On two sides of the room, beautiful drapes covered large windows that reached from the floor to the ceiling. In one corner of the room, a seating area was furnished with several low sofas and strange-looking round pillowed chairs. In the center was a low glass table supported by an ornately carved animal she recognized as being like the one she had seen on the doors. She felt a slight tug on her hand and realized her amazement had frozen her for some time. She looked up, and the soldier who was smiling down at her held his free hand forward, gesturing her toward the far end of the room. She looked in the direction he was indicating, and behind a grand dark desk she saw the tall stranger who had visited her family's home. He rose from his chair and came around the desk directly toward her, his smile as gentle as she remembered, and as he approached her, she felt again the assurance which came to her when she looked into his eyes.

"Well, my desert flower has finally arrived," he said as he reached for her with both hands. She released the hand of the soldier and went to him. His large hands grasped her tiny waist, and he picked her up easily and held her.

"You are even more beautiful than I remembered," he said. "Are they taking good care of you?"

Sharifa could not speak, but managed to nod her head. She suddenly hated her shyness and wanted to say something.

"Sawsan and Nofa gave me a bath," she said.

"Yes, and I can still smell the perfume. You smell just like the desert flower that you are. I must remember to compliment them on their selection of your clothes. I know they didn't have much time." He looked to the soldier who had brought Sharifa into the room and gestured with his head, and Ahmad immediately left the room, closing the door behind him.

"I wanted to see you before I began some meetings this evening," he said. "Tomorrow, I must go away, and I may not see you again for a long time."

"Are you going back to my village?" she asked. She somehow had a vision that this grand man could do the impossible and make her family return.

"No, but to other villages just like yours." He moved to one of the strange chairs and sat down with her on his lap. "Your village is gone, Sharifa, and nothing I nor anybody can do will bring it back. I am very sorry for the sadness you feel, and I feel your sadness, too. The only happiness is that you were not also destroyed by the enemy, and that I found you, and you are here and safe."

"Who is the enemy?" she asked.

He took her hand in his, turned the palm upward and spread her fingers so that she could see the blue star. Her hand was tiny next to his.

"That is the enemy," he said.

"But who are they?" she asked.

"Have you ever seen that star before?"

Silent tears were on her cheeks as she nodded her head, unable to speak.

"Where?" he asked.

She tried to tell him about the plane which had come so close to her, but the words wouldn't come. She tried to hold back the tears, but couldn't, and she buried her head in her hands, the movement in her shoulders the only clue to her quiet suffering. He stroked the back of her head and waited until the spasms slowed.

After some minutes, she began to breathe normally, and she raised her head. With a soft linen cloth he gently wiped the tears from her eyes and cheeks.

"Was that star on the airplanes which came to your village?"

She nodded, looking directly into his eyes. She could see the kindness there, and feel the caring he had for her.

166

"That star belongs to the enemy," he said. "They are people who lived in our land many years ago and worshipped the God of Abraham. They left, but now they want to return, and they want us to leave. I put that star on your hand, and it will stay there always to remind you of those who would drive us and our people from our homes."

"But it is our home," she said, and the tears began again. This time she was determined not to lose control, and she continued to look directly at him, letting the tears stream down her cheeks.

"Do not be ashamed of the tears, my little desert flower. This enemy has brought tears to many of our people. It is our sacred mission to force them to leave our homeland and never return."

Sharifa didn't know what to say. She was confused by all that had happened and what she was being told. Who were these people who would drive someone from their home? Why couldn't everybody live together? There was no one else anywhere near their village. Why did they want her family to leave? Nothing made any sense to her.

He traced the star in her hand with his finger.

"You must always remember," he said, "this star is the enemy. It will be with you always, just as the memory of your family will be with you always. One day, you will have the opportunity to do something about the killing of your family. But you must wait until it is time. Every time you look at your hand and see that star, remember the enemy who killed your family and the obligation you have. The Zionists and the Americans are the enemy, little desert flower, and as Allah is our God, I swear to you that one day we will drive all of them from our lands. You and I. You and I and all of our people who have suffered at the hands of these enemies. Do you want to do that?"

She looked into his eyes, but then lowered her head. She understood his words, but knew, even at her age, that she was just a little girl. She couldn't drive anybody from her home. What could she do against the airplanes which bombed her village?

"What's the matter?" he asked as he gently put his finger under her chin and raised her head. "You are an Arab. You don't have to lower your head to me or anyone else. Never again."

"But I am too little," she said.

"Oh, is that it?" he asked with a smile. "Yes, you are small and yes, you are a little girl. But one day, you'll be big and be able to join the battle to make our homeland free of these enemies. Don't you worry, because you will get your chance."

She knew that what he said was true, but in her heart, she wanted to be able to help now, and knowing she couldn't made her feel useless. She started to lower her head again, but remembered what he said and raised her head and looked into his eyes. When her eyes met his, she knew then that he was right. One day she would return to her village in victory. The thought of that victory made her feel better, and she smiled.

"That's my little desert flower. What you must do now is listen to Sawsan and Nofa and do everything they say. They are going to help you and make arrangements for your education and watch over you as you grow to be a woman. I may not see you often, but you must know that I will always be thinking of you. I have something to help you remember me. Keep it with you always and every time you look at it, know that I am with you." He reached into his pocket and withdrew a silver chain. He took the pouch from her pocket, removed the locket, and placed it on the chain. As he put the chain around her neck, she bent her head forward so that he could latch it, and then straightened to look into his face again. He placed the chain and locket under her dress and took her hand and pressed it to her chest so that she could feel the locket under the delicate material.

"You see, even though no one else can see the locket, it is there for you to feel and touch and know that I am thinking of you. Every time you think of me, touch this; every time you think of your family, touch the star on your hand."

She felt her fingers on the locket, and the touch brought her comfort. She placed the tips of her fingers on the star in her hand and looked into his face.

"Your education is most important now, since one day, our people will need educated men and women to help in our battle. You must believe that everything you learn is learned to help in the fight against the enemy. Allah will always be by your side, and I will always be in your heart." As he spoke, he reached down and took her hand and opened it to the star on her palm and brought it to his lips and kissed it. He then leaned forward and kissed her forehead.

"Now," he said, placing her on the floor and rising from the chair. "It is time for you to go with Sawsan and Nofa, and for me to get to work. There are many people waiting for me, and we don't want to disappoint them." He smiled down at her, and she smiled back at him. He started to walk her to the door. As he got to the door and reached for the handle, she put her arms out to him. He bent to her, and she put her arms around his neck and squeezed as hard as she could.

"I will do well at my learning," she said. "I will make you proud of me."

"It's not only me that will be proud, but Allah will be proud and your family will be proud also. I know you will do well, and don't forget, if ever you need anything, you must let me know. Tell Sawsan or Nofa or even Ahmad. It may seem that I am not around too often because I am very busy, but I can and will always come when you need me."

"I know," she said. She backed up and raised her face to his and looked into his eyes again

"I love you, little desert flower," he said, and she went out the door.

MARCH
1990

weapons systems--pentagon adv20 3-90
PATRIOT missile explodes in failed test launch
USWNS Military News
adv mar 20 1990 or thereafter

By GEORGE GROWSON

WASHINGTON—The Army announced today that a test of the
PATRIOT missile at White Sands Missile Range ended in
failure when the missile exploded several seconds into the
flight, but that the cause of the failure was not
immediately known. This test was the eighth in a series of
tests to demonstrate the capability of the modified PATRIOT
system to engage short range ballistic missiles, the first
such capability in a fielded Army system.

A spokesperson for the Army stated that all conditions
for the test were normal and that investigations to
determine the cause of the failure were underway. The test
program has been placed on hold until the investigation
into the incident is complete, but the schedule for the
fielding of the upgraded system is not expected to be
delayed.

EIGHT

"Ladies and gentlemen, would you please buckle your seatbelts for the approach and landing in El Paso." Jeff put away his papers and his briefcase in the overhead compartment. He looked out the window at the area around El Paso. The area was ugly with sand dunes and scrub brush. He looked down, trying to recognize the places on the Rio Grande where he had gone dove and quail hunting when he had returned to Fort Bliss from Vietnam. As the plane made its final approach, he could see signs of the wildlife which thrived in the harsh environment of the rocks and sand.

As the plane made a slight bank over Hueco Tanks and lined up for runway 31 at El Paso International, the sprawling city came into view. It was different from towns back east which started gradually and became more dense as you got closer to town. Around El Paso and other desert towns, there was desert and then, abruptly, there was city. Fort Bliss became visible, with its large buildings housing the U.S. Army Air Defense Artillery School which trained officers and enlisted personnel to operate and maintain the Army's Air Defense systems. Jeff could see the familiar training areas with the sprawling fields of asphalt where U.S. and foreign countries housed their missile and gun systems.

The plane touched down with a bump and screech, and then slowed and turned to the terminal, a modern complex in a style which suited the southwest flavor of the town, the cultural center of the region's Tex-Mex food and country music.

"Ladies and gentlemen, welcome to El Paso International Airport, serving the twin cities of El Paso, Texas, and Juarez, Mexico. The local time is 6:17 PM."

An Army staff car and driver were waiting for Jeff in front of the airport. The driver put his carry-on bag in the trunk and drove directly to the Chaparral House, the visiting VIP quarters of Fort Bliss.

"Is there anything I need to do for you this evening, General?" the soldier asked as he put Jeff's bag down.

"Yes, if you could wait a few minutes, I need you to drop me at Carlos and Mickey's Restaurant. Do you know where that is?"

"Yes, sir. Will you be needing a ride back here later?"

"No, but thanks, anyway. I'm having a dinner meeting with someone, and he'll give me a lift when we're done. What are the arrangements for the morning?"

"I'm to pick you up at oh six forty-five and take you to the helicopter pad here on the post. A chopper will fly you directly to the launch site, and someone will meet you there. I'll pick you up at the pad when you return and take you to the airport. Anything else?"

"Thanks, no," Jeff said. "After I have dinner, I plan to crash and get a good night's sleep."

Jeff put his overnight bag in the bedroom and went back to the waiting Army staff car. When the driver dropped him at the entrance of the restaurant, Jeff found Johnny Madkin at a table in the bar, nursing a Lone Star beer.

"Welcome to the sunny southwest," Johnny said as he stood. He sat as Jeff took a seat and ordered a Coors Light.

"Thanks for coming down," Jeff said. Johnny lived in Las Cruces, New Mexico, a small town some 45 miles up the Rio Grande River and a quicker drive into the test ranges.

"No problem. Any chance to get out on the town and hear some of El Paso's finest is an opportunity and not a chore."

"I'm afraid I'm not going to be much help in the country music department tonight," Jeff said. "After we're done, I'm in the bag. I've had a long day, it's nearly eight o'clock at home, and six forty-five is early in the morning."

"Yeah. And these old bones will be able to count every one of these beers. I've got a room next door, and if it's OK with you, I'll fly out with you in the morning."

"Glad to have you. We'll drop by and pick you up."

"Band comes on here in a bit," Johnny said. "So you're gonna get country whether you want it or not. Have you eaten?"

"No, and I will take you up on that. Can we eat here in the bar?"

"You bet." Johnny signaled for the waitress and they ordered another round of beers and the house specials—chili rellenos, refried beans and guacamole salad.

"You ready to talk a little business?" Johnny asked.

"You bet. Shoot."

"The flight tomorrow is scheduled for ten in the morning. We've set up an intercept that'll really stretch PATRIOT's capabilities, since it's right on the edge of the performance envelope. Raytheon didn't want to go that risky this early in the program, but Steve Smith met with them last week, and it was decided to keep the flight as planned."

"Are there any special conditions?"

"The usual and a few extra. The flight time window is a little tighter than normal because of the location and low altitude of the intercept. They had to exercise the range extension and close the White Sands National Monument, and they don't like to keep it closed for very long. We have some extra safety radars uprange to track the PATRIOT and the Lance missile that will be used as the target vehicle, just to make sure that they don't get off course."

"What about the firing window?"

"Tight as a widow's purse strings. Once the target is under way, the launch window for PATRIOT is just a matter of seconds. If we fire too early, the intercept will be out of effective range, and if we wait too late, the Lance will hit the ground before our missile gets there. Steve's people and Raytheon have made enough computer runs of the software logic to cover every contingency in the world, and we don't expect any problem, as long as the target flight is on the right path."

"Well, that's a problem. PATRIOT will have to work in a real attack,

177

anyway, so we'd better be ready to do it in a test."

"That was Steve's official government position to Raytheon, and I guess the argument held."

"Is there a back-up target missile?" Jeff asked.

"Two," Johnny said. "But it's going to be tight if we aren't successful on the first shot because of our limited slot of range time. I'm going to check with the range control people again first thing in the morning to see if they can't cut us some slack, but I don't hold much hope."

"How 'bout my baby?"

"The PATRIOT system is running perfectly. We haven't had any down time in over a week."

"And the crew?"

"The crew has been on the system for over a month now, and they're really good. I don't know of any problems that could cause anything to go wrong."

The food came and they ordered another round of beer as they started to eat. A band was setting up in the corner. After some tuning up and individual picking, the group started with a particularly loud version of Hank Williams, Jr.

"I told you you'd get a fix," Johnny said, having to raise his voice noticeably to be heard over the band.

"Yeah, but I'm not sure I'd call that country music."

□□□□□

The helicopter banked as it turned away from Highway 54 toward the Army test ranges at McGregor and Oro Grande and over the back gate of White Sands to Launch Complex 38. Jeff was looking forward over the pilot's shoulder when the launch site came into view. Without the camouflage nets, the PATRIOT was easy to find by the big face of the radar silhouetted against the morning sunrise. From the air, the stabilizing outriggers made it resemble a giant beetle poised in the middle of a huge sandy expanse. A short distance away, the launcher was already loaded with two PATRIOT missiles in their box-like canister, erected by the launcher to their firing elevation and pointed downrange. As they approached the landing pad, Jeff could see the thick mounds of dirt forming the berms that protected all of the equipment in the area.

The helicopter touched down, and Jeff waited for the dust to settle a little before he jumped down and walked toward the complex, which housed the equipment, test facilities, and government and contractor personnel. Johnny Madkin jumped down right behind him.

"We're right on time," Johnny said. "The pre-flight briefing is about to start. We should be about two hours from flight time."

They went inside the building and everyone stood as he entered the briefing room.

"Take your seats, folks," Jeff said.

There was a routine briefing during which everything that was expected on the flight was covered in some detail. The main point was that because the test was the actual firing of a "hostile" missile at the PATRIOT, safety was an even higher priority than normal. If anything varied from normal or the track data from the range safety radars indicated either missile was outside of its safe zone, the missiles would both immediately be destroyed in flight. Everything was on schedule.

"Cut 'em down and ask questions later," was the way Johnny had put it.

After the briefing, a special ceremony was held outside on the pavement around the PATRIOT radar. Jeff presented awards to several key soldiers, contractors and government civilians for their work on the system over the winter.

The Army photographers finished their work for the awards ceremony, and the crowd went back to their individual work stations to get ready for the test. Jeff walked over to the van that housed the Engagement Control Station and went inside. The crew was in place, going through the checks to make sure the system was ready. Jeff recognized one or two of them, but not the one he wanted.

"Is Sergeant Johnson still on this crew?" he asked one of the crewmen.

"No, sir, he transferred a few months ago to one of the other units."

"Do you know which one?" Jeff asked.

"No, sir, but they can tell you in the personnel section," the young soldier said.

So much for that plan.

Jeff moved back to the office complex and found Johnny.

"Did you ever talk to the sergeant who was at the console the last time I was here?" he asked Johnny.

"No," he answered. "He transferred from that unit about a week after the flight. I've been near the console on every flight since then, and I haven't seen any entries made during that time. You said it wasn't that important, so I let it drop. Do you want me to try to find out where he was transferred?"

"No," Jeff said. "You're right. It wasn't important. I've just about convinced myself it was a dream, anyway. Maybe I've been spending too much time in Washington lately. It does strange things to your mind."

"I heard that," Johnny said smiling. "Every time I have to go there, my wife tells me I don't make sense for a week."

❑❑❑❑❑

At range safety radar site number seventeen, Sergeant Johnson did the final checks on the Westinghouse FPS-16 radar which would be used as one of the range safety radars for the PATRIOT flight test. He went inside the cement block building that housed the data processing, power, control and communication equipment for the target tracker.

"Everything OK outside?" the chief of the station asked.

"Looks good," Johnson said. "I've got some more checks to make here on the inside, and then we'll be ready. Why don't you make us a fresh pot of coffee, and I'll finish up here."

"Sounds good to me. Four o'clock was early this morning, and I believe it's going to be a two-pot day."

When his boss left the room, Johnson called up the computer software routine which allowed the operator to input the conditions for the radar. He scrolled down through the list of data and stopped about half the distance from the bottom. The entry was for radar elevation above sea level and was set correctly at 3,025 feet. He then closed the routine and went about his other checks.

"Here's a fresh cup," the Section Chief said as he came back into the room. "All done with the checks?"

"All set," Johnson said as he took the hot cup. "Everything should go just as planned. This should make some people very happy."

"Great. Now all we have to do is sit and wait."

"Yep, just wait and watch." Johnson said. He turned back to the radar console, and the other man could not see the small smile on his face.

❑❑❑❑❑

Jeff had taken his familiar spot behind the console operator in the PATRIOT Engagement Control Station. The operators were performing the ritual of taking the system through all the normal steps leading to an engagement. Jeff eased himself toward the door, slipped out and onto the small metal platform attached to the back of the van and waited. He looked toward the desert in the direction of the launcher, hidden from view by the dirt berm.

He actually saw the missile before he heard the launch, and when the noise and buffeting pressure of the rocket hit him like a clap of close thunder, he braced himself against the metal rail and watched as the missile sped downrange. Suddenly, something went very wrong. Seeing the missile come apart before he heard the noise was like watching a silent movie. There was a puff of smoke in the front of the missile and the nose cone seemed to expand as the missile came apart. Burning pieces flew in every direction, and then there was a large fireball from the rear of the missile body. The burning pieces of the motor spewed from the white hot mass and formed elaborate arcs of smoke trails, looking very much like a July 4th fireworks display.

Then he heard the explosion. It was a loud double blast as first the warhead exploded and then the rocket motor blew when the motor casing split. The additional pressure from the explosion physically pushed him back a little on the platform, and he wondered for an instant if he was in danger, but decided he wasn't. He watched, mesmerized by the sight.

181

Thoughts were already racing through his mind. What could possibly have happened this early in the flight? How would he plan the damage control? What would his supporters say or do? He wasn't concentrating on what went wrong, only what he would do now. He would have to get the full story together quickly before speculation and rumor destroyed the program.

Johnny Madkin came running from the launch control building.

"Jesus, did you see it?" he asked, out of breath.

"Yeah," Jeff said, looking at the smoke trails and the still falling debris.

"What happened?" Johnny asked.

"No idea," Jeff said. "It just blew. Looked like it came from the warhead. I thought you might know."

"No. All we saw on the indicators was that the flight just stopped."

"What about the Lance?"

"They blew the Lance from Range Control as soon as they heard what happened here."

Jeff still stood without moving on the small platform. He stared out into the desert as though he expected the answer to come from there.

"It's the first time she ever let me down," he said, disappointment showing in his voice. "I feel like I want to shout at her and let her know what she's done."

"I know how you feel," Johnny said.

"Damn," Jeff said as he looked at the smoke cloud one last time and turned to step down off the platform.

❑❑❑❑❑

Inside the office building, there was chaos. Most people were looking at data records dealing with their special part of the system, trying to find any indication of what went wrong. Others were bringing new computer printouts into the room or shouting instructions or numbers across the room. Jeff made his way to the office of Lester Grounds, the Raytheon Test Director, who was on the phone as Jeff came in the door.

"Hell no, I don't know what happened," Lester was saying. "It just blew."

He put his hand over the mouthpiece and said to Jeff, "Boston. Three vice presidents have already wet their pants and the Program Manager wants my head detached from my body and sent to Congress as a peace offering."

Jeff smiled an unhappy grimace and went to a chair against the wall.

"Look, we're trying to find out," Lester said, speaking back to the phone. "And I'm sure we'll know something in an hour or so. It can't be that difficult."

He put the phone down and sat down hard in his desk chair.

"Tough day at the office, Lester?" Jeff asked.

Lester responded with a very tired look.

"I'm not being flip. Just wanted to let you know I'm an ally."

Lester looked out the window.

"Damn," he finally said.

"I already said that."

"Damn. I haven't been able to find out what happened because the phone was ringing as soon as I got to the office."

"Go ahead and do what you have to," Jeff said. "I'll catch the phone. I don't think anybody will give me much trouble."

"Thanks, Jeff," he said as he started for the door. "I'll get to you as soon as we have anything."

Jeff reached for the phone to call Steve in Huntsville.

"The news is not good," he said when Steve was on the line.

"I already heard," Steve said. "Any ideas?"

"No. Premature destruct on the missile. It happened only a few seconds into the flight. The motor was still burning. As of now, we don't have the slightest clue what happened."

He could sense the pain at the other end of the line.

"What about the backup missile?" Steve asked.

"No sense firing again until we know what happened on this one. I think we are probably past the launch window, anyway. By now, the tourists are back at the monument. We'll have to wait for another day."

"Damn," said Steve.

"That seems to be the consensus of the day," Jeff said. "I'll be in touch."

The phone was ringing before he got back to his seat. He moved around the desk and sat in Lester's chair as he picked up the phone.

"Test Director's Office," he answered.

"I am calling from Senator Hastings' office looking for General Weyland." It was Suzy.

"Speaking," he said. He instantly felt better just hearing her voice.

"I heard there was a problem. The Senator asked me to check."

"Jesus, it's only been thirty minutes. It really doesn't take much time for bad news to travel, does it? How did you hear?"

"The Senator knew when he called me, but I don't know where he heard it."

"OK," Jeff said. "Yeah, you might say we had a problem. Don't know yet whether it had to do with the basic system or the modifications we put in or something altogether separate. In fact, we don't know diddly."

"Well, look at the bright side," she said.

"Which is?"

"There have been seven unqualified successes. Whatever went wrong here can probably be explained. You're too far into tests now for it to be anything seriously wrong with the system. I think you'll find your support here strong enough to weather this."

"You're probably right," he said.

"You know I'm right," she said. "Even so, as soon as you find out what happened, please let the Senator know. He says it's important."

"There goes my plan to keep it under wraps until I have a good story."

"Can you do it?"

"OK," he said.

"In the meantime, practice what you preach and keep thinking positive thoughts."

"I suppose you have an example or two of those, also."

"How about Friday night?"

"Yeah, I'd say that definitely qualifies as a positive thought."

"And then there was Saturday morning."

"Double ditto for Saturday morning." He was feeling better already and it must have shown.

"See? Now you'd better go," she said.

"I'll call you tonight, if there is a tonight."

"OK. Good luck, and dwell on those positive thoughts."

The second line was ringing before he got the phone down. Now he knew what the Test Director had meant as he pushed the other button.

It was Johnny. "Come over to the Data Reduction room. I think we've got something."

"On my way," he said.

□□□□□

The range safety Section Chief was on the phone to range control. Sergeant Johnson moved his chair so that the other man could not see his activity and opened up the software program that controlled the data set for the radar. He quickly scanned down the list of parameters and found the entry he had identified before the flight. He moved his fingers discretely on the keyboard until the elevation number had been changed to what he wanted. Satisfied with the entry he had made of the incorrect setting, he sat back in the chair.

"Hey Chief," Johnson called over his shoulder. "I think you better come look at this. I think someone may have made a big mistake."

"Whadaya mean?"

"The elevation of the radar is supposed to be 3,025 feet, but it's entered as 2,035 feet. Somebody got the 2 and the 3 backwards, and it's off by over a thousand feet."

"Damn."

□□□□□

The Data Reduction room was filled with tables stacked with computer printouts and data charts. Johnny was at a small group around one of the tables and motioned for Jeff to come over.

"This is Sammy Herborn and Bobby Rose with Raytheon," he said. "They're the lead engineers of the technical team from Boston."

The young engineers were seated in front of a large printout opened almost to the end.

"General," Sammy said, "this is a printout of all of the data communications with the missile, both messages sent to the missile and those sent back. It includes all of the detailed telemetry data as well as the operational commands and communications."

He flipped back a few pages. Jeff looked at the numbers and was staggered at how much data was flowing between the ground and the missile. The flight had only lasted seconds, but the printout was at least 6 inches thick.

"Right here at three point six two seconds, there was a command sent from the ground to destroy the missile. We're trying to check now to see what could have caused it. But it's for sure the missile was cut down by a ground command and not something wrong on the missile. That's all we know right now."

"What could cause that to happen?" Jeff asked.

"Unfortunately, a number of things," Bobby said. "Even more unfortunately, we don't have a separate list of things to check, and some of the data may not be in these files. If it was a normal system function, we could find it pretty easy. But since it wasn't, we might be here a while."

"What types of things wouldn't be on the printouts?" Johnny Madkin asked.

"Say there was a failure in an obscure piece of the hardware that rendered the flight unsuccessful. In a test configuration, there would be special commands to terminate the flight for safety reasons. Those commands would only show up in these records if it was a piece of hardware we normally monitor and record. If the particular piece of hardware is one which wouldn't cause an abort in wartime, we probably don't have it recorded."

"So what's the process now?" Jeff asked.

"We've started several things. First, we're looking for the obvious. Was the missile out of control, that sort of thing. Second, we have people running checks on the computer code, finding every place the command destruct data bit is registered. That's a painstaking process."

Jeff had a thought. "Do you know Max Fisher?" he asked.

"Better than I'm willing to tell people in public," Sammy said. "He's our boss. We've already talked to him three times. He's doing the software code check I mentioned back in Boston. We're working the data part from here since we have the printouts."

The Test Director came up to the table.

"Well, you boys can stop your looking. They found the problem. One of the range safety radars had an improper setting in its data base that made it think the missile was off course, and it automatically sent the destruct signal."

No one spoke. Jeff could tell they were all having the same feelings. Relief that it wasn't their system. Anger that a trivial human error could have erased the unbelievable number of hours that had gone into this test.

"I am exercising executive privilege and hereby declaring it Miller time," Jeff said.

Sammy Herborn flipped the printout closed.

"Ordinarily, I wouldn't," he said, "but since you're the General…I guess I should call Max." It took Jeff a second to realize he was talking about Fish.

"Give him my love," Jeff said as they all started from the building.

❑❑❑❑❑

Sergeant Johnson pulled into the roadside bar and went to the phone. He hesitated a moment and then headed for the building. Inside, he sat at the bar and ordered his longneck.

He finished his beer and ordered another. He was on his third when he went to the phone. After the coded ring and hang up, she answered as usual on the first ring when he dialed again.

"Hello."

"Your hero has been successful again." His voice was beginning to slur from the quick beer.

"What does that mean?" The response was very cold.

"It means whatever your man in Boston did to the system, the missile blew up just like you said it would, and everybody believes it was a human error on my part just like you said they would because I changed the software after the flight."

"Don't be so specific on the phone."

"Well, both of the tests are done. The one where I made the entry in the console and now this one where the missile blew."

"Say what we agreed."

"What your messenger told me to say last week, or what you told me to say when you were here last year?" The beer had really started to work on his mind. "I can still remember what you looked like when you were conducting business between my legs."

"Have they stopped their investigation?" She showed no sign that she wanted anything but the business at hand.

"I think so. Yeah, sure. At least nobody's looking in the software just like we planned. I changed the entry to make it look like it was wrong before the flight and they all think that was what blew the missile. My chief had to go over to their site and give them the details, and nobody seemed to suspect anything like what you did, whatever it was, that made the missile blow. When he came back, he said they were all going to town to have a beer."

"And you decided to join them?"

"Nah, I'm at a club on the highway."

"Did anyone suspect you?"

"I told you I was successful, didn't I? It wasn't easy though. I had to really be good, and I was. I'm always good. I changed the numbers after the explosion and nobody's the wiser."

"Have you arranged for your next transfer?"

"Yeah." Johnson grimaced as he looked off into the desert. "Your General did his homework, and I got my orders yesterday, but I don't know if it's going to work. The people where I am are so happy with my work, they are going to try to get me to stay."

"You can't let that happen."

"They told me some general had arranged it. What did you do for him?"

"That doesn't concern you."

"I bet it don't. Same things you did for me, huh? Maybe you need to come out here and do 'em again and help me think of a way to make this work." He was having fun, and he could feel himself becoming aroused.

"That won't be possible." The tone of her voice was not meant to console him, but to chastise.

"Maybe I just won't be able to arrange it unless you do." He had decided to push it a little further. "After all, I don't think you can finish whatever it is you're trying to do without me."

"I said it is impossible."

"Well, then, maybe you should find yourself another fetch 'n' carry boy, because I'm getting tired of this shit."

"That won't be necessary. You will do what you are told."

"Well, I suggest you look somewhere else."

"Then I suggest you look up the penalties for treason in your country."

"What's that supposed to mean?"

"It means that every conversation we have had is on tape as well as a record of the payments we have made to you and the payments we have made to the other debts you owed, which were substantial. If this operation aborts, I will not hesitate to make sure the FBI knows of your role."

He slammed the phone down.

"Whore bitch," he said to the idle pay phone. He kicked at the wall of the phone booth and went back into the bar and ordered another beer. He kicked at the barstool, but missed and nearly fell. He cursed her aloud so that the few other customers in the bar looked at him. He looked back at them hard and wondered if one of them would be the one who broke his legs when he couldn't come up with the money he owed. He took the beer and went back to the phone and dialed the number again.

"Hello."

"OK. I'll do it. When do I get my money?"

"Same time, same place," she said and hung up.

"Damn," he said to the dead receiver.

Celia Mitchell hung up the phone and turned back to the video on the TV. The tip of her tongue traced the smile on her lips as she watched the tape of her latest bedroom scene starring General Grant.

189

JANUARY
1974

Middle East diplomacy—pentagon adv12 1-74
Kissinger optimistic about peace in Israel, Egypt, Iraq
USWNS Military News
adv jan 12 1974 or thereafter

By GEORGE GROWSON

WASHINGTON—Today it was announced that Secretary of
State Henry Kissinger took a hopeful step toward peace in
the Middle East during yet another round of "shuttle
diplomacy." The Secretary has traveled extensively between
Israel, Egypt and Iraq to try to finalize the agreements
for peace in the area. Agreements have been signed between
Egyptian President Anwar Sadat and Israeli Premier Golda
Meir. The Secretary's office today released an optimistic
statement saying that Iraq has finally consented to
participate in the talks, which could lead not only to
peace, but potentially to a form of disarmament.
Meanwhile, long lines continue to be the case at the
fuel pumps in the United States as a result of oil
embargoes still in effect by the Organization of Petroleum
Exporting Countries (OPEC). There have been rumors that
some of the Arab nations involved may be considering
lifting the embargo in order to regain the revenue they
have lost, but as of now, the embargo seems to be solid.

NINE

January 12, 1974

Coventry School for Men and Women

Shropshire, England

4:30 PM

Sharifa bounded down the steps of the classroom, holding her books tightly to her chest. She was excited about the prospect of the afternoon and evening since today was the final tryouts for the girls' field hockey team, and tonight was her first official date. But she had to hurry if she was going to make the field in time. She had to first go by her dormitory room and change clothes, but from there she could ride her bicycle.

"See you at practice, Sharon?" It was her best friend, Julia, just coming down the street past the classroom building. She was with a group of boys, one of which was Sharifa's date for this evening. Julia was already dressed in her hockey uniform and headed toward the practice field.

"You bet," Sharifa said. Having multiple names was as natural to her as having multiple languages. She put them together with the countries. England was English and school and Sharon. Home was Arabic and the desert and Sharifa.

"I was hoping you'd miss and give the rest of us a chance," Julia shouted, but Sharifa could tell it was a friendly gibe. Eye contact had been made between Sharifa and Andrew, her date-to-be, and they were both slowing their pace.

"Oh, do knock it off, you two," Julia said.

Sharifa waved to the group as they went down the street, and Andrew was still looking over his shoulder as she rounded the corner and came onto the street for her dormitory. When she saw the car in front of her building, any disappointment at knowing she would miss her tryout and probably her date was driven away by the excitement she suddenly felt, knowing she was about to see Al Hamie again. She ran directly toward the car, and Ahmad was out and waiting as soon as he saw her. Seeing him stand beside the car, she realized again how huge Ahmad was. He was well over two meters and solidly built. Ahmad had been Al Hamie's personal driver and bodyguard for Sharifa's entire memory, and seeing Ahmad always meant that seeing him was not far away.

How long had it been since she had seen him? This was her senior year at school, and he had not come to visit her. She had not seen him at all except when she was home while the school was closed for the semester break, and then it had only been a quick visit in his office. She had been able to tell from the look in his eyes that he was under a lot of pressure and was very worried, and she knew from the newspapers and what little television she was able to watch that things were difficult for him.

Battles on several borders with other Arab countries were not uncommon, and not all of them went his way. He was often portrayed as a difficult person by the press, but Sharifa knew this was because of his firm anti-American and anti-Zionist beliefs which he would not compromise. More and more, however, the nations of the Arab world were beginning to look to him as their leader. He was not an outward radical like some, and he did not grovel to the Americans as did others. He was a stable, conservative leader of his country, adhering to the codes demanded by the tradition and religion of their people, and she saw him as the only hope for the future of the Arab world.

"Hello, Ahmad," she said in English as she approached the car. She knew he wouldn't speak back to her. Ahmad spoke no English, and while he was with her in public places outside of their own country, spoke as little as possible. He nodded with a smile and opened the passenger's door for her.

"Do I have time to freshen up a little?" she asked in Arabic, lowering her voice.

Ahmad nodded yes.

"Will we be overnight?"

Ahmad shook his head no.

196

"Late this evening?"

Ahmad nodded yes.

As she bounded up the steps to her room, he waited in the limousine. She wasn't gone long, but took the time to call Andrew's room and leave a message with his roommate that she would have to miss their date. She said that her father had come to town unexpectedly, and she would have to spend the evening with him. She then called the athletic department and gave them the same message. She changed from her classroom outfit, which she thought was childish, and put on an expensive outfit Al Hamie had sent for her birthday. She tried to tell herself it wasn't a little test to see if he would recognize the clothes, but she also knew it didn't matter if he did or didn't. She knew in her heart how much he loved her and that the enormous pressure he was under didn't allow him much time for shopping for schoolgirls' clothes.

She leapt down the steps in front of the dormitory building and before Ahmad could get out to help her, she was already in the car on the front seat beside him.

"You should ride in the back seat," he said in Arabic.

"Why?" she teased.

"Because that's where important people ride. Drivers and soldiers ride in the front seat."

"I just wanted to talk to you. I can't talk to you if all I can see is the back of your head. Don't you want to talk to me, Ahmad?"

He blushed at her forwardness.

"Yes, of course I do," he said. "But you should act like the important person you are."

"How are Sawsan and Nofa?" she asked, completely ignoring his request.

"The same as ever," he said. "They never stop asking questions about you and giving me instructions for you."

"Did they send me anything?" she asked, knowing the two women would never let Ahmad go without something for her.

"Yes," he said smiling at her.

"What is it?" she asked, excited.

"I was made to swear by Allah that I would not tell you, and to instruct you that you were not to ask any more questions of a person who is as weak to your manipulations as I am."

"Do you know?" She pulled her knees underneath her and turned to face him on the seat of the car.

"They made me promise to keep it a secret," he said. "Please do not make me suffer their attentions by failing to keep my promise."

"Ahmad, you're not telling me what I want to know," she teased. "You know what it is and I want to know." Ahmad was totally committed to her, and Sharifa knew she was a big part of what very little enjoyment ever came into his life. He was also one of the few people in the world who completely understood her entire life, and she felt a bond with him in serving the person they believed would be the leader of the new Arab nation.

"Patience, please. Did you get the package that was sent last week for your birthday?"

"Yes, it was these clothes that I have on now. Aren't they pretty?" she said. "How far will we have to travel?"

"Not far," Ahmad said. "He is waiting for us near here. And yes, the clothes are very pretty."

When she thought of Al Hamie, her hand instinctively went to her chest and the locket there. She could feel it through the fine silk of the blouse. She fingered the locket and then finally pressed it with the palm of her hand. She wondered if Ahmad noticed her breasts and decided he probably hadn't. She sat back to watch the familiar countryside as Ahmad maneuvered the big Rolls Royce through the small village which was mostly houses and shops for the people who supported the school. They were headed toward Liverpool. She had met him there once before, but a very long time ago. She had been in a different school then with a different name. Ahmad had come for her and they had flown together to Liverpool and then driven to a house in the hills outside the city. It had been a grand weekend by the sea. That was the last time she recalled seeing him really relaxed and able to spend some time by himself and with her. Since then, it had always been rushed evenings or quick visits to his office. Sharifa didn't mind this for herself, but she was worried about him.

198

"How is he?" she asked Ahmad.

"He is well. The others give him a difficult time." She knew by "the others" Ahmad meant the leaders of the other Arab countries.

"Why can't they see what he is trying to do?"

"Some are too busy getting rich from the Americans, and the rest are too busy building bombs to blow up the Zionists. He is in the middle."

"But surely they can see that his way is the only right thing for our people."

"Not if you're one of the people getting rich or bombing Zionists. His way is too complicated and dangerous for them and takes too much time."

"But in the end, his way will do exactly what they are trying to do, only his solution will be permanent. He will send the Zionists back where they came from, and unite our people everywhere, and then we can once again be the masters of our own destiny."

"Yes, desert flower. But his way takes time, and the others want immediate results."

"But it will be so temporary," she said. "Not a lasting solution that will allow all of our people to be free from outside influence forever."

"I know that."

"Yes, you're right," she said. "I know I'm preaching to the choir."

"What?" Ahmad asked, obviously confused.

"'Preaching to the choir' is an American expression meaning telling something to someone who already knows and believes it."

"A strange expression," he said. "Are you learning many American ways?"

"Learning, yes," she said. "Liking, no. Americans are worse than we were taught. They are selfish, self-indulging, and uncaring people who mouth reverence to their God, but then live their lives as though he doesn't exist. They wouldn't last one week in the desert."

"Yes, I know," he said.

"The last time I saw him was over the holidays. He looked very tired."

"It is always very tense for him now. This weekend will be good for him. He will stay by the coast for several days and try to relax. There will only be a few meetings." Sharifa was not surprised or hurt that he was going to be in England for the entire weekend, but she would only see him for this evening. She knew that he would give her all the time he could, and that the other meetings he must attend were important for the future of their people. Some of the meetings were so secret that all of the staff except Ahmad and the security guards were taken away. "He would like to see you again on Sunday afternoon before he leaves, but it is not possible for you to stay with him until then."

"I understand," she said. "When will he leave for the homeland?"

"I do not know," Ahmad said, but she realized as soon as she had asked the question that even if he did know, it would not have been proper for him to tell her. She felt a slight embarrassment and lowered her head and looked at the floor of the car. Ahmad reached across the seat and placed one of his huge hands on her arm.

"It is understandable to want to know, little desert flower. I, more than anyone, know how you feel about him, because I feel the same way."

She didn't respond, but instead lowered the back of the seat and rested her head. It was a few moments before he noticed that she had reclined.

"If you like, you may get in the back seat and take a short nap," he said.

"No, thank you," she said with the slur of sleep already in her voice. "I'll stay right here with the unimportant folk."

◻◻◻◻◻

Sharifa was awakened by the sound of the limousine's tires on a gravel driveway. It was dusk, but she could recognize the house from her previous visit. Through the trees, she could see the lawn which she knew gradually dropped to the sea. The house was as she remembered it—tall and very much English. As soon as Ahmad stopped, she was out of the car and headed for the front door. Before she got to the door, it opened, but by a hand that she could not see, and when she looked in, it was clear someone was standing behind the massive carved door. She went in and looked around the edge of the door and screamed in delight as Sawsan peered back at her.

"Ahmad said there was a surprise, but he wouldn't tell me," she said, grasping Sawsan in a big hug.

"I made him promise," Sawsan said. "And the one who controls the food is in total control of that one. He eats like a herd of horses."

"No herd of horses could live on the small portions of food you give me," Ahmad said as he came in the door smiling.

Sawsan shot him a look.

"But no horse ever had food which tasted so good," he added quickly, still smiling.

"If I fed you everything you wanted to eat, you wouldn't be able to get into that car, even if it was twice as big as it is," Sawsan said. "Back up, little desert flower, and let me look at you. Aren't these the clothes he sent you for your birthday?"

"Yes," Sharifa said. "Do you like them?"

"You look beautiful," she said. "Al Hamie will be so pleased." Sawsan looked strange to her without her traditional robes. She remembered that in this house, all of the people traveling with him dressed in the western style, but it still seemed odd to see Sawsan, in particular, without robe or veil. For her part, Sawsan seemed totally comfortable dressed as a typical British doweress in well-chosen and obviously expensive clothes.

"He's in the garden, but he has someone with him. He said to fix you something to eat, and he will be in soon."

"I'm too excited to eat. I am going to walk down by the water. Come with me, Sawsan, so we can talk of home, and Ahmad can come for us when it is time."

"Yes, my little one," Sawsan said. "I have many things to tell you."

The two women left the house by a side door and went down a path that led to the water's edge. Sharifa strained to see into the garden to get a glimpse of him and to see who might be with him. She so wished that she could be a part of the conversations he had with the others. She was confident that she could convince them of the wisdom in his planning, and that she could be an asset to him by being with him rather than away at school. She knew she could learn by tutors and private study. But she had never even approached the idea with him. He always seemed to know exactly what he wanted her to do, and in the end, she always felt that what he wanted her to do would be the best thing.

They walked by the shore for a long time and talked of Nofa and of Sharifa's friends from home. After awhile, they had exhausted all of those topics and got to the one on which they always spent the most time when they were together.

"Tell me how he is," Sharifa said. "I asked Ahmad, but that's like talking to a tree stump."

"He is better than you might think," Sawsan said. "Do not be fooled by his tired look. Yes, he is tired, but he really believes that he is making progress with the others. His heart is happy, and he is looking forward to your visit."

"Does he get enough sleep and eat well?"

"No, but what man on an important crusade does?" Sawsan asked with a shrug and a helpless gesture of her hands. "But he is healthy. The doctor examined him in detail just the other week and said that he was fine. The others may wish that he would join Allah in the sky, but that is not going to happen."

Sharifa heard a bell and, peering toward the house, saw Ahmad standing under a light by the back door, looking in her direction. Her hand went to the locket as the two women turned toward the house and quickened their pace, though careful to maintain the demure presence expected of women in their culture.

"In the study," Ahmad said as Sharifa got to the house. She went in the door and, with Ahmad close behind her, found her way through the hallways to the door of the study. Outside the door, she stopped to look at herself in a mirror at the end of the hall. With her fingertips, she touched her hair until it was just the way she wanted, took a deep breath and nodded to Ahmad, who then knocked on the large carved oak door and went inside, leaving her in the hallway.

In only a few moments, Ahmad opened the door and held out his hand to her and walked her into the study. Al Hamie was standing beside a desk carved in the same style as the door. Ahmad dropped her hand, turned, and left, closing the door behind him. Al Hamie's face lit in a broad smile when their eyes met, and her instinct was to run to him, but she knew that was not proper. As she approached, he held out his hand to her, and she bent her head to kiss it. He grasped her by both shoulders and leaned forward to kiss her gently on each of her cheeks, then put both arms around her and held her to him.

"You are more beautiful than ever," he said, holding her at arm's length. "The beauty of all of the flowers of the desert combined does not equal your radiance."

"You honor me with your admiration," she said, letting her head bow slightly in ritual humility.

"Remember what I have told you, little desert flower," he said as he gently cupped his hand under her chin and raised her head. "Bow your head to no one."

"I bow my head to you out of respect," she said. "For there is no one greater on this earth."

"But you must learn to be proud as well as humble."

"Yes," she said. "But I will never be so proud that I will not bow my head to you."

Lifting her hand, he turned her palm upward, revealing the blue star. He paused. "Always remember our enemies."

"Yes," she said. "I will remember them forever in a secret part of my heart."

"How are your studies?" he asked as he sat in a large comfortable chair and motioned for her to be seated also.

"Fine. I should be graduating in a few months," she said, sitting on the floor in front of him. "My grades are good and I have been interviewing with colleges."

"You are too modest. I understand that your grades are among the best in your class, and there are several universities who are aggressively recruiting you to come and study with them."

She blushed at his knowledge of her performance, although she was pleased that he had taken the trouble to find out about her schoolwork. She was not a natural academic and had worked hard to achieve the results that placed her at the top of her class.

"Do you have a preference for my university?" she asked.

"Only that it be in America," he said.

He saw her negative reaction.

"What should I study there?" she asked.

"You must learn the enemy, little desert flower. And there is no better way to learn than to live with them as one of their own. Study the people," he said. She nodded her head. She understood that her choice of studies would be up to her, but would be secondary to learning and adapting to American ways.

"I will," she said.

"This summer, you will be tutored in American ways and manner of speaking. You will attend the university as an American citizen." She nodded, excited by the inference that she would spend the summer at home near him.

"And how are you?" she asked. "Sawsan says that you do not get enough to eat or enough rest. You look tired." He smiled at the mention of Sawsan, and she remembered the feeling that had come to her all of her life when she had seen that smile. There was no single word which could describe it. Peace. Security. Happiness. Confidence. Love. All of these and more ran through her whenever she was this close to him and could see his smile and look into his eyes.

"I am well," he said. "Which is more than I can say for all of our people. We are being murdered and driven from our homes every day, and no one seems to care."

"You care," she said. "And I care. And Ahmad cares. And Sawsan and Nofa and all of those around you care."

"But we are not enough," he said. "We must have the leaders of the other Arab nations with us. Without them, we are only a lone voice whimpering in the desert."

"But why won't they listen?" she asked.

"Two simple words," he said softly. "Greed and passion."

"Can't you reason with them?"

"We are trying," he said. "But even as we speak, our people are killing each other by the hundreds and thousands every day. I assume you have read in the newspapers of the wars in our homeland. We don't have to wait for the Zionists to come and kill us, because we are going to do it to ourselves."

"Can't it be stopped?"

"We cannot allow our people to be ruled by extremists who make their own interpretations of what Allah has given us as his Holy Word, or by those who would allow the Americans and the Soviets to rule Arab nations through money and weapons."

"Will you be able to stop them?"

"Yes, but that is not the final threat, or even the most important threat. While we fight among ourselves, the Zionists become stronger every day and the Americans become more intertwined with the weaker nations of our people. The Americans continue to supply the Zionists and Arabs with weapons bought with money from cheap oil that our people gladly sell them. It is inevitable that one day we will have to face the Zionists and the Americans in battle, and I pray earnestly that we do not have to fight our own people at the same time."

"Surely, none of our own people would ever side with the Zionists against you."

"The world is a strange place, little desert flower, and greed and passion will make men do things they would not otherwise have done."

"Our enemies must laugh at us as we kill ourselves," she said sadly.

"Our enemies are not only the Zionists and the Americans, but the other Arab nations who side with them for American money, technology, and weapons."

This was the first time that she had ever had a political discussion with him, and she felt proud to be hearing his words firsthand. She wanted to let him know that she was ready to help in any way he wanted, but she didn't know how.

"I feel so helpless."

"You shouldn't," he said. "You are doing the right thing to help our people. The day will come when we will need committed patriots who know the ways of our enemy. Your education in America will be a great benefit to your people. When it is completed, you will be asked to make great sacrifices."

205

She looked into the eyes which could say so much without words being spoken. Then her glance dropped to her feet and the floor.

"I will do whatever you ask of me," she said.

"It may be difficult," he said. "Do not make commitments lightly. The road ahead is very steep and very dangerous. Many of our people will suffer and die and others like you will be called upon to make sacrifices beyond any they have made before."

"I know what it means to suffer," she said. "And I know what it means to sacrifice. I am prepared to do whatever you need to support the battle."

"I know, little desert flower," he said. "I know. And one day, it will be your time. But now, it is time for you to be educated. You have made me proud by your accomplishments in school. It is through these accomplishments that I know the commitment you have for our people. I know you will not disappoint me in America."

"I will not," she said.

"Now let us have dinner. Sawsan has prepared food she brought all the way from home just for this meal with you. She is very proud of herself."

Sharifa cleared the papers from her desk. This was going to be a three-day weekend, and she wanted everything to be ready to go when she returned to work on Tuesday. Vern Stork, one of the senior partners of the law firm, had invited her to the Cape, and she was looking forward to the time away from the office. She heard the phone ring on the receptionist's desk, and while she knew there was probably no one else in the office this late on a Friday afternoon, she let it ring a few times anyway just to be sure. No one answered the insistent ring, and, finally confident she was alone, Sharifa picked up the phone.

206

"Good afternoon, Stork, Schaffer, and Aronson. This is Celia Mitchell, may I help you?" she said into the receiver.

"Yes, you may, Miss Mitchell." The English was just a little too perfect, and her heart skipped a beat at the note of familiarity.

"Are you able to speak privately?"

"Yes."

"Do you believe this line is free?"

"Yes."

"Then would you hold just a moment, please?" The caller didn't wait for an answer and then there were several clicks on the line. She then heard a truly familiar voice in an even more familiar language.

"Hello." Ahmad said.

"Hello!" She almost shouted into the phone. "You'll never know how good it is to hear your voice."

"Is the line secure?" he asked.

"Yes, I told you the last time that they have these lines checked every month."

"Good. It is good to hear your voice, also. Are you free for the weekend?"

"The weekend and then some. Monday is a holiday here for Founder's Day or some such. When can you pick me up?"

"Right away. At least as soon as you can be ready. If you can arrange it, Tuesday off in addition will help some. How long will it take you to be ready?"

"Tuesday's no problem," she said, her mind going through a mental checklist. "I'll have to make a phone call or two and take care of some other business, but I should be ready in about an hour and a half. That good enough?"

"That will be fine," Ahmad said. "Drive to Logan Airport and park in Public Parking Section B3. I'll find you."

"That's a twenty-minute drive tacked on my hour and a half. How about six-thirty."

"Six-thirty will be fine. I'll see you there."

Her heart was pounding as she put down the phone. Luckily, she had a way to get in touch with Vern. She chuckled as she thought that what she would like to do was to call his wife and tell her he wouldn't really be competing in the sailing regatta this weekend after all. "All in due time," she thought. She wrote a note to Vern: "Congressional subcommittee has convened this weekend and will be in session until Wednesday. Please tell Harold—CM." She knew that Vern would understand the coded message that she was called away for personal reasons and couldn't make their rendezvous. He would also cover for her with Harold Simmons, her boss, for Tuesday off. She was neither disappointed nor concerned as she wrote the message since she knew Vern would stop at the office on his way to their meeting and would at least be able to make other plans.

Driving to her apartment, she ran through her mental checklist again, but there was nothing pending which couldn't wait until Wednesday. She had an exchange agreement with her neighbor to take care of each other's cats, but that was all she had to arrange. Packing was no problem since she kept a separate set of clothes ready to go. Each month, she went through them to keep them current and ready, and although she hadn't used them in over two years, she never failed to do her monthly check of the traveling wardrobe and accessories packed away in a black leather traveling bag.

Three days, she thought, and got excited again as her fingers played with the locket around her neck. She wondered if that meant she was going to be able to go home to see the places she hadn't been in over four years and to see Sawsan and Nofa again and eat some of Sawsan's cooking. The life she lived deprived her of any really good Middle Eastern food. Occasionally if she was out of town on a business trip by herself, she would go to a Middle Eastern restaurant. But she couldn't at home. Nobody talked about it much, but most of the people in the office thought she was Jewish. Years of practice had taught her how to hold her hand so the star was not visible, but once or twice, she had slipped. Once, Vern Stork had told a terribly crude Arabic joke, and when he noticed her nervously stroking the palm of her hand, he offered an apology and asked if he had offended her, but she said no. That night while Vern slept, she had lain in his bed while tears of shame for what she was doing flowed across her cheeks. With all of her strength, she had pressed the locket into the star of her hand and prayed to Allah that her time should come soon.

At her apartment, she packed quickly, loaded the car and left a note on her girlfriend's door. As she took a hot shower, she tried to decide how to wear her hair. Her long black hair was nearly to the center of her back, and she had changed to a popular new American style. She thought it was attractive, but he might think it was too American and too blatant an attempt at sexuality. She decided to go with her everyday style since she wanted him to see her just as she was. That way, if he wasn't pleased with what she was doing, he could let her know.

At Logan Airport, she followed the signs to Section B3 without any problem. She spotted the black limousine before she was even in a parking place. By the time she was out of the car, Ahmad was coming to help her with the luggage.

She wanted to hug him in the American style, but knew that wasn't wise, so she went to the rear lid of her black Japanese sports car and was removing the two black leather bags as Ahmad reached her. Without a word, he took the bags, carried them to the limousine and deposited them in the open trunk. He then opened the passenger door for her, but she walked by that door and went to the front door, giving him her best "I've come a long way, baby" look as she passed him. Ahmad smiled as he closed the back door, went around to his side and got in the driver's seat. When his door was shut, she threw herself at him across the seat and grabbed his huge body and kissed him hard on the mouth.

"You are learning too many American ways," Ahmad said, pleased and proud of this attention, but embarrassed at her forwardness.

"If you knew the American ways I was learning, you would do more than blush," she said, smiling at him. "God, I have missed you so. Are we going home? Please tell me we are going home."

"To the desert, but not home. At least not first. I think he wanted an extra day so he might send you home to see Sawsan and Nofa. Nofa is not well."

"Where are we going then?" she asked.

"In time, little one. Did you bring your Arabic passport in addition to your American?"

"Yes."

"Good. I need you to give me the Arabic passport now. Use the American if anyone asks to see one. I will get the Arabic one stamped with the proper stamps you will need to get back into the United States. Are you sure you were not followed?"

"Yes, I'm sure I wasn't followed. Who would want to follow me anyway?"

"Anyone who knew who you are."

"And who am I?" she asked, a slight mocking tone in her voice.

"Someone who knows Al Hamie, and can lead others to him," Ahmad said.

"Touché," she said

"What?" he asked.

"It's a French fencing expression meaning, well, I don't exactly know how to explain it."

"It's all right," Ahmad said. "I think I understand. We're here already. Help me with the guard so I don't have to speak." The limousine was at a small gate with a guardhouse. The guard came to the car and Ahmad rolled down the window and handed him a pass. The guard took a long look in the window at Sharifa, who had raised her skirt well above mid-thigh and made direct eye contact with the guard as his eyes went from hers, to her legs, back to her eyes. He handed the pass back to Ahmad and waved them on, and Ahmad drove through the gate and onto the concrete of the airfield.

"I meant for you to speak to him."

"That was easier."

"I noticed."

There was a row of planes and Ahmad drove beside an aircraft with markings she did not recognize. She knew little about planes, but knew enough to know it was a jet used by executives for long distance flights. Although there were several stewards helping with the luggage and arrangements, Sharifa didn't say anything as she boarded the plane. She had learned that until you are fully aware of your surroundings, even a few poorly chosen words could give away more information than was intended. Inside, there were a half dozen seats, all of which were the size of commercial overseas first class lounge chairs. She went to the front row and sat on the port side without fastening her seatbelt. Ahmad came from the doorway and moved up the aisle to the seat beside her. The engines were starting as he sat down, and he began to fasten his seatbelt. He looked at her and smiled.

"You are very beautiful," he said. "He will be very pleased."

"Thank you," she said, and looked at the floor in front of her seat.

"Does it take much time?" he asked.

"What?" she asked.

"I'm sorry," he said. "Your hair. Does it take much time to prepare it in that manner?"

"No," she said and looked at him and smiled. He had never been so personal with her before. Maybe it was because of the excitement when she first saw him and kissed him. She probably shouldn't have kissed him with such passion, but she felt so much more for him than the American men she had kissed with a passion she didn't feel. But now she had embarrassed him, and he was looking at the floor. Neither of them spoke for a while, even though his speaking had told her it was all right to use Arabic on the flight.

"How long will our flight be?" she asked.

"Many hours," he said. "The last two seats on your side make into a bed and there are bedclothes in the overhead compartment. When you are ready to sleep, the steward will make the bed for you. There is also a bathroom with a shower in the rear of the plane."

Sharifa wanted to ask many more questions, but had learned to be content with what Ahmad told her. At least she knew they were going to Arabic territory, and that she might get a chance to go home and see the people and land she really loved. The plane was moving and soon they were airborne, and she could see the lights of Boston fade quickly behind her.

"Will we have to stop for fuel?" she asked.

"No," Ahmad said. "The plane has been especially equipped for this trip. We have extra fuel tanks on the outside of the plane that will be jettisoned when they are empty."

"How long is our flying time?"

"I haven't figured it out in hours," he said. "But there is a flight schedule on the door behind the pilot if you want me to get it for you. It tells what time we will be arriving in Tripoli. From there we will have a long drive into the desert mountains. You should get as much rest as you can while we are flying. There are some sleeping pills in the bathroom if you want."

"No thanks." As she settled into her seat she looked again at Ahmad. "You don't approve of me, do you?" she asked.

"What do you mean?" He seemed surprised.

"I mean my lifestyle."

"I don't know anything about your lifestyle. I am concerned only for your welfare."

"My welfare or my chastity."

"Your chastity is not my concern, but yours, and maybe the concern of Al Hamie. But not mine."

"But my welfare is?"

"Yes. Have you not always known that?"

"Yes. Maybe I just want somebody to be concerned about my chastity, too."

"Do you need that?"

"If you knew the life I live, you wouldn't need to ask that question. I have become something I never dreamed I would be."

"Do you enjoy it?"

"I try not to think about it."

"And what are you?"

"A person who does things that would not please Allah."

"Maybe. But the reasons you are what you are would please him. The fact that you have allowed yourself to become something you abhor in the service of our people will be judged a sacrifice worthy of praise."

"You think?"

"I know."

"Good. Come sit by me so I can use your shoulder."

❑❑❑❑❑

An official car from the government of Libya was waiting beside the plane when it taxied to a stop. Sharifa was moved from the air-conditioning of the plane to the air-conditioning of the car so swiftly she almost didn't notice the heat which felt like the inside of a blast furnace. By the time Ahmad got in the car, the trunk was being closed and then they were off. She knew it probably wasn't a coincidence they had arrived during late afternoon since now they would drive in the safety and coolness of the night. She had not slept as well on the plane as she had hoped because she had been excited about the trip, and the ride had been bumpier than usual.

She ended the long car ride with her head in Ahmad's lap and his jacket over her body. She slept soundly, awakened only by the sound of doors opening. As she sat up and stretched, Ahmad was out of the door and seeing to the luggage.

She had been to Libya many times before during her childhood, but had never been to this place, a stark, yet striking house set among the large hills. She was sure that in the light of morning, there would be beautiful views of the countryside. Each of the Arabic leaders maintained special places like this one for important meetings which were not ostentatious in the western style like America's Camp David, but built so that guests could appreciate the land, mountains, desert and water and feel close to Allah as they planned for the future of their people. Sharifa loved these places, and the opportunities they had always afforded her to be with Al Hamie during these meetings were the most special of all of their times together.

When she arrived at her room her luggage was already there, and a maid was unpacking her clothes and placing them in a dresser and a wardrobe.

"Is there a bath?" Sharifa asked.

"Yes, and plenty of hot water," the maid said. "Would you like me to prepare a bath now?'

"Yes, please," Sharifa said, looking forward to relaxing in the hot water.

The morning sun provided the anticipated views of the surrounding mountains and a valley below them. The house was situated on a craggy plateau far into the hills, and through the doors of her bedroom, there was a patio on which Sharifa was served her breakfast. Seeing the steep and twisting road approaching the house from the valley below, she was glad she had been asleep during the drive. In the hazy distance, she could see the desert floor which the sun was just beginning to touch, wiping away the evening coolness. She longed to be in that desert, and was looking forward to the possibility of her visit home. As the maid was taking away the dishes, there was a knock at the door. When the maid opened it, Ahmad came into the room and greeted Sharifa.

"There is a meeting at ten o'clock. He would like you to meet with him at nine and then to attend the meeting with him."

Sharifa was startled. She had never been to the working sessions of one of these meetings.

"Are you sure he wants me to attend?" she asked.

"Yes, he was very specific. He is looking forward to seeing you and he asked me how you looked."

"And what did you tell him?" She raised her eyes to look directly into his.

His eyes met hers as he spoke to her with an almost reverent tone.

"I told him just what I told you, that heaven and earth together could not even approach your beauty."

Her face flushed, but she maintained the contact with his eyes.

"Where do I meet him?" she asked.

"He will come to you here."

She looked at her watch, but it was still set on Boston time.

"It is seven o'clock," Ahmad said. "You have plenty of time."

"Easy for you to say," she said, smiling. "But to get this ragged body in presentable form, I'll just have enough time."

"He has sent the clothes he wants you to wear."

"Yes, I saw them." The clothes in the wardrobe were a blend of Arabic and western styles. She had seen a Palestinian spokeswoman on television recently, and she had been dressed in a similar style. Very professional and eastern enough to notice, but western enough to be friendly to the news media. She had known the clothes were from him when she saw that they

214

were white. He always liked her in white.

"I will be ready," she said.

At precisely nine o'clock, there was a knock on the door. Ahmad came onto the patio where Sharifa was waiting at a table with a carafe of strong Arabic coffee.

"You are ready?" he asked.

"Yes," she said, rising from the table and moving to the rock wall at the edge of the patio. Ahmad walked with her and closely inspected the grounds over the wall and the surrounding area, then turned, took the maid with him, and left the room without closing the door. She sat casually on the edge of the rock wall and looked at the valley which was now in full sunlight.

She was full of questions about why she was going to attend the meeting and what would be discussed. Would she be required to say anything? She had never known of a woman in these meetings. Then she realized she had never known who had attended at all, male or female. Hearing a noise, she turned to see him coming through the glass door, and she stood and faced him.

"Hello, Sharifa. Ahmad was right. You are more beautiful than ever," he said. "Yes, my desert flower, you have blossomed into a woman, and a most attractive one."

"I am glad you are pleased," she said, looking at the floor in front of her feet, and then raising her head she saw that his eyes were as gentle as ever, but that his face had aged. He was still handsome and a picture of strength, but the last two years had not been kind.

"I am glad you could come. I hope it was not inconvenient."

"No. Not at all. I was happy to get the invitation."

"Ahmad has told you of the schedule for today?"

"Yes," she said.

"Then sit, and let's have a coffee and talk about what will happen."

They moved to the table, and she poured the coffee after they were seated.

"Do you miss our coffee?" he asked.

"Yes, and I miss the desert, our food, and our people but, most of all, I miss being able to serve you."

"But you live well? Your needs are met?"

"Yes," she said. "Too well. I have every convenience, and I am becoming just like the Americans. I have a beautiful apartment, a glorious new car, a closet full of expensive clothes, and more money than my entire village saw in a year."

"And how does that make you feel?"

"I feel bad because I know many of our people are doing without even the basics of food and clothes, yet I have so much." She could not look at him as she spoke those words, but looked toward the valley below.

"You should not feel guilty. I have told you that you are in training for important activities."

"I want to help the struggle of our people, but I have not been able to make any contribution."

"That is about to change," he said.

"You mean I will be able to come home?" Her heart nearly leapt into her throat with anticipation of his answer.

"No, not yet. But you will begin to serve."

"I will do whatever is required of me."

"I know that, and the others know that. They, too, have watched your growth. We believe you are ready."

She was stunned. To think that the leaders of other nations were even aware that she existed was unthinkable, but to know that they had somehow been apprised of her life was beyond her imagination.

"At today's meeting, you will be introduced, and you will listen to the conversations. If you are asked a question, respond honestly. But unless you are asked, do not volunteer your opinion on any matter."

"Yes," she said.

"Remember that I have told you that when the time is right, you may be asked to make sacrifices for your country and for the Arab people?'

"Yes," she said.

"That time has come. We are now ready to put you in positions of importance in America. We have some ways of helping, but your relationship with me must not be disclosed."

"That has been done. No one knows my origins. They all think I am an American Jew."

"Well, so far, no one has checked too deeply. The jobs we have in mind will call for extensive investigations into your background. The paperwork for your life history has been prepared with the utmost care and at great expense. It will bear scrutiny, but you must make no mistakes which will compromise the facade."

"Mistakes will not happen."

"I know, little desert flower. Now tell me about your job and what you are doing."

"I am a lawyer in a small Boston firm working mostly for political clients. It is rumored that the firm has strong ties to the Kennedys, although I have never met any of them nor handled any of their affairs. There are frequent trips to Washington, and I have been several times."

"How did you manage to get this particular job?" She knew he already knew the answers, but was pleased that he wanted her to tell him. She had the impression he might be rehearsing her for the later session with the others.

"After my graduation from Harvard Law School, I received many job offers. I sent home a list of those I thought most appropriate and received a reply that this firm was chosen."

"Yes, I remember now. We chose them because of their Washington ties. I take it the ties are mostly to the Democrat party?"

"Yes, as far as I know. All of our clients seem to be Democrats."

"So I am told," he said. There was a long silence as he stood and walked to the rock wall and looked at the valley below.

"It was a valley very similar to this in which your family lived."

"Yes," she said. "The same thought occurred to me this morning as I watched the sun rise over the mountains." At the thought of her family, she instinctively placed her fingertips on the star in the palm of her hand. She was ashamed that she hadn't thought of them in a long time.

He turned and held out his hand for her to come to him. She rose from the table and went to his side. He took her hand and opened her palm. He placed the tip of his finger in the center of the star.

"On the blood of your mother and the blood of your father." There was an awkward silence until she realized she was to repeat after him.

"On the blood of my mother and the blood of my father."

"On the blood of your sister and brother."

"On the blood of my sister and brother."

"On the blood of all your sisters and brothers who have fallen to the enemy."

"On the blood of all my sisters and brothers who have fallen to the enemy."

"I swear by the Almighty that I will make any sacrifice."

"I swear by the Almighty that I will make any sacrifice."

"And that I will never rest until the enemy is driven from our home."

"And that I will never rest until the enemy is driven from our home."

"To your own death."

"To my own death."

He released her hand and grasped her by both shoulders. He pulled her to him and kissed her on each of her cheeks. She knew that as he did so, he could taste the salt of the tears which were there. But they were not tears of shame. Not any more. Never again.

❑❑❑❑❑

Sharifa was glad that she had been instructed to remain silent. With the people in this room, she could not have spoken even if she wanted. The room was not crowded, but the leader of every nation of the true Arab coalition was there. Not those nations who curried favor with the Americans, and not those nations who had made peace with the Israelis. These were the last of the true believers, including the Palestinians. But she was not the only woman there. She saw the same woman she had seen on television, and they made eye contact and exchanged knowing smiles as kindred spirits. Most of the faces were familiar to her from the news media. They were mostly dressed in native garb, but several were dressed in western style or, as in Al Hamie's case, in uniforms. They exchanged traditional recognitions with each other as they took their places at the table, but the meeting was clearly a business gathering. Greetings were typically Arabic and had none of the fluster of western show. Most of the leaders made eye contact with her as they sat, and she bowed her head to each with respect. Soon, everyone was seated, and Al Hamie rose from his position at the head of the table.

"Thank you all for coming. I will make my introductory comments very brief and then we can get to the agenda for the meeting. I have called you together because I believe we are at a major turning point for our people. A point where we can, if we will but work together, rid ourselves of our enemies forever. If we each continue on our own independent paths, we will never overcome the Zionists and the Americans, but if we come together as one great Arab spirit, then no one can defeat us."

Sharifa could see several of the principals at the table showing various signs of discomfort. This line of talk was the reason they had come, but, as many of them had felt the impact of his military, they could not help feeling hesitant. They weren't going to let themselves be put into a position for another taste of the same.

"I know that we must each be careful," he continued, "but what I propose now is a two-point agreement which begins our cooperation in a small but beneficial manner, one which allows us to grow as we are successful, and one which won't damage us if we aren't. First, we need to pool our finances for an Arab-controlled foundation of technological excellence for the development of our own weapons. This foundation can have a different center for each of our countries and we may then share the results. One country can develop the technology of missiles, another airplanes, another warships, and so forth. Individually, we don't have the capacity to produce a well-rounded force of our own, and we will always be getting second-class weapons from the Americans, the Russians, and other industrialized nations. But if we come together, we can build our own force, a truly Arab force.

"Second, we need to develop and refine our capability to gather intelligence on our true enemy, and to exchange this intelligence with each other. Let me reiterate that I said intelligence on our true enemy. There are those who will continue to gather intelligence on their Arab neighbors,

219

and we expect them to keep this information to themselves."

Sharifa noted more squirming. He was known to have the most sophisticated intelligence apparatus in the Arab world. He knew as much about the activities of the men in this room as they knew themselves, or so the stories went, and Sharifa believed the stories.

"I propose we build a center of intelligence, staffed by the collective resources of the members here and dedicated to the gathering and dissemination of information on our true enemies. Maybe," and at this point a small smile escaped, "maybe we will find this to be such a big job we won't have time to be looking under our Arab brother's bedcovers." Bits of muted laughter could be heard around the table.

"In connection with this center, I propose we develop a cadre of our Arab family who can pass as members of any of the nations who are our enemy. These will be the most important links in our intelligence plan, because their usefulness will extend beyond the ability to supply information on our enemy. With our funds and backing, they will inevitably be able to reach positions of influence in our enemies' governments. These dedicated patriots will be able to provide us what we have never had before: knowledge of our enemies' intent and perhaps even an influence on their actions. I have brought one such patriot with me today who is ready for such a mission."

Sharifa immediately knew that he was speaking of her and as she felt the eyes of the room move to her, she swelled with pride at the thought of being chosen as the first of these patriots. Now she knew that she had been brought to this meeting to show that this part of his plan could work. She noticed several of the leaders at the table cast discreet looks in her direction, and some even nodded and smiled at her. She fought the temptation to lower her eyes.

"Trust me, my brothers," he continued. "Now we fight with each other, but the day is coming when we will have to fight the Americans and the Zionists together. There is no escaping it. If we fight them as individual nations while we are still fighting each other, we can only lose as we have lost in the past. If we fight them together as one force with Allah on our side, we can only win. I pray to Allah with all my being that we can come to an agreement, for if we cannot, our cause is surely lost."

As he sat down, there was a buzz around the room, and Sharifa closely watched the members. With almost no exceptions, leaders were conferring with their advisors rather than other leaders. The most outspoken and independent of the leaders dressed in traditional desert robes rose to speak, and as he stood, his hands arranged his checkered headdress and then flipped it over his shoulder.

"We are most honored to be invited to this meeting," he said. "I, too, believe that we must be together or we will all be crushed by the Americans, the Zionists or their Arab puppets. But how can I expose my backside to a neighbor who continues to drop bombs on me? How can I build weapons and then give them to another neighbor who may use them against me? How can we guarantee Arab unity when we can't even guarantee Arab peace?" He ended his questions with his hands outstretched and sat down. There was another buzz of discussion around the room, this one louder than before. Sharifa looked at him and was surprised to see him looking at her. She looked into his eyes, and he smiled that peaceful smile she loved.

The leader of one of the smaller countries stood. The noise of the group slowly lessened.

"I support these proposals. As you all know, though our country is small, it is one of the poorest." There was some chuckling at this. It was quietly known that this was one of the wealthiest of the Arab families, although the people of his country were indeed poor. "We are proud, and we do not want to be dependent on America or anyone else, but we have no way to secure our economic and military independence unless we can unite with other Arab nations. That is what we want to do, and that is why we are here."

"That is why we are all here," another stood and said. "But we must first have assurances that the benefits of these cooperations will not be used against our own countries."

With that, Al Hamie rose again, and waited while the room slowly became quiet as before.

"I have developed the beginnings of an agreement among our countries for that purpose. It is far from complete and will require much work before it is finished. I propose we form an organization which would operate somewhat like the United Nations, but be composed only of those Arab nations of our choosing. This organization would have the authority to impose discipline on any member nation which used the benefits of our collective efforts on other member nations. I believe such an organization would work."

"And who would be the leader of this group?" came a quick question.

"The leader doesn't matter," he said. "The group would vote on any action."

"And how would the world see this group?"

"The world wouldn't see this group at all. We would meet in secret, just as we are doing here. For all the world knows, we are meeting to discuss the price of real estate in the desert. Surely, we wouldn't tell our friends across the oceans that we have instituted a new organization to spy on them and infiltrate their governments."

There was a lot of murmuring around the room, but she could tell he was gaining on them. The simple fact was that what he said was true. It was what he had been saying for many years, and now he had put forth specific proposals which made a lot of sense to them. The room filled with many conversations, which was typical of an Arab conference. As he worked his way around the room, she could see him talking to each of the leaders individually, explaining his ideas and getting commitments to at least consider the plan. Occasionally, he would glance at her and smile as she watched him with admiration and love.

□□□□□

She couldn't be happier, and she wished she never had to leave. Her life had no real memories that went before this room of hers. She had vague memories of her parents and her love for them, but her mind had blocked out all of the specifics before waking in this room those many years ago. He, Sawsan, Nofa, and Ahmad were her family, and this was her home.

Early in the morning, she had ridden out into the desert on her horse, an Arabian she had named Satan after the black stallion in the books she had read as a young girl. The horse had been a present from him when she had graduated at the top of her class from prep school in England. Satan was still a strong stallion, large and black, and was kept in good condition by the stable crews. She loved to ride him as fast as he would go and let his black mane flow with her black hair until those watching couldn't tell them apart. She had returned from her ride and taken a bath in the very tub in which she had her first bath. Sawsan had tended to her needs, but had a new helper. Nofa was getting old and was sick. They had gone by to see her this morning, and the visit had cheered the old woman.

She was not surprised to see all of the western conveniences which had been added to her room. From makeup to hair dryer, everything was there. As she finished dressing, there was a knock on the door, and Ahmad was there when she opened it.

"He would like to see you before we leave," he said.

"I'm ready," she said. "Let me get one last thing." She returned to the table and picked up the chain and locket and handed it to Ahmad to put around her neck. She tucked it safely under her sweater and pressed it with the palm of her hand, making sure Ahmad could see that she was pressing it against her breasts. She looked directly into his eyes as she turned to the door to leave the room, but Ahmad gave no outward sign of noticing her attentions, and followed her as she left the room.

He was in his study, and no matter how many times she had been through the procedure before, she still got butterflies in her stomach as she waited when Ahmad went in. Never before had she been turned away, but she was always fearful that he wouldn't have time or some emergency would arise to prohibit their meeting. Presently, Ahmad opened the door and reached out his hand. She put her hand in his huge grip, and he led her into the room, left and shut the door behind him.

"And so, another visit has come to an end," he said, coming to meet her. There were the familiar kisses on each of her cheeks.

"Yes, it has been wonderful. I am so pleased you arranged it."

"It may be the last visit for awhile. At least until you get settled and we can make some plans."

"Settled? I thought I was settled."

"I would like for you to use whatever contacts and influence you have and relocate to Washington. There, I would like for you to secure a job in the office of a United States Senator. I believe you work with a Mr. Stork?"

"Yes," Sharifa said. "I am sure he will be helpful."

"I understand your relationship is such that he will. You have done well. I will also have some of our people who spend a lot of money with Mr. Stork speak to him and solicit his assistance. Here is a list of four senators. Any of them will suffice. Two are close acquaintances of Mr. Stork. There is also another list of other prominent Washington politicians, bureaucrats and military personnel. I would like for you to get to know each of them as well as you can. Intimately, if possible. On each of these, I want you to develop your own personal information file. Ways in which they can be influenced. Vulnerabilities. Weaknesses of the flesh. Some of that information is already included with the list. Some are marked as only rumors which I would like for you to confirm. A time will come when you will have to use this file to get information from these people or to influence their actions."

"I understand," she said, putting the envelope in the pocket of her jacket.

"Some of these are women," he said. "Will that be a problem for you?"

"No," she said, but she avoided any contact with his eyes as she answered.

"If you encounter any situations in which you need help, you should communicate them to me." Sharifa remembered the promotion which had been blocked for her at the law firm by an ambitious young lawyer. She had made the point in her communications, and shortly, the young man had not been in his job. Sharifa had not asked what had happened to him, and she had been given the promotion the next month.

"This may not always be pleasant," he said. "Especially if you have developed a fondness for any of these people."

"That will not present a problem," she said.

"If my plan for our people is to work, I must be able to show the others what I propose is possible. That alone will be worth what we have sacrificed to achieve your position. You will be the foundation for bringing the Arab nations together, and will be a hero to your people."

224

"I am honored by the faith you have placed in me," she said.

"In all of this, it must never be revealed to anyone in America, friend or enemy, why you want the information or why you want certain things done. It must be made to seem there is some other reason."

"Yes."

"Once you are settled in Washington and have secured a position, contact Ahmad in the same manner you have in Boston. In the meantime, there are additional funds in the safety deposit box in your bank. Feel free to use this money in any way you see fit to support the mission you have been given. That is its purpose."

"I will spend it wisely," she said

"I know you will." He came to her and was about to place his hands on her shoulders. She reached for his hand and knelt to the floor. With bowed head, she brought his hand to her lips. Holding his hand, she rose and looked into his eyes. He kissed her on both cheeks and embraced her.

"I love you," she said.

"Yes, and I love you, too, little desert flower. Go with Allah."

Middle East crisis--pentagon adv2 8-90
Iraq invades Kuwait
USWNS Military News
adv aug 12 1990 or thereafter

By GEORGE GROWSON

WASHINGTON—Massive tank and foot soldier units from Iraq
today invaded the country of Kuwait in a lightning attack
reminiscent of the German blitzkrieg of World War II. The
entire country was overrun in a matter of hours. Some
limited resistance rapidly faded as the magnitude of the
invading forces became apparent. Thousands of Iraqi tanks
and tens of thousands of troops poured over the border into
Kuwait.

Kuwaiti refugees fled across the border into Saudi
Arabia seeking safety from the invaders; it is rumored that
the royal family of Kuwait is establishing a government in
exile in Riyadh, the Saudi Arabian capital. Casualties in
Kuwait are unknown, but stories of mass executions of
Kuwaiti loyalists, including women and children, are
already circulating.

TEN

They'll have to come to me.

The television in the corner flashed from Atlanta newsrooms to Baghdad motel rooms, dramatically illustrating the full-scale invasion and thus the full-scale war. The television reporters predicted the American reaction, and Jeff was convinced that the president would use this opportunity to make sure he would never be called a wimp again. Recognizing his potential role in the conflict, Jeff had called a mandatory attendance staff meeting for nine o'clock. His plan was to work out the logistics of placing PATRIOT in the war, should that step be necessary. In his view, U.S. involvement in the war was inevitable, and he was going to be ready.

The group attending the meeting was the smallest required to get the job done. A television in the corner broadcast CNN with the volume muted. Jeff wanted it on so that the staff would know why they were there before the meeting even started. Broadcast TV was never watched in a military office unless there were far-reaching national consequences at stake. Jeff had his own sources of intelligence through Army channels, and was pretty well abreast of the military situation, so the TV was there mainly for the effect.

It was entertaining to watch the news reporters pretending to be seasoned military experts. The media was already beginning to bring in analysts from the outside, many of whom were retired military personnel Jeff had worked with in the past.

As Jeff entered the room, all of the attendees stood.

"Take your seats," Jeff said. "We have a lot of work ahead of us. While I have received no official direction, I am convinced that once the military situation in the Middle East is fully assessed, it is inevitable that some defense against Iraq's surface-to-surface missile force will be required, and PATRIOT is the only hope of providing that defense. Before you say it yourself, I will say it for you. Our program is not yet ready, and we are unproven as a missile killer. We have had only one test since the failure this spring, and although it was successful, we have not thoroughly demonstrated that we can kill Iraq's missiles. Our systems are not deployed in any region remotely close to the area of interest. We have no missiles other than three experimental prototypes, and we're nine months and a lot of money we don't have away from an up-and-running production line.

"But my instinct is that we will be asked to participate. At least we will be asked *if* we can participate. When I'm asked that question, I want to be able to give the best informed answer I can. So here's what we need:

"We are going to prepare a plan to take us from where we are today to a full scale deployment of PATRIOT in the Middle East. We'll need several alternative plans that can go with whatever might develop in the area. The primary plan to take the systems into Saudi Arabia will receive the highest priority. From there, we'll need a backup in case Iraq continues their advance and captures Saudi before we can get U.S. forces in that country. The plan also needs to include an option for deployment to Israel."

Jeff passed a stack of papers down the table and asked each person in the room to take a copy.

"We need to be able to answer a lot of questions. If the accelerator were pressed to the floor, how quickly could missiles be produced? How many by when? How quickly could soldier crews be trained? Could we use contractor personnel if it were necessary? How many systems could be sent, when, and from where? What equipment would be required to transport the PATRIOTs and their crews to the Middle East? What seaports and airports could be used? What critical tests would need to be completed? How long would it take? What's the total inventory of Iraq's surface-to-surface missile arsenal? What types of warheads do they have? What is the maintenance status of our fielded PATRIOT systems? What supply of repair parts is available? I have all of this and some more on the handouts, with assignments. Steve Smith will be the central point for coordination."

"The real kicker," Steve Smith said, "is how many systems will be required. We'll start some analytical runs with our computer simulations to try to get a handle on not only that, but also on where the systems should be geographically placed. I think we have some idea of the location of the most valuable Saudi assets, but a lot will be contingent on where the U.S. forces settle if and when they go into the area."

"We'll just have to make some assumptions," Jeff said. "We can refine them as we get more information during the next few days. The important thing is to get started and establish a baseline set of analyses which can show what PATRIOT can and can't do as far as protecting assets. I can almost guarantee you that someone will ask for that in the next few days."

"We already have some information we generated in contingency exercises this summer," Steve said. "We'd planned on using that type of data to support the funding battle for the completion of the program. It won't match the current situation exactly since Kuwait is no longer with the good guys, but it'll be pretty close and a good starting point."

"Good," Jeff said. "We'll need to work the performance aspect of our story hard. What PATRIOT can and can't do is the heartbeat of this story, and it has to be told right."

"The biggest hole we have is information on the type and quantity of Iraq's missiles," Steve said.

"Tell me about that," Jeff said.

"Hussein has modified the SCUDs he bought from the Soviets. We don't know anything about those modifications, except some sketchy information from some unclassified journals. Saddam fired some of the modified types in the war with Iran, but what they are exactly, we don't know. Worse still, we don't know how PATRIOT will perform against them."

"What's our best guess?"

"We don't have a clue."

"Get a special task group working on that," Jeff said. "Get some people from the Missile and Space Intelligence Center in the group, and let's get the best package we can."

An outline was developed for a complete plan which would be prepared as a presentation. This was to be the number one priority of the project. The group would meet every morning at eight and afternoons at three to review the status of all areas of the plan. A first draft with blanks for any unknown information would be reviewed on the second day.

Jeff returned to his office and sat down to formulate the overall plan from the top level.

Laura stuck her head in the door. "General, someone's on the phone who says he is from the Chairman's office."

"Well, that didn't take as long as I thought it would," Jeff said.

Everyone in the Army knew what "the Chairman" meant. The Chairman of the Joint Chiefs of Staff. In this case, General Colin Powell.

"General Weyland speaking."

"Sir, this is Colonel Sampson from General Powell's office. We're forming some preliminary plans here, and those plans include PATRIOT. We've contacted Fort Bliss for assistance on the PATRIOTs which are currently deployed, but we also need some help in the anti-missile area. I can't say much on the phone, but we're going to want to talk to somebody in your office about what PATRIOT can and can't do."

"We stand ready to help in any way, Colonel," Jeff said. "We just started this morning pulling together some information here on that very thing. Is there anything you need right away?"

"No, I just wanted to make contact to let you know that what we're doing is probably going to involve PATRIOT. When will you be ready to make a presentation here?"

"By the first of the week for sure."

"That should be good. I'll be in touch as things develop."

Jeff hung up the phone and wrote a note to be copied for each of the participants of the morning meeting to let everyone know of this latest development. As he walked out the door to hand the note to Laura, she met him coming in. "There's a Mr. Max Fisher from Raytheon on the phone for you."

Jeff returned to his desk. "Hello, Fish. How's everything in the frozen north?"

"A perfect summer day. I called to let you know what I've found on your piece of hidden software." It took Jeff a moment to remember what Fish was talking about.

"I'd forgotten," he said.

"In fact, so had I," Fish said. "I'd made a so-so look after you were here this spring and found nothing. I decided it was going to take some special effort and made a plan to get to it, but never did."

"So why now?" Jeff asked.

"You remember the failure we had when the range safety radar blew up the missile?"

"Yeah, I remember. Not a good day." Jeff remembered the frustration he'd felt and the problems that failure had caused the program.

"Well, before we found out the range safety radar had blown the missile, we started an exercise here to trace all the software links to the command destruct to try to find out what happened."

"Yeah, I remember. Your man Sammy Herborn told me at WSMR," Jeff said.

"We shut that down after we got the word on the range safety radar, but the printouts were completed and stored in the computer room. I was going through the other day cleaning out some space and saw the printouts. Out of curiosity, I started looking through them and found something interesting."

"What was that?" Jeff's mind was on his task at hand and he wasn't concentrating on Fish's monologue. He had a legal pad on his desk and was making some notes on the plan to put PATRIOT in the Middle East.

"I started sketching out all of the software routes that could produce a command destruct, and there was one that didn't fit. That's a pretty sensitive function, and I'm damned familiar with anything that could cause a missile to blow. One route came from an area of the software that didn't make any sense."

"Yeah," Jeff said. By now, even Fish could tell he wasn't interested.

"Sir, would you like for me to call you back some other time?" Fish asked.

"No, go ahead, and don't call me 'sir'."

"Well, I printed out this section of the code and there was no reference to the command destruct. I thought maybe the software had been changed since the flight, so I went to the PATRIOT library and got the tapes for that flight. I printed out the same set of software, and still nothing."

"So what does that mean?" Jeff asked, trying hard to sound interested.

"Nothing yet. I took the flight tape and reran the trace software we used when we had the failure. It gave me the same results."

"So what do we have? A glitch in the software, maybe?"

"No. I'm almost finished. I did a bit-by-bit scan of the software on the tape. There's a small chunk of program on the tape that the reader wouldn't take. It has to be the section of code that deals with the command destruct, because all other references are accounted for. To go beyond this point is going to take some heavy work, but I just thought I'd let you know what I've found."

"Is that it?" Jeff asked.

"Except for several observations. First, that little bit of code was not put there by Raytheon, at least not officially. We have very rigid standards for deliverable operational code, and it definitely doesn't qualify. Second, I don't know if it requires an input from the operator or not like you saw, but what we have here is definitely a piece of unauthorized code of some sort which deals with the command destruct."

"What are you going to do now?" Jeff was interested now, but his mind kept turning back to his mobilization plan.

"Well, if you want, I can keep trying to find out what this code is. We have a little slack time now, and I should be able to get to it."

"I have a feeling your slack is about to go away."

"You mean the Iraq thing?"

"Yeah. The Iraq thing."

"Are we going to play?"

"Probably. Everything's uncertain at this point. If you have any loose ends, better start tightening them up."

"I heard that. I'll be in touch."

"Yeah. Thanks for the call. Good work, and keep me posted, will you?"

"You bet, Cap'n."

As Jeff hung up the phone, Laura looked around the corner again. "General, Colonel Sampson is on the line again."

Jeff picked up the phone again.

"This is General Weyland, Colonel. You're working fast."

"Good morning again, General. Sir, General Powell would like to talk to you. If you'll wait just a second, I'll let him know you're on the line."

After a long pause, a familiar voice came on the phone. "Good morning, General Weyland. This is Colin Powell."

"Good morning, General," Jeff said. Jeff wondered if he was going to feel this intimidated when he got to the Pearly Gates and was introduced to St. Peter. He decided not.

"First," General Powell said, "I want to congratulate you on the success you've had with your program there. I have to be objective as the chairman, but I can't help taking great pride in an Army program that has been as successful as yours."

"A lot of effort by a lot of people has gone into the program, sir."

"If I was calling you to chew your tail because of a failure, would you be putting the blame on others, General?"

"No, sir."

"No, you wouldn't, would you? No program succeeds without an outstanding leader. Other things and other people are required, but no undertaking succeeds without a good leader."

"Yes, sir. Thank you." Jeff waited.

"I'm going to assume you are knowledgeable about the full situation. I am most interested in what you think your program can do for us in what may or may not become a major conflict which may or may not involve U.S. soldiers. I know what Iraq has and what you claim your missile can do. Are you prepared to stand behind those claims?"

"Yes, sir. The only question is one of time. I assume we don't have much."

"That's an understatement and an area over which we may not exercise complete control. I need to know what you think of all this. When do you think you could come to Washington?"

"I told Colonel Sampson that we will have a preliminary presentation by the first of the week."

"I'm more interested in what you think, not so much what you can present. And I'd like to meet you before all of this gets so tangled that we won't have time to talk. When can you come?"

"I can be there as soon as you need me, sir. There's a flight tonight."

"That should work. I have some meetings across the river in the morning. Why don't you plan to be here right after lunch?"

"I'll be there."

"Is there anything we can do for you from this end in the meantime?"

"We seem to have a great big zero when it comes to knowing what Saddam has done to modify his SCUDs. Any information you can provide in that area would help."

"I'll have Colonel Sampson get some people working on it."

"We'll be setting up a special working group here for that purpose. Have him get in touch with Steve Smith."

"Good. When you get here, ask for Colonel Sampson. He'll know what's going on."

"Yes, sir."

"I'll see you tomorrow, then."

❑❑❑❑❑

Doug Glover left the Raytheon plant at Andover and drove to the White Horse Tavern. He ordered scotch and took it with him to the pay phone.

"Hello." The voice brought a flood of memories and a quick arousal.

"I think we may have a problem," he said.

"What kind of problem?" The voice reminded him of black silk.

"They're looking at the software again."

"I thought you said they couldn't find it." Just a hint of accusation.

"I said they wouldn't see it if they weren't looking."

"Why are they looking?"

"I don't know. I just know they are."

"Who?"

"My boss, Max Fisher again. As far as I know, he's the only one. But he's enough. A guy who knows the software as well as he does will find it sooner or later if he knows to look for it."

"How did you find out he was looking?"

"The first time was when I called you several months ago. After that, Max had me make some runs for him on the machine. The setups seemed to indicate he was looking for something below the master code. I made sure the runs wouldn't show anything. Then he quit. Then it started again in the last few days. He was looking at some old printouts and asked me about the code."

"Did you find out who he's talking to?"

"His name is Weyland. General Weyland. He and Max are old buddies from when Max was in the Army."

"Is he still looking?"

"I don't think so, but I don't know. He usually asks me to make the runs for him, and he hasn't made any runs this time. He was just looking at these old printouts. We're starting to get real busy here thinking we're going to send the system to the war. Do you want me to ask him about it?"

"No, just keep your eyes and ears open."

"I'm scared. If Max finds that code, he'll know there aren't many people who could put it there."

"Don't worry. I told you we would take care of any problems."

"You told me lots of things."

"What do you mean?"

"Are you coming here soon?"

"No."

"Can I come there?"

"No."

"Why?"

"That's over now. Just do what you're told."

"I can still remember the weekend we had in the apartment in Washington. I've never felt like that with a woman before."

"And how are your wife and children?"

"Fine," he mumbled into the phone.

"Do you still have the pictures I sent you?"

"No," he said and immediately put his hand over his mouth, choking back a wave of nausea. "I told you the last time that I shredded them." She had sent two pictures to his office. One was of him and his wife and children in front of their church and the other was the two of them in the bed of the apartment in Washington. A note made it clear there were many more.

"Do you need me to send you some more?"

"No."

"Good. You call me if you find out anything else." She hung up.

He went back to the bar. The bartender looked at him with that professional bartender question on his face, and Doug raised two fingers to indicate he wanted a double.

ꆆꆆꆆꆆꆆ

Jeff strained to see the house numbers on the dark street. He found the address written on the piece of paper in his hand, parked the car, and followed the curved sidewalk to the front door.

"Well, I'll be." The woman who answered the door was about forty, blonde and attractive.

"Jan," Jeff said. "It's good to see you."

"Billy said you were coming by, but I didn't believe it. It's good to see you, too." She put both arms around his neck and they held each other tight.

"Hey there, not too much of that," Billy said as he came around the corner. "You know how these bachelors can be, Jan." They all laughed.

"Can I get you something before you two settle in?" she asked.

"If you have any Jack Daniel's, I'll have some," Jeff said.

"Billy brought some home. He said you wouldn't have changed." She went off toward the back of the house.

"We can talk in here," Billy said, and headed for the living room.

They exchanged family stories for a few minutes while they waited for Jan to bring the drinks.

"So what's on your mind?" Billy asked. "You sounded sort of mysterious on the phone."

238

"Well, I'm not sure where to begin or even if you're the right person to talk to. I know you transferred to the Intelligence Corps after we left Vietnam. Other than the fact that you went to work for the government after you retired, I don't know what you've been doing."

"Why don't you just tell me, and then I'll let you know what I think." Billy said.

Jeff went through the story as best as he could. He started with the accidental glimpse of the operator's entry into the console and his casual inquiry into the incident and ended with Fish's call earlier in the day.

"Christ, I bet I haven't thought about ol' Fish for ten years," Billy said. "How's he doing?"

"Great," Jeff said. "He's in a good position at Raytheon and has a good professional reputation. He has a gaggle of kids and I'm the godfather of his oldest."

"So what are you looking for from me?" Billy asked.

"I was wondering if you had run across anything like the bad guys tampering with the software on Army systems."

"What is Fish doing now?"

"Probably nothing. When he called, I was preoccupied with the activity in Iraq and really just put him off. Later, I started thinking about it some more, and decided it was probably too important for the brush-off I gave him. I called Fish back late in the afternoon, but couldn't get an answer. I'm going to call him in the morning and have him step up the intensity."

"It sure would be interesting to know what that little bit of code does," Billy said.

"It's interesting you haven't said if this is your job. From your tone, I assume you're interested."

"Sure, I am. For old time's sake if nothing else."

"Fish made it clear that analyzing the code wasn't going to be easy," Jeff said. "I don't know whether that means a few hours or a few months. Plus they are about to be hit with a lot of activity based on the developments in the Middle East."

"Is PATRIOT going to Saudi Arabia?" The question seemed to be of more than passing interest to Billy.

"I may know more about that after my meetings tomorrow, but right now, I haven't the foggiest. My guess is it depends on whether we send in U.S. troops. It's my opinion that if we do, we'd be crazy to send them in without some protection from Iraq's SCUDs. PATRIOT gives at least the hope of that. It's not perfect, but it sure beats the next best alternative."

"Which is?"

"Which is when you hear the SCUD coming, you crawl into a hole, tuck your head between your legs and kiss your ass good-bye."

"Nice alternative."

"You really didn't answer my question," Jeff said. "Have you seen any other evidence of the bad guys tampering with operational software code on U.S. weapons?"

"No, this would be the first, if that's what it is. What you could easily have is some eager young engineer who put a piece of test code in the software for an experiment or something and then forgot to take it out."

"I didn't ask him that specific question, but I got the sense that Fish was convinced an accident was not a possibility. The code appears to have some technique which allows it to hide itself and not be easily discovered. That doesn't sound like an accident to me."

"Does anyone else have direct access to the code except Raytheon?"

"Not at the moment. The government will bring on its satellite system for control of the software worldwide in the next month or two, and then all of the software will be controlled from Huntsville. But for now, it's all still done by the contractor. There's the ability to make small changes at the range for tests, but that's monitored pretty closely, and again, it's only done by Raytheon. One slip of the finger by an overambitious programmer could foul up a lot of work."

"Tell me about this satellite system."

"It's pretty straightforward. There are several hardware versions of the PATRIOT system in the field. Some are in various stages of receiving upgrades, some belong to foreign countries which may not have the latest changes, and some are just newer models. We'll maintain the correct software configuration for each of these different hardware versions in Huntsville and send out the proper code changes via satellite whenever there's a change. That saves us from having to send out classified tape cassettes all over the world and precludes the probability that a human error will send the wrong tape to an operational site or that a tape will be lost and fall into the wrong hands. It's also a lot quicker and the record keeping is better and easier."

"So there will be an operational link into the software to all PATRIOT systems all of the time?"

"In peacetime, it will be only at scheduled times. During combat, it will be operational 24 hours a day. That way, we can get the latest changes to the critical sites essentially instantaneously."

"Do you have any real reason to believe there's a connection between the entry you saw in the console and the hidden code Fish has found on the tape?" Billy asked.

"Good point. No, I don't. In fact, I can easily convince myself that there is no connection, and that they're both completely independent occurrences. That's why I came to you—to see if there is any history of this type of thing that might make this case into something."

"No, there isn't, and I tend to agree with you," Billy said. "It probably is just a coincidence and nothing to it. I'll check around with some friends and see if anyone else has ever run across something like this and also make some phone calls. But my guess is it's going to be a dry well. Tell me about your meetings tomorrow."

"Not much to tell," Jeff said. "The Chairman wants my opinion on the situation and what PATRIOT can or can't do to help. I assume he's considering a deployment of U.S. troops to the area and they're worried about what Saddam can do with his missiles."

"A good thing to be concerned about," Billy said. "Have you seen the intelligence estimates on how many missiles the ol' boy has?"

"Yes, I have," Jeff said. "My two main concerns are not so much how many he has, but how has he modified them and what type of warheads he has on them."

"Both of those are good questions, and I'm afraid we don't really have solid answers for you. We know he has chemicals since he used them in Iran. We think he has biologicals, but we're not sure if either one of them is on the SCUDs."

"What do you know about his modification of the SCUDs?"

"Not much more than you can read in the papers," Billy said. "The Al Hussein is his modified version of the SCUD-B he bought from the Ruskies. It's several feet longer for added propellant, which allows it to fly to about 400 kilometers. I've seen copies of your presentation on the missile threat in the Middle East. You're pretty much on target with what we see there. There are a few pieces of new information we have that you don't. I'll see they get to you."

Jeff gave Billy a quick look at the reference to the presentation, showing that he didn't realize his material was being reviewed by intelligence organizations. Billy noticed his reaction.

"Look," Billy said, "I can't call you on the phone and tell you stuff out of channels. One way to help, though, is to get a copy of what you're thinking and if you're getting off track, send a little subtle help your way."

"Subtle help?" Jeff's face showed his puzzlement.

"Yeah," Billy said. "Remember this spring when you were doing your analysis of the Korean theater? Midway through the exercise there was a new intelligence analyst at Redstone Arsenal from Washington on a temporary assignment who had some free time and helped you with updated estimates on the North Korean missile inventory. Remember that?"

"Yeah," Jeff said, "he was a sharp young man, very helpful. I don't think our work would have been nearly as good if he hadn't been there. He seemed to always be able to get the interesting pieces of data we couldn't."

"The truth is," Billy said with the beginning of a smile, "your results would have been almost meaningless without his input."

"Do I infer that you sent him to Huntsville to keep me from making a public display of my stupidity?"

"No," Billy said with a big smile. "That would have been outside my area of authority and a blatantly illegal use of government funds. Plus, it's a violation of the intelligence community's sacred code."

"Which is?"

"Don't tell 'em nothing."

242

"I think I'll have a little more of your Jack, and maybe a place on this couch doesn't look too bad for the night."

The conversation drifted to the inevitable.

"Have you talked to any of the other guys besides Fish?" Billy asked.

"Not in several years," Jeff said. "But I think about 'em often."

"Yeah, me too. Every now and then something comes up at work that takes me back to those times, and I think about those guys. It was a good group,"

"You can say that again,"

"It was a good group," Billy said with a one-sided smile. "We really stuck by each other."

"I know what you're thinking by that smile," Jeff said. "And we made a commitment we weren't going to talk about that night ever again."

"Yeah, but it was a hell of a night. You'll have to admit that."

"I'll drink to that," Jeff said.

"Have Guns, Will Travel," Billy toasted and held his drink upward.

"To the Paladins, one and all," Jeff responded, and touched the glass of his best friend.

"To those still with us…"

"And to those who aren't…"

"Forever and ever…"

"Amen."

Middle East crisis--pentagon adv7 8-90
Iraq masses troops in Kuwait—Saudi Arabia seeks U.S. support
USWNS Military News
adv aug 7 1990 or thereafter

By GEORGE GROWSON

   WASHINGTON—Iraqi tanks and troops continued to pour into
the Emirate of Kuwait today. There is no official estimate
of how many Iraqi soldiers have now crossed the border, but
the number is assumed to be in the hundreds of thousands.
Today in an official press release, the U.S. State
Department said that troops, tanks, and equipment are being
massed in battle positions near the border between Kuwait
and Saudi Arabia. King Fahd of Saudi Arabia has reportedly
dispatched his grandson, Prince Khalid, on an emergency
mission to the United States for meetings with President
Bush and his staff. The prince seeks commitments of rapid
U.S. support in the hopes of preventing an invasion of
Saudi territory.

ELEVEN

August 7, 1990

The Pentagon

Washington, DC

10:15 AM

Somehow, Jeff didn't feel intimidated this time. His relaxed meeting with the Chairman the previous Friday, as well as the way General Powell had made him feel at ease, produced an almost casual atmosphere for this follow-up session. At Friday's meeting Jeff had given his opinion on PATRIOT's capability to engage Iraq's SCUDs. They also had to consider whether or not the U.S. could get PATRIOT to the Middle East in time to be of value if a conflict occurred. A major portion of the discussion had centered around the time left until PATRIOT had to be in the theatre. No one knew Saddam Hussein's plans or timetable, or whether he planned to continue his invasion into Saudi Arabia immediately or sit tight and regroup in Kuwait to see what the west would do. The meeting in General Powell's office had lasted about an hour. After that, Jeff had gone over the draft outline of his plan with Colonel Sampson, who had made some suggestions for improvements to the schedule. Jeff had been surprised that General Grant had not been at that meeting, but, as instructed, he had kept him informed throughout the process.

The room was starting to fill. Staff assistants were coming and going, arranging briefing papers at the places where their bosses would sit. Jeff recognized many of the names from previous meetings, but a lot of them were new. He didn't know how many would attend, but there was a seat designated for the Secretary of Defense. He also noticed that his boss, Lieutenant General Grant, was to be seated next to General Powell.

Jeff was ready. He and his staff, with help from Raytheon, had put a plan together which covered most contingencies. Several major decision points had been inserted in the plan so that corrections could be made as the military situation developed.

Colonel Sampson entered the room and stood just inside the door. As the room quieted, he announced, "Ladies and gentlemen, the Chairman of the Joint Chiefs of Staff," and everyone stood.

As General Powell came into the room, he said, "Please, take your seats. The Secretary will not be here when we start this morning. He is in a meeting with the President at this moment. He asked that we start without him, and he will join us later if he has time. I have asked General Weyland to give us an update on the PATRIOT. He has developed a plan for the deployment of the system to the Middle East which he will share with us now. General Weyland."

Jeff stood and went to the front of the room by the projection screen.

"Good morning, ladies and gentlemen. As General Powell said, I am General Jeff Weyland, Project Manager for the PATRIOT Air Defense Missile built for the United States Army by the Raytheon Company. With me today is Dick Teacher, Vice President for new programs of the Raytheon Company. We have been fielding PATRIOT since the first units were initially deployed to the U.S. Army Europe in 1985, but we are still in a full-blown production program as only about 50 percent of our objective PATRIOT force structure has been manufactured and is operational. Since the days of the initial fielding, we have been working on modifications to the system to provide an anti-missile capability."

Jeff's first chart illuminated the screen.

"The first portion of this effort, called PATRIOT Anti-missile Capability Phase One, or PAC I for short, was fielded last year and is illustrated on this figure. This was accomplished primarily in the system's software and provides a very limited—and I stress limited—anti-missile capability, which gives the PATRIOT system the ability to protect itself and not much more. While it does not contribute significantly to the battle strategy of other Army forces, this limited capability should not be overlooked, since it helps to ensure PATRIOT's presence on the battlefield, even when the going gets a little rough."

248

Jeff made brief eye contact with General Powell, who was watching him intently. When their eyes met, General Powell seemed to relax a little, sat back in his chair, nodded at Jeff, and smiled.

Weren't sure of me, were you?

"This capability was developed because of the rising threat to U.S. forces from attack by surface-to-surface missiles from the Warsaw Pact countries and unaligned Third World nations. The value of PATRIOT to the theater is such that it has to be able to survive attack by missiles and, once they are launched, the only way to do that is to shoot them down. The inherent capability of the system, as it was originally developed, allowed only this self-defense capability."

From the corner of his eye, Jeff could see General Grant scanning the audience, judging reactions to the meeting and the material. Jeff wasn't sure how he was going to respond to all of this. After his meeting with General Powell, he had notified General Grant's office of the schedule for the presentation and asked that, in the interest of time, they not have a trial run with his office. That request had been approved though, Jeff suspected, not without some resentment. General Grant now found himself in the uncomfortable position of having the whole world hear something from his organization while he heard it for the first time, a position he obviously didn't like.

"As we went through the PAC I program, it became apparent to us that additional upgrades could be made to the system that would significantly improve this capability to engage missiles. Some hardware changes to the radar, some more extensive software changes, and some improvements to the PATRIOT fuze and warhead would provide protection not only for ourselves, but to a small region around us as well. This program has been named the PATRIOT Anti-missile Capability Phase Two or PAC II. The changes proposed in this upgrade are not insignificant and not inexpensive, but the PAC II is the only viable and affordable option the country has for providing some level of defense against missile attack for the tactical theater in the very near future. The expected improvements gained from this upgrade were considered sufficient to allow approval for development in the fall of 1989, and we began initial testing last year. We now believe we have the right configuration and are ready to proceed."

Jeff advanced the slide projector. "This chart shows the PAC II test firings we have conducted during this spring and summer. There have been nine tests and eight successes. The one failure was attributed to a non-PATRIOT malfunction in one of the range safety radars, which caused an erroneous command destruct of the missile after a few seconds of flight. On the lower portion of the chart, the targets which were used for the tests are shown together with a comparison to the missiles believed to be in the inventory of Saddam Hussein."

Jeff pushed the slide advance button again.

"This next chart shows the original schedule for the modification program which would take PATRIOT through fielding and upgrade of all U.S. units deployed worldwide. If we get the go-ahead for the program this fall, the first production missiles will be ready for testing late in the spring of 1991. It should be noted again that this is not yet an approved program, and funds for this activity have not yet been allocated. The approval process for that decision is scheduled to take place this month, but I assume that decision will be delayed by higher priorities until the present crisis in the Middle East is resolved."

A slight murmur of discussion started in the room. Jeff spoke a little louder to get everybody's attention.

"This overlay on the chart shows in red the changes which we feel can be made to the schedule to produce the fastest fielding possible. The three main areas affecting the schedule are the production of the upgraded missiles, the modification of the ground systems, and the training of the soldiers. The major bottleneck is the availability of the missile. Currently, there are only three PATRIOT missiles of the PAC II variety in the entire inventory, and all three are at White Sands Missile Range with *Experimental* printed on the side. There are no production missiles available, there is no production line to produce any missiles, and there is no current capability to produce the numbers which would be required to support a major deployment of U.S. forces or to support an allied offensive.

"This next chart shows the number of missiles that could be produced by a maximum effort to modify and expand the basic PATRIOT production lines at Raytheon and Martin Marietta in Orlando. As you can see, if we go to three shifts per day, seven days per week, the numbers grow rapidly. The first missiles would be available by late next month; by sometime in late January, we would have enough missiles to carry on a protracted conflict." Jeff could hear another buzz of muted conversation around the room in response to the numbers and dates, but he couldn't hear whether this group thought they were going to be good enough or not.

"This next chart shows the transportation needed to airlift PATRIOT to the Middle East." This time, there was no mistaking the reaction of the audience. There was an audible gasp at the number of Air Force C5-A aircraft flights required to move the systems, personnel, and associated equipment across the Atlantic, through Europe, and into the Middle East.

"It's clear from these numbers," Jeff continued, "that a significant portion of the country's airlift capability will have to be dedicated to this mission. Not only will it have to be dedicated, it will have to be done early. I strongly recommend that as soon as the ground equipment could be made ready, both it and the troops should be sent to the theater. The reason for this, as I mentioned earlier, is that this equipment is still experimental. The test area at White Sands is similar to the Middle East, but we will need to know how the hardware is going to react in that specific environment and what, if any, changes are going to be required. The more time the troops can have with their hands on the equipment in the environment where the potential conflict will occur, the more likely it's going to work right when it's needed.

"I would now like to discuss the capability PATRIOT has to engage the missiles in the Iraqi inventory. Of their missiles, we are primarily concerned with two: the 150 kilometer range SCUD-B and the Al Hussein. The Al Hussein is a 400 kilometer range modification of the SCUD-B which was upgraded by Iraq after it was received from the Soviet Union. This first chart shows the areas Iraq can engage with those two missiles from the known fixed launcher sites within the country. This overlay shows how those areas increase if mobile launchers are used from other likely positions within Iraq. This last overlay shows the increase in the areas if the mobile launchers are moved into Kuwait."

"Is there any evidence that the mobile launchers have been moved to Kuwait?" The question came from a Navy uniform Jeff did not recognize.

"None that I have, Admiral," Jeff said. "But you can notice from the chart that it doesn't really matter much, since most of the high value targets in Saudi can be hit without moving launchers into Kuwait. We don't have a good handle on how many mobile launchers they have, but that number is probably more than whatever the official estimate is. Saddam Hussein learned the lessons of camouflage and concealment well, and those launchers could be anywhere, disguised as gas tankers or just hidden in a barn.

"This next overlay illustrates the area on the ground which could be protected by twelve PATRIOT batteries deployed in Saudi Arabia. I use the term *protected* with some degree of reservation. There are several aspects of engaging these missiles with PATRIOT which are somewhat uncertain. First, we have a limited amount of test data. On the one hand, there are more tests we could do. On the other, that would consume missiles which might better be saved for engagement of SCUDs until we know how much time we will have. But without additional tests, we just don't have much hard information on how well our warhead will perform in combat.

"Second, we're not really sure of the kill we can achieve. Obviously, we don't have SCUDs to use for practice, and since we've never even seen one of these Al Husseins, we're not really sure how hard or soft they are. All we have is our calculations and a lot of laboratory data on things we think look like them.

"Third, our design goal was for what we called a mission kill. That is, we wanted to protect specific areas on the ground during combat. That means if we didn't cause a catastrophic explosion of the incoming missile's warhead, but did in fact cause it to miss its target, we had achieved our mission. If the enemy's missile landed somewhere else and detonated, it could still cause damage in a real-life situation, but we would have achieved our immediate mission by knocking it off course from its intended target.

"Fourth, *protected* has to be understood to be within some statistical uncertainty. Not every shot will be a success. This chart shows our current estimate of the probability of a successful mission kill in several different environments. Not only will the things I mentioned earlier have an effect, but factors such as weather, the distance the PATRIOT missile has to fly before the intercept, and any debris which might be in the sky will all influence the probability of a successful intercept.

"Last, there's a lot, and I mean a lot, of uncertainty about the warheads Iraq has on their SCUDs and which ones they might use against our forces. The business of engaging something other than a conventional high-explosive warhead is still more art than science. If Iraq chooses to use chemical, biological, or even nuclear warheads, the decision quickly becomes one of national policy rather than PATRIOT capability. That's an oversimplification, but still true."

"Do we think he will use them?" General Grant asked.

"I think," General Powell said, "that we will have to assume he will use everything he has. We will have to prepare ourselves for the worst."

"This map shows the deployment of PATRIOT systems around the world. The systems owned by the United States are shown in green, while those from our allied nations are shown in blue. This overlay shows which systems would be easiest and quickest to get into the Middle East theater. Of course, that would be a decision for someone outside my office, but as the developer, we keep up with this information. I would assume others would come to the same conclusions my office has about which ones to move. I discussed this with General Smythe at the U.S. Army Air Defense Artillery School at Fort Bliss, and he concurs with the plan. The systems kept on the highest state of alert for reaction to situations such as this are at Fort Bliss, and they should be the first to go. The next priority is the units deployed on fixed sites in Europe, specifically in Germany.

"This last chart is a summary of what I have presented in the performance area. Remember that these numbers are largely the result of computer simulations and not a lot of test data. The numbers are based on the deployment of the twelve systems I mentioned earlier, and they reflect our best estimate on the percentage of SCUD missiles we could expect to kill outright with an unqualified kill, as well as the percentage we would expect to at least damage or knock off course."

"Why would we care about knocking them off course since we think the missile is so inaccurate anyway?" More input from the Navy, Jeff noted.

If there was going to be any real competition for the PATRIOT in the future, it would be from the Navy's Aegis system with the Standard Missile.

They're stewing in their juices at the attention the Army's getting.

"Even though we believe the SCUD missiles are inaccurate, the targets are large—Riyadh airport, for example, or large concentrations of Allied ground forces. A few SCUDs landing in the port where the Navy is unloading their ships could disrupt the entire timetable of a deployment."

"Are they really that inaccurate?" General Grant asked.

"They certainly were at one time, but we don't know if the Iraqis have made any improvements to the missile guidance. We don't think so, though I imagine there are people in this room who could address that better than I. But if they have, then they can choose their targets with care and engage them with precision. In that case, knocking the missile off course would be a good thing. In either case, there isn't any way to know what the result will be on each firing. You can't choose which target you will kill and which you will cripple. These numbers are what we believe the statistical average will be in the long haul."

"One thing which hasn't been addressed here is cost. Do we know what this speed-up is going to cost?" The question came from Dr. Itsu, the lead cost analyst from the Office of the Secretary of Defense.

"No, Tom, we don't," Jeff answered. "I do have data on what the original program was expected to cost and those estimates are in the packages I provided. They are, incidentally, the same numbers we gave your office this summer. We have done some simple calculations on shift premiums, special fast freight for some major items, those sorts of things, but it's all premature. One thing is sure—it will cost a lot, maybe even double the original estimate." There was another buzz around the room.

"You haven't shown any information on Israel. Do you recommend sending any PATRIOTs to Israel?" asked the Deputy Under Secretary of Defense for International Affairs.

"Mr. Blair, Israel has purchased two PATRIOT units under a foreign military sales case from Raytheon, and those systems are in storage in the country now, awaiting completion of crew training at Ft. Bliss. Those systems are not modified to the PAC II level. Clearly, additional U.S.

PATRIOTs owned and manned by the United States can be sent to Israel, and a good degree of protection can be provided to that country. What we require is a detailed numerical evaluation which looks at the launch points within Iraq, the trajectory the SCUDs would have to fly to make the longer trek to Israel, and where PATRIOTs could be deployed. That research is underway in Huntsville, but no useful information has yet been produced."

"What if the launches came from within Syria?" asked the Assistant Secretary of the Army for Research and Development. "Wouldn't that make it easier for them and tougher for us?"

"Mr. Secretary," Jeff responded, "we will obviously continue to make estimates of as many contingencies as time permits. We have created a team of analysts composed of government folks and contractors. They have been organized into three shifts to study all those possibilities. But the truth is, we just don't have that information yet."

"I was really looking for your opinion rather than an analytical result."

"My personal opinion is that Saddam Hussein does not seem to be putting his troops or equipment on the border with Syria yet, so it doesn't appear that he will attempt a hostile takeover there. The Syrian government may give him permission to bring his equipment in, but I personally doubt that Syria wants to risk totally losing its stable relationship with the West. Based on that, I believe the chances are slim that we will see SCUDs launched from within Syria. However, if he moves his military on Saudi Arabia and is successful in taking all or a large part of that country, I believe all bets are off, and we will have to reassess the situation. Other Arab leaders may rally to his side if they see him start to win against the United States and Saudi Arabia, which he considers to be our puppet. I couldn't even make an educated guess about what might happen then."

"You showed coverage that could be provided by twelve PATRIOTs in Saudi Arabia," said the Army Assistant Chief of Staff for Intelligence. "Why twelve, and have you considered where we might place them if Saudi Arabia is lost before we can get our forces into the theater?"

"To answer the first question, twelve was the number that gave us full ground coverage of the areas we considered to be high priority assets. Those would be deployed as two battalions of six batteries each. As we get further into the analysis, we may find we'll need more systems to engage the numbers of SCUDs available to Iraq. I can't imagine we will need any fewer, but more is a possibility that depends on the quantity of men and material the U.S. sends into the country. As to the second question, we have started an evaluation of areas both within Saudi Arabia in fall-back positions from the current border and areas outside the kingdom where advantageous positions for systems like PATRIOT exist, although there aren't many. Preliminary results from those evaluations should be available by the end of the week. A personal speculation at this point is that there will be at least two fall-back lines within Saudi Arabia where positions could be established with PATRIOTs, but that obviously depends on whether or not the combat forces are deployed."

"If you are going to meet the schedule you projected, when do you need the go-ahead?" General Powell brought the room to silence with his question.

"Our plan calls for a decision by the day after tomorrow. After that, almost everything will be delayed until we get a full go-ahead. There's a lot we can do without the decision, but there is also a lot we can't. It all depends on the availability of money."

As Jeff scanned the room, he noticed that General Powell was now looking directly at him. Jeff glanced around the room, but when he looked back, the General was still watching him. Soon the room quieted as most people noticed the Chief was going to ask another question.

"General Weyland," he said, "we appreciate your putting this presentation together for us. Now I would like to ask a couple of final questions." His face grew even more intense. "We are going to have to make some very important decisions in the next couple of days which are going to profoundly affect the course our country takes. To do that, we need to have the best information possible. In our business, there are seldom any guarantees, so we have come to rely on judgments and commitments. I ask you. In your judgment, are the plans you have presented here today realistically achievable?"

"Yes, sir, they are." Jeff could feel the sweat under his collar. He wanted to look toward General Grant to gauge his reaction, but could not break the intense stare from General Powell.

256

"And do you give your personal commitment to making them a reality?" The eyes never wavered.

"Yes, sir, I do."

"Well, folks," General Powell said, "unless anyone has any more questions for General Weyland, I think we are finished. I would like to see the members of my staff in my office for a few minutes. General Weyland, thank you very much."

❑❑❑❑❑

"I hope you're aware of the position in which you have placed the United States Army," General Grant said.

"Yes, sir, I am," Jeff said. "General Grant, I am confident that..."

"I don't give one big goddamn about your confidence, Weyland. I'm talking about where you have placed the Army. If we decide to send PATRIOT to the Middle East, and I can't imagine that not happening after your Pollyanna presentation this morning, the Army will have to move ahead with this development without the benefit of a proper evaluation of its merits. Don't you understand that?"

"I understand that that may be the result of the session this morning, but I don't think I had any other choice."

"You had the choice of letting the Army make that decision, General, not the Chairman of the Joint Chiefs of Staff."

"General Grant, I was asked by the Chairman to give my honest appraisal of the role PATRIOT could play in a potential conflict. I did that and no more."

"What you did was give one man's opinion—yours—in place of the leadership of the Army. If that group believes your preposterous claims and then you can't deliver, that stink is going to be rubbed all over the Army. You'll be long gone by then, but it will be the Army who gets the rap for not being able to deliver in a national crisis."

"Sir," Jeff said, "I believe that schedule is achievable. It won't be easy, and I will need some support and quick funding, but it can be done."

General Grant was completely ignoring Jeff.

257

"We probably have some time to recover. I can't imagine that group making any major decisions before the weekend." General Grant was starting to get red in the face. "In the meantime, I want you to start to develop some realistic numbers, and I mean realistic numbers, on how long all of this is going to take, how much it is going to cost, and just exactly how well it is going to work. And I don't want any more mumbo jumbo about 'mission kills' instead of 'catastrophic kills' or 'statistically in the long haul' or 'maybe there are improvements to the guidance.' I want hard numbers. If this thing goes the way I think it will, that whole area over there is going to be filled with high priority assets on the ground, and moving something off course isn't going to be worth a damn. If you can't kill them in the air, you can't do the job."

"Yes, sir," Jeff said. "Do you want me to bring that data to you or to General Powell?"

"What the hell do you think? You're damn right, bring it directly to me. And I want to see it before anybody else even knows it exists. Do you understand that?"

"And if General Powell calls me direct?"

"You just better hope he doesn't." General Grant was up behind his desk and pacing. "I'll send a message down to his office to let his people know I am in charge now, and they'll have to start coming through me."

"Sir, I would like to back up just a minute and try to get you to understand what I was trying to say about PATRIOT's capability in this area."

"General Weyland, I am going to say this one last time. I don't give a rat's ass about what you think your system can or can't do. The issue is that the United States Army is supposed to make the decision on what the United States Army wants to build, not some smart-assed Ph.D. Brigadier General from some Ivy League school."

"Yes, sir, but...."

"Bullshit, General, you gave that group a hyped-up sales pitch just so you could get your program funded and accelerated. You saw that as an opportunity to bypass the entire Army decision-making process and get the golden ring."

"No, sir, I...."

"Don't contradict me, Weyland!" General Grant was shouting and his

258

face was fully flushed. "If you don't begin to get a firmer grip on the reality of who runs this man's Army and who you report to, you may find yourself reporting to a general court martial. Do you understand that?"

"Yes, sir."

"It is my opinion that you have oversold the performance of an experimental system on which there exists almost no meaningful data. If this is true, and this damn thing doesn't work as well as you have advertised, that in itself would be a serious offense. Men may die, Weyland, because of your goddamned schoolboy approach to problem solving. If that happens, and I believe it will, I am going to personally look you up after this thing is over and make sure you get what you deserve!" Saliva was spurting from General Grant's mouth as he yelled.

"This thing of yours is no good for the Army, and before everything is over, you assholes are going to be put in your place. Once you and those dumb sons-of-bitches upstairs realize that systems like this won't work in combat, they'll take another look at how fucked up this high-tech Army they've created really is. Then they'll know that what we need to depend on is men and steel, not transistors. Men and steel, Weyland. When the critical time comes, your sorry goddamned things will fail, and we'll have to rely on men and steel. You mark my words."

General Grant had now come around the desk and was towering over Jeff and bellowing into his face. Jeff knew people outside could hear. He was starting to get nervous, but he didn't know what to do. General Grant's adamant prediction of failure apparently had more basis than the rhetoric of a skeptical observer.

"Sir, you seem to have some information on the performance of PATRIOT which I should know before we make final recommendations on taking the system into a combat zone. If that's the case, I would sure appreciate it if you'd tell me. You said it first—men's lives are at stake here."

General Grant reacted strangely to Jeff's response. He backed away from Jeff and seemed to stare off into space. He walked to the window and looked out. He stood there silent for what seemed to Jeff to be a very long time. Jeff barely heard him when he responded.

"No, General," he said almost in a whisper. "I don't have any information you should have before sending this system into combat. You may leave now."

Jeff started for the door.

"Weyland?" General Grant called him, but was still looking out of the window.

"Yes, sir," Jeff said.

"Just remember, the data comes to me first," General Grant said, almost mumbling. "The data comes to me first."

"Yes, sir," Jeff said and continued toward the door. He looked over his shoulder and General Grant was standing by the window with his hands raised to his face. His head was down, almost bowed and his shoulders had lost their military squareness. His slumped body looked much smaller to Jeff than just five minutes before.

"The data comes to me first," Jeff heard General Grant say again as he pulled the door shut behind him.

ꙥꙥꙥꙥꙥ

"Well," Steve Smith asked as Jeff closed General Grant's office door, "are you still in one piece?"

"To tell the truth, I'm not really sure," Jeff said. "Let's get somewhere we can talk."

They wandered through the Pentagon maze until they came to one of the cafe shops which had a few small tables, ordered Cokes and sat down.

"Steve, I just saw something I really don't understand. General Grant was so certain that we were going to fail that I was almost having doubts myself. Then all of a sudden he seemed to collapse right in front of my eyes. He completely quit communicating and seemed to withdraw into a shell. It was bizarre behavior to say the least."

"Why was he so convinced that PATRIOT will fail?"

"I have no idea. Until we had that meeting with him before we started the testing, I thought he was a supporter. When he turned on me at that session, I knew we had an uphill battle making him

260

understand, but I sure didn't think it was going to be like this. It's one thing to show someone information and let the numbers speak for themselves, but it's something else to try to reason with someone who has his mind as preset as he does. I can't think of any reason for him to feel the way he does."

"Is there some one aspect of PATRIOT that gives him a particular problem?"

"Not that I could tell," Jeff said. "He just seemed convinced that we won't be able to follow through on the plans we presented at the meeting this morning. And I mean convinced."

"What's our plan now?" Steve asked.

"Same plan," Jeff said. "We have to put together the numbers on the basics for General Grant. I want to do that as simply as possible. We'll answer exactly the questions he's asked. Separate from that, full speed ahead on the planning for the accelerated development and fielding. I feel in my bones that General Powell will direct PATRIOT into the area if the President sends U.S. troops into the Middle East. Fact is, he doesn't have any other choice. Whether PATRIOT is good or bad is almost moot; she's all there is, and everybody knows that. If he doesn't do it and we take a hit from Saddam's missiles, he'll be the goat. So if we go in, it's coming. You can count on it."

"I don't think there will be much General Grant or anybody else can do, even if they wanted to," Steve said. "I also don't think he'll buck this thing up the line. When he sees her numbers, even he will see he's fighting a losing battle."

"The only thing is that I have this nagging feeling that there's more to his attitude than shows on the surface. There may be a hidden agenda here, and if so, we're not done with General Grant."

"Let's hope he's playing straight; he's been enough of a pain already," Steve said. "OK, I've got my orders. When are you coming back to Huntsville?"

"Tomorrow," Jeff said with a slight hint of a smile. "Tonight I'm going to do a little reconnaissance and see if I can get a handle on our support on the Hill."

Steve returned the smile.

□□□□□

General Wesley F. Grant felt the silky flesh next to his. How she kept him so close to climax for so long without going over the edge was beyond him. She looked up at him and her eyes smiled as her tongue moved slowly around him. The pleasure she showed at such times heightened the eroticism, and he wondered what he would do without her. He could never go back to the life he had before.

He looked at her in the mirror on the ceiling and admired her covetously. Her head lay on his leg, her hand with the blazing red nails gently teasing his nipples. He was glad he had lost that twenty pounds and still worked out. If he hadn't, she might not be as attracted to him.

He was glad they were able to separate their lovemaking from their business. Politics and the military made strange bedfellows. But now there was a war starting, and things might have to change a little. He hoped it wouldn't interfere with his visits with her in this apartment. He wondered again how much she was paying for a place this nice. He had asked her, but she had made some vague response about family money.

He felt her moving and reached down to stroke her face. She crawled on top of him and sat upright. He stared at her, her hair falling down over her beautiful breasts. God, she was gorgeous! He entered her, and she moaned as she ran her tongue over her lips. She leaned forward until her breasts were suspended just over him and her nipples grazed his face as she rocked. Her moaning became more pronounced as she moved faster. He drew in her buttocks, moving with her thrusts, matching her rhythm. She shook her head wildly, her hair stinging his face and chest.

Her moans became guttural cries, then grew higher. When he began to moan, she moved her hands and knees wide until she was on all fours straddled over him. With his final release, he drove himself into her and she immediately stiffened, arched her back, and pushed down hard on him. She gasped for air, then collapsed as the perspiration from their two bodies soaked the silk sheets.

□□□□□

In the living room, he fixed two drinks while he waited for her to come from the bedroom. When she came into the room, she was wearing the black gown again. He handed her the drink, and she took a sip and then put the glass on the table.

"What's the feeling on the Hill about Iraq?" he asked.

"They want to know how much a war costs," she said.

"Really?"

"They're scared we can't afford it."

"But will they support it?" he asked.

"Probably," she said. "The Democrats' main concern is that the President might come out of this looking so good that he'll win the next election."

"Goddamned politics!" he shouted. "Why can't the sorry bastards at least leave election politics out of international crisis decision-making? Every goddamned decision made in Washington today has to do with some sonofabitch getting elected instead of what's best for the country."

"I know it makes you mad, Wes, but that's the way we make our living on our side. Don't you understand that?"

"Understanding and liking are two different things," he said. "Does the Senator understand that we may have to postpone the little episode with PATRIOT until after this thing is over?"

"No. In fact, he was excited about it. We can't let PATRIOT get so firmly established during the war that our plan won't work afterwards."

"But we're talking about a war here, Cel, not some test range."

"But the Senator has a plan for that. Don't you worry."

"What kind of plan? The damn thing either works or it doesn't. And if it doesn't, people are going to get killed."

"All of that has been thought through and included in the plan. You just need to do your part."

"Well, I'm trying," Grant said. "In fact, I made some moves in that direction today. I believe I may be able to keep PATRIOT out of the war altogether. That way, we avoid the problem completely, and then we can pick back up after the conflict is over."

"That's not what the Senator and his people want you to do. They want you to do everything you can to make sure that PATRIOT is a key part of any forces we send. He said to tell you it was very important."

"That makes no sense to me at all. Like you said, if it works, then we can't undo the glory it will get, and like I said, if it doesn't, people might lose their lives."

"I'm not sure I understand either, Wes, but that's what he said. From what I've been able to hear, they don't think it will be used much, and when it is, it won't matter much."

"That doesn't sound like much of a plan to me, Celia. I would prefer to keep the system from going to the area at all."

"No, that's not acceptable. PATRIOT must be a part of any deployment."

"I'm not sure I can make that happen. The performance of the system will speak for itself."

"The Senator's office has been notified of the President's feelings about a quick response force to be sent into the area." She gathered her legs under her on the couch and turned to face him. The gown fell open enough to show there was nothing on underneath.

"The 82nd Airborne Division will be deployed immediately from Fort Bragg. Senator Strong wants you to make sure that PATRIOT goes in as the second unit."

"That may be only a matter of a week or so. I saw a briefing today that said PATRIOT can't be ready for months, maybe even late January."

"The PATRIOT systems can be shipped in now. Any modifications required can be made later wherever they are positioned, and the new missiles linked up as they become available."

"You sure have learned a lot about this process in a few days."

"The Senator asked me to organize the office for the crisis. It still isn't one of his main interests. He and his staffers are still working on the new health care program full time, so this got dumped on me. I thought it was great since it gave me more time with you."

"Yeah, that part's neat all right, but not the part about PATRIOT. I'm not sure I can make it happen. In fact, I'm still not so sure it's a good idea."

"Oh, it's a good idea," she said with a bright smile. She went to the bar and fixed them both another drink. Her gown was open in the front and he watched as she moved across the room. He looked away from her as she turned to him at the bar.

"Tell me again why it isn't a good idea just to keep the system at home during the conflict? PATRIOT is not on the current list for deployment, at least not the list I have seen. Why not just let nature take its course?"

"No. It's a perfect opportunity to show the world our side of the argument. No one's going to get hurt. The Air Force will have so many planes there, the Iraqis will never dare to fly planes over Saudi Arabia. They only have a few SCUDs, and they don't even know where they are going to land after they fire them. So whether PATRIOT is there or not won't make a difference to anybody but us. And to us, it's everything."

"I don't see it that way," he said. "I..."

"It doesn't matter how you see it, Wessy. Now you just need do this thing the way the Senator's people want it so we can continue to have a good time."

"Are you threatening me?" he asked.

"Only if I have to," she said. She put her hand on his leg and began to stroke.

"I'm afraid the little games aren't going to work this time, Cel. This is serious business. We may go to war. Do you know what that means?"

"I know exactly what a war means, General." She pulled herself away from him, straightened her gown and stood looking down at him. "I know far better than you about war. But this war will be fought with PATRIOT. You will get PATRIOT into the area, and there will be no more discussion." She moved away from him toward the bar.

"Listen, Cel. Let's not fight. This is just something I can't do." He watched as she picked up the remote from the television and moved to the center of the room. She pointed the remote at the television and pressed some buttons.

"What are you doing that for?" he asked as the picture began fading in. "You know I don't like television."

The picture on the screen was two lovers in the throes of sex. He watched, not knowing if this was another of her little games until he realized it was the two of them in her bedroom. A flash on the screen and the video was him and his wife walking in their front yard. Then another flash to the bedroom and to a vivid display of some of her toys in full use. Then his wife at the grocery store. Then him alone on the bed. Him in his uniform leaving the Pentagon. Close-up of him alone on the bed.

His jaw had fallen as he looked from the television to her to the television and back to her.

"I don't understand," he said.

"You're a big boy," she said. "Figure it out."

"You rotten bitch. Who do you think you're dealing with? This kind of low-life blackmail won't work with me. I'll have your pretty ass in jail."

"Maybe so, but don't forget there is a soundtrack which goes along with those tapes and in this room also. If I go to jail, so do you."

She paused. "Wes, look. The Senator and his people have guaranteed me there will be no bad side effects. It's just important that it go their way. We don't even have to tell them that I had to show you the tape, and everything can be just like it was. It's not going to make any difference anyway. And then we can still have each other. Otherwise, your wife is not going to be the only person who sees and hears these tapes."

She pressed her body into his and her voice softened. "On one side is complete disaster for you and me, and on the other side is a chance for us. And the great part is that no one will ever know. They said I can destroy the tapes when this is all over, and then we would have each other forever. Nobody is going to get hurt over this. The SCUDs can barely find Saudi Arabia, much less U.S. targets. Let's give it a try. If it doesn't go like we think it will, we can fix it then."

"How do they know he won't use many of his SCUDs?" he asked.

She was smiling now as she turned off the television with the remote and started to pull the top of the gown down over her shoulders.

"The same way they know everything, Wessy. Here, quit pouting and show me what you can do," she said, pushing her bare breasts against his chest.

weapons systems--pentagon adv16 1-91
U.S. begins liberation of Kuwait with massive air strikes
USWNS Military News
adv jan 16 1991 or thereafter

By GEORGE GROWSON

WASHINGTON—Today, the United States announced the beginning of a combat air campaign against targets in Iraq and Kuwait. As White House Press Secretary Marlin Fitzwater announced, "The liberation of Kuwait has begun," several news agencies reported massive bombings of targets distributed over the entire country. Mr. Fitzwater appeared tired as he addressed the United States' participation with the Arab Coalition in the undertaking. "This is a joint multi-national effort to restore the country of Kuwait to its rightful government," he said. "The United States and our allies are committed to the stability of the Persian Gulf."

TWELVE

January 16, 1991

Crown Plaza Hotel

Crystal City

Arlington, Virginia

7:00 PM

"I'll be damned! He really did it!"

Jeff rocked back in his chair as he listened to the chaotic reports from Baghdad on CNN.

"Didn't you think he would?" Steve and Jeff had been in meetings for two days at the Pentagon, describing the status of the PATRIOT units that had been deployed to Saudi Arabia. Tension and excitement were high everywhere, but there had been no direct indication of when the offensive would be launched. The United Nations deadline for Iraq to withdraw from Kuwait had come and gone on January fifteenth, and that had been the target date for Jeff and the PATRIOT plan. But as the deadline passed with no sign of any activity, Jeff had begun to develop doubts.

"One part of me thought he would," Jeff said, "but I would be lying if I didn't say that way down deep inside, another part of me still thought he wouldn't. I'm proud of him. They can say what they want to say, but this time we have a president who has big brass balls."

"I just know that if he hadn't, a lot of people here would've done a lot of work for nothing."

"In a way that's true, but maybe what we have done is prevent a war. Getting ready for a fight is one thing—and this has been a real circus—but if he could have found a way around it, we would've all cheered him."

"It doesn't feel like it's been nearly five months since the day you got the call from General Powell."

"Yeah. 'General, please get PATRIOT deployed to Saudi Arabia with all due haste.' I could taste parts of my stomach in my mouth."

"I'm glad we weren't responsible for the actual movement of PATRIOT units."

"Yeah. If we'd had much more to do, I don't think we would've made it."

A lot of Jeff's time had been spent developing the capability to update the software by satellite. With the system going into combat for the first time, Jeff knew they would probably need to update the software on a moment's notice. With the satellite, they wouldn't have to fly new tapes over on the twenty-hour trek from White Sands to Saudi Arabia and then get the copies to each PATRIOT site, some of which might be in active combat. That new process had taken a major effort to secure the additional funding, get government control of the software, and then make all of the necessary tests once the systems were in place in the Middle East.

It was all complete now. PATRIOT had been the second major U.S. unit to go into the theater, right behind the 82nd Airborne. Jeff was watching the activity on television like most other Americans.

I've done my job. She's ready, and she'll do hers.

"Where's Suzy?" Steve asked.

"I'm surprised she hasn't called," Jeff said. "We'd arranged to meet for dinner tonight since I'm going back to Huntsville in the morning. After the activity started in Saudi earlier today, I tried to get her at her office, but she'd already left. I don't want to leave this television, but since I don't have any way of getting in touch with her, I guess I'd better go on and meet her."

❑❑❑❑❑

"Someone followed me here."

Jeff could tell something was wrong as soon as he saw Suzy. When he arrived at the trendy Georgetown restaurant, she was already at a table and was obviously nervous.

"You mean like some guy in a James Bond movie?" Jeff asked, the kidding in his voice thinly disguised.

"Jeff, I'm serious," she said. "He followed me from my apartment in a white car, and I'm sure I saw the car come in the parking lot as I came in the front door."

"OK, I believe you. Let's just not let it spoil our dinner. To say I've had a tough day is a major understatement. I've been looking forward to a visit with my good friend Jack and a rare steak since morning."

"I don't feel like eating," she said.

"Are you really that upset? I just assumed it was some clown who passed you on the street and followed you to see if you were alone."

"Maybe, but it could be something more. The world is full of kooks."

"And you're an attractive woman living alone in a very violent city."

"Jeff, a reminder of how violent my city is wasn't what I needed right now."

"Would you rather leave?" he asked.

"Oh Jeff, if you don't really mind, could we? I can't shake the feeling he's here looking at me, and it gives me the creeps. I'm sorry about dinner, but we can go somewhere else."

"How about we pick up some Chinese and take it back to your place?"

"That would be great." She was already standing as she spoke.

"On second thought, your apartment complex may have been where the trouble began. If the creep sees you with me and sees my uniform, he'll have second thoughts, whatever his first thoughts were."

Jeff stood a little taller as he rose from his chair, took some bills from his wallet, and put them on the table.

"Give me your keys, and I'll go get the car and pick you up at the door."

"No way," she said. "Now that you're here, I'm not going to let you get out of reach."

"OK, hold on tight and I'll try to summon some old reflexes that I haven't used in decades."

He put her arm through his and scanned the room as they negotiated the other tables and headed for the door. There were no single men at any tables and nobody watching them as they went through the dining area. No one was moving in the bar, where there were only a few couples.

He waited just outside the door for a moment, peering at the parking lot and street, but saw nothing unusual and no white car. She said nothing as they walked quickly toward her car. He let her in her door, locked it, and came around to the driver's side. As he opened his door, he took one last look in all directions, but didn't see anything unusual. He got in on the driver's side, started the car, and pulled out of the lot. He drove quickly for a few blocks, then pulled into a small parking lot, made a U-turn, and paused close to a building so the car couldn't be seen from the street.

"Do you know what the car looked like?"

"Big and white and fairly new," she said. "That's all I could tell."

They waited a full five minutes. No white car came up the street, nor any car driven by a lone man. He pulled back into the street.

"I think we shook him, whoever he was."

"Or you think my imagination got a little carried away."

"If I thought that, I wouldn't have traded my steak for Chinese," he said, reaching across the seat for her hand and pulling her over to him.

"We can still go out if you'd rather. I know I was probably being silly, but it seemed so real."

"No problem, your place is fine. That way, we won't have to have a designated driver and I can have my Jack and ply you with spirits at the same time."

"And what will you do with me once I'm plied?"

"Why, I'm the Plied Piper, didn't you know? The truth is I would rather be in front of a television right now, anyway. We're missing war as interpreted by the pissants."

"What do you mean?"

"You don't know? The bombing of Iraq started early this evening. I went by the Pentagon before I came to meet you, but there's no indication of what Saddam's reaction is going to be, and it's kind of a tense moment in history. To be honest, if I'd had some way to get in touch with you, I would have been on the late plane to Huntsville this evening. The war is being reported by all of the networks and CNN, and it's really interesting to see them at work."

He drove the car across the Memorial Bridge and went down onto the

George Washington Parkway to make his way back toward Alexandria. He pulled up onto Route One South through Crystal City and into their favorite Chinese restaurant along the strip.

"Come in with me, and we'll have a drink while they dish up some food," Jeff said as he got out of the car.

"Like I said, buster, I'm hanging onto you for the night. I sure wouldn't want you to find another plyee in there and not come back."

Dan Wu made his usual fuss over them when they ordered. He made a double fuss when he found out they weren't going to stay. He put them at a table in the bar and brought a bottle of plum wine. In a few minutes, the food was ready, and they stood to leave. Jeff paid for the bottle of wine, which they also took with them.

As he pulled back onto Route One, he noticed the car in his mirror right away.

Damn. New and white and big.

Suzy saw him looking in the mirror.

"It's him, isn't it?" Her voice had a slight waver. "I can tell without even looking back."

"I don't know, but maybe. Let's just see."

Jeff made an abrupt right turn and the white car followed, but at a distance.

"I don't think he knows we've spotted him," Jeff said, watching in the mirror.

Jeff circled the block and turned back onto Route One as though he had forgotten something and was going back to the restaurant. As he passed the restaurant, he increased his speed, crossed three lanes of traffic and slid onto the ramp for Interstate 395 South.

"What are you doing?" Suzy asked.

"I don't know. I just wanted to make sure he was really following us."

"Is he?" She sat rigidly, not looking back toward their pursuer.

"Yes." Jeff continued increasing speed as the white car began gaining.

"Oh Jeff, I'm scared."

Jeff looked down at the speedometer, which indicated he was nearing ninety.

"Maybe a traffic cop will come after us," Suzy said.

"I don't think that would do much good. He'll just go away and come back later, and then we'll not only have the white car to deal with, but a speeding ticket besides."

"Somehow, a speeding ticket doesn't seem like our biggest problem right now."

"Well, whoever's driving that car probably knows where you live, so it has to be settled in some way. If we can get the license number, then we'll have something."

By this time they were getting out of the dense commercial area. "Funny what goes through your mind," Jeff said. "When I lived out this way with Beth, it took me 45 minutes to get to work every morning. I just made the freeway distance in 10 minutes."

He pulled off onto the next exit ramp. Suzy had huddled down in her seat and was concentrating on the front windshield. She had moved away from Jeff and was clutching the arm rest.

"I'm going to try to find some way to get his license number."

"Why don't we just stop someplace and get help?"

"I already thought of that. He'll just leave and then where'll we be? I want to try to get his number. Can you get it if I try to get us into position?"

"I'll try. I think I have something here to write with."

"Get ready." Jeff began slowing the car. In the mirror, the white car was getting closer. Ahead, there was a fairly large bridge, and Jeff let the car drift to the center of the road. For just a moment, Jeff took his eyes off the mirror as he approached the bridge. The lights in the side mirror caught his attention and by the time he looked in the rearview mirror, the car was beside him.

"Christ!" Jeff shouted as he slammed on the brakes. "Now! Get the number as he goes past!"

In that instant, the other car rammed them and shoved them toward the bridge abutment. Jeff kept his foot hard on the brake and forced their car into the other vehicle and away from the bridge structure. The shrill sound of metal on metal tore the night. Thoughts raced through his mind as the cars pushed at each other like bumper cars at an amusement park.

274

He wanted to look at Suzy, but he couldn't take his eyes from the white car, and the driver behind the wheel who was looking back at him.

He had hit his brakes first, so the white car was moving faster and sliding up toward the front of Suzy's car. He prayed the bumpers didn't hook. As if the other driver realized his original plan wasn't going to work, he pulled away from Jeff and accelerated across the bridge. Jeff pulled hard left on the steering wheel to avoided the bridge abutment and kept his pressure on the brake until they came to a stop on the side of the bridge. The white car had disappeared over the crest, and all was quiet except for their breathing.

"Jesus, are you all right?" he asked. He slid across the seat and pulled her to him. She was crying and shaking, but seemed in control.

"I'm OK," she got out between gasps for air. "Let's get out of here before he comes back."

"Do you have any idea what this is all about?"

"No," she said. "And I don't care. Let's just go."

"Did you get the number?"

"No. I'm sorry, it just happened too fast."

"Yeah, me too. I'm not sure what shape the car is in," he said. "I'm going to get out to check it over."

"No, please," she said, trying to talk while holding back the sobs. "Jeff, let's just go."

"OK."

He started the car across the bridge. The car seemed to run all right, and he didn't hear anything which sounded too ominous. He was about to turn around on the far side when she screamed. He looked up and saw the white car coming directly at them. He slammed the car in reverse and pressed the gas to the floor. He looked over his shoulder to try to drive backward, but his first glance back to the front told him that was going to be useless. He slammed on the brakes, shifted the lever into drive and hit the gas again. He could hear Suzy screaming as the cars bore down on each other. Jeff swerved hard right, and their car climbed the sidewalk of the bridge and braced itself against the guard rail. The white car swerved and pulled hard toward him.

Steady, boy. Steady. Steady...Now!

Jeff pulled hard left on the wheel and stepped down on the accelerator just as the white car reached the front of Suzy's car. The sudden motion seemed to startle the other driver.

Jesus, he's going fast.

Suzy gripped the dashboard with both hands, her arms locked. Her eyes wide, she watched in disbelief as the white car approached. Jeff drove hard into the other car's front fender with all the force he could muster.

As the two cars collided, the impact threw Jeff and Suzy hard against their seatbelts, and Jeff's head hit the steering wheel. The white car ricocheted off Suzy's car, careened across the bridge, jumped the sidewalk, crashed through the guardrail and stopped, hanging over the edge. Jeff and Suzy hung limp in the car, their ragged breathing the only sound. Jeff raised his head and looked toward Suzy.

"Are you OK?" he asked.

"Yes, I think so. How about you?"

"OK now. I think I blacked out for a second." Jeff struggled loose from his seatbelt and tried to open the car's door, but it wouldn't move. He banged his shoulder against the door, and it groaned as it gave way. He turned sideways in the seat and pushed with his feet to get an opening wide enough to squeeze out.

He slowly approached the white car, which was perched at a precarious angle over the edge of the bridge. The streetlights from the end of the bridge barely gave enough light to see, but he could make out the driver's head protruding through the broken windshield.

No seatbelt.

Jeff forced himself to approach the car. He reached for the handle but the door was stuck. He heard a creaking sound and the car began to tilt over the side of the bridge. For a moment, he held onto the handle before realizing it was useless. He watched as the car completed its roll through the air and he heard the loud smack as it landed upside down in the water. He reached the rail just in time to see the wheels disappear under the white foam.

❑❑❑❑❑

276

This time Jeff didn't need to look for the number to find the house as he pulled into the driveway. Suzy got out on her side, and he slid across the seat to go out her door. His side of the car was a giant tangle of metal.

He rang the bell and waited. Billy opened the door.

"Hey, boss, what's up?" Billy asked. "And who's this goddess you've brought with you?"

Jeff had forgotten that Billy and Suzy had not met.

"Suzy, this is Billy. Billy, meet Suzy Morris. As they say in today's lingo, she's my significant other."

"Well, well. Hey there, lady. I'm pleased to meet you, but I can't compliment you on your selection of escorts for the evening." Billy had opened the door wide as Jeff and Suzy came into the house.

"I'm more than her escort for the evening, and you can skip the line of bull. She knows all about you, and I mean all."

"Hi, Billy," Suzy said, managing a smile. "Yes, I'm afraid I've heard more than a few war stories about the two of you."

"Well, come on in, and I'll go get Jan to put on some coffee."

"No coffee, we just need to talk," Jeff said as they went deeper into the house.

In the light of the house, Billy saw the seriousness of their faces and the cut across Jeff's forehead.

"Hey, Jeff, what's going on?"

"You tell me, buddy."

"What do you mean, Jeff?"

"I came to see you to ask about what might be some bad boys messing with my system. Something I can't figure out, so I came to my friend for help. Then, the next time I come to town, someone tries to put me in the river. So I'm asking you again, buddy. What's going on?"

"Slow down a bit," Billy backed up a step. "You've lost me. I don't have any idea what you're talking about. Let's go sit down, and I'm going to get some coffee going. I feel a long one coming on."

Billy left, and Jeff and Suzy sat in the room in silence. Finally, she spoke.

"I've heard you talk about him ever since I've known you. Do you really think he could be behind this?"

"No. No way. But I don't have that same confidence about the people he works for. Besides, I just didn't know anyplace else to go. I don't know what made me react like that when he opened the door except for the trauma of the evening."

"So tell me what's happening," Billy said as he returned to the room.

"Billy, I'm sorry about snapping at you, but it's been a hell of a night. There's no way of telling who's responsible, but it surely couldn't have been you."

"Responsible for what? Will you please tell me what has happened? What happened to your head, and what does this have to do with me?"

"Nothing, I don't think. Go check on that coffee, and then I'll tell you about the night."

"OK, liquid refreshment coming up." As he left the room, he looked over his shoulder at Suzy. "I hope you haven't believed many of his lies about me."

He returned shortly with a bucket of ice and the bottle of Jack Daniel's. He put the whiskey on the table and sat across the room from Jeff.

"OK, so tell me what happened."

Starting at the beginning with Suzy's being followed, Jeff and Suzy recounted everything until the car went off the bridge.

"Jesus!" Billy said. "A hell of a night. Did you call the police?"

"No, I came straight here. That is, after a little sheet metal work on the car so it could move."

"Why here?"

"I obviously wasn't thinking straight, but I went through everything in my mind. You were the only connection I could come up with. As soon as I tell you my concerns about the PATRIOT, someone tries to kill me. The people you work for have a reputation for doing crazy things like this."

"That's mostly in the movies. For the moment, I'm going to let it pass that you had those thoughts about someone who saved your life. Why do you think it was you he was after? It could have been Suzy."

"Given a clearer thinking head, it almost has to be. But Christ, why would anybody want to kill Suzy?"

Billy looked toward Suzy. "Can you think of any reason?"

278

"No," she said, clearly amazed at the idea. Jeff could tell that with this new revelation she was about to cry.

"I don't think that's where it's coming from," Jeff said.

"Well, first," Billy said, "I think we need to do something about the car in the river. We either need to call the police or take care of it some other way. If we don't, and the police find out later, there will be serious problems."

"What do you mean, take care of it some other way?" Suzy asked.

"I don't know. Wait here a few minutes while I make a phone call."

Billy went into the next room. They could hear enough of the conversation to know Billy was telling someone an abridged version of what had happened. Shortly, he hung up and came back into the room.

"So you thought I was going to have you put away, huh?"

"Not you, dummy, the people you work for. I hear a lot of stranger stories of what those clowns do."

"Your boyfriend here," Billy turned to Suzy, "seems to think I work for some very strange people."

The phone rang, and Billy called to the back of the house that he would get it. He returned after a short conversation.

"Well, the police don't have anything on it yet. Obviously nobody saw the crash, and nobody crossing the bridge has noticed the damage or bothered to report it."

"You can find out that quick?" Suzy was surprised.

"Seems you can't do anything today in law enforcement without putting it into a computer. Every call made to the local police is recorded on a data processing machine of some sort almost as soon as the conversation is over. It's just a matter of checking the files."

"And having access to the files," Jeff said. "I told you he works for some strange people. So what now?"

"You tell me. You're the one with the car at the bottom of the river."

Jeff winced at the reminder of that little detail. "Well," he said, "I suggest we try to be logical and walk through all of the possibilities to see if we can come up with any reason somebody might want to kill one or both of us. If we come up with something there, then maybe we can decide what to do."

"OK," Billy said. "Good plan. My vote for the top option on the list is that he's a stalker who by random choice locked onto Suzy, and got mad when you spotted him, and then just went off the deep end. He was probably cruising and looking for single females."

"OK, that's one," Jeff said. "And probably the right one. Next would be that something big in Suzy's office is about to happen, and she knows something she shouldn't."

"Where do you work?" Billy asked.

"Senator Hastings's office," Suzy said. "But I've been sitting here thinking about that very thing and I've drawn nothing but blanks. There is no significant legislation pending. There's nothing I'm involved in that has any great significance."

"Well," Billy said, "it could be something that you actually don't know you know. One of those kinds of things. Jeff, the next option has to deal with you."

"The only thing I have that could possibly be even remotely that big is the deployment of PATRIOT to the Middle East. But that's pretty far fetched."

"Anything past the first option is going to be far fetched. As I said when we started, the first option is probably the right one. Especially in this city. It happens every day since the crazies have taken over."

"While I can't picture it actually happening, I can imagine there are a lot of people who don't want PATRIOT to be successful in the Middle East."

"I'd say that's an understatement," Billy said.

"But it all started with him following me," Suzy said.

"Well," Jeff said, "we haven't exactly hidden our relationship, but we have been discreet. I can't imagine that someone who wanted to get to me would know to start by trailing Suzy. Not only that, but my job is done. At this stage, I'm not sure I could stop PATRIOT from working right, even if I wanted to."

"I agree," Billy said. "And that takes us back to option one."

"That really gives me the creeps," Suzy said.

"Is there any chance this is something to do with the conversation we had when you visited me the last time?" Billy asked.

280

Suzy looked from Billy to Jeff. "What conversation was that?" she asked.

"I told him about the entry I saw at White Sands this spring, as well as some input I had gotten from Raytheon."

"Well?" Billy said.

"With all that's been going on, I haven't even thought about that since our last conversation. That has to be the least likely of all. Plus it still puts us back to how he started with Suzy if it was me he was after."

"Don't forget, buddy, your first reaction when it happened was that conversation. That's why you're here, remember?"

"Yeah, and I also thought it was your organization that was behind it, remember? Both were equally crazy, it turns out."

"Touché. How many people know about that incident?" Billy asked.

"I've only told a few. But I have no way of knowing how many they told if anybody. Fish may have some other people working on it at Raytheon by now, but as busy as they've been, I seriously doubt it."

"Fish?" Suzy looked to both of them, obviously confused again.

"You know, Max Fisher. I told you about him. He was with us in Vietnam and now works for Raytheon on the PATRIOT software."

"Oh, yes. I remember. Now that I think about it, I told somebody," Suzy said.

They both looked at her.

"Who?" Jeff asked.

"Celia Mitchell was in my office one day when I was talking to you on the phone, and you were telling me about the flight. When I hung up, she asked me what it was about and I told her."

Billy looked toward Jeff.

"No way," Jeff said. "She works for Senator Strong, and he's been one of my strongest supporters. That doesn't compute."

"Don't forget about her connection to General Grant," Suzy said. "That computes for sure."

"Who's General Grant?" Billy asked.

"Besides being the biggest ass in the United States Army, he's my boss."

"Why would we suspect him?"

"Because Suzy thinks he's tied to Celia Mitchell, and he doesn't like me or PATRIOT."

"How is he tied to Celia?"

"With a love knot, if you believe Dr. Ruth here."

"You don't believe he's a possible?"

"No way, Billy. The man is a thirty-year, three-war veteran. He may be an ass and an idiot, but he's not a traitor or a murderer."

"OK," Billy said. "Then we're all blanks except option number one."

"So what do we do about the car?" Jeff asked.

"I vote I get some people to take care of it. If it turns out to be something ordinary, we can then get the local police involved. If it's something more than ordinary, at least we won't have any outside involvement."

"Can you make that happen?"

"I already have. There are people on the way to the scene right now."

Jeff looked at Suzy. She had wrapped her arms around herself and looked very defenseless.

"Well," he said. "I think we're right and he was a crazy. That being the case, I am almost glad it ended the way it did. At least now we won't have to worry about him stalking Suzy."

"And I hate to admit it about myself," Suzy said, "but I feel safer with him gone, too."

"Tell me again about Celia Mitchell asking you to fill her in about your phone conversation," Billy said to Suzy.

"Why are you interested in that?" Jeff asked.

"Because if for whatever reason we find out the right answer is not option one, the only thing I've heard here tonight that could be a possible is the link from you to Suzy to Celia Mitchell to General Grant back to you. In fact, to both of you at one time."

"But that's a real long stretch," Jeff said.

"So humor me for a minute," Billy said. "Suzy?"

"Well, she was in my office, and we'd been having some girl talk for some time when Jeff called. I talked to him for five minutes or so which was mostly him telling me about the flight, and after I hung up the phone, she asked me about the conversation."

282

"Did she ask about the mission and whether or not it went well?" Billy asked.

"No. Now that you mention it, she specifically asked about the entry. It didn't seem odd at the time, but that was all she asked about."

"Had you said enough on your side of the conversation with Jeff for her to know there had been such an incident?"

"I honestly don't remember. Maybe or maybe not."

"But that was the only thing she asked about?" Jeff was now interested.

"Yes."

"Did she ask directly about the entry or just what you were talking about?" Jeff asked.

"I'm trying to remember. She asked about the entry, but I don't remember if I'd mentioned that from my side or not."

"Try harder," Jeff said.

"I am trying," she said, but she was starting to cry.

"I think maybe we've had it for the night," Jeff said. "I don't think there is anything there, anyway. I'm going to take Suzy with me and get us some sleep."

"Good idea," Billy said. "Where can I get you in the morning?"

"Here's a mobile number I'll be at until I leave town." Jeff wrote the number on the back of a business card. "I'll also put down the number of the motel where I'm staying. I'll get another room under your name and Suzy can stay with me tonight."

"I'll be in touch," Billy said.

□□□□□

The sound of the ringing woke Jeff with a start. He tried to move, but was stiff from bruises. By the time he realized he didn't want to try moving again for several months, he recognized that it was the phone ringing. He opened his eyes and looked at the bedside clock. He heard Suzy answering the phone from her side of the bed and then a sleepy chuckle and she handed the phone to Jeff.

"It's Billy," she said and sat up in the bed.

"I take it you've got something on the car," he said when he got the phone to his ear.

"Yeah," Billy said sounding wide awake. "But you're not going to like it."

"It wasn't option number one, huh?"

"Doesn't look like it. Your boy is an Arab. His original home is listed as Bahrain, but that's what they all put when they don't want you to know where they're really from. He didn't have any ID, but we ran his soggy little prints through our soggy little print matchup machine and got a positive ID. He's moved around a lot. Immigration shows him coming into the country day before yesterday on a flight from London to JFK. No information before that for nearly six months. We're trying to run a correlation on his earlier comings and goings with other sinister happenings, but that probably won't yield much. These people change IDs like you and I do underwear."

"Maybe he's a violent type and just decided to have some kicks for the evening during his trip. Maybe he just happened to see Suzy first."

"Yeah, right. I think this boy knew exactly what he was after. The only thing we don't know is whether he meant to kill or warn."

"What about the police?"

"We handled that. Kept you two out of it. Not to worry except for what you tell Suzy's insurance company. Good luck with that."

"You said warning. Do you think it might have been a warning?" Jeff asked, already knowing his opinion of the answer.

"Possibly, but not probably. If it was, it wouldn't have worked. What they wanted was to make it look like an accident. Then, if we're right about the only other option for why, the push on the software entry would just fade away. Not only do I think it wasn't a warning, I think that because he missed, you're relatively safe now."

"How do you figure that?"

"OK, follow the little bouncing ball. Whatever the game is with the software, it needs to be a secret. The only way to keep the secret was to remove you. You're the only one pulling the wagon. Everybody else is riding. Now that the bad guys took their best shot at you and missed, they'll

284

probably go into deep cover. If you have figured this out and told someone like me, then your untimely death brings on the Cavalry. Follow?"

"I think so. Why not bring on the Cavalry now, anyway?"

"Because we probably can't flush them out of their deep cover. All they would have to do would be to take their little chunk of software code and run. We not only would never find them, we might not ever know what they were up to or even whether we stopped them."

"This still seems far fetched. Are we really saying that we think General Grant tried to get me killed?"

"Again, possible, but not probable. I don't think we have enough information to determine who is or isn't involved. We're running detailed background checks on Celia Mitchell now. Her security check for her secret clearance in the Senator's office was OK, but those aren't very deep. So far, though, she looks clean. And clearly Grant is, too, on paper. So we don't really have much."

"So Suzy and I are supposed to go back to business as usual?"

"That's the best I've got. We have a channel that we can use to make sure the river swimmer gets the recognition he deserves in the Middle East. That way, whoever sent him will know he tried and failed, rather than skipping with whatever money he had been paid in advance."

"I talked to Fish after we got here. The printouts he had were all trashed during a housecleaning, but he is going to print out some new ones in the morning. I told him to do it himself and not get anybody else involved. He said he should have them ready by mid-morning."

"I'll continue to work the information on Mitchell and Grant. What we really need, though, is to know what's in that hidden software."

"This is the craziest scheme I've ever heard, but I don't have a better plan. Look, I think I'm going to change my schedule and head up to Boston to work with Fish. I also think I'm going to take Suzy with me."

"I think those both might be good ideas. How do we stay in touch?"

"I'll forward all my calls from my cellular phone to wherever I happen to be. You should be able to get me on that number just about any time."

"Good luck, buddy."

"You too," Jeff said as he hung up.

weapons systems--pentagon adv 17 1-91
Israel shelled with Iraqi SCUD missiles
USWNS Military News
adv jan 17 1991 or thereafter

By GEORGE GROWSON

WASHINGTON—Statements released today from the U.S.
military headquarters in Saudi Arabia indicated that Tel
Aviv and Haifa were hit last evening with seven SCUD
missiles. There was no significant damage. One additional
SCUD was aimed at a military base in northern Saudi Arabia,
but was intercepted by a U.S. PATRIOT missile. While the
U.S. is trying to prevent a retaliation by Israel, it is
not known at this time how that country will respond. The
White House announced today that additional PATRIOT systems
from the U.S. 32nd Army Air Defense Command in Germany will
be immediately airlifted to Israel to assist in the
protection of that country from SCUD attacks. The member
nations of the Allied Coalitions convened last night in
hope of maintaining the fragile relationships and
agreements which hold the group together. President Bush
has stated that without unified Arab support, he will not
pursue military actions against Saddam Hussein.
From an outsider's view, it would appear that the
breakup of the Arab support is imminent. If the SCUD
missiles continue to hit Israel, the Israelis will surely
join the hostilities. Such a development would most likely
prevent most Arab nations, with the possible exception of
Saudi Arabia, from participating in U.S. efforts. One great
unknown is whether those Arab nations will remain neutral
in the face of Israeli entry into the war or switch their
allegiance and their military resources to Iraq. The entire
situation hinges on whether President Bush can make good on
his promise to protect Israel from the Iraqi SCUDs, and
what Israel will do in the event he can't.

THIRTEEN

Jeff walked rapidly through the halls of Raytheon. He saw many familiar faces as he worked his way toward the back of the building and Fish's office. He was somewhat surprised he hadn't picked up a Raytheon escort at the reception desk, and expected to be waylaid by a corporate executive any minute, since it was the first time he had ever arrived at a contractor facility unannounced.

As he entered Fish's office, he noticed another man was already there.

"Hello, sir," Fish said as he stood up to shake hands. "Sir, this is Doug Glover. Doug, this is General Weyland I've told you about. We were together in Vietnam."

"Glad to meet you, sir. Max has told me a lot about you," Doug said.

"Well, when you're ready for me to tell you the truth, let me know. And for god's sake, will you people quit calling me 'sir'."

"Old military habits die hard," Doug said. "Especially when I see those stars on your shoulders. I'm going to go and let you two have some privacy. But, General, I just want to let you know how proud we all are to be a part of what's been done these last three months. Especially after we shot that SCUD down last night. We all know that without what you've personally done, PATRIOT wouldn't have even gotten the chance to be there, much less be shooting down SCUDs."

"Thanks, Doug. I know how you feel. I'm as proud as you are just to have been a part of it. Now we've just got to make sure she continues to do her job. Do you guys have the data from the firing last night?"

"Not yet," Fish said. "It's supposed to be coming in on the wire pretty soon. Since it's a lot of data, they edited it some over there because it's hard to get a phone line for that long. But from what I've heard, there won't be much to look at. The shot was picture perfect. It looks like we had a direct hit, and the SCUD fireballed in the sky. If Dan Rather isn't a good witness to a kill, I don't know who is."

Doug left and Fish said, "He's the guy who makes most of my runs for me on PATRIOT software. Nice guy."

"Did you get the data I asked you about on the phone?"

"Yeah. At least, it should be on the printer now. Why don't I get Doug to have the printouts brought here?"

"No! Did you make the runs yourself?"

"Sure. You were pretty adamant about that when you called this morning, although I don't know why."

"Let's just say that something has happened to move this thing up on my priority list. If someone at Raytheon has in fact played with PATRIOT software, then that person is probably still here. I don't want to take any chances."

"So what happened?"

"Somebody tried to kill me last night," Jeff said. His face reflected the chill he felt from the memory.

"Over this?"

"Fish, I have absolutely no idea. All I know is what happened. As to why, this thing I asked you about seems like the most stupid idea in the world. Without what happened last night, I would still have this so far on the back burner it would fall off the stove. But the truth is that I can't come up with any other leads; this is the only possibility. I met with Billy last night, and we decided that until we had a better idea, this is the one we are going to pursue."

"Billy Walker?"

"Yeah."

"Jesus. You and Billy at it again. And now me. Boy, this'll really be like old times. Just what is it you two think this piece of software does?"

"We have the same set of blanks there. That's why I'm here. I'm hoping that between the two of us, we can figure it out."

290

"If what you say is right, it probably wouldn't be best to work here. Why don't we take the printouts I have and go somewhere else?"

"Can you get away from here with all that's going on?"

"If I tell them I am going with the PATRIOT Project Manager, I sure can. We're going to need some help, though. I can tell you from what I saw the last time I looked at this material, it's over my head, and it's going to take some research and a lot of work."

"No help from anybody here. Too risky. If all of this craziness is true, then somebody in this building is probably involved. We'll have to figure it out by ourselves. Suzy's waiting in the car—she was with me last night. Is there any place we can get some good reference material?"

"The best in the country is right down the road at the MIT Research and Engineering facility. I think my card will show I'm still a member in good standing, and they have some small rooms where we can work. I also have a small contract with them, so if we can't break the code ourselves, maybe we can get some help."

"OK, let's do it. You go get the printouts, and I'll meet you at the front door. And don't tell anyone what you're doing."

"Be right there," Fish said, and started down the hall.

❑❑❑❑❑

Jeff pulled to the front door of the Raytheon facility and saw Fish waiting for him with one cardboard box in his arms and another at his feet. Suzy got out of the car and opened the back door.

"Hello there," Fish said as he put the first box on the seat. "My name is Max Fisher, but you can call me Fish."

"Hello, Fish, I'm Suzy Morris, but you can call me crazy for being here."

"Crazy was when you got mixed up with that guy," Fish said as he put the second box on the back seat.

Jeff glanced at Fish as he closed the door. "What's in those two boxes?"

"These are the printouts I made this morning."

"But two boxes full! I thought we were talking about a page or two."

"Hey, Cap'n, I told you this wasn't going to be easy. The specific part we are interested in is only a few pages. The rest is the system software that communicates with this code we're looking for. If we want to know what's going on, having it all is the only way."

"This may be harder than we thought," Jeff said, looking across the seat at Suzy.

"Look, folks," Fish said, "if this was easy, I'd have it done already. I told you before, Cap'n, and I'm telling you now, we're after someone who's smart and didn't want his stuff to be traced or decoded."

"So you're saying we're looking for the proverbial needle in the haystack?" Suzy asked.

"No, I'm telling you that if it was that easy, I'd have left it at home for my kids to do. Take a left, then go around to the right on Hartwell Road.

"The actual material we'll be looking at is three pages at the most. The problem is, it isn't a piece of code as you and I know it. It's just a string of numbers which mean something to the computer, but not much to anybody else. Think of it as wandering through the woods. If you have a pretty good sense of direction and a compass and you know where you want to go, you can generally get through the woods pretty well. All we've got are the numbers that say how many steps and then which way to turn. It's dark and we don't have a compass and very soon we're going to be bumping into the trees. What we've got to find out is where did he start from, what does he see at each point he stops, and what does he do then? That way, we can find out where he's going. All that without the benefit of light or compass. Understand?"

"Not one word," Jeff said. "But I'm ready to start learning. We've got to find out what that piece of software does."

"Does this have something to do with what's going on in Saudi?" Fish asked.

"We don't have any idea," Suzy said. "The only clue we have is that the man who tried to kill us was from the Middle East."

"Last night must have been some shock. You doing OK?"

"Except for some bumps and bruises," she said. "We would've been killed if we hadn't been very lucky."

"See, Crazy, I told you he wasn't any good for you."

Suzy chuckled in spite of herself. She really liked this man and understood why he and Jeff were so close. There was a bond there that even a brief observation showed went way back. It was the same bond she had seen between Jeff and Billy. She was confident that this man could help them.

"Take a right at the bottom of the hill, and then it's just a couple of blocks down. My pass will get us into all of the unclassified areas," Fish said. "I think that'll be all we'll need. They do a lot of government classified work here, including some for PATRIOT. If we need to get in one of those areas, you may have to use some of your well-placed pull."

"I know someone who's pretty well placed," Jeff said. "But under the circumstances, I'd just assume no one knew I was here."

The gate guard looked at Fish's pass and waved them through. Jeff recognized the complex and realized he had been here before, but had never been in the area into which Fish directed him to drive. They parked in front of an older building several blocks behind the main facility. A sign above the building identified it as the software laboratory.

The Massachusetts Institute of Technology Research and Engineering facility had broken away from the Institute where Jeff had received his doctorate. It was now a completely self-supporting, non-profit organization which conducted independent research on almost any subject for both private business and the government. It retained its ties to one of the nation's top technical institutes and, as a result, could use the students as virtual slave labor. As they started for the building, Jeff realized it was bigger than he had remembered.

Jeff and Fish each carried one of the boxes inside the building as Suzy held the door. As they walked down the central hall, Jeff could see work rooms of various sizes and private offices on each side of the hallway. Near the center of the building, the wall turned to glass and gave a full view of a major computer facility which, judging from all of the activity around it, was very busy.

"I burned a lot of midnight oil in that room when we were developing PATRIOT's software," Fish said as they passed the computer room. "In the early days when I first got out of school and went to work for Raytheon, we didn't have a computer like the one that would eventually be in PATRIOT, so we wrote some special software for the mainframe they had here that would make it resemble our future PATRIOT computer when we got it built. A lot of the early work on our programs was done here. Nowadays, that's a pretty common thing to do, and they call the process 'computer emulation,' but in those days, it was all smoke and mirrors. We had to kind of feel our way through the process."

"Why is PATRIOT's computer different from any other computer?" Suzy asked.

"Speed," Fish said. "The computer is built by Raytheon for PATRIOT and nothing else. It is designed to run the special JOVIAL code which was written just for PATRIOT, and that allowed the boys in the lab to really tune the computer for its exact needs. Of course, you have to realize that was in the late sixties and early seventies. Today, you can get that kind of speed in something you carry around in your pocket, but we're still on our original machine. We've improved the memory and a lot of the other peripherals, but we've stuck with the same central processor. It's too hard to re-code all the software to go to a new machine."

"It's really that hard to re-code?" Jeff remembered the pressure he was under from the Army to switch to a standard computer language.

"Actually, the re-coding isn't the problem. It's the verification and validation that everything works exactly right. The computer programs are large and complex, and there are many paths that might not be actually used for years at a time. Each engagement has its own specific variables: aircraft type, environment, and location in the sky. So, each may call for a particular piece of software code that may never be used again. There are so many different combinations of intercepts that it's impossible to know if you've covered the entire set of potential paths through the system software. And if you miss even one, Murphy's Law will getcha, you betcha. We've been using what amounts to the same software for nearly fifteen years, and that's a lot of confidence to throw out the window."

Fish showed his identification card to a receptionist at the desk and asked if there was a room where they could work. The receptionist led them past the desk to a room with a conference table, chairs, and several smaller tables. Fish thanked her as he put his box on the table.

Suzy sank gratefully into a chair, leaned her elbows on the table and started massaging her temples.

"I'd like you to tell me what you can about what's going on before we start this," Fish said. "I know you said Billy is involved, and I know a little about what he does for a living, so I know you may not be able to tell me everything. But at least give me a hint of what we're looking for."

"I'll tell you everything I know. There is no reason not to at this point. In a nutshell, I saw the entry I talked to you about. I mentioned it to you, Steve Smith, Suzy, and Billy."

"I mentioned it to a woman I work with," Suzy continued, "who happens to be unusually friendly, if you get my drift, with Jeff's boss, General Grant."

"Billy says he didn't tell anybody any specifics," Jeff picked up the story again. "But the next thing we know, this Arab tries to kill us last night. We honestly don't know if there's any connection, but it's all we've got right now. Billy has a hunch that whoever put that code there doesn't want it found and believes that if I accidentally disappeared, then they would be safe."

"That part's probably true. Nobody else has asked me to look for it and I had quit until you called again. So if you had gone away for any reason, I probably would've let it drop."

"We need to find out if that software is anything worth killing somebody for, and if so, what it is, and who put it there," Suzy said.

"OK, I'm ready to get started."

"One last thing," Jeff said. "If this is really something sinister, it almost had to be put there by someone who works for Raytheon. From what you tell me, that means someone who works with you. As we go through this, keep in mind who that might be. It would have to be somebody with access, knowledge and opportunity. There can't be too many people like that around."

"Depending on the time frame, that could be one of a hundred or maybe less, but I'll keep it in mind."

"OK, where do we start?"

"And how can we help?" Suzy asked.

"The papers in the box I carried are in the numerical order of the utility subroutines of the system. Crazy, if you will take those out and arrange them on that table over there so we can find and use them easily, that would be a help. Cap'n, the big printout at the top of the other box is the system code. Down the left hand column, you'll see entry points every few pages that are more or less in numerical order, but some of the numbers might be missing. If you would tear the printout apart at each of the numbered entry points, use that marking pen to mark the entry number on the front of the section, and lay them out on the other table in numerical order, then we can find stuff more easily when we need it. I am going to the reference desk to get some technical material I think we might need."

It took Suzy and Jeff nearly an hour to get all of the printout material laid out on the tables. Fish sat at the conference table with some textbooks, working with a pencil and paper and a small part of the code.

"Cap'n, how close can you judge the exact point in time when the entry was made at the keyboard?"

"The best I can recall, it was after target track, but before missile away. I don't remember if it was before the engagement decision. Is that important?"

"I don't know yet. If you remember, I said the other month that what had put me on to this is that one of the connections to the missile destruct command was to this little bit of code. But if the entry was made before the missile was launched, that doesn't seem to be consistent."

"What've you got so far?" Jeff moved his chair over to Fish.

"Not much," Fish said. "But look at this."

"Hey, if you two guys are going to dig into that, then why don't I go and get us something to eat?" Suzy said. "It was early this morning when we started in Washington, and I haven't had anything to eat except airplane food. I'm starved, and my head is pounding."

"Good idea," Fish said. "There's a little cafe in the last building we passed before this one. They should have some sandwiches there."

"So what do all of these numbers mean?" Jeff asked as Suzy left the room.

"Each number is an instruction," Fish said. "The trick is to pull each number, look it up in the machine language book to see what the instruction is, see what register it applies to, and then see what the machine does with it. It's tough to track it all the way through, and I'm not making much progress."

"I'm still not sure I understand," Jeff said. "Why don't you show me an example, and then maybe I can help."

"OK. Take this sequence of numbers here. The first number translates into a formula for addition by using this table here in the book. The second number is the location of the first number to be added, and the next number is the location of the second number to be added. The last number tells us where to put the results of the addition."

"How do you know that you aren't writing over something when you put the results into that location?"

"You may or you may not. If you're smart enough to get this far, I guess it's assumed that you're smart enough to keep up with all of that. At any rate, when you get down into this kind of code, you're on your own. This is raw machine language. There aren't any further steps the machine is going to take except execute. No compilation, no error checks, nothing. Just execute. If it's right, it's right, but if it's wrong, you're dead and there isn't any way to know why."

"Then why use this kind of language at all?"

"The first reason is speed. By using very carefully designed machine language instructions, you can gain speed over standard, easier-to-use-languages. For sections of program that are separable and small and will be used a lot of times during the course of the intercept, it can be worth it to code them in machine language to save the time."

"And the second reason?" Jeff asked.

"It's the only way the code can be hidden. Regular language stuff like FORTRAN or JOVIAL has to go through a compiler, and that would've been immediately recognizable as code that didn't belong. If there's really a piece of code here that doesn't belong and that was hidden on purpose, it had to be in machine language to be that way."

"You said 'if'." Jeff was obviously puzzled. "I thought we knew for sure it was there."

"We know something's there. We still don't know what it is and what it does and why it's there. There's always the chance this is something that can be explained. Hell, it could be something that does absolutely nothing and was there from a long time ago and because it can't be seen or felt, it would never have gotten removed."

"But I thought you said it was wired into the command destruct circuit."

"Wired into and being used are two different things. It could still be completely passive."

"OK, what can I do?" Jeff asked.

"The same thing I'm doing. You start from the bottom and go up, I'll continue down from the top. When we meet in the middle, we'll at least have all of the instruction set. Then we can begin to see if we can make sense of what the code does."

"OK, boys," Suzy said as she came into the room with a bag. "Have we deciphered the master puzzle yet?"

"No," Jeff said, "but that bag sure smells good. I didn't realize how hungry I was until you mentioned it."

With the sandwiches finished, they worked for two more hours. Jeff had made almost no progress except to learn that he was no good at this. Fish was ahead, but a long way from being finished. Jeff put the printout on the table.

"OK, Fish, this is what we're going to do. I'm going to take this lady to someplace safe. Then I'm going back to Huntsville to see if I can get some more help working the problem. You take your part and go back to your house and work there. I'll call you when I get to Huntsville as soon as I have any more information."

"Now wait just a minute," Suzy said. "I don't plan to be put someplace while you two carry on."

"No, I think that's a good idea. They must be about to go crazy in Huntsville without Jeff there through this," Fish said.

"Yeah, I really need to check in. Let's pack this stuff up and get on the road."

"I'll make us copies of the material we need from these books. That

298

way, we can each have a set of what we need. I'll keep the printouts with me for reference. You should be able to get a set from the Missile Command people in Huntsville. Will they give you any static about doing that for you?"

"No. In fact, I think I'll call Steve and let him know what's going on and have him start that ball rolling. It should be ready by the time I get there. Is there any way we can print off the hidden code in Huntsville?"

"Not easily. I had to make some really complicated setups to get it. I'll make a copy, and that way, no one in Huntsville will know what's up. If the bad guys have people in Raytheon, they may well have them in Huntsville."

"Good thinking."

Fish left to make the copies. Jeff could tell Suzy was not happy.

"What's the matter?" he asked.

"Put me someplace safe for a couple of days, huh?" she said. "No way, buster. I'm staying with you."

"I'm going to be moving fast, and we don't know where this thing is going to lead. Besides, you're going to really like where I'm going to take you, and we'll have tonight all to ourselves."

"We'll see. At least the tonight part sounds OK," Suzy said, as they began to pack the boxes.

◻◻◻◻◻

Fish closed the trunk lid of his car. He had stopped by his office to pick up some additional materials he might need for the long night's work ahead. He backed out of his parking place and turned right. As he left the parking area, Doug Glover exited the building by the same door. A green delivery van started and pulled beside his car, and Doug got in the front. As the van left the parking lot, two additional cars fell in behind.

Fish drove, completely lost in thought about the hidden code. He was not thinking about how the code got where it was or what sinister purpose it was for, but rather about how to identify it. He was also concerned about the security of his department. If this had indeed happened at Raytheon, then he was ultimately responsible. He did not notice the small caravan of vehicles following him several hundred yards back. He drove at a leisurely pace, turning the code over in his mind. He made the turn on to Route 128 and headed west toward his home.

Several miles later, he left the interstate and headed north for the peaceful drive through the rural Massachusetts countryside. The ride allowed him time in the morning to go over his plans for the day and a few moments to relax and unwind on the way home. He passed the White Horse Tavern on his right and noticed the early evening crowd was already gathering. Fish had long since given up alcohol, but still enjoyed the one evening a week he spent there with others from work. They kidded him good naturedly about not drinking, but he had made a promise to Sarah when their first son was born.

The van and two cars took the same exit and followed some distance behind. They lost sight of the car, but Doug Glover directed the route. He knew where Fish was going, and he had already planned where to make the contact.

Fish turned right on the narrow country road that led to their small farm home. This was the part of the drive he enjoyed most. There were no buildings within sight of the road for nearly ten miles and very little traffic. In his rearview mirror, he noticed the van approaching from behind. One car pulled out to pass the van and then another. He realized that the cars were going faster than was wise on the narrow winding road. Instinctively, he lessened the pressure on the accelerator, expecting that the cars would pass him. Both cars started around him together. When the first had pulled back into the right lane, he saw brake lights. Fish smiled to himself, thinking that the driver had realized the road couldn't handle those speeds.

The brake lights glowed as the car braked sharply. Fish looked to his left for the other car, but it was directly beside his rear fender. He braked and then increased the pressure on the pedal some more when he realized he was going to have to slow a lot to avoid hitting the car in front. Too late, he realized it was a trap as he looked into his mirror and saw the van closing in on him. As he stopped behind the lead car, he thought he saw Doug Glover, but the man turned his face away.

A man got out of the car in front and came back to the driver's door. Fish locked the door and started to slide across the seat to the passenger's door, but someone was already there. Fish saw the pistol and heard the shot at the same time the glass of the window shattered. A hand came in and opened the door from inside.

"Out," came the command. Fish sat on the seat.

"Who are you?" Fish said. "You must've made some kind of a mistake."

"No mistake, Fisher," the voice said. "We can do this alive or dead. Makes very little difference to me. Now get out of the car." Fish's mind was racing. His first thought was of the notes in the trunk from his work on the hidden code. He slid across the seat and got out of the car.

"I'm telling you, you're making a mistake. I am an employee of the Ra..."

The blow hit him just below his right ear, and he fell to the ground.

"Get him in the van," the man with the pistol said.

When Fish regained consciousness, he was tied, gagged, and blindfolded. The van was moving through some rough areas and the bouncing was painful. There was no carpeting or cushioning of any kind in the bed of the van, and he could feel the wetness on the side of his head which he assumed was blood. At least he was alive, he thought, and he began to try to formulate a plan in his mind. The only thing he could come up with was to kick and fight and run like hell when he was untied or do nothing and wait and see what was going to happen. The van stopped, and Fish could hear people moving inside and outside the vehicle.

There was some mumbling from outside the rear of the van. He heard the doors opening and sensed people getting in. Rough hands brought him to a sitting position. There was a hard slap across his face, and Fish could taste his own blood.

"Now, Mr. Fisher." Same voice. "We are going to ask you a few simple questions. If you answer, you'll be OK. If you don't, it won't be pleasant. Not pleasant at all. Do you understand?"

Fish didn't move. He sensed the blow coming before it landed. He flinched, but it didn't help much. The impact to the right side of his head rolled him onto his side. Rough hands pushed him upright.

"Do you understand?"

Fish nodded his head yes.

"I really don't want to use a lot of time here. We know who you are, who your friend is you've spent the afternoon with, and what the two of you are doing. What we don't know is how successful you've been. Tell us."

"I have been at the library at the MIT Research and Engineering facility working on the next version of the PATRIOT software. I don't..."

The blow caught him in mid-sentence and by surprise. He could feel the flesh of his cheek tear and the blood spill down his face. When he was pushed upright, the side of his face was numb. Another blow came to the side of his ribcage. He thought he heard the cracking of bone.

"I said I don't have a lot of time, and I don't plan to waste much of it here with you. What you can tell me will make my job easier, but it's not absolutely critical. Now once again, and this will be the last time I will ask. Tell me the results of your work this afternoon."

"My name is Max Fisher. I am an employee of the Raytheon Company. I have been at the MIT research laboratory doing research for the next version of PATRIOT software." He wasn't sure how many times he had been hit and he braced himself for another blow. It came, and then another and another.

There was silence in the van, and then movement. He heard the back doors open and close and heard voices outside. As Fish slipped from consciousness and the blackness came to him, he smelled something. Damn, he thought. Sarah's going to be upset. I shit in my pants.

□□□□□

"You told me your parents' home was nice, but I never imagined anything like this. Why would anyone ever want to leave this place?"

Suzy was on the couch in front of a roaring fire, lying with her head in Jeff's lap. Jeff had called ahead, and they had driven the three hours to Jeff's family home. The Thomases had prepared a grand meal, New England style with all the trimmings. After his parents' death, there was plenty of money left to maintain the house, so he had asked the Thomases to stay.

They lived there now and kept the house ready for what they knew would be his eventual return. Jeff and Suzy had eaten and drunk their fill and were now relaxing and trying to forget the events of the last few days.

"Wouldn't it be nice to have a pause button on life so that we could just stop at this place and this time and not have to leave until we wanted?" she asked.

"I know. I also wish I had a fast forward so we could get through this thing."

"What's does it all mean, Jeff?"

"I don't know, sweetheart, but we're sure going to find out."

"How, if we can't break the computer code?"

"We're bound to break the code eventually. If we can't get it done soon, I'll get more help."

"But then whoever sent the first man may find out what we're doing and send some really heavy stuff."

"They may have already. That's a chance we'll have to take. That's why I want you to stay here until we get this thing put to bed. I want you to call your office in the morning and tell them you'll be out of town for a few days. Take vacation or sick leave or whatever you have to do."

"Do you think a few days will be enough?"

"I have no idea. But if we haven't made real progress by then, we'll have to turn Billy and his people loose. We've got to trust somebody, and he and Fish are at the top of my list."

"Mine too."

Jeff started to say something else, but when he looked down at Suzy, she was fast asleep. He slid out from underneath her and replaced his lap with a pillow. He went to the table and took the material Fish had copied for him from an envelope. He continued to translate the machine language code the way Fish had instructed him. It was a painstaking process. He called Fish to see if he was making progress.

Sarah Fisher answered the phone on the first ring. "Why, no, he's not here. I called the office about sundown, and someone said they had seen him briefly a short while earlier, but not since. They assumed he had come home. It's not unusual for him to work this late, but it is unusual for him not to call."

"Let me give you a number where I am," Jeff said. "Have him call me when he gets in."

"Jeff, is there something I should know?"

"I don't think there's a problem, Sarah. Just ask him to give me a call, would you, please?"

"Of course," she said, but Jeff could tell he had not soothed her concern very much.

He immediately called Billy

"What's up, boss?" Billy asked.

"There may be another problem. I dropped Fish at the Raytheon plant around four o'clock. He was going to get some more material from his office and then work at home. I just talked to Sarah, and he isn't home yet and she says he's not at his office. Can you get some people checking on it?"

"You bet. Are you making any progress on the code?"

"No, not really. That's going much slower without Fish. I sure hope he's all right."

"Well, let's not get too worked up until we know something."

"It smells, Billy."

"Yeah, I know. I'll get some people right on it."

As Jeff hung up the phone and turned back toward the table and the work, he saw Suzy standing in the doorway watching.

"You heard?" he asked.

"Yes," she said. "Are you sure we're safe here?"

"If there's a safer place, I don't know where it might be."

"How about on the steps of the Capitol, screaming our lungs out that something is wrong?"

Jeff chuckled. "The problem with that is it's too crowded, plus they would come for us with straitjackets. I think we're doing the right thing. We've got to sort this out."

"I wonder if Fish would think we're doing the right thing. Wherever he is, I sure hope so."

"Me, too," Jeff said as he bent to the papers on the desk.

"I'll make some coffee," she said, and turned to leave the room.

□□□□□

The ringing of the phone woke Jeff with a start. His neck hurt when he moved his head, and his back ached as he tried to sit up. With some effort, he stood and walked to the phone.

"It's Billy, I've got bad news."

"Fish?"

"Yeah, the local cops found him about midnight. He's in a coma, but alive. It took a while because he didn't have any ID on him. They'd assumed it was a robbery since his wallet was missing. One of my people checked the police reports after you called me and made the match from Fish's physical description. He called the local police and they made the match from the prints we sent by telefax. The body was in a ditch not far from a place called the White Horse Tavern. The police assumed he had too much to drink. They thought he probably stopped off to have one or two, had too many, and flashed a thick wallet. Someone followed him out and did him in, stole the wallet, and dragged him to the ditch. He would've been dead if he'd stayed in that ditch much longer. They wouldn't have found him yet except that a biker had a flat and was walking his bike along the side of the road."

"That story is bull," Jeff said. "Fish didn't drink and he had just left me with the code to go home and work. He wouldn't have stopped at some damn bar."

"Hey, slow down, boss. I know all that. I have some of our people up there working the problem. The local police are a little nervous about all the attention from Washington, but we convinced them we're FBI and we're there looking for drugs. They seemed satisfied with that."

"What are you going to do?"

"I've already started a heavy investigation with my people, and we'll find whoever's responsible. I just hope we can find them before whatever this is all about takes place. Are you making any progress on the code?"

"No. I was really counting on Fish. Has anybody talked to Sarah?"

"Yes, she's with Fish at the hospital. He's getting the best care they got. Doctors give him less than 50-50 on recovery, but my money's on Fish."

305

"I'm going to leave Suzy here and catch the redeye to Huntsville. There's no way I can break this code myself, and I've got to have help. I've got no choice but to pick a few people I think I can trust and get them working. Have you come up with anything yet?"

"Nothing on General Grant, but we may have our first break on Celia Mitchell. Seems there's an irregularity in her birth certificate. The permanent record can't be found in the hospital where her birth certificate says she was born. It's only a little thing, but it's a flaw and we're going to run it down. Takes time for that sort of thing."

"What else?"

"We've tapped the phone in her apartment, but not much there. I figure if this is what we think it is, she'll have a separate phone in another name."

"How did you get a warrant?"

"I didn't."

"I thought that was illegal without a warrant."

"It is. You want me to take it off?"

"No."

"Good, I had it put on when I first heard about Fish. When do you think you may have something on the code?"

"Today. Tomorrow. Next week. Never. Who knows? One minute I tell myself it's just a few numbers and can't be that hard, and the next I don't think I'll ever make sense out of it. Trust me, I'm doing the best I can, and I'm going to get some more help."

"OK, buddy, stay in touch."

"Right," Jeff said as he hung up the phone. He looked out the window to see the moon just coming over the mountains. Turning back into the room, he saw Suzy standing in the doorway watching him.

"Something's happened to Fish, hasn't it?"

Jeff nodded.

"How bad?" she asked quietly.

Jeff scrubbed a hand over the stubble on his face.

"Well, he's alive, but it's bad. That's another reason I think you should stay here."

"I'm coming with you."

"Look," he said, "we've been through this already, and you'll be a lot better off here. You'll be safe and comfortable, and the Thomases can look after you."

"Wrong. First, how do you know I'd be safe here? Second, I do not want to be looked after. At least, not by anybody but you. Third, I'll be able to help if I'm with you, and that's where I intend to be."

January 18, 1991
Huntsville, Alabama
9:00 AM

Jeff had no choice but to use his badge to get into the Technical Laboratories of the U.S. Army Missile Command Research, Development and Engineering Center. He had flown to Huntsville on tickets he purchased with cash at the window, under a false name. In Huntsville, he and Suzy had registered as Mr. and Mrs. in a no-tell motel under the same name he used on the airplane. He had taken a taxi from the airport to the motel, and when morning light came, he had called Steve to pick him up. He was able to convince Suzy that she had to stay in the room. She didn't have a clearance to get in the laboratories on Redstone Arsenal.

Steve was obviously curious when he picked up Jeff, and it took most of the car ride to tell the full story.

"If you tell me much more, I'm going to get paranoid again," Steve said when Jeff was finished. "So that's why you needed the printouts."

"Yep, and I've got copies of the other material we need with me. We're going to have to work this problem ourselves. We'll need at least one more person we can trust, but no more. I don't want anybody else getting involved. For all we know, there are people in Huntsville involved, too."

"I heard that. Now I really am getting paranoid. I have just the man waiting for us here. He is the same person who made the printouts from the Software Engineering Directorate. Since Ben Peeples was killed in that break-in, he knows this code as well as anybody except probably Max. If we can't get it done with him helping us, then it can't be done."

As they entered the room Steve had reserved, Jeff recognized the young engineer and was pleased with Steve's choice.

"Sir, this is Ralph Jameson. Ralph, General Weyland."

"Pleased to meet you, sir. I've always been an admirer of yours."

"Thanks, Ralph. Has Steve told you what we have to do?"

"No, sir," Steve said. "I'm not real sure I even know why I'm here."

"OK," Jeff said opening his envelope and pulling out the material from Fish. "Let's take the printouts you have and spread them on the tables in order of subroutine number and system entry points. What I have here is some machine language code which is buried somehow in the PATRIOT operational code. It's on all of the tapes and apparently in all of the systems, but seems to hide itself pretty well."

"Excuse me, sir," Ralph interrupted. "Did you say there's some hidden code in the operational PATRIOT systems?"

"Yes, that's what I said. Fish found it and got these printouts. At least it was in the version of the code he had. Whether it is in the deployed system or not, we don't know yet."

"Excuse me, sir. Fish?" Ralph asked.

"I'm sorry, Ralph. Max Fisher at Raytheon is an old friend, and I know him as Fish. Our job is to find out what the code does. Between Fish and myself, we've decoded most of the instruction set, and I was just about ready to start trying to match the instructions to the system code entry points when I had to quit and catch the last flight here last night."

"Have you made much progress?"

"Sorry, no. I have a gut feeling the problem is simpler from here on given what we have done, but we still have a long way to go. I'm afraid that from this point on, I'm not going to be much help. I'm really more than a little out of my field."

"That's OK, sir," Ralph said. "It'll take me a few minutes to familiarize myself with what you've done so far, and then I think we can work the problem. I've done a lot of machine language programming myself since I've been here, so I'm as familiar with this as anybody."

The phone in the corner rang and Steve answered. A couple of yeahs let them know it was for him. He made several glances at Jeff which seemed to indicate it was bad news. He asked a few questions and then hung up the phone.

"Bad news, guys. Iraq has sailed more SCUDs at Israel. A lot of damage was done."

"I heard that on the news this morning," Jeff said. "What about the U.S. PATRIOTs that were sent there from Germany? Didn't they try to engage?"

"Yeah. Killed several of the SCUDs. We already knew that from what we heard last night. Now it seems like the PATRIOTs which were fired at one or maybe two of the SCUDs were apparently bad missiles and self destructed after just a few seconds of the flight. Also seems as though those were the two SCUDs which did all of the damage on the ground. There's a big shouting match on what happened, and it seems the top shouter is the President. Jeff, with all due respect to your problem here, I think I'd better get back to the office."

"I agree. Only I'm coming with you. Ralph, do you think you can work this by yourself?"

"No problem, General. I'll give you guys a call when I've got something."

weapons systems--pentagon adv18 1-91
U.S. PATRIOT missiles fail to intercept Iraqi SCUDs
USWNS Military News
adv jan 18 1991 or thereafter

By George Growson

   WASHINGTON—At least one SCUD missile landed in an
apartment complex in Tel Aviv last night, killing two and
injuring more than 70 people. It is not known how many
other SCUDs were launched from Iraq. Several PATRIOT
missiles were launched, but their effectiveness is unclear.
Witnesses said that one PATRIOT exploded in a giant
fireball just a few seconds after launch. This PATRIOT may
have been intended to protect the apartment building that
was destroyed by the SCUD. U.S. officials would provide no
comment on the missile attack or the performance of the
PATRIOT missile that may have detonated prematurely.

FOURTEEN

January 18, 1991

Redstone Arsenal

Huntsville, Alabama

11:45 AM

Chaos was the only way to describe the scene when Jeff and Steve arrived at the PATRIOT Project Office building. Reporters, television crews, and an assortment of well-wishers and sightseers milled around the entrance to the building. Jeff had been warned by Steve, and he had hoped that his civilian clothes would disguise him. As they approached the building, a reporter recognized him, and their hopes fell of making it unscathed through the zoo.

Jeff could see the reporter giving his preliminary buildup into a hand-held microphone. When Jeff and Steve got to the edge of the throng, the reporter approached them.

"General Weyland, as manager of the PATRIOT Project, can you give us a comment on the performance of PATRIOT in the war?"

"Fellas, you're going to have to let me get to my office before I can give you any comment. So far, I don't know a whole lot more than you do."

Jeff tried to push his way through the mob.

"Can you make any comment on the PATRIOT that failed yesterday and the Israelis who were killed?"

"I am very saddened by the loss of life in Israel, but we haven't confirmed that a PATRIOT failed in an engagement. There are many reasons a missile could blow up like that."

"Could you give us some examples?"

"No. After we get the data back from Israel and get a chance to look at it carefully, we'll have a statement for you."

As he said these words, Jeff was running the possible reasons for failure through his mind. With an impact like an electric shock, the similarity of this failure to the one at the White Sands test hit him, and he began to push his way even harder through the crowd.

"How many PATRIOTs have been fired so far?"

"I don't think we're going to release that data yet—there isn't any reason to tell Saddam Hussein everything we're doing."

"Do you know how many SCUDs have been destroyed?"

"Same response," Jeff said.

There were guards at the door, and Jeff tried to get their attention so they could help him get through the crowd.

"Do you know how many PATRIOTs have failed like the one did yesterday?"

"Look, I said that we don't know yet if there even was a failure. When we find any answers, we'll make an official announcement."

"Will you do that release from here or Washington or Riyadh?"

"I don't know."

"Who is in charge of the investigation into the failure of the missile?"

"I don't even know if there is an investigation. I've said twice now that we don't even know for sure there was a failure."

Jeff put a little irritation in his voice in an attempt to get the reporters to back off. The relationship between the events which had just happened and those of last spring was running full speed through his mind.

As he neared the door, the guards made a path to the gate and ushered Jeff and Steve through. Once on the inside of the protected area, they headed for the elevator.

"Whoo! I can't imagine why anyone would want to live like that on a permanent basis," Steve said. "That was scary."

"Yeah. I can picture tomorrow's headlines. PATRIOT Chief Contradicts Army Story on Failure. Then we'll have that to contend with in addition to everything else."

Steve and Jeff slid their badges through the card reader, and Steve pushed the elevator button for the second floor. As the door closed, they could still see the guards holding back the crowd pressing toward the building.

"Did the similarity between what we've heard about the missile failures in Israel and the one that failed at White Sands last March occur to you?" Jeff asked.

"Not really," Steve said. "I mean, of course it occurred to me, since those are the only real failures we've had. But the one last March blew because of a range safety radar, and there are no range safety radars in Israel. At least I don't think there are."

"Still seems odd to be just a coincidence. At least two of the missiles we've fired in the last year have failed, and they both failed in exactly the same manner in both testing and combat. I think that deserves some investigation. Not only that, but Fish said the command destruct last spring may have come from the code we're trying to identify."

"What are you saying? You think all of that is somehow related?"

"Let's get at least one small group working that hypothesis, even though it's way out in left field," Jeff said. "Just until we're sure it's wrong."

"OK," Steve said, "I'll put some people on it."

When the elevator door opened, the scene was not much different from that at the front of the building. There was a mob in the hall in front of Jeff's office, but this time instead of reporters, it was government employees. They gave him a little more respect than the reporters had and parted as he came from the elevator. Everyone was talking excitedly and shouting cheers to him. Suddenly, the entire crowd erupted into a great cheer as he made his way down the corridor toward his office. Over the door was a banner with big letters reading "PATRIOT 15—SCUD 1." Just outside his office door, he stood on a chair and faced the excited crowd of his co-workers.

"Folks, you have every right to be proud today. From all indications, our system has performed exceptionally well in her first test in combat."

The crowd interrupted with cheers. He could hear individuals shouting "We showed 'em" and "Give'em hell, Gen'ral." His pride was obvious as he continued to speak.

"This week, we've shown the world what our country's technology can do when used to ensure peace for the free world."

More cheers.

"The system we have managed from this very office has backed up the solid positions of our Army, our President, and our country. There were some who said it wouldn't work, but it does. There were some who said we couldn't get it there in time, but we did. And there were some who said our President didn't have the guts to use it, but he did."

Louder cheers.

"Now I don't mean to detract from the enthusiasm we're all feeling, but there's still a lot of work to do. First, we need to find out what happened last night, and if there's a problem, get it fixed. We need to maintain the pressure for more missiles. We don't know how long this war is going to last, and we don't know how many SCUDs Iraq has and plans to fire. After I get the dust to settle in my office here, I'm going to come around to see each of you and let you tell me what we should be doing to better help the young men and women who have put their lives in harm's way for their country. Now let's go to work for them, and let's show that bastard Saddam Hussein what we can do."

There was a big cheer as he stepped down off the chair, and the crowd began to disperse.

He went down the corridor towards his office and through the double doors of the Project Manager's suite. Laura was there waiting for him.

"I'm proud, too, sir," she said. "We were beginning to worry about you when we didn't hear."

"Thanks, Laura," Jeff said. "I hope you'll understand that I don't mean to be rude or insensitive, but I don't have any time for small talk right now. We've got a real problem on our hands."

"I hear you, and I'm ready," Laura said. "What can I do?"

"First, do you have a number for Billy Walker?"

"Yes, and he's already called this morning."

"Good. Get him for me. What else?"

"There are also calls from General Grant's office and General Powell's office and several press calls. Those are just the important ones. There's a stack of other ones, from the mayor on down."

"Just hold them all and get Billy on the line for me, will you? And you might get someone to get us some sandwiches. Have whoever is in charge of our control room get Steve Smith up to date on last night, and then have Steve come see me."

"Yes, sir. Anything else?"

"Look, Laura. Some really weird things have been going on, and I don't have any choice but to trust you. Would you call the Starlight Motel and ask for room 124? Suzy Morris should answer, and just tell her I don't have time to talk, but I was just checking on her. Tell her how crazy everything is here, and that I will call her as soon as I can. Don't let anyone else hear the call nor let anyone know where Suzy is."

"Got it," she said.

"Thanks."

Laura pulled the door closed as she left, and he was alone with his thoughts. The intercom buzzed.

"General, Billy Walker on line two."

"Billy, Jeff. Have you heard what happened last night?"

"Yes, but I didn't think it was tied to what we're doing. You think it is?"

"I don't know, but the more I think about it, the more I think it is. We had a missile blow like that at White Sands during a test last March. It was explained at the time by a malfunction in a range safety radar, but I think it's too much of a coincidence that the only two missiles we've lost have been to the same phenomenon. That's just too improbable."

"What makes you think it's tied to the hidden software?"

"One thing Fish said keeps coming back. He said that when the missile blew at White Sands, and they were running software checks before we discovered the radar malfunction, the printouts showed there was a direct link from the missile destruct function to the hidden code. That's what put him onto it in the first place. I can't help but think they may all be coming from the same basic cause."

"If we can find out what's in that software, we might know the answer to all of this."

"I agree, and I've got the best man Steve could find working on it. He seemed optimistic, but so did I when Fish and I got started. Have

317

you got anything new?"

"Not much, but we're closing in on Mitchell. She definitely was not born in the hospital listed on her birth certificate. That could be just some simple administrative error, but I'm going on the assumption that she has a completely fake background."

"Have you found her yet?"

"No. I've requested a tail on her, but so far they haven't been able to find her to start. She's not in her apartment or her office and neither phone has been used. We'll keep trying. I told the guys to follow but not pick her up if they locate her."

"What about Fish?" Jeff asked.

"Holding his own. They think he's got a fighting chance."

Jeff looked up, saw Steve at the office door, and motioned him to a chair until he finished the conversation with Billy. Jeff turned to Steve.

"Are we in touch with the PATRIOT unit that fired the failed missile last night?" he asked.

"Not on a moment-to-moment basis, but we can set up a link if you want us to."

"Yes, I do. I'd like to talk to the Battery Commander. Which battery was it?"

"Bravo Battery, 4th Battalion of the 43rd Artillery. Captain Jerry Maxwell."

"I remember him. See if you can get me patched through to him either from my office or down in the control room."

"Yes, sir. It might take a few minutes."

"Any feedback from the lab yet on the software?"

"Nothing. I'll give Ralph a call and see how he's coming."

"Good. First priority on the call to Israel."

"Yes, sir," Steve said as he left the room, and Jeff picked up the stack of message slips Laura had handed him.

Jeff called to General Powell's office and reached Colonel Sampson, who relayed General Powell's thanks and congratulations for a job well done. Ordinarily, that would have been a moment for Jeff to stop and finally feel a little pride himself, but he almost brushed Colonel Sampson off because of his preoccupation with his problem. There was no answer at General Grant's office.

January 18, 1991
U.S. PATRIOT Compound
Tel Aviv, Israel
8:00 PM

"There's a call from the states for Captain Maxwell." The clerk yelled down the hall at Sergeant Johnson.

"Who's it from?" the sergeant asked over his shoulder.

"General Weyland, the PATRIOT Project Manager."

"Tell him the Captain ain't here."

"Where do I tell them he is?"

"Shit, I don't care. Tell 'em he's missing in action."

"Yeah, right. What if they want to talk to you?"

"Then come get me. I'll be down at the launcher area."

"That ain't gonna get it."

"Then tell them to call the battalion commander. I've got work to do, and talking to some general who's got a bug up his ass ain't part of it."

There was a knock at the door, and Steve stuck his head around the corner.

"Odd piece of data," Steve said.

"I'm not sure what could be considered odd in the midst of what's going on around here. What's up?" asked Jeff.

"Captain Maxwell is officially listed as missing in action."

"He's what?" Jeff was up and out of his chair and coming around the desk. "How could somebody be missing in action from a PATRIOT site?

319

None of the sites have been hit, have they?"

"No, nothing like that. It appears that after the engagement last night, Captain Maxwell left the compound for what he said was a walk and hasn't been seen since. They're eight hours ahead of us so that means he's been missing almost a full day now. He's either AWOL or something's happened."

"Who is the First Sergeant there?"

"Sergeant First Class Johnson is acting since they left Germany. The regular First Sergeant was ill and couldn't make the trip."

"Can I talk to Sergeant Johnson?"

"I'm sure you can. It'll take me a few minutes to set up the call again. I'll have them patch it through to your office."

"Thanks," Jeff said as Steve left. He walked back around his desk and sat in deep thought.

Jeff reached over and hit the intercom. "Laura, see if you can get me Johnny Madkin at White Sands."

He leaned back in the chair. Something about the name Johnson kept ringing in his head.

"Johnny Madkin on line one," Laura's voice said to him over the intercom behind his desk. He picked up the phone.

"Johnny, I need some information."

"You and most of the rest of the world. Is this about the flight last night?"

"Yes and no. Do you remember the flight last January when I visited the range and there was a question about an odd entry made by the console operator?"

"Yeah, I remember. You had us check into it for a while and then it just dropped. What's up?"

"Do you remember the name of the operator who was at the console and made the entry?"

"No, not off the top of my head. Hang on a second."

Jeff could hear the phone clank as Johnny put it on his desk. He heard Johnny going through a file cabinet.

"Staff Sergeant James E. Johnson," Johnny said when he returned to the phone. "I remember him. Good looking young NCO. Big fellow. Smart."

"Do you know if he's still at White Sands?"

"I doubt it. Most of the troops who know anything at all about how to operate PATRIOT are in Saudi Arabia now."

"Did any from White Sands go to Israel?" Jeff asked.

"No, not unless they had transferred to Germany in the meantime. All the units and personnel from here went to Saudi. The ones in Israel all came from Germany. Do you want me to check and see where he is now?"

"Yes, and could you get back to me as soon as possible?"

"Sure, what's up?"

"Probably nothing. I'll tell you about it when you find him. Is there any activity out there?"

"We're setting up for a shot tomorrow. We're going to try to replicate the firing that went bad last night to see if we can reproduce the problem here. The data collected on the tactical firing sites is slim compared to what we can get here, so if we can make the system fail the same way, we can almost assuredly find the cause."

"Good luck on that. Keep me posted."

"You bet," Johnny said, and they hung up.

Steve was waiting at the door.

"Gets a little odder each time," he said. "Sergeant Johnson was there when I placed the call for Captain Maxwell, but now nobody can find him. They believe he's still at the site, but no one seems to know where. They're going to keep looking and get back to us."

"OK, route the call to me when it comes."

"OK, boss," Steve said. Laura was coming in as Steve left his office.

"Colonel Sampson is on line three. Want something to eat?"

Jeff nodded yes as he picked up the phone.

"I hope your day is going better than mine, Colonel."

"If it is, then you're really having a record setter. I just got off the phone with the Chairman who just got off the phone with the President who just got off the phone with Mr. Shamir, who is pissed as hell."

"How could he tell?"

"Good line, sir, but not much help. We thought we had it under control, but as they start to approach night time over there, nerves get edgy again."

"So what's the situation?"

"We don't have a lot of time here. The President believes that the next time the Israelis are hit bad, they'll strike back and then there's no telling what might happen."

"What do you want from me?"

"The President wants some assurance that you can stop the SCUDs."

"I've given all the assurances I can. I said there were no guarantees. Some are going to slip through."

"I know that, sir. I guess the chairman just wanted you to know the critical nature of the situation."

"Right. Tell him I'm aware."

"Yes, sir."

"Also tell him it's my opinion that if PATRIOT hadn't been there, we would have passed the boiling point long ago. Make sure he and the President understand that."

"Trust me, General, they do, and they appreciate what you and your people there have done. They just want to make sure nothing is left to chance."

"Thanks."

Jeff flopped on the couch as he tried to run all of the pieces through his head. He kept trying to convince himself that the failure or failures in Israel and White Sands were not related, but his mind wouldn't let it happen. He pulled out his phone book and dialed the Starlight Motel.

"Hi, Cap'n. How goes the ship."

"Bouncing on heavy seas. Everything OK there?"

"I'm fine, except for going a little stir crazy. There's not even a TV in this room."

"Remind me, and I'll get you a pocket TV when we do this the next time."

"If there's a next time for this episode, buster, you'll need more than a pocket TV to make me happy."

"I bet you say that to every guy who puts you up in a luxury motel."

"They usually leave me with something to eat."

"Is the door bolted?"

"Yes."

"Has anybody been there?"

"Only the cleaning crew. I asked them to come back later."

"Good. Pack the bags. Until this is over, we'll stay someplace different each night."

"When will you be able to get away?"

"No idea. Just be ready."

"Will do."

"If I can't make it soon, I'll get Laura to bring you some lunch."

"I can wait. I have some crackers in my bag."

"Suzy?"

"Yes."

"I love you, and I'm sorry I've put you in this situation."

"It's not your situation. It's ours. And it's not you who put me here, remember? I did. Is it going to be OK?"

"Yes."

"Certain?"

"No."

The intercom buzzed.

"I've got to go."

"I love you, too."

"Thanks."

Laura's voice was on the intercom as soon as he hung up.

"General, Johnny Madkin on line two."

"I've found your sergeant," Johnny said. "I think you said he was in Germany, and you were right if you did. He left the unit assigned to do the test that day and worked as an operator for the range for a while. He then requested and received a transfer back into PATRIOT and is assigned to the 32nd in Germany. I don't know which unit yet, but we should know that soon."

"What did he do when he was assigned to the range?" Jeff asked.

"Don't really know what he was doing. He was assigned to range support. I'll poke into that, too, and get back to you with both those answers."

"OK. Thanks, Johnny."

Jeff hit the intercom again and asked Laura to get Billy on the phone. In just a moment, he was there.

"OK, buddy," Jeff said, "I've got another one for you."

"Well, this is getting better by the minute. I've got new data for you, too. You first."

"The young sergeant named Johnson who was at the console when the entry was made that day subsequently was transferred to range support. I don't know for sure yet, but I'll be willing to bet that he was somewhere around that range safety radar the day the missile blew prematurely. It also turns out he has now been assigned to a PATRIOT unit in Germany. There is also a Sergeant Johnson assigned to the unit from Germany that had the missile blow last night."

"If that's the same Sergeant Johnson, he's been a busy young man. Do you have his full name?"

"James E. Johnson. Sergeant First Class. Why don't you see what you can find out about him?"

"Will do," Billy said. "Ready for my data?"

"Shoot," Jeff said.

"Your girl Celia Mitchell travels under an alias. Sharon Reynolds. Been pretty busy, too. Made several trips to El Paso and Boston."

"Any travel outside the country?" Jeff asked.

"Not that we know of. Not even a passport in that name. But that doesn't mean much. It doesn't take much to create an alias just for airline travel and car rental inside the U.S. A passport is something else. If she travels outside the country, she probably has a deep cover ID for that with separate passport and the whole works."

"How did you get on to the Sharon ID?"

"Found it in a hidden safe in her apartment. Checked the travel times in the airline log against the records of her vacation. Matched up pretty good."

"You went into her apartment? Christ, Billy, are you trying to get us all sent to jail?"

"Did I say we went into her apartment?"

"No."

"Good. Damn, you scared me. That would really be beyond my bounds, not to mention illegal. It seems to me you need to quit asking so many questions if that's going to be your reaction to the answers."

"Have you found her yet?"

"No, but we're running this Sharon Reynolds ID through everything we can. She'll turn up."

"What about Grant?" Jeff asked.

"He's still at the Pentagon."

"I couldn't get an answer at his office just a little while ago."

"That's because he's down in the situation room," Billy said. "Want me to get a number where he can be reached?"

"Christ, you're not tailing him, too, are you?"

"No. It's more like we just made sure we had somebody in the meetings where he was. My guy will find some way to stay with him for the day. Want the number?"

"No, I really don't want to talk to him. I was just returning a call."

"OK. Remember, there's no sure indication he is one of the bad guys. Maybe he's just being used somehow. Stay in touch, buddy."

"Yeah, you bet," Jeff said as he hung up.

Steve had his head in the door as Jeff finished the conversation with Billy.

"Sir, Ralph Jameson is on the phone. He says that he is not finished yet, but he has a sketchy outline of the code logic. Do you want to hear it?"

"I sure do. That code may be the answer to all of this."

Steve came in the office and hit the intercom. "Laura, put Ralph Jameson onto the boss's line."

A short pause and Laura said, "Line two, General."

Jeff hit the speaker button on the phone so both he and Steve could hear Ralph.

"That didn't take long, Ralph. You work fast," Jeff said.

"You guys were closer than you thought. Whoever did what you gave me had done most of the hard work." Jeff thought about Fish, lying in his hospital bed.

"If I can assume you did it correctly," Ralph continued, "then I think I have a rough feel for what the code is doing."

"OK," Jeff said. "Let's have it."

"It appears to be some type of safety check."

Safety check?

Jeff's heart sank. Safety check wasn't what he was expecting at all.

The voice on the speaker continued. "The code is intended to check on certain events, settings and inputs that occur during the flight. If all of these conditions are not satisfied, it triggers a sequence of events that eventually will send a destruct command to the missile."

"What are all of these things, the code checks?" Steve asked.

"I don't know them all, yet, and that may take a while. I'll have to go to each of the sections in the system software to see what's there. I just thought you might want to know what I found out so far."

"Can you make any sense of why this code is there?" Jeff asked. "It seems to be maybe something not totally abnormal."

"No. It may just be something that was there from a test a long time ago, and either on purpose or accidentally got put in background and then never was discovered."

"Could that happen accidentally?" Jeff asked.

"Yes. No. Maybe. I don't know. All of the above," Ralph said. "Maybe there was actually a bad spot on the disk and the computer somehow hiccuped at the same time and registered the wrong location or something. Seems unlikely, and I don't even know if it can happen. It just seems equally unlikely that someone did it on purpose. Especially with logic that will cut down a missile. That's pretty sensitive stuff."

"You bet," Steve said. "Look what happened last night."

"You think this is what did that damage last night?" Ralph asked.

"Nobody has the foggiest," Jeff said. "You keep digging in that software and maybe we'll find out."

"I heard that," Ralph said.

326

"Good work," Jeff said. "Stick to it, Ralph, and keep me posted."

"Okay, sir," Ralph said, and they hung up.

"I'm going to the control room," Jeff said to Steve as he came from behind the desk.

"You think they may know something?"

"I just want to check on what's been going on since last night."

"OK. I'm going back to my place and see if I can make any sense of the stack of messages on my desk."

Jeff created quite a stir as he came into the room. An Army Warrant Officer was in charge. The operation in the room had been on three shifts per day, seven days per week, since August. Jeff knew the men and women in this room had not had a normal day off since the day Saddam Hussein invaded Kuwait. Not Thanksgiving, nor Christmas, nor New Year's. From this room, all coordination for the manufacture and transportation of PAC II missiles had been managed.

Charts on every wall from floor to ceiling described each missile by serial number and where it was in the process of manufacture, delivery or use. A fair number of the missiles had red lines drawn through them indicating that these were the ones that had been fired. The status of all deployed units was displayed, showing the readiness of each PATRIOT unit worldwide. Communications were in place with Saudi Arabia, Israel, key U.S. Army, Air Force, and Navy installations, and the Pentagon. The room had operated as the nerve center for PATRIOT deployment and operation since the conflict began.

"Hello, Mr. Jorgenson," Jeff said to the Warrant Officer in charge of the shift. "How 'bout filling me in on where we stand."

"Sure thing, sir," he said. "If you'll come right over here to this first board, I think I have a summary that will tell you everything we know."

"There are 632 PAC II missiles which have completed manufacture and been shipped to the Middle East. These missiles are in the hands of U.S. PATRIOT units in Saudi Arabia and Israel. Of those, sixty-seven have been fired to date. I don't have the numbers of the SCUDs that have been successfully engaged, but I believe the number is around twenty-eight. There are four confirmed misses. One of those, PATRIOT just plain missed,

I guess by the law of averages, but the other three appeared to be bad missiles."

"When you say 'bad missiles,' what do you mean?"

"I mean they were never brought under control by the ground crew and never responded to our commands, so they were destroyed."

"When you say 'destroyed,' do you mean from the ground?"

"Could be either way. If the missile doesn't receive any command from the ground after a certain period of time, it'll blow itself. By the same token, if the ground doesn't receive any information back from the missile, it'll command the missile to blow."

"And you're convinced it was one or the other of those cases last night?"

"Well, I was until you asked, because those are the only normal cases with bad missiles. But obviously you have a reason for asking that makes me question that. Why do you ask?"

"What if the communication was good, both from the ground up and the missile down, and it still blew? What would you conclude then?"

"One last check is on the missile to see if, internally, the system is responding as it should. If the missile commands a fin to turn and it doesn't, for example, the system can tell that, and in cases where the abnormality is judged to be such that the system can't complete its mission, it'll blow the missile."

"So what happened last night?" Jeff asked.

"So far, we don't know. The data's not back in the States yet. It probably will go to Raytheon first, and they'll look at it, but I don't know if they have it yet."

"Find out for me, would you, and let me know which of the circumstances you described seemed to be the case last night."

"Yes, sir. Anything else?"

"Yes, you mentioned there were two more missiles that also failed. Do you know what happened to them?"

"No, sir, except it was the same type of thing. Missile blew shortly after launch. Actually, there were three others. The one last night was not in that count. So now there are four."

"In Israel and in Saudi Arabia?" Jeff asked.

"No, sir, only in Israel."

Jeff raised his eyebrows.

"Do you consider that strange?"

"Yes, sir, now that you mention it. We've fired a lot more missiles in Saudi Arabia, but none have failed in this way. Only in Israel."

"Did the missiles get the same treatment going to Israel as the ones going to Saudi?"

"Yes, sir. Identical conditions for the transportation of the missiles. But the radar and computer systems are a different story. Israel has systems from Germany that were airlifted after very short notice last week. The ones in Saudi have been there since August and September."

"Were the failures in Israel from one site or multiple sites?"

Mr. Jorgenson looked at the boards. "From two sites. Both of the sites protecting Tel Aviv. The sites protecting the harbor and the military bases haven't had any failures. But this sample size is so small, I don't know if that means anything."

"See if you can get some data on how all of those missiles failed, and get that to me. Who's working this at Raytheon?"

"We were interfacing with Max Fisher, but he's out sick. We're now talking to a guy who works for him by the name of Doug Glover. Seems pretty sharp. I'll get on the horn to him right away."

"Thanks, Chief," Jeff said. "You guys are doing a great job. Maybe this thing won't take much longer and we can have a few days off."

"Well, sir, I remember the way I spent the last war, and this room doesn't seem too bad. Having to work a few holiday shifts beats the hell out of slogging through rice paddies."

"You're right on that score. I remember those paddies, too," Jeff said, and smiled as he left the control room.

When Jeff arrived at his office, there was a message to call Ralph Jameson. He called Steve into the office and got Ralph back on the speaker box.

"I just found one more piece of data," Ralph said, "and I thought I would pass it on."

"Go ahead," Jeff said.

"Well, like I said before, there's a list of things the code checks to see if it wants to blow the missile. I've identified several things that appear normal, but I came across one I don't understand. The code checks for a bit in the data coming to the site on the satellite receiver. If the bit is not set a certain way, it'll execute missile destruct."

"That doesn't seem too unusual," Steve said.

"It didn't seem too far out to me either until I checked the list of items on the satellite message. The bit which is being checked is a spare and has never been used. I called to check with the communications people, and they checked the actual messages going out right now; that bit location is never used."

"So what's in the location for that bit?"

"Nothing. It's left blank."

"So the space would be there if someone wanted to use it?"

"Not only that, but since it's not being used by our communications setup, it probably wouldn't be noticed if it was being used for some other purpose."

"Are you sure about this?" Jeff asked.

"Yes, sir," Ralph said. "The missile checks bit location forty-six on the satellite message, and depending on how that bit is set, it will command a destruct of the missile."

"Anything else?" Steve asked.

"It also looks for an input from the keyboard. There's a short code it looks for to tell it there is an input coming. Then there's just a scrambled bunch of letters it checks against. If it doesn't receive the message or the letters don't match, it blows the missile."

"Thanks, Ralph," Jeff said, and abruptly hung up the phone and looked at Steve.

"This is either nothing or a mistake gone awry, or somebody could hold PATRIOT's performance in their hip pocket."

Laura's voice on the intercom said, "General, Johnny Madkin is on line one."

"What's up, Johnny?"

"I did some more checking about Sergeant Johnson and found out that when he left here and went to range support, he worked the radar system over there."

"Things are getting stranger by the minute. Okay, thanks Johnny. I'll talk to you later."

Jeff reached back to the desk and hit the intercom button an angry blow. "Laura, get Billy Walker on the phone for me. Right away."

"Yes, sir."

Jeff and Steve sat quietly in the room, each feeling his own heartbeat as they waited for the phone.

"Line two, General."

"Billy, Jeff. New information. The hidden code contains instructions to check a supposedly unused bit in the satellite communications message and blow the missile for certain settings. Turns out we have three other missiles which have blown like the one last night. All engaging SCUDs attacking densely populated Israeli civilian areas. And get this. It looks like our Sergeant Johnson was the operator sitting at the console of the range safety radar that blew our missile last summer."

"Are you really insinuating that someone has tapped into the communication link to PATRIOT and can turn it on and off?"

"I know it sounds like I've been watching too many *Twilight Zone* reruns, but yes, that's what I think," Jeff replied.

"And our same Sergeant Johnson definitely seems to be up to his neck in this somehow. I've talked to several people about him, and guess what? He's now assigned to the PATRIOT system that experienced the failure last night."

"I know. He also seems to have disappeared. I tried to call him a short while ago at the firing unit. He can't be found, and the Battery Commander is listed as missing in action."

"Well," Billy said with a deep breath, "at least there's not much doubt any more if we have something sinister afoot. It appears we have a big time conspiracy to deal with here. Do you want us to bring in General Grant?"

"No, we really don't know for sure yet if he's involved. None of this points to him. Have you found Celia Mitchell yet?"

"No. Dropped off the face of the earth, that lady did."

"I have an idea. Suzy and I are coming to Washington on the next plane. Can you meet us at the airport?"

"I'm at your disposal, buddy. Will we need any cavalry?"

"Not for what I've got in mind. We'll have to follow our noses after that."

"I'll see you at the airport. As soon as you get your schedule, have somebody give me a call."

"Right. Thanks, buddy."

"Yeah, well. Let's just make this one count. Big stakes."

"Right. See you in a couple of hours."

"Yeah, see ya."

Hitting the intercom button once again as he rose from his chair, Jeff said, "Laura, call Suzy for me, please, and tell her to be ready to move. I'm on my way."

January 18, 1991
Washington, DC
9:45 PM

"Welcome to our nation's capital, buddy. What's this plan you want help with?" Billy said as Jeff and Suzy climbed into the car in front of Washington National Airport.

"I want to meet with Senator Hyman T. Strong," Jeff said.

"Senator Strong?" Billy's reaction said this wasn't going to be easy. "Why don't you just go straight to God, himself? I'm not sure I can get us to him, especially tonight."

"I figured we might have to wait until tomorrow morning, but we think he may hold the key to this thing," Suzy said. "I also have the feeling that as a United States Senator, he might be willing to cooperate once he gets a feeling for the full scope of what's going on."

"What role do you figure he plays?" Billy asked.

"I don't really know," Jeff said. "He's as liberal as they come. I mean way left. But for some unknown reason, he's a major supporter of PATRIOT."

"So?"

"It's the only weapon I know of that he supports," Suzy said. "That makes no sense at all to me, but it's another piece of this puzzle that doesn't fit."

"And the fact that Celia Mitchell is his secretary, I think, is no coincidence," Jeff added.

"Let me see if I can get a home address on him," Billy said as he reached for the cellular phone on the console of the car.

There was a strained conversation with whoever answered the phone. It was clear that the person on the other end of the conversation didn't want to give Billy any information on Senator Strong. Billy hung up in frustration.

"Well, it seems that even in today's environment, some things are still sacred," Billy said.

"You mean a senator has privileges that even you can't break?"

"Not all senators. Just this one and a few more like him. You have to realize that in addition to being a member of the Senate Arms Services Committee, he's also the Chairman of the Senate Select Committee on Intelligence. As such, he controls the budget for such paltry organizations as the one I work for."

"So no help there?" Suzy asked.

"Right. That's a dead end. In fact, I may have done more harm than good. I've now been forbidden to have any contact with the good senator. I'll also get the opportunity to explain to my boss early on Monday morning just exactly why I wanted such information as that in the first place."

"Sorry," Jeff said. "I didn't mean to get you in hot water."

"No problem. It just means we'll have to go to plan B."

"Which is?"

"Which is, to coin a phrase rapidly gaining prominence, 'the mother of all black books.' Do you have an office in this town with a computer and a modem?"

"Sure. In Crystal City, right around the corner."

"Do you have a key to the building and access to the computer?"

"Of course. Take a left. Is this going to get you in more trouble?"

"No. But I say no only because I don't think there's any way I could be in more trouble than I am already. Besides, if I'm as good at this as people tell me I am, they'll never know it. And if they do, it traces to your computer, not mine."

"Thanks a lot. Take a right and then left into the driveway."

Billy parked the car in the front lot of the high-rise office complex and they went in the building, up the elevator and to the suite rented by the PATRIOT Project Office. Jeff opened the door and then used a second key to open a door into a small room with several computers.

"Take your pick. They all have phone hook-ups."

"This is really a nice set-up. A fella could run a real undercover operation from here. If I'm ever in a pinch, would it be OK if I used this place?"

"Be my guest," Jeff said.

Billy sat down in front of an IBM PC and turned it on while Jeff and Suzy watched. When the screen began to glow, he worked quickly, obviously familiar with the machine.

"That's a talent I didn't know you had," Jeff said. "You're pretty quick with that thing."

"Quick won't mean diddly if I get the wrong code." Billy reached inside his jacket, pulled out a small address book and began to look for something in particular.

"I thought writing down codes was against the rules for you guys. Don't they make you commit everything to memory?" Suzy asked

"A, I don't trust my memory. B, 'they' didn't give me these numbers. C, these numbers are in such a deep personal code, I myself have trouble figuring them out, and I made up the code. Don't ask me to explain it to you or I'll have to shoot you, and that would make Jeff mad all over again."

They watched as Billy worked the machine. He referenced the small address book several times. There were obviously several missed entries on the machine, but finally Billy put the book down and looked at Jeff.

334

"This is it. Do you want his address or phone number?"

"What about both?"

"Nothing's too good for my buddy. Get ready to write fast. They won't stay on the screen long."

"Why?"

"As soon as we see it, everybody else does and somebody knows we're looking, so we have to be out of there before they can trace the call, and that's an automatic process."

"How long does the trace take?" Suzy asked.

"Too long, if the perpetrator, that's me, knows it's there, which I do. Don't worry." He looked at Jeff. "Just be prepared to work fast and then get out of here fast."

"I thought you said it was too slow to trace back here," Jeff said.

"It was, but that was last year. One never knows how quickly technology moves. Let's just don't take any chances. Ready?"

"Ready," Jeff said.

Suzy was holding her breath as Billy clicked the keys and called off the address in an upscale section of McLean, Virginia, and the phone number.

"Got it?" Billy asked.

"Yep. Shut 'er down."

Billy's fingers moved rapidly over the keys.

"Done. Let's get going."

⌑⌑⌑⌑⌑

Billy had no trouble finding the address Jeff had written on the small pad. They cruised the street a second time.

"I guess the best thing to do is to pull into the driveway and knock on the door," Jeff said.

"Maybe we should call first," Suzy said.

"And say what? I want to talk to you about the possibility you may be involved in a plot to aid an enemy of the United States? I don't think so."

"OK, what's your idea?" Billy asked.

"How about you let me and Suzy out, and we'll go up to the door.

335

That way, I can call you on the cellular if I need you." Jeff reached over the back seat and pulled his small portable cellular phone from his carry-on airline case.

"OK. I'll cruise the block until I hear from you." Billy pulled over to the curb by the driveway, and Jeff got out of the car, with Suzy following him.

They walked the length of the driveway and down a small rock path toward the front door. At the door, Jeff rang the bell and waited. Nothing. He rang the bell again. Finally, he could see some movement on the other side of the door. When it opened, Jeff's heart skipped a beat. The three-piece suit and the bulge under the armpit made it clear this was no butler. Feeling Suzy behind him helped Jeff resist the urge to turn and run.

"I need to see Senator Strong," Jeff said.

"I bet you do," the suit said. "OK, boys. Bring 'em in."

Jeff started to take a step backwards, but two more suits came from the bushes on either side of the path. One of them grabbed Suzy's arm while the other shoved Jeff a step closer to the doorway.

"Hey," Suzy said as she tried to pull her arm away, but couldn't.

"Why don't you come with us, and let's talk a little," the first suit said as he gripped Jeff's wrist.

"What are you doing?" Jeff asked, struggling a little. When the grip tightened significantly on his arm, he could tell he was well outmatched. Struggling would not be a wise thing to do. "I want to know what you're doing. And let go of me."

"I think," the first suit said, "you better be quiet and realize just how precarious your situation is. I'll ask the questions, and you'll answer them. Do you understand?"

Jeff nodded his head.

"Good. First, who are you?"

"I am Brigadier General Jeff Weyland, Project Manager of the PATRIOT Air Defense Missile."

"And who is she?"

"This is Suzy Morris. She is the Administrative Assistant to Senator Hastings."

"Well now, General, do you want to tell me just what a general in the

United States Army is doing poking around in a computer database where he's not supposed to be?"

Damn, that was fast.

"It's imperative that I speak to the Senator."

"We'll get to that. For now, how 'bout you tell me just how you got into that database?"

Another suit came from the back of the house with a portable cellular phone and handed it to the first suit. He spoke into the phone several times, then smiled as he looked at Jeff.

"Bring him to me," the suit said into the phone without taking his eyes off Jeff.

"Maybe we'll ask your buddy how you got into that database."

They all stood there silently for a while, and then they heard steps coming up the gravel path Jeff had traveled just a few minutes before.

"Well, would you look here?" the first suit said as Billy came into the light. "If it isn't our brother in spirit. What the hell are you doing here, Walker? Let him go, fellas. Them, too," he said, motioning to Jeff and Suzy.

Jeff rubbed his wrist, and Suzy straightened her jacket as she glared at the suit who had been holding her.

"I asked you, Walker, and I want an answer. What are you doing here? You're going to have a lot of explaining to do."

"My friend here needs to talk to the Senator," Billy said.

"I already heard that verse from your buddy and his friend here. Tell me something new and clever."

"All I know to say is that this is a matter of national importance."

The suit rolled his eyes and made a face that let it be known he didn't think much of Billy's national emergency.

"Look," Billy said, "you know how much trouble I'm in by being here, so you know how important I think it is. I'm asking you, Al, in the name of all that we believe in, let this man talk to the Senator."

"Who is he, exactly?" the man named Al asked.

"He's exactly Brigadier General Jeff Weyland. The man in charge of the PATRIOT missile."

"Why does he need to talk to the Senator?"

"That's between him and the Senator," Billy said.

Al looked at Jeff and Suzy.

"PATRIOT, huh? You guys've really been showing 'em the last few days, haven't you?"

"Yes, we have, but it might all be for nothing if you don't let me talk to the Senator."

"Why didn't you just call him and visit him in his office like everybody else does?" Al asked.

"Because, asshole," Billy said, "there are bad guys involved, and we're not sure who they are."

"You guys see bad guys behind every lamp post."

"Listen, Al," Billy said. "Did you hear the story on the news about the PATRIOT that blew up last night and the Israelis that were killed?"

"Yeah, I heard something about that. Why?"

"This has to do with that problem," Jeff said. "Four PATRIOTs have blown up just like that, plus one at White Sands last summer during a test."

"What does this have to do with Senator Strong?"

"We think the Senator may have some information that can help us find out what's causing them to fail," Suzy said. "If we can't find out why, more lives are at stake. It could even bring Israel into the war. We need to talk to the Senator." Al looked at her and then to Jeff.

"Do you have some ID?"

"Yes," Jeff said, and he and Suzy both showed their government badges. Al looked at them for a long time.

"Wait here," Al said and went into the back of the house.

Billy, Jeff and Suzy silently looked at each other and waited. In a few minutes, Al came back and waved his hand in the direction of Jeff and Suzy.

"If the two of you will come with me, the Senator will see you," he said.

"Thanks," Jeff said, as he and Suzy followed Al into the house.

"Funny thing," Al said as they started up a staircase. "The Senator said he kind of expected somebody to come and see him. He seems nervous about it."

338

They went down the main hall on the second floor of the house. Billy knew that Senators lived well, but the opulence of the house surprised him. It went beyond living well to extremely luxurious. They entered a small sitting area with a fireplace. The Senator, wearing pajamas, a robe and slippers, was seated in a rocking chair in front of the fire.

"Come and sit, General Weyland," the Senator said without rising or offering his hand. "I see you've brought someone else."

"Yes, sir. Senator, this is Suzy Morris."

"Please have a seat, young lady."

"Thank you," Suzy said, and sat in one of the armchairs.

"General, I know we haven't met," Senator Strong said. "But I've heard a great deal about you and your missile over the years. Please, sit down."

"Thank you, Senator. I'm flattered that you have heard of me. PATRIOT I expected, but not me."

"Oh, yes. You have quite a reputation among my colleagues. A good one, I might add." He turned to Suzy. "Haven't I seen you before?"

"Yes," Suzy said. "I work in Senator Hastings's office."

"I thought so. I seem to recall Hastings saying you really ran his office."

"Thank you, Senator," Suzy said.

"I wonder if we might talk about PATRIOT?" Jeff asked.

"You want to know about the plan, don't you?"

"Plan, sir?" Jeff leaned forward in his chair. The Senator was speaking very low.

"Yes, that plan of General Grant's."

"Well, yes, sir. I think that's what I'd like to talk about. What plan did General Grant tell you about?"

"He never told me a damn thing. As a matter of fact, I never spoke with him about it. He sent all of his communication through one of my assistants."

"That would be Miss Mitchell?"

"Yes, Celia. Do you know her?"

"I've met her once or twice. She's a friend of a friend, so to speak. She's actually a better friend of Suzy's."

"Well," the Senator said, "I got all of my information from General

Grant through her. She explained the plan to me. It wasn't much of a plan, though. I never did like it."

Jeff could feel him slipping away. At first, it had seemed that the Senator thought Jeff knew everything, and he was scared and nervous. Now, he seemed to realize Jeff was in the dark, and he was getting a little more confident and less cooperative.

"Tell me about the plan, sir."

"Well, as I said, it wasn't much of a plan. I'd really rather not talk about it if you don't mind. Politics, you understand."

"Yes, sir, I understand. Senator, if I might, I have a friend downstairs who would like to tell you a few things about Miss Mitchell."

"What kinds of things?" He seemed interested in that.

"Some information we've picked up on her background."

"Well, she has a secret clearance, you know. All the people in my office do."

"Yes, sir, but would you listen to what Mr. Walker has to say?"

"Walker?"

"Yes, sir. Billy Walker. He's a friend of mine who's been helping me on this."

"Billy Walker, huh. Hasn't he testified in front of my committee before? Works out at the funny farm?"

"Possibly. Let me get him."

Jeff went to the door and found Al was standing just outside.

"Get Billy up here," Jeff said to Al.

He could tell Al wasn't happy, but he motioned for one of the suits down the hall to come stand by the door as he went downstairs. Jeff went back inside the room with the Senator. He sat in the chair the Senator offered, and neither spoke until Billy arrived.

"I thought so," the Senator said with a sneer as Billy came into the room. "The spooks have arrived."

"Billy," Jeff said, "the Senator doesn't want to talk about anything much, and in a way, I don't blame him. I think, however, if he heard a little of what you've found out about his assistant, Miss Mitchell, he might have a change of heart."

340

"OK," Billy said as he pulled a little pad from his coat pocket. "Celia Mitchell, alias Sharon Reynolds, alias Sharifa Martouf. Works for Senator Strong as Celia Mitchell. False birth certificate for clearance and other U.S. papers. Travels in the United States under the name Sharon Reynolds. No ID beyond credit cards and driver's license. Travels internationally as Sharifa Martouf on Bahraini passport. Primarily exits and enters the U.S. through British Virgin Islands. Passport shows no other stamps. Leaves the country once or twice a year. Known final destination is in Palestine where she has been seen in the company of known Palestinian terrorists. Traveled to El Paso, Texas, and Boston, Massachusetts during a time of clandestine Palestinian terrorist activities in those areas. Keeps regular contact in this country with runners for the PLO. Bottom line. Confirmed agent of a spin-off Palestinian Liberation Front terrorist group. Other members of the office say she is the Senator's closest advisor on military affairs."

Jeff was looking at Billy with his mouth slightly open and continued to stare for a few moments, not realizing Billy was finished. He flinched slightly as Suzy nudged him from behind.

"Thanks, Billy. Why don't you leave us alone with the Senator again for a few minutes?"

"OK," Billy said as he moved to the door. "If you need me, I'll be right outside."

"Now Senator, I think you need to tell me what you know."

"Yes," Senator Strong said. "How much of this is going to get out?"

"If what you tell me is what I think it's going to be, not much, and none from me."

"Well, I've not done anything that I didn't think was best for our country. You understand that, don't you?"

"Yes, sir. Now will you tell me about Miss Mitchell and General Grant and the plan?"

"Where in the name of all that's holy did you get all of that information on Celia Mitchell?" Jeff shouted. "I thought you were keeping me up to date."

The three of them were back in the car leaving Senator Strong's home. The three suits—who had turned out to be Secret Service agents—were satisfied that no harm was done; they had finally agreed, under more pressure from the Senator, that no report of the evening's activity should be forthcoming.

"Well, I must have forgotten to tell you the new data."

"Forgotten! Goddamnit, I asked you twice since I got here tonight what else you had on her and General Grant, and you said nothing new. What else do you know?"

"That's pretty much it."

"Where did you pick up that information?"

"Well, actually, buddy, since you keep asking so many questions, I made a lot of it up."

Suzy was laughing.

"I thought so. I knew it as soon as I heard 'known Palestinian terrorist.' Christ, Billy."

"Come on, Jeff," Suzy said. "Don't you think you're being a little rough?"

"I don't think it's funny and I don't know why, but that's what I figured the whole time you were telling him. Do me a favor, and don't ever do that to me again."

"Did it work?"

"What do you mean, did it work?"

"Did he talk?"

"Yes," Suzy said, still laughing.

"Well, sure he talked; wouldn't you? And now we need to talk. Head towards the airport."

"Well?" Billy was smiling.

"Well, what?"

"How about something like 'Nice job, Billy' or 'Attaboy, Billy.' Some little something that recognizes that you were captured by the Secret Service and would now be in handcuffs or somewhere in a cell if it wasn't for ol' Billy."

"Yeah, okay. Thanks."

"I can tell your heart's not in it, but that'll do for now." Billy smiled as

342

he looked at Suzy. "I should have left him with the police that night in Saigon."

"Okay, that's enough."

"So tell me, what'd the Senator have to say?"

"Plenty, and I think if we work this thing between the three of us, we might just be able to piece together what's going on. Celia Mitchell came to the Senator with a story that General Grant had information that the Army was covering up serious performance deficiencies in PATRIOT. These deficiencies were of a type that would not show up until late in the test program when PATRIOT was trying to demonstrate performance against the most sophisticated targets. There was an inference that General Grant might even be in control of the exposure of these failures. The story line was that General Grant was opposed to PATRIOT because he thought too much of the Army's development and purchasing money was going to high tech weapons with doubtful payoff and not enough to weapons made of hard steel like tanks and rifles. He knew the Senator was opposed to expensive weapons of any type, so he offered up a plan. The basic idea was that the Senator would support the program within the Senate Armed Services Committee and get the funding committed. When the program ran into technical difficulty, he would then come out as a disillusioned supporter. By that time, the Army would have put all of its eggs into the PATRIOT basket, and when it was canceled, there would be nothing to take its place. General Grant, who had opposed the program from the beginning, would then step in and offer a compromise from the Army to save significant amounts of money, but keep the fighting force alive with guns and tanks."

"But instead of complex testing, we got a war," Billy offered.

"Right. The Senator seemed to think the process would be put on hold."

"Sometime last fall," Suzy said, "he began to suspect that Celia might be in charge instead of General Grant. She would bring him what were supposed to be messages from the General, but when he would disagree, she would make a very persuasive argument."

"You know, there is a far out but distinct possibility that this whole thing was developed just for this war," Billy said.

"I know," Jeff said. "Let's finish this first, and then we can try to develop an overall theory."

Suzy picked up the story again.

"Senator Strong said he argued that PATRIOT should not be sent to the Middle East since these performance deficiencies could cause problems for the U.S. forces there. Celia countered that General Grant gave his personal assurance that no U.S. forces or missions would be put in jeopardy. He had hard information that the use of SCUDs would not be a factor in the conflict. That way, the failure of PATRIOT would be highlighted and their plan would become much more realizable."

"What did he think when the SCUDs started falling this week?"

"That's when he got nervous. Especially when he saw the news from the failure splattered all over the paper this morning and learned about the Israeli citizens that were killed. When we got there, especially with all of the fanfare, he thought we knew everything and had come to arrest him."

"If you ask my opinion, we should."

"Now, with all of that information, can we piece together the whole plan?"

"Seems to me, you've got it," Billy said. "What else is there?"

"Who does Celia Mitchell work for?" Suzy asked.

"Beats me."

"Why go to all of this trouble to protect a few SCUDs? Our data says they're not very accurate anyway."

"I see your point," Billy said. "OK, let's list what we do know. The command to blow or not blow the missile comes in over the satellite. The entry on the keyboard last January was probably needed since there was no satellite on the system at White Sands during those tests. It was a test of their own to make sure the system was working. Same goes for the test failure in March. They wanted to make sure they could blow the missile. You poke into the problem, and they poke back. Fish pokes into the problem, and he's in the hospital. PATRIOTs are failing at random in Israel, and we've got a missing captain and sergeant. What else?"

"For one thing, Ben Peeples, the analyst working the problem in Huntsville, was also killed."

"Given the sophistication of the technical process they've set up, it appears to me that the failures are probably not random."

"Is there anything that ties all of the failures together?"

"They were all failures on SCUDs aimed at civilian targets in Israel," Suzy said.

"OK. Let's try this," Billy said. "A major thrust of Saddam Hussein's strategy is to get Israel into the war. Why not use the SCUDs to hit Israel until they can't stand it any more and enter the war?"

"That would surely break the coalition," Jeff said. "But he knew the U.S. was developing PATRIOT upgrades which could stop his SCUDs, so he developed this scheme to keep them from working."

"But why only selected PATRIOTs?" Suzy asked. "Why not just blow them all up?"

"Several answers to that." Billy was on a roll now. "If every PATRIOT failed, the fact that it was something more than a random failure would be obvious and the problem would be too easy to find and fix. And if PATRIOT was a total failure, then the creative mind of the U.S. would find some other way to stop the SCUDs."

"Like?"

"Like putting so many B-52s over central Baghdad that Saddam Hussein would think it's an eclipse of the sun."

"But we're already bombing him," Suzy said.

"Sure we're bombing him, but what we've done is nothing compared to an all out attack with B-52s. Remember?" Billy looked at Jeff.

Yeah, I remember.

"Yes," Jeff said.

"You can't see 'em, and you can't hear 'em," Billy said. "Then slowly the ground around you starts to shake, and then you feel 'em and then hear a distant rumble that grows louder and louder. The ground shakes until weaker buildings fall, and you get concerned for your own safety. Then later you learn the center of the bomb drop was miles away. It's an awesome experience, and one I hope I never have again."

"OK," Jeff said. "I agree we could stop the SCUDs another way if we had to."

345

"A way much less pleasurable to Saddam Hussein. And besides, if that didn't work, I wouldn't rule out nuclear, given the stakes."

"Yes."

"So the plan for the failed PATRIOTs was simply to support the strategy to get Israel into the war and break the coalition."

"And do it in a way that no one would know it was happening until it was too late."

"Right."

"I can't believe it," Suzy said. "Celia seems like such a normal person."

"So did Ted Bundy," Billy said.

"I still wonder if all this is really worth it," Suzy said.

"Probably a good plan," Jeff said. "I think the theory is right. If they can get Israel into the war, the coalition will break apart. If the coalition breaks, at least some of the Arab countries will side with Iraq. If enough of them break away, they will be tough to beat, even for the U.S. Probably, we would stand either alone or with just the Saudis. Hell, with Israel in the fray, not even Saudi is a sure bet."

"Not too good a position to be surrounded on four sides by the likes of Saddam and Muammar and the boys," Billy said. "If whoever's behind this can pull it all off, he'll be King of the Middle East and owner of eighty percent of the world's oil. At that point, he would have almost an iron grip on the economies of most countries of the world."

Jeff shuddered at the reality of this thought. "How about General Grant?"

"What about him?" Suzy asked.

"Where does he fit into Billy's theory?"

"You tell me," Billy said. "I don't know him."

"My guess would be that he has somehow been duped and is an unknowing participant. She probably told him pretty much the mirror image of what she told Senator Strong. In a way, I kind of feel sorry for him."

"She could dupe me any time she wanted. And you wouldn't need to feel sorry for me."

"You've seen her?" Jeff asked.

346

"Seen the pictures in her clearance file," Billy said. "Quite a fancy little terrorist, I'd say."

"Funny, I never thought of her that way," Suzy said. "She always seemed sort of cold to men."

"If what we think is true, she probably wanted to make sure she didn't get involved with anybody else in any way. It would have messed up the master plan. So what do we do now?"

"I've been thinking about that," Jeff said. "I think what I want to do is get the final piece of data that says we're right in all of this."

"Which is?"

"Tomorrow, there's a missile firing at White Sands. They want to try to duplicate the failure so it can be found and fixed. Suzy and I will catch the red-eye flight tonight and work with Johnny Madkin to answer that question tomorrow. Given what we know now, that shouldn't be too hard, and I believe the first order of business should be to get the PATRIOTs fixed for battle."

"OK. On this end, I'll make sure we find Miss Mitchell, and we'll also keep a closer eye on General Grant."

"Good plan. There isn't cellular phone coverage at White Sands, so I'll call you when I can get to a regular phone."

They had arrived at the airport.

▢▢▢▢▢

The large black limousine did not move from the parking place reserved for diplomatic vehicles. Two men in service uniforms got out of the front doors just as Suzy and Jeff were making their way to the American Airlines ticket counter. They opened the rear doors of the limousine, and three men dressed identically in immaculate black suits emerged and moved toward the American Airlines entrance. The uniforms followed some twenty feet behind.

Jeff finished purchasing the tickets and left the counter to find Suzy, who was waiting for him at the coffee shop. When he got to the coffee shop, he didn't see her right away. Just as he was about to return to the

347

American ticket counter to look for her, a man who looked vaguely familiar approached him.

"Pardon me, you are General Weyland, correct?"

"Yes, have we met?"

"No, I don't think so. I am Prince Bandar Bin Sultan, Ambassador to the United States from the Kingdom of Saudi Arabia."

Jeff remembered now why the man seemed familiar. He had seen him on television several evenings earlier.

"I'm very pleased to meet you," Jeff said. "But right now, I'm sorry that I can't stop and talk. I am trying to find my friend, and then we have a plane to catch."

"Yes, of course, Miss Morris. I have met her at several social functions in the city. You are a lucky man, General. She is with my friends, and if you could just join us for a just few minutes, I assure you we will get you to your plane on time." The English was perfect New England, and the smile was perfect Washington. The suit was not from Macy's and the shoes had never seen a store shelf.

"She's with you?" Jeff asked. "I don't understand."

"If we could just have a few minutes of your time, I am sure you will understand everything."

"Mr. Ambassador, anyone who can make me understand everything right now has got my attention."

"Well, maybe not everything." The million dollar smile flashed again. "But at least why I am here to talk to you. Please follow me."

They walked a short distance to a door in the hallway. In front of the door was a large man in a service uniform who appeared to Jeff to be a chauffeur or maybe a bodyguard. Jeff noticed the barely perceptible nod from Bandar, and the uniform turned and opened the door. He bowed slightly and discreetly as Jeff and Prince Bandar moved into the room.

Inside, there was a small room set up for airport waiting. Low, well-padded black leather chairs were placed around several small cocktail tables scattered around the room. At the end of the room was a bar behind which stood another man in the same uniform as the man outside the door. Suzy was sitting at one of the cocktail tables and had obviously been served. She

348

smiled and raised her drink to Jeff as he and Bandar entered the room. Two other men stood across the table from Suzy.

"Gentlemen, this is General Weyland, the United States PATRIOT Project Manager. General, I would like to present Prince Fisal ibn Sultan. At present, Prince Fisal is known as Lieutenant General Fisal ibn Sultan, Commander of Arab forces in the coalition. Also with us is General Aziz of the Saudi Air Defense Forces."

"I am pleased to meet you, General Fisal. General Aziz and I have met on several occasions."

"Yes, well," Bandar said. "Their visit to your country at this time is on business which we cannot discuss here. However, we have become somewhat aware of your situation and would like to offer you any assistance which may be of value."

"Somewhat aware of my situation?"

"Yes."

"How aware and what type of assistance?"

"We are aware that there has been an attempt on your life, that the attempt is somehow tied to PATRIOT's performance in the Middle East, and that you are attempting to solve the puzzle of what is happening."

"And the assistance?"

General Fisal responded. "Clearly our country cannot openly support any activity which is dedicated to assisting Israel. On the other hand, it is very much to our benefit for the Arab coalition to remain intact. If Israel enters the war, it will be impossible for that to happen. It is said in some quarters that if the coalition fails, our kingdom may cease to exist."

"I've heard that myself," Jeff said.

"It is a very complex situation for us. We are therefore prepared to offer you anything within our ability you may need to assist you in solving that puzzle."

"Such as?" Jeff asked.

"As a start, a secure place for a few days for Miss Morris."

Jeff looked down at Suzy and saw in her face the immediate rejection of that notion. He smiled and faced Bandar again.

"That won't be necessary," Jeff said. "We've convinced ourselves that we've passed the stage of a physical threat to either of us."

"Very well," Bandar said. "We will leave it to you. Here is my card. I have written on the back a private number where I can be reached personally. Please don't hesitate to call me if there is any assistance our country can provide. We have vast resources and some sources of information which may surprise you."

"I understand your offer, and I thank you," Jeff said.

"Very well, then," Bandar said offering his hand to Suzy to assist her to her feet. "You must go now, so you will not miss your plane. Please, let me hear from you."

"Trust me," Jeff said. "If I need you, I'll call."

"That is all we can ask," Bandar said.

weapons systems--pentagon adv19 1-91
29 injured in Tel Aviv due to PATRIOT missile failures
USWNS Military News
adv jan 19 1991 or thereafter

By GEORGE GROWSON

WASHINGTON—Over the weekend, Iraq proved that they still have the capability to launch SCUD missiles, targeting Tel Aviv one night and Saudi Arabia the next. Twenty-nine people were injured in Tel Aviv. Though PATRIOT missiles aided in the defense of Saudi targets, they appear to have been less successful in Israel. President Bush praised Israel for their great restraint in not retaliating after these attacks.

Also, at a briefing in Riyadh, Saudi Arabia, Saudi Arabian officials announced that three more planes had been downed over the weekend, one of which was a U.S. F-15. Under pressure from the media, the spokesman also confirmed that not all of the Iraqi mobile SCUD launchers had been destroyed.

At home, President Bush expressed anger at the treatment of coalition POWs held in Iraq. In a harshly worded letter to Iraqi officials, he charged them with violating the directives of the Geneva Convention and committing war crimes against those prisoners.

FIFTEEN

As he moved quickly down the sidewalk, General Grant looked tired from the strain of all that had happened during the last few days. His stride lacked the military sureness of days past. His uniform jacket was wrinkled. The military hat he usually wore with pride was missing, and he had not shaved. The door to bungalow 3 was open a small crack, and it swung inward on his first heavy knock. He went into the front room of the building, but no one was there. He silently looked at the television where he had watched videos of himself, his lover, and his wife. The memory was still strong. He tried not to think about it.

He walked across to the bedroom and stood in front of the closed door. He opened the door, took one step into the room, and looked down to see her lying on the bed. She was nude, lying partly on her side, and smiling up at him. Her long black hair was spread sensuously on the white silk sheets, and the barest tip of her tongue was tracing small circles on her crimson lips. A whiskey bottle and an empty glass were on the table beside the bed. As he came in the door, she cupped her lower breast, squeezing the nipple between her thumb and finger. Her other hand was between her legs, keeping a gentle, rocking rhythm with the radio in the living room. He started to say something, but found he couldn't speak. He watched her for a long while, mesmerized by the sight.

Without stopping any of her activities, she looked at him and finally spoke, almost in a whisper.

"Did you do what I asked?"

"Yes," he said, not able to take his eyes off her hands.

"All of it?" Her eyes rolled slightly and then closed briefly.

"Yes," he said again, hanging his head as he spoke.

"How did it go?"

"You told me PATRIOTs and SCUDs were not going to play a part in the war."

"I told you no one was going to get hurt," she said.

He seemed relieved that at least her voice was gentle and not harsh like he had heard it before.

"But people are being hurt and killed," he said. He had reverted once again to the sound of a little boy pleading to his mother. She smiled at him through barely open eyes.

"So how different is the world going to be with a few less Jews? Relax, mighty General, none of your precious Americans are being hurt. This will be over in a few days if you did your job right."

"I just don't understand," he mumbled.

"Of course you don't, Wessy. Now tell Celia how everything went when you did what I asked."

"I'm not sure," he said. "General Weyland is well liked and well respected. What I said came as a shock to everyone. I'm sure there're some who'll check more closely."

"Did you call all of the other organizations?"

"Yes."

"And how did that go?"

"About the same. I tried to get a person at each place who wasn't close to Weyland. He has some very loyal friends at some locations."

"So you got everything done?"

"Yes."

"You're sure?"

"Yes."

"How long do we have?"

"I don't know. It's hard to say. Two days, maybe three, but I would only count on two."

354

"Good. Your job is done, then."

His shoulders slumped even lower as he exhaled, somewhere between a sigh and a moan.

"You have done well." Her body was rocking faster now, and her hand was taking longer strokes between her legs. His erection was straining his uniform trousers as he watched her on the bed.

"Believe me," she said. "The day will come when you will be proud of the role you played."

He pushed the door closed and began to remove his tie.

"No need for that," she said.

"I need you today," he said. "You said that if I did this one last thing, we could be together."

"That was before," she said. "Now your job is done, and you can leave."

"But I thought you wanted us to be together." He dropped to his knees beside the bed to look into her face.

Her breath was coming faster. A laugh came from somewhere deep in her throat and ended in a moan he recognized from their times together in this bed. "Celia, please."

Her deep laugh got louder and her moans were reaching a higher pitch.

"Celia, please," he begged again.

"Celia, please," she mocked him as she turned to him, her face barely inches from his. He could feel her breath, hot and moist. "Celia, please," she said again.

"I only want..." his voice trailed off as he watched her hands.

"No!" she shouted, suddenly violent. "Celia doesn't please. Not you. Not ever again. Now get out!" He felt her saliva sting his face, and then she turned from him.

He stood, the sudden shock of what he had heard pushing him back. With his hands, he wiped her spit from his face, which had flushed to a brilliant crimson. Her lips were curled in what looked like a combination of anger and pleasure. The deep, throaty laugh started again. He couldn't take his eyes from her as he backed across the room. He reached behind his back to find the knob and felt his way through the door. Only when he couldn't see her did he turn and start forward toward the front of the bungalow. He could still hear her laughing at him as he crossed the room where he had experienced so many hours of perverted pleasure.

Laughing at him.

He stumbled across the room to the door. As he pulled the door closed, he heard the loud cry she used to say only he could provoke. In the living room, the television seemed to be laughing at him also. He reached for a lamp on a table at the end of the couch, and its cord ripped from the wall as he hurled it at the mocking screen. His lips curled in an angry smile as the television exploded in front of him, and he turned to leave the room.

Laughing at him.

He didn't even pull the door shut as he half ran and half stumbled down the one step and started across the courtyard. He sat on a small brick bench near the center of the courtyard and lowered his head to his knees. After some time, he stood and turned to leave again. He held his hand over his mouth but could not hold back the vomit.

January 19, 1991
U.S. PATRIOT Compound
Tel Aviv, Israel
6:00 PM

The cluster of several hundred soldiers gathered at the gate, waiting with their passes to be released to the local area. The military police were preparing to start the evening ritual. The gates opened, the crowd pressed forward, and Sergeant First Class James E. Johnson inconspicuously worked his way to the middle of the crowd.

He had been through this process before, and knew that the MPs did not check passes closely and did not look at any identification. Identification was only inspected on return to the compound. He pulled the expired pass

356

from his wallet and held it toward the MP as he went through the gate. The MP looked at him briefly and then looked back toward the gate house toward the sergeant who had brought Johnson's picture and description to the gate an hour or so earlier. He nodded toward Johnson who was now in the flow and moving through the gate.

The police sergeant left the gatehouse and quickly moved ahead of the crowd. Johnson saw him from the corner of his eye and worked his way toward the opposite side of the cluster of soldiers. When the police sergeant made a move in the same direction, Johnson bolted. Four MPs materialized from behind the row of buildings outside the gate, and Johnson found himself running directly toward them.

The crowd of soldiers pulled back as they saw the MPs and realized something out of the ordinary was happening. Johnson doubled back into the flow of traffic and pushed his way through the crowd which broke away to give him room. When he came out on the far side of the sea of bodies, he broke into a run in the direction of a small group of buildings. He heard the shouts behind him, but didn't take the time to look.

He ran down a small alley and came out on a street filled with vendors selling fresh vegetables. He ran down the street. Ahead, a small car was pulling out of a parking place and heading in his direction. He got to the car just as the driver was about to increase speed. He grabbed the door handle and jerked the door open. The man shouted something at him in a language he did not understand. People on the street stopped and looked.

Johnson reached inside the car and grabbed the man by the collar of his shirt. As the man's heavy body began to move, Johnson grabbed the top of the car to give himself more leverage and pulled harder. The man finally came out of the car, and Johnson flung him to the ground and jumped into the moving vehicle. He slammed his foot on the accelerator, and the car sped down the street. In the rear view mirror, he could see the military police coming around the corner into the street. They had their weapons drawn but did not fire. He saw a main street ahead, turned into the flow of traffic, and slowed.

□□□□□

January 19, 1991
New Mexico Highway 54
10:00 AM

As a junior officer, Jeff had traveled Highway 54 many times. Those were the days before his rank allowed him to travel the route by helicopter. Now, as the car crested each small hill in the desert, memories of those earlier years came back, and the distant mountains made him feel like he was coming home. Driving in the desert took such little concentration that he had time to think. He kept going over the entire set of strange events in his head. He marveled at the fact that if he hadn't seen the entry on that day last January, none of this would have been discovered; perhaps tonight, Saddam was planning to make the big splash which would draw Israel into the war. If he and Billy were right about Saddam's plan, the future of the whole world could have been decided by dumb luck.

I'll be goddamned.

"What?" Suzy's question made him realize he had been thinking aloud.

"Just thinking how crazy this whole thing is," he said.

"Crazy is right, but it's not a strong enough word. I still have a hard time with all this. It just seems impossible that Celia is in the middle of it."

"If we're right, she could be the central figure. If Billy can't find her, we may never know the full story."

"Do you think it will be over soon?"

"Yes."

At the guard gate, he presented his military identification and Suzy's capitol pass. The guard waved him through, and he drove the short distance to Launch Complex 38, the PATRIOT test site. He parked the rental car in his reserved parking place and they walked to the office building. Just inside the door, a young female guard in a glass booth controlled the turnstile restricting access to the building. He looked at her and smiled, waiting for her to activate the mechanism that would let them through and into the building.

358

"I'm sorry, sir, but you are not authorized in this building," the guard said. She seemed to be slightly embarrassed.

"Janie, I'm General Weyland." He thought maybe she didn't recognize him since it was the first time he had been there without his uniform.

"I know who you are, sir," she said sheepishly, "I just can't let you in."

"Why not?"

"I don't know, sir. That's just what I've been told."

"By who?"

"By Mr. Anderson."

"And who is he?"

"The Director of Security for the installation."

"Would you call Mr. Anderson for me Janie, so I could talk to him?"

"Yes, sir." As Jeff turned to Suzy with a question on his face, Janie reached for the phone and dialed. Mr. Anderson obviously answered and she began to explain to him what was going on at the gate.

"He wants to talk to you," she said, holding the phone through the window to Jeff.

"General Weyland here," Jeff said.

"General, this is Bob Anderson. We've never met, but I am the Director of Security for this facility. I have no understanding of why, sir, but just about two hours ago, we received a telefax from Washington directing that your name be taken off the access list for the area. I'm sorry, sir, but I just can't let you in."

"Who was the message from in Washington?" Jeff asked.

"Well, I don't really know whose office it came from, but it was originated under the authority of a Lieutenant General Grant. It was endorsed by the PATRIOT Project Office, which was all I needed. Even with that, it still seemed strange to me, so I had someone call and talk to security at PATRIOT to see if they would authenticate the order. Sure enough, they did."

Jeff hung up the phone without saying good-bye.

"Can I use this phone?" he asked Janie.

"Only for local calls. It won't go off the range."

"Thanks."

"Who are you going to call?" asked Suzy.

"I'm going to see if Johnny knows what's going on," Jeff replied, pulling his small phone list from his wallet. After four rings, a female voice Jeff did not recognize answered.

"Mr. Madkin's office."

"This is General Weyland. Please let me speak to Mr. Madkin."

"Mr. Madkin is not in, sir. May I help you?"

"Yes, you can tell me where I can reach Johnny."

"I wouldn't know that, General. He didn't say where he was going or when he would be back."

"What time is the firing today?" Jeff asked.

"I wouldn't know that either, sir."

"Thanks," Jeff said as he hung up the phone. He tried the Raytheon test director's line with the same result. He thanked Janie, who had listened to the entire proceedings, and they walked outside the building and stood beside his car.

"What now?" Suzy asked.

"I'm trying to figure that out. If..."

"ONE HOUR TO TEST."

They heard the announcement over the loudspeakers mounted on the buildings.

"REPEAT, ONE HOUR TO TEST. ALL PERSONNEL ARE REQUIRED TO BE INSIDE AUTHORIZED SHELTERS FIFTEEN MINUTES BEFORE TEST. REPEAT, ONE HOUR TO TEST. NEXT WARNING IN FIFTEEN MINUTES."

Jeff looked in the direction of the building that housed the operational test activity. The fence separating the outer area from the restricted test area was attached to the building. The PATRIOT vans were also attached to the building, but on the inside of the fence.

"In the past, I'd always thought of those fences as insufficient security. Now they look a hundred feet tall."

"Jeff, you're not thinking of doing something crazy."

"No. Not yet, anyway. Let's go see if we can find Johnny."

They started walking in the direction of the operations building. Several people were outside, either taking a smoke break or carrying papers from one building to another. He didn't see anyone he recognized.

They climbed the stairs leading to the platform beside the operations building door. Above the door handle was a cipher lock. There were six numbers in a circle around a knob which would open the door. He punched the three numbers of the combination and tried the knob. Nothing. He tried again. Still nothing.

"Either I've remembered the numbers wrong, or the combination has been changed since I was here last."

"Why not just knock?"

While they were standing there looking at each other, the door was opened from the inside. Someone had obviously heard him trying to work the cipher lock and had come to check.

"Thanks," he said, starting in the door. "I guess I forgot the combination."

The man moved to block them from entering. It wasn't an overly hostile move, and the man didn't seem hostile, just curious.

"Do you have some identification?" he asked.

"Yes," Jeff said, and retrieved his military identification from his wallet. "Here it is. I am General Weyland, the PATRIOT Project Manager."

"It takes a Range Badge or an escort to get in this building."

"OK, would you do me a favor and find Johnny Madkin for me. He'll escort me."

"Just a minute." He shut the door and was gone.

Jeff and Suzy waited for what seemed a long time. The people standing outside smoking were trying not to make eye contact, but they were obviously getting curious. Just as he was about to knock on the door, it opened again. It was a different man.

"I'm General Weyland. I..."

"I know who you are, sir. I just talked to you on the phone. I'm Bob Anderson, and I thought we understood each other. You do not have access to these facilities, and I have the responsibility and the authority to keep you out. Now you will either have to leave the premises, or I will be forced to call the military police." With that, he shut the door.

They walked back to his car. He reached for his cellular phone. He turned it on, but there was no service.

Damn.

He threw the phone on the seat and stood by the car.

"What now?" Suzy asked.

"I don't know. I don't know whether to wait for Johnny to walk across the open area, go get the military police myself, or just leave."

Finally, he motioned to Suzy and they got in the car. He started the engine and left the complex.

"I've got to find a phone," he said. "Keep your eyes out for one."

"Jeff, I don't understand what's going on," she said.

"Me either, sweetheart. But if I can get to a phone, I'm sure going to find out."

He drove to the small snack bar known as PATRIOT Patty's. Remembering there was a pay phone on the side of the building, he parked the car next to the booth. He got out of the car, went to the phone and took the receiver off the hook. He flashed Suzy a smile when he heard the dial tone. Using the list in his wallet, he dialed a number and then a charge card number. Several rings.

"Hello?"

"I'd like to speak to Billy Walker, please."

"I'm sorry, there is no Mr. Walker at this number."

"I'm sorry," Jeff said. "I must have dialed the wrong number."

He checked his list and dialed the number again.

"Hello." Same voice.

"I'm sorry to bother you again, but I am looking for Billy Walker. I reached him at this number yesterday."

"I'm sorry, sir, but there is no Mr. Walker here."

"Is this the..." Jeff hesitated. "Can you get a message to Mr. Walker for me?"

"Sir, I'm sorry. But, as I said, there is no Mr. Walker at this number."

"Thanks," he said, and hung up the phone. The muscle in his stomach was going into overdrive.

He dialed Billy's home number. Six rings. No answer. He tried the cellular phone number Billy had given him. Same result. He hung up and returned to his car.

"I can't find Billy," he said.

"Jeff, this is scary. Where could he be?"

"I have no idea."

"What about your office?" she asked.

Jeff ran back to the phone with Suzy right behind him. He dialed one more set of numbers.

"Hello," he answered on the first ring.

"You sonofabitch! What're you doing?" Jeff shouted, turning and giving Suzy a thumbs up.

"Me a sonofabitch? You're the sonofabitch. Why haven't you gotten in touch before now?"

"How the hell was I supposed to know where you are, and what are you doing in my office, and why can't I get into my own test range?"

"You want those questions answered in the order you asked them or is there some specific priority you might assign to some in particular?"

"No. Why can't I get into my own test range?"

"Because you are no longer the PATRIOT Project Manager. Next question?"

"Why are you in my Washington office?"

"Because I have been forbidden to talk to you, and they took away my number drop and turned off my home phone and cellular phone. I figured you would remember you said I could work out of your office in an emergency, so I came here."

"That's crazy as hell."

"Did it work?"

"What?"

"You said it was crazy. I asked if it worked."

"Yeah, I guess. But it was Suzy who remembered, not me."

"Hell, it was her I was counting on anyway. Next question."

"How did you get in my office?"

"That's so easy, I'm not even going to answer. Next?"

"Who did all of this?"

"The man you were feeling sorry for, General Grant. Seems he met with the Army high rollers and told them you had been acting very strange lately. You'd hardly been in your office for the last three or four days. You popped up unannounced at Raytheon and left without saying anything to any of the brass. You made an odd call on Senator Strong in the middle of the night, although it appears the Senator is keeping to his word and is not the leak. I think Miss Mitchell was having him watched. At any rate, the brass tried to get you to come forward so they could get your side of the story, but you couldn't be found, which just complicated things. So they agreed with General Grant and relieved you of your job, and now you are listed as Absent Without Leave. You're in a heap of trouble, ol' buddy."

"Thanks a lot. I suppose you argued my case."

"Yep, for a while. If you remember, I'm in a little trouble with those same people myself, no small thanks to you. Especially when they found out about the visit to the Senator's house. When they put the pressure on Al, he squealed like a stuck pig. I always said you could never trust the Secret Service."

"How about Celia Mitchell?"

"I got a hot line on her. After he convinced the powers-that-be that you were one taco short of a combination plate, General Grant went to see her. We found their little lust nest. Unfortunately, there was only one man trailing our General. He called for backup when Grant went in the bungalow, but the visit wasn't long. Grant came out in a hurry before the second tail could get there. The first tail stayed with Grant, and when the second tail got to the bungalow, the girl was gone. Nice place. We found everything but her traveling ID with the passport. She has a lot of interesting equipment. State of the art in video and audio, if you get my drift. Plus a library of tapes. Ought to make for some interesting viewing someday."

"So you lost her?"

"Yep, that's the long and short of it. Actually, we never had her. Not only that, but all of the hubbub at the bungalow got a lot of attention. As soon as my management found out who we were tailing and who had requested it, they really shit a brick. I'm sort of on restriction right now."

"What does that mean?"

364

"It's sort of like being grounded when you're a teenager. You aren't supposed to do anything that's fun."

"Does that mean you can't help me any more?"

"I said 'not supposed to,' asshole. Why do you think I'm here in your office?"

"Won't you get in more trouble?"

"Well, my organization has a funny history. When an employee—such as myself—gets in real trouble—such as I am—but sticks to his guns and eventually is found out to have saved our country from the bad guys—such as I will—they tend to overlook a lot of things. I'm going on the assumption that we're on the right track, and we're doing our country a big favor and are going to save everybody from George on down a lot of heartache if we can pull this thing off. If we're right, I'll be OK when the dust settles."

"I'm worried."

"Congratulations. At least we're making progress."

"Shut up a minute, will you?" Jeff said. "Whoever is pulling the strings on their side must know that their house of cards can't last more than a day or so. I think they're going to make their move soon."

"I agree. Maybe even tonight. Can you get the job done there?"

"Well, right now, the biggest problem I have is to get into that van. I'm really not welcome at the launch site."

"There's one more thing I need to know," Billy said.

"What's that?"

"Are you on any of those video tapes?"

"Christ almighty, Billy!"

"Well, I need to know. If you are, then I can protect you."

"No, I'm not."

"Shame," Billy said. "I was hoping to get to see you in action."

"Are you looking at those tapes?"

"I had to do something while I waited for you to call. Besides, it was for professional reasons. By the way, you need to get some better video equipment in your office here. I'm losing some of the detail."

"Now I find out you're a pervert, too."

"Well, we've got to find out who else she had on the hook, don't we?"

"Christ, yes. But that can wait until later."

"I was just killing time until you called. Listen, if you can't get to the people there, then you haven't made any progress. I assume the system will receive the right data from the satellite and nothing will happen to the missile. Just another wasted shot."

"I've got a hunch and an idea," Jeff said. "Call the Research, Development, and Engineering Center at Redstone Arsenal and talk to a man named Ralph Jameson in the Software Engineering Directorate. Ask him for the codes for the keyboard. He'll know what you mean. Make sure you copy down the codes exactly. I'll call you back at this same number later."

"Where are you going?"

"I think I know a way to make them talk to me."

"There's some more bad news," Billy said.

"It can't get much worse than it already is."

"I'm afraid it can. Your house in Massachusetts was burned last night. It appears to have been a firebomb."

"What! What about the Thomases?"

Suzy heard the added tension in his voice and moved closer to him.

"They were in the house, but got out when the alarm sounded."

"Thank God for that. You think this was connected?"

"Has to be, unless you can think of another reason someone would throw a half dozen incendiary grenades into your home."

"I don't understand what they thought they would have to gain by that," Jeff said.

"Well, I've thought about that while I was sitting here watching the world's greatest lover and waiting for you to call."

"And?"

"My guess is that they were on your trail and got as far as the house. At that point, you hadn't gone fully underground. They thought you were there and went after you. When you weren't there, they left their calling card."

"Why?"

366

"As a warning of some sort. They want you to know the extremes they're willing to take to either find you or keep you under wraps until they've done whatever it is they're going to do. After all, with hundreds or even thousands dying in Kuwait every day, what's a few more bodies over here? The Thomases heard them talking. They were looking for Suzy."

Jeff's breath caught and his heart began to pound harder. He reached over and pulled Suzy to him.

"They said something about looking for the girl and going to Atlanta."

"Billy?"

"Yes."

"Are you thinking what I am?"

"Apparently not. Enlighten me."

"If that was a warning, then they must have something else they're going to try."

"I'm still a blank, buddy."

"Christ, Billy. If they can't get to me, then they'll try for the something they know is more important, and if they knew about Suzy, then they know about Cindy!"

"Jesus. Is she still in Atlanta?"

"Yes."

"Then I'm headed there. Do what you have to on your end and meet me."

"Where, Billy? And how will you get there?"

"I have some IOUs serious enough for some folks to take some risks. I'll call them in and get an F-15 to Atlanta. I can be there in less than an hour. Write down this number."

Jeff wrote down the number Billy gave him and hung up the phone.

"We can leave here now and nobody would blame you," Suzy said as they got back to the car.

"Except me," he said. "Besides, with the current state of affairs, we don't have any way to get to Atlanta except by a commercial flight, and the next one doesn't leave El Paso for five hours."

"What's the idea you mentioned?"

"I'm going to get their attention," he said.

Jeff drove back to the launch complex. He parked as close to the operations building as he could while staying out of sight.

He rolled down his window and waited. Pretty soon, he heard the announcement.

"FIVE MINUTES UNTIL TEST. ALL PERSONNEL SHOULD BE IN SHELTERS. REPEAT. FIVE MINUTES UNTIL LAUNCH. ALL PERSONNEL SHOULD BE IN SHELTERS."

Jeff looked at Suzy and then his watch. He looked at the corner of the building. A small van was connected to the building on his side of the fence with a cable; there was a satellite dish antenna on top of the van. He had seen the exact same antenna when the system was demonstrated for him in Huntsville. He waited, trying to judge the last minute before the mission began.

Just do it. Now!

He opened the door to the car.

"Jeff, be careful," Suzy whispered.

He walked toward the main door of the operations building. Beside the door was a set of fire fighting materials. A barrel of sand, a barrel of water, a few buckets, and an ax. He picked up the ax and headed for the small van with the satellite dish. Rounding the van, he followed the cable with his eyes. It ran from the satellite dish antenna around the side of the van and into a port on the side wall.

He looked around one more time, took a large swing with the ax, and came down on the cable. One swing was all it took to cut the cable clean. He leaned the ax against the van and walked back to the car. Suzy's look told him she felt what he felt. They had crossed another boundary. Neither spoke.

He started the car and moved to the other side of the parking lot where he could see both the front of the building and the van.

They heard the siren indicating the missile was about to launch. Soon after he heard the boom and the roar, and looked downrange to see the missile. He tried to judge about where the missile had been when he saw it blow this past summer. At just about the same spot, he saw the curious sight for the second time in his life. The nose cone of the missile shattered, and then the motor case erupted in a spectacular display, just as he remembered. He also remembered his feeling when he had seen it for the first time. It was a moment before they heard the explosion, and then all was quiet as they waited again.

"Christ, Jeff," Suzy said finally. "What now?"

"We wait," he said.

Eventually, two men came out of the building and walked to the satellite van. They entered the van for a few minutes and then came back out and walked around to the side where the antenna was mounted. Jeff couldn't see them while they were blocked by the van, but when they returned to the front, they were talking animatedly and walking at a fast clip toward the door of the operations building. They went inside; shortly after, a group of about ten men came out, Bob Anderson and Johnny Madkin among them. They all went to the van and around to the back side. One man was carrying the ax when they returned to the front of the van. Most of the group went back to the door of the operations building, while Johnny Madkin and one man Jeff didn't recognize started for the administration building.

After the door had closed behind the group, Jeff started the car and drove slowly toward the two men walking across the blacktop. Johnny recognized Jeff and said something to the other man, who continued walking. Jeff stopped the car, Suzy opened the passenger door, and Johnny got in. They drove out of the parking lot and onto the range road.

"Jesus, Jeff, what are you doing here?"

"Trying to do my job," Jeff said. "Johnny, this is Suzy Morris."

"Nice to meet you. You're in big trouble, Jeff. Jesus, what's going on?"

"I think I know, but it's so complicated you won't believe it. Johnny, do you trust me?"

He could see Johnny was uncomfortable.

"Well, sure, Jeff, but I don't understand. I could get in trouble just talking to you. Tell me what's going on, and maybe I can help."

"Is there a backup missile?"

"Sure there is. There always is, you know that. Why?"

"Is there a backup target?"

"Yes, but why do you want to know that?"

"Because I want you to fire that backup missile, and I want to be in the van when it goes."

"I can't do it, Jeff. It's impossible, even if I wanted to. Anderson is about to go into cardiac arrest. When he saw the ax beside the van, he started screaming that he knew you had done it, and he was going to have your stars and see you in prison."

"Well, he can have my stars. Right now that's not too important. I just want to fire that missile."

"Jesus, Jeff. Did you cut that cable?"

"Yes."

"By all that's holy, Jeff, why?"

"How long have we known each other, Johnny?"

"Twelve years, but Jesus..."

"Do you doubt my loyalty to our country?"

"No, but..."

"Do you believe we both want the same things for PATRIOT?"

"Yes, Jeff, but why did you cut that cable?"

"To make the missile blow, Johnny. The signal to bypass the destruct command comes in over that satellite. If the system doesn't get the signal or it isn't entered on the keyboard, the missile blows. Listen, it's a very long and complicated story. They've already tried to kill me, and Max Fisher is in a hospital in Boston. They probably killed Ben Peeples in Huntsville. Last night, they firebombed my house and nearly killed the people in it. I believe they might've gone after my daughter now to try to control me. The Commander of the Battery that fired the bad PATRIOT missile night before last is missing in action. The people behind all of this are the people who put out the bulletin taking away my position. It's time for you to make a hard choice, Johnny. I'm telling you that our country is under attack. A different kind of attack than is going on in the Middle East, but an attack just as serious and just as well planned. It involves what's happening right here, right now. It involves that entry I saw Sergeant Johnson make on the console last year. Sergeant Johnson was then and is now working for these people. We've got to show what's been done to this system and what needs to happen to fix it, probably within the next twelve hours, or it'll be too late. You need to reach way down in your gut and ask yourself who you think I am. I need your help, possibly to save our country. Will you do it?"

Johnny looked at the floor of the car for a long time. He turned his head and looked first at Jeff and then directly at Suzy.

"Please," she said.

"But we have received an official notice that you're not the PATRIOT Project Manager any more," Johnny said, looking back to Jeff.

"None of that matters. This is just me and you. You either believe in me or you don't. Which is it?"

Johnny looked out into the desert for a long while.

"OK. I'm with you," he finally said. "What do you want me to do?"

Suzy exhaled and let out an enormous sigh.

"I need you to go back to the operations building and get the system turned on for the backup flight. Say you have a hunch what was wrong and think you can fix it. Once you have things under way, get loose and come to the door and wave at me. I'll come in and wait somewhere out of the way until it's close to the launch time. Wherever I wait, I'll need a phone that can make long distance calls. When it gets to about ten minutes before launch, then you come and get me and take me to the van."

"I don't know if it'll work, but I'm willing to give it a try. The hardest part will be to convince people that I know what went wrong, but I can't tell them or show them. I'll have to think of something. Then we will have security to deal with. Once Anderson knows we're going to fire again, he'll have his people all over the place."

"That's why I need to get in the building now."

"OK, let's go."

"How much time do we have?"

"No more than an hour. After that, the range will shut us down, even with the priority we have."

"OK. You ready?"

"Ready."

Jeff turned the car around and headed back to Launch Complex 38 for the third time that day.

□□□□□

January 19, 1991
Israeli Jordanian Border
10 Miles East of Jericho, Israel
9:00 PM

Sergeant Johnson ordered another cup of coffee. He was sitting in a makeshift outdoor cafe in a position to observe the activities at the border crossing to Jordan. The beginnings of a plan were formulating in his mind, and he was trying to work out the details. The ride across Israel had been uneventful, and as he drove through Jerusalem, there was no evidence that he was being sought. As a precaution, he had ditched the first car and stolen another. He had to kill the stupid Jew, but that also gave him some less conspicuous clothes. He had been sitting in this cafe watching the border for thirty minutes.

There was a fair amount of pedestrian traffic, and the guards were not checking the passes too closely. Several buildings were scattered along the street leading up to the gate, and there was one building in particular that seemed to be abandoned. The door in the middle of the building was standing open, and he had walked to it a while back and checked the inside. The light was dim through the dirty windows, and the few pieces of furniture inside indicated that the room was once some sort of restaurant; the dirt and dust made it clear the building had not been used for some time.

Many people going to the border passed directly in front of the building he had inspected. Most of the traffic was in groups, but occasionally there were isolated individuals.

He drank some more of the strong coffee and watched the traffic. Shortly, he spotted a man coming toward him who was close to his size and appearance and on the same side of the street as the building. He stood, dropped some bills on the table, and headed in the direction of the abandoned building. As he walked, he removed a knife from his pocket and held it in his left hand concealing the blade under his sleeve. He timed

372

his arrival so that he reached the man just as he was arriving at the abandoned building.

"Do you speak English?" he asked.

"Only a little."

"I would like for you to do me a service," Johnson said.

"I don't understand."

"I want to pay you," Johnson said. He reached into his pocket and extracted the large roll of Israeli and American money. The man's eyes widened at the sight of the cash.

"You want to buy something?" the man asked.

"Yes." Johnson looked around as though he were looking for a place they could talk. "Let's go in here," he said, and motioned with his head toward the abandoned building.

"Yes."

They entered the building, and Johnson shut the door behind them. He turned to the man, and without hesitation plunged the knife directly into his ribcage. The man's mouth opened to yell, but he could make no sound as he slowly sank to the dirty floor. Johnson quickly went through the man's pockets and found his wallet and identification papers. He dragged the body behind the counter at the rear of the room.

He waited a long while before he returned. He watched the border traffic for another fifteen minutes until he spotted a large group approaching. No one seemed to notice as he stood and fell in with the group. As they approached the gate, each person showed identification to the guards, but no one spoke unless the guards asked a question. Johnson had his identification ready when he got to the guard and held it up. The guard did not take the card, but just looked at it and motioned him through.

⊓⊓⊓⊓⊓

The parking lot of Launch Complex 38 was empty, and Jeff pulled the car up to the operations building. Johnny got out and went up the steps to the locked door. He hesitated a second at the lock and then reached out, entered the three numbers, and opened the door. Jeff and Suzy watched from the car as the door closed. They waited. Several minutes later, the door opened, and Johnny came to the platform, looked in the direction of the car, and nodded. Jeff and Suzy came to the platform where Johnny was holding the door open.

"It looks clear," Johnny said. "Move quick."

They made a quick left, hurried down the hall, and turned right at the second corridor. Several offices down the corridor, Johnny opened a door to an office marked "PATRIOT Project" and they went in.

The front reception area was empty and Johnny headed through to the back offices and entered a door marked "Private." As Jeff followed him into the small room, he bumped into Johnny, who had stopped. It was a small conference room furnished with tables and chairs at the tables and around the wall. Sitting at the first table was Bob Anderson and the man who had been walking across the blacktop with Johnny. At the second table was Al. Several other men stood against the wall.

"Uh, oh," Suzy said quietly to Jeff.

"Come in, Johnny," Bob Anderson said, "and shut the door. Welcome back, General. You've made this a lot easier. I'd already called the military police after we found the cable was cut on the satellite. Then when Terry here told me he saw Johnny get in the car with you, I called them back to tell them to look for you on the road. Then Al here shows up with a very impressive badge and seriously wants to have a conversation with you. I'm surprised they didn't pick you up, but, as I said, this just makes it easier on everyone. Johnny, you're going to have some explaining to do, also. I'm afraid you're going to be in as much trouble as your friend here."

Jeff stepped past Johnny and stood directly in front of Bob Anderson. He looked at Al.

"I'm glad you're here," he said.

"Maybe you are and maybe you aren't," Al said.

Jeff turned back to Bob Anderson.

"Mr. Anderson, Johnny is not responsible for any of this. I'm the only one who has been out of line..."

"I have to disagree with you, General. You are here, in this building, and it was Johnny Madkin who brought you here. I think we will want to

374

hear why he did that, and what the two of you planned to do next. I think a lot of people will be interested in answers to those questions."

"Mr. Anderson, I'm going to tell you the same thing I told Johnny. There is a matter going on here which is of grave importance to our country."

"We understand all of that, General Weyland," Al said, getting up from his chair. "But the problem has gotten a little bigger than that."

"Bigger than what?" Jeff asked. "I thought we were together on this."

"We were last night," Al said. "But several things have changed since then. I have directions to bring you in."

"In? What do you mean, bring me in?"

"That's a pretty straightforward term, General. You watch the movies. I'm taking you in."

Several of the other men moved in around Jeff, Johnny, and Suzy. Jeff recognized some of them from the session at Senator Strong's house.

"Let's call Senator Strong and see what he thinks," Jeff said.

"Senator Strong has apparently already done some talking," Al said. "It looks like he's had a change of heart, and that's why we're here."

"Well then, let's get on with it," Jeff said. "I need to get into that van."

"General, I don't think you've heard me. You're not going into any van, and you're not going to fire any missile. You are under arrest pursuant to a federal warrant for conspiracy against the security of the United States, and you and I and this young lady are leaving here now. Together."

"You don't understand," Jeff said. "The..."

"I understand perfectly, General. It's you who doesn't seem to understand. You have been declared a fugitive and I have direct orders to take you into custody. The discussion part of this activity is over and we are now entering the implementation stage. We are most definitely leaving. Now you have the choice of coming peacefully or forcefully. Which is it going to be?"

Suzy had moved beside Jeff and was holding his arm tightly. Jeff let the air go out of him as he dropped his shoulders and nodded to Al.

"Good," Al said. "General, if you and the young lady will come with me, I have a car waiting."

□□□□□

January 19, 1991
Jordan-Iraq Border
11:00 PM

Sergeant Johnson pulled off the side of the road and parked the stolen car where he could observe the activity at the border gate. The road was busy with cars and trucks going each way. Long lines of oil tanker trucks were going in both directions across the border.

He studied the border activities until he was ready. Then he started the car and took his place in the line. When he reached the guard, he rolled down the window.

"Do you speak English?" he asked.

The guard said something he did not understand.

"Can you get someone who speaks English?" Johnson asked.

The guard turned over his shoulder and shouted. Several soldiers came to the car.

"Does anyone here speak English?" Johnson shouted at the small group.

They spoke rapidly among themselves. The guard motioned Johnson to drive the car over to the side. Several more soldiers came over and walked in front of the car. When he stopped the car, one soldier opened the door and motioned for him to get out. He got out and stood leaning against the car and waited.

Three more soldiers came over. One pointed a rifle at Johnson while another searched him, taking his Army .45 caliber pistol, his knife, his money, and the wallet and identification he had stolen at the border in Israel. The soldier handed the wallet to the third soldier, who appeared to Johnson to be an officer. The officer looked at the papers in the wallet.

"This is you?" he asked, looking at the identification.

"No," Johnson said, relieved to find someone with whom he could communicate. "My identification is in the car. I am an American."

The word "American" created a stir among the soldiers.

376

"I am Captain Hassan. What do you want?"

"I have been working for your country. I seek political asylum in Iraq."

"You say you are an American soldier, yet you have been working for our country?"

"Yes. In the United States and in Israel. There are people in your government who will know me." Johnson moved to reach inside the car, but several soldiers jumped and pointed their rifles to block his movement.

"Please," Captain Hassan said, showing perfect teeth with a polite smile. "Allow me." He moved to the door of the car and sat in the driver's seat. He looked around until he found Johnson's small bag which contained his wallet and considerable cash. He opened the wallet and found Johnson's military identification. He got out of the car and stood facing Johnson.

"This is you?"

"Yes, Sergeant First Class James E. Johnson, United States Army."

Captain Hassan said something to the group of soldiers around them and there was a lot of discussion.

"You will wait here," Captain Hassan said. He spoke to the soldiers, turned and walked back to the border inspection building. The soldiers talked among themselves, taking great interest in Johnson. After waiting some fifteen minutes, Johnson saw the Captain returning with another officer. When they approached, the second officer spoke.

"I am Major Amin," he said. "What is it you want?"

"I am Sergeant First Class James E. Johnson of the United States Army. I have been working for the country of Iraq. I have left my post in Israel and seek political asylum in Iraq."

"You are from America?"

"Yes," Johnson said. "From Texas."

"Are you a Texas cowboy?" the Major asked with a broad smile.

"No," Johnson said, and managed a small laugh. "I am a soldier in the Army."

"Why do you want to come to Iraq?"

"I have worked for your country, and now I am not welcome at home."

"I see," Major Amin said. He turned to the Captain and said something sharply. There was a stir among the soldiers. The Captain said something and several soldiers left the group. The Major turned back to Johnson.

"You will come with me." He turned and walked toward the building at the border crossing.

□□□□□

The five of them walked through the Flight Control building of Holloman Air Force Base. Al was beside Jeff, and two other agents were behind them on each side of Suzy. Jeff looked at the doors on the side of the corridor. There was a delivery truck loading just outside. Al leaned over close to him.

"Don't even think about it, General," he said. "My orders are to bring you in, and trust me, I'm very good at following my orders."

They made the turn at the end of the corridor toward the gates for private aircrafts.

"I want to try one more time to make you understand the significance of what's happening," Jeff said. He had tried to get a conversation started in the car, to no avail.

"And I'm going to tell you one more time that the people I work for know everything you know, and there's nothing for you to say to me."

"There is a national crisis."

"That part you have right," Al said.

"But the solution is at the firing range, not here."

"That part you may have right, too," Al said. "But you're not going to be part of it."

They arrived at a gate with no visible activity. There was one person present in civilian clothes. Al stopped the group, made a motion to the other two men and left them standing there while he went over to talk to the person who seemed to be waiting for him.

The two men talked, and as the conversation progressed, it got more animated. Al seemed to be getting excited and looked at his watch. He glanced at Suzy and Jeff several times and gestured in their direction; when he finished talking, he came back to Jeff.

378

"General, I'm not sure, but I may owe you an apology," he said.

"Why's that?" Jeff asked.

"Well, we'll all know in a little while." Al motioned toward a door beside the gate. The person waiting at the gate had moved to the door and unlocked and opened it. Once inside with the door shut, Jeff turned to Al.

"Now, can you tell me just what's going on?"

"No," he said. "And the truth is, I'm not so sure myself now. We're going to wait here for a few minutes."

"Bullshit. I'm not going to just sit here and wait while a major conspiracy is being orchestrated against my country and my daughter may be in danger. I want some answers."

"I don't have any answers, General." Al seemed a bit unnerved. Jeff pressed.

"If you don't have any answers, then by God, I'll get some. I want to use a telephone."

"General, if you'll just have a little patience, I think we'll all have the answers you're looking for."

"Patience? How can you expect..." Suzy shouted.

The man from the gate opened the door and looked at Al. Al made a slight nod and the door was closed.

"Just what the hell is going on?" Jeff asked. "I want a phone."

"Just a few more moments now, General."

The man from the gate opened the door and came in again. There was someone behind him, and Jeff froze when he saw President George Bush. Behind the President were General Colin Powell and a man Jeff thought he recognized as Brent Scowcroft.

"Mr. President," Jeff could hardly get the words to come. Suzy moved close beside him as he shook the President's outstretched hand.

"Hello, General," the President said. "I'm sorry if we've inconvenienced you. I thought what was happening was important enough that we should talk directly to each other."

"Mr. President." The shock was too much. Jeff released President Bush's hand and the President turned to Suzy.

"And you, Miss Morris. We've met before, if memory serves. Senator

Hastings has told me a lot of good things about you. We could use people like you at the White House." He grasped Suzy's hand with both of his.

"Hello, sir," Suzy said.

"I assume you know these other gentlemen," he said, looking back at Jeff.

"I know General Powell," Jeff said and shook the offered hand.

"And this is Brent Scowcroft."

"I'm pleased to meet you," Jeff said.

"From what I've heard, General Weyland, the pleasure is mine."

"Well, I suppose you're wondering what's going on here," the President said. "And since I'm told that time may be critical, let me try to explain in as few words as I can. General Powell briefed me this morning about General Grant's strange actions. Colin was troubled because his confidence in you led him to believe that all was not as it seemed to be."

Jeff stole a look at Colin Powell, who nodded his agreement.

"Then I received a call from Senator Strong, who filled me in on your visit last night. He was mighty concerned that he'd done something that could very much endanger the fighting men of his country, and he wanted me to know. He feels responsible for whatever may be happening."

Jeff put his arm around Suzy's shoulders.

"From our understanding of the scheme," he said, "the Senator's role was very small and he was unaware of the involvement of foreign influence. We went to him only as a source of information."

"The three of us," the President continued after nodding his acceptance of Jeff's statement, "have been in California at a secret meeting with representatives of the Arab nations in the coalition. When we heard you'd been found, we diverted the plane on our way back to Washington to come here and meet with you. Apparently, when I asked that they find you, someone in the Secret Service misunderstood the why and the how."

Jeff looked at Al, who mouthed an apology.

The President continued his discussion.

"The matter in which you are involved is of the highest importance to America. If what I understand of this plot is true, then it's vital that it not succeed."

"I agree, Mr. President," Jeff said.

"Part of our problem is that we don't really have the full story. Apparently only you have that."

"I can tell you everything I know," Jeff said.

"Please do, but be as brief as possible. I have some other information when you're finished that may bear on the problem. Time may be more critical than you think."

"Yes, sir," Jeff said. He quickly explained his theory of the plan to inhibit PATRIOT performance intercepting SCUDs aimed at Israeli population centers. When he finished, the President looked to Brent Scowcroft.

"That seems to track with what we were told," he said. He looked back to Jeff. "And you believe you have all of the pieces to the puzzle?"

"I believe I will have as soon as I can make a phone call or two. I have some people working at Redstone Arsenal on the final pieces now, and they're waiting on my call."

"Good. General Weyland, we've been informed that Iraq plans an all-out SCUD attack on Israel very soon. Our own spy satellites have picked up additional movement in possible launch areas. It's imperative that PATRIOT be repaired or fixed before that or we might lose Israel's cooperation. They're at the brink already, and a major loss of Israeli life will probably put them over the edge."

"If I'm right, Mr. President, a major loss of Israeli life is probable unless we can fix this thing."

"If that happens, General, the entire war effort will fail. Our Arab friends have made it clear again today they will not participate further if Israel enters the war."

"I understand."

"I hope all of us in this room understand," the President said. "We have over a half million American soldiers on Arab soil. If the coalition doesn't hold firm, there's no telling what situation those young men and women will face. It has the potential of being the greatest catastrophe in our country's military history."

Al's beeper went off. The President looked over his shoulder with minor irritation and then back to Jeff. Al left the room.

"Is it possible to correct this sabotage of our PATRIOT missiles, General

Weyland, and let them work their magic tonight?"

"Yes, Mr. President," Jeff said. "It is possible. If what I believe to be the plan is correct, the problem can be fixed with relative ease."

"Well, then. Maybe we can avoid this thing."

Al came back in the room with a portable phone. "Sir," he said, "I have someone who needs to talk to General Weyland." He handed the phone to Jeff before anyone could protest.

"General Weyland," Jeff spoke into the phone.

"Jeff, it's Billy."

"Are you in Atlanta?"

"Yeah, but there's not good news, buddy. She's missing and the bad guys have left another calling card." Jeff's stomach knotted and the fear was plain on his face.

"What kind of card?"

"Cat."

Jeff couldn't bring himself to ask.

"You need to get here fast. I've got guys all over the town. We've got a lead, but don't have them in sight yet. You still got the number I gave you?"

"Yes," Jeff said. He could feel his body going numb as he handed the phone to Al.

"I take it that was not good news," the President said.

"No," Jeff said. "It wasn't. It appears they have my daughter."

"Oh, Jeff!" Suzy cried out.

"Where?"

"In Atlanta. Some of your people are looking for them, but they haven't found her yet."

"General Weyland, I understand and can fully sympathize with your situation. But, I'm going to have to ask you to do something that I'm not real sure I could do myself."

"Mr. President, you don't have to ask. If you could make a helicopter available for me, I'm going back to the launch site."

"I'll get you your helicopter, but I can do better than that, General. We flew out here in a specially outfitted SR-71 Blackbird airplane. Air Force One is standing by in New Orleans, and I'll have it come and fetch me

382

here. When you're finished in White Sands, use my Blackbird to go to Atlanta."

"Thank you, Mr. President."

"No, General. Thank you. I thank you and your country thanks you."

▢▢▢▢▢

"TARGET ENGAGEABLE."

The scene in the van was familiar. On the console in front of him were the codes he had received from Ralph Jameson. The first set of two letters was a code to tell the hidden software that an input was coming. Jeff entered the two letters on the keyboard. A question mark came on the screen. Jeff could feel his own heart beating. He entered the other set of letters, "AFIRAHS."

Ralph Jameson hadn't been able to make any sense of the letters, but Billy had seen Sharifa spelled backwards even as he wrote the letters down. When he gave the codes to Jeff, Billy had paused for a moment before asking if Jeff recognized the code. Jeff hadn't looked for any sense in the letters, so as soon as Billy asked, he took a second look. Spelling something backwards is always the first thing to try, and sure enough, big as life, there she was. If they needed any hard data to connect Celia Mitchell to this complex scheme, this was it.

After he entered the letters, nothing else happened, and the screen was blank. Ralph Jameson said that was to be expected. If the letters were wrong, it would give you the question mark one more time. Two strikes and you were out, and the missile would blow. No second question mark, and you were home free. It was still in question whether the codes were the same on the tactical systems as they were on the lab systems at Huntsville and Raytheon.

"MISSILE AWAY."

Jeff moved quickly to the back of the van and slipped outside the door to stand on the small platform. With a boom and a roar, the missile rose above the berms around the launch area. Jeff stood tensely watching as the missile gained altitude, and his hands involuntarily rose as the missile

383

climbed through his own mental reference of the danger zone. By the time the missile reached burnout of the rocket motor and started major maneuverings downrange, his arms were fully extended over his head. He would never remember what he yelled as the missile rapidly faded from sight.

Bob Anderson was in the van when he returned. That was an unusual situation, but this was an unusual day.

"I have a telefax for you," Bob said, and handed him a single piece of paper. Jeff had to move to the corner of the van to find a small light from one of the electronic racks by which to read. It was instructions from Ralph Jameson for the software changes to negate the buried code. Jeff would need to combine the information from Ralph with what he had observed in the van to make the final corrections. Obviously, Ralph had not been on the list to get the message from General Grant. There was a footnote. Ralph said that he hadn't been able to go through the system at White Sands since they had lost satellite communications with Launch Complex 38 several hours before for unknown reasons.

"Sir, there's a phone call for you. You can take it in the Director's office."

Jeff left the van and went into the first office in the corridor. He reached for the phone on the desk and punched the blinking light.

"General Weyland."

"They want to talk to you." It was Billy.

"You've got her?"

"No. One of them came to us. He wants to talk to you."

"Put him on."

"Hello, General. I am sorry we have..."

"You're going to be a lot sorrier if you don't let her go."

"I'm afraid you aren't in much of a position to be making threats, General." The voice spoke in perfect English, but with a flat calmness and lack of animation.

"I believe I am. Trust me. If anything happens to her, you will not survive."

"That may be, General. But you must understand that is a sacrifice I am prepared to make. Are you?"

384

"What do you mean?"

"Are you prepared to trade my life for hers?"

"What do you want?"

"I believe you have received the instructions on the repair of the system, correct?"

Jeff looked at the piece of paper in his hands.

"So?"

"It is up to you to distribute this software change, yes?"

"Again, so?"

"We would like for you to make a slight error in writing the directions for the correction to the software. No one will ever know that it was anything other than an honest mistake. You are under a lot of strain."

"No."

"Think about it. You have the changes required, and everyone is waiting on you. You have the future in your hands, and you cannot be checked. All of the available test missiles have now been fired, and there is no way to check what you will do. It would be easy for you to save your daughter's life."

"No," Jeff said, but his voice had lost some of its firmness.

"In that case, General, perhaps you should listen to something."

There was a slight pause, and then he heard a faint noise in the background. As it became louder, he could recognize it as a scream. It didn't stop. Jeff gripped the phone until his knuckles were white.

"Now, General, let me ask you again."

"It's good that you are prepared to make death your contribution," Jeff said, his teeth clenched tightly, and the muscles of his jaw working.

"General, I will say once again that you are in no position to make useless threats. Your attitude will only worsen things. There is no need for her to endure more pain. She has suffered enough already. Her death will not be kind. She is a very pretty girl, and it would be such a waste." The phone went dead.

His hands shaking, Jeff pulled out the piece of paper with the number Billy had given him and dialed.

"He's gone," Billy said when he answered. "He had a phone with him, and he patched into wherever she is."

"Was it real?"

"Seemed like it. Could you recognize her voice?"

"No," Jeff said faintly. "All I heard was screams." He was choking back the bile in his throat. "Can you trace it?"

"We're working it already, but probably not, since it was cellular. When can you get here?"

"I don't know. How long does it take at three times the speed of sound?"

"I'll be waiting when you land. Sounds like you've had some interesting company."

"Right. But that's not the company I want right now."

"We'll find her, Jeff."

"I know," he said, his voice cracking, "but will she be alive?"

Jeff sagged into the desk chair as he fumbled the phone back into its cradle. Suddenly feeling old and tired and sick, he stared blankly at the wall. He knew he needed to, had to, move, but for the moment, his body refused to budge. Through his mind, as if in a slide show, flashed a series of images. Cindy at eight, all bony knees and freckles. Teenaged Cindy proudly waving her brand new driver's license. Cindy frowning as she put the finishing touches on a painting, a dab of blue paint on her cheek.

Slowly Jeff's gaze traveled across the objects in the room and rested on the piece of paper in his hand. He still couldn't move as he looked at the cryptic instructions on the sheet. Under his hand, a snapshot tucked into the blotter on the desk caught his eye. The photo showed a small girl, probably Lester's granddaughter, perched atop a black and white pony. The child's face glowed with joy. Immediately, Jeff was reminded of his horse ride with four-year-old Cindy, and across those years, he remembered her words, "Daddy has to go. He has to help other little girls."

He stared at the piece of paper in his hand with the code changes written on it. He scrubbed his hands over his face and breathed a great sigh. Gently touching the snapshot, he pushed himself to his feet and left the small office. He found Johnny Madkin waiting for him in the hallway.

"Get me some paper, will you, Johnny? I've got to write the instructions for changing the software."

weapons systems--pentagon adv19 1-91
Saudi Arabia, Israel brace for SCUD attacks
USWNS Military News
adv jan 19 1991 or thereafter

By GEORGE GROWSON

WASHINGTON—There has been a lull in the fighting between
the Allied coalition and Iraq. It is speculated that Saddam
Hussein is either preparing for a major assault or has
expended all of the SCUDs he has available. In an
announcement made earlier today, U.S. military officials
stated that 415 additional air sorties have been flown over
Iraq and Kuwait during the day. As Saudi Arabia and Israel
prepare for another night with the fear of SCUD attacks,
discussions continue among the United States, Israel, and
the Allied Arab nations. There is increased speculation
that Israel may enter the conflict; Arab members of the
coalition have refused comment on their reaction should
there be such a development. President Bush canceled
several appointments today and has turned his full
attention to the conflict in the Middle East.

SIXTEEN

The small window allowed Jeff a limited view of Dobbins Air Force Base, but he could tell that the arrival of the SR-71 was causing quite a stir. Several people had stopped what they were doing and were staring at the world's fastest airplane. Traveling over three times the speed of sound, the plane had made the trip from White Sands Missile Range in just over an hour.

When the plane came to a stop by the hangar, the canopy popped open, and Jeff and Suzy removed the helmet and harness system which strapped them into their ejection seats. Jeff recognized Billy in the driver's seat of a gray sedan. Billy didn't get out of the car, but waited just outside the ring of people and service vehicles rapidly gathering around the Blackbird.

A portable staircase was wheeled to the plane and Jeff and Suzy climbed out. A man in an Air Force uniform was waiting for them as they reached the bottom of the ladder.

"Good afternoon, sir," he said as he saluted. "I'm George Adkisson, the Commander of Dobbins Base. Welcome to our facility."

"Thanks," Jeff said, returning the salute. "I'm glad you had a runway to accommodate the plane. There aren't many around, and we couldn't get clearance to fly into any civilian airports."

"We made the changes a few years back to handle this plane and some other special military aircraft. This is quite a plane, and the first one I've seen up close. Is there anything I can do to help you, sir?"

"Not for me personally," Jeff said. "But if you could get some fuel for the plane and something to eat for the pilot, we'd appreciate it."

"No problem," Adkisson said. "Will you be staying long?"

"I really don't know," Jeff said. "We have some pressing business in Atlanta, and we'll leave as soon as we've finished."

"Will you need ground transportation?"

"Thanks, but no," Jeff said. "There's a car here for us. If you could just assist the pilot and provide some security for the aircraft while I'm gone, I'd appreciate it."

"Surely," Adkisson said, and he turned his attention back to the plane as Jeff and Suzy hurried toward the car and Billy.

Jeff and Suzy got in the car, which began moving before they had closed their doors. Billy turned on a siren, and the crowd of people immediately parted for them.

"Where is she?" Jeff asked as soon as he had the door closed.

"We don't know. We're trying to pick up her trail, but can't. She was in her studio this morning, but didn't say anything to anyone about leaving. She just isn't there now. She isn't anywhere we've looked."

"Do you have other people in town now?"

"About fifty and more on the way. The President had already called my boss and given full clearance."

"Do you have a plan?" Jeff asked.

"No more than what we're doing. We're going down every alley we can," Billy said.

After they passed the main terminal building and went through the gate of the military installation, a black limousine pulled in front of them.

"Uh oh," Billy said. He put the gearshift into reverse and started to back away.

"Wait," Jeff said.

A lone man got out of the limousine from the front passenger door wearing a familiar chauffeur's uniform.

The man looked in Billy's car and motioned back to the limousine. Another uniformed man got out and opened the rear door for a lone passenger.

"Saudi intelligence," Billy said. They waited as the man approached the car.

"I wondered if they would come," Jeff said.

"Come, hell," Billy said. "What do you mean, come?"

"I called for their help. I used the radio on the plane."

"And you just happened to have a contact number for Saudi intelligence?"

"No," Jeff said. "I actually happened to have the number for the Saudi ambassador who had offered his help."

"Bandar?"

"Himself."

"Someday when we're all old and gray, that's a story I'd like to hear."

Jeff opened his door and walked around to meet the Saudi. Billy got out and stood by the door. The man nodded to Billy as he approached and Billy returned his nod, but they exchanged no greeting.

"You must be General Weyland," he said, holding his hand toward Jeff, but his eyes remained steadily on Billy.

"Yes," Jeff said. "Do you have something for me?"

"The men you are looking for are in three rooms on the seventieth floor of the Westin Peachtree Plaza. Rooms 7035 through 7039."

Billy nodded and looked toward the other car.

The Arab finally looked away from Billy and turned his eyes to Jeff. "I bring you greetings from our King. He wishes me to convey that he is a great admirer of the PATRIOT, and he wishes you well in your quest." With that, he spun on his heels and returned to the limousine.

"Well, I'll be damned," Billy said as he turned to the car. By the time Jeff reached his door, Billy was on the radio.

"Code Blue, Code Blue. This is Pretty Boy. All units. Suspects are..."

Jeff and Suzy listened as Billy gave instructions over the radio. He maneuvered the car onto Interstate 75 and sped toward downtown Atlanta, the siren's blast parting traffic.

"I'm going to be straight here, buddy. There's no way to know if she's alive. If it was her on the phone, then she's probably OK. Either they killed her right away or they've kept her as a bargaining chip in case it comes to a negotiation. Assuming the latter, we still have a chance."

"Where's the hotel?" Jeff asked.

"Downtown. Nice place—pedestrian access to sights and restaurants, all the conveniences. In fact, these people may have had these rooms on a permanent basis, as a lot of other countries do."

Billy got off at Williams Street in the heart of downtown, then took an immediate right to avoid the traffic at the Merchandise Mart. Jeff fell against the car door as Billy jerked left onto Techwood and pulled up at the hotel. He brought the car to a stop next to several men, and Jeff and Suzy followed him to the small group.

"Any change?" Billy asked.

"No," one of the men answered. "They're still in the room."

"How many?" Jeff asked.

"We don't know for sure," the agent said. "We've bugged the hall, and we believe the one who visited Billy is in the room. That's all we know for sure. We don't know yet how many there are, or even if the girl is in there."

The girl.

"There's some more news," another agent said, walking up to their group. "We've taken the rooms on both ends of their set and installed some more listening devices. We've been able to hear some individual words, but no sense of any conversation yet. But we can tell there are at least two female voices in there."

"Speaking English?" Billy asked.

"Some English and some something else, probably Arabic. They're not talking much. One of the female voices only speaks English, but she's talking so low we can't understand her. We have some better sound equipment and an interpreter on the way."

Billy and Jeff exchanged a look, and Billy motioned for Jeff and Suzy to move away from the others. They walked back toward the car and stopped out of listening range from the other men. After some more talk, Billy came back to Suzy and Jeff.

"Look, buddy," Billy said. "This is going to be a hard decision for you."

"Seems like the day for that," Jeff said.

"My reasoning is that any confrontation or attempt to negotiate is going

392

to end up with Cindy looking down the end of a gun barrel. I don't think we can give them any warning. I also don't think we ought to delay. Every minute we wait gives somebody in that room more of a chance to spot us. We're trying to be careful, but if somebody comes out in a hurry, they're liable to see something that'll tip them. I think the best plan is to go in with guns blazing and take out as many of them as we can before they have a chance to react."

"You're right," Jeff said.

"You like the plan?"

"I mean it's a tough decision."

"Well?"

"Yeah, you're right. It's the only thing that makes sense."

"It's up to you, buddy. If you want, we can try to negotiate."

Jeff looked at Suzy and then back to Billy. Suzy took his hand and lifted it to her cheek.

"No. I agree with you. That's a loser."

"OK. We'll go with my plan. I want you to know I have my best men here. If she's alive, we'll get her."

"I'm going in with you," Jeff said.

"Jeff, that's not smart. You need to leave this to us."

"If that was your daughter, would you stand out here and watch?"

"No." Billy turned, walked back to the group of men and had a short discussion. Suzy moaned quietly and turned pale when Billy returned with a handgun for Jeff.

"This is the best there is at short range. You ready?"

"Yes," Jeff said.

He looked at the pistol, which felt strange in his hand. It wasn't that he avoided guns, but they just didn't fit into his lifestyle. He hadn't held one since Vietnam. This one was light and fit well into his hand as he wrapped his fingers around the ivory grips. He shoved it into his belt and turned to Suzy.

"Don't even say it," she said, meeting his gaze. "If you can go, so can I. I'll wait in the hall while you go into the rooms."

"OK. Let's go," Billy said. He went back to his men and gave some instructions.

393

□□□□□

Alleh Abdul Mohatma turned the big missile transporter onto the sandy road leading into the desert, following the vehicle in front of him. The entire convoy of SCUD launchers and support vehicles was driving without lights, but they were used to it. It was necessary if they were going to avoid the American airplanes and accomplish their mission. In the faded light of the moon, dust could be seen rising from the desert ahead where other MAZ transporters had reached their firing locations. Alleh and the others had been concerned about the large number of launchers to be used on this night. After the firings, it would be impossible for all of them to hide quickly enough to evade the aircrafts which were sure to come. Some would be lost for sure.

The small truck leading the group pulled off the roadbed, and Alleh followed the guide truck in front of him. Finally, the lead truck turned right into a small depression in the desert. When the truck stopped, Alleh checked the compass on the dash of his transporter and drove in a large circle to point the missile in the direction written beside the compass. He then pulled forward toward a pole, positioning the heavy eight-wheeled truck so that his driver's side front fender was nearly touching the pole. He left the engine running and jumped down from the driver's compartment to begin his flight preparation for the missile.

A second truck drove up beside his. When the door opened, Alleh was surprised to see an American in the front compartment. All of the drivers and crews had heard about the American who had escaped from Israel and made his way to Iraq. One of the other operators had told of seeing him in the village earlier tonight. Alleh had listened as they all joked about the Americans who were leaving their posts because they were so scared of the Iraqi SCUDs. Johnson's defection had bolstered their respect for their Supreme Ruler. Only a truly great man could strike such fear in the minds of their enemies that they would run in the face of battle.

The truck carrying the fuel for the missile had arrived and Alleh put on the protective suit required for the process. This was the one part of the job all the operators feared. The red fuming nitric acid would

394

destroy any flesh it touched, and there were many stories of men who had been burned to death due to their own carelessness. He pulled the hoses from the fuel truck and prepared the missile. The guidance and survey teams were positioning their instruments around the area. Two more missile transporters were going through similar procedures several hundred yards away.

❑❑❑❑❑

Jeff, Billy and Suzy stepped from the elevator on the seventieth floor as a half dozen men emerged from a room several doors down. One nodded at Billy and moved cautiously down the curved hallway.

"Their rooms are all the way on the other side. It's a round building with a circular floorplan," Billy whispered to Jeff. They followed the other men. Another door opened a little way down the circular hallway, and more men came out.

"We'll go in all three rooms at the same time. Remember, these men will kill without thinking. If you hesitate, even for one split second, they'll kill you and then Cindy."

Jeff's mouth was too dry to make any words. He nodded to Billy and removed the pistol from his belt. He could see the men positioning themselves on either side of the doors. There were four men at each door— two on one side and two on the other. An additional two men at each door had a large, heavy cylinder with handles on each side. Everyone was against the wall waiting. Billy motioned to the third door.

"This is our door. From the listening devices, it appears this is where they're keeping Cindy."

She's on the other side of that wall.

Jeff looked back toward the elevator and made eye contact with Suzy. She was leaning against the wall with her hands gripped in front of her. Jeff motioned her back into the alcove for the elevators, and she gave him a look which told him everything she felt. He nodded to her, and she disappeared around the corner.

Jeff moved into position behind Billy, tucked his elbow in tight, and raised the pistol to a vertical position. At Billy's gesture, the battering ram teams moved into position. They moved the heavy crash poles with slow swings until they were rocking like synchronized pendulums. On Billy's signal, all three crashed into the doors simultaneously and the teams poured into each of the rooms. Jeff followed closely behind Billy.

"Federal agents!" Billy shouted. "Everybody stay still!" One man started up from his chair. Before Jeff could even think, Billy fired twice, and the man went down. A face looked around the corner from the next room, and Jeff fired twice in that direction, but couldn't tell if it was a hit. Cindy was tied on the bed. Jeff heard gunshots in the other rooms as he ran to his screaming daughter.

Baby.

He wanted to hug her, but he was concerned about her injuries. Billy disappeared through the door and into the next room. More gunshots sounded.

"All clear, room two," came from the adjoining room. Jeff heard a similar call for room one.

He sat on the bed beside Cindy and touched her face. He took a quick look at her and saw bruises and small cuts, but nothing seemed serious. A large bruise on her cheek was swollen enough to force her eye half closed. She had stopped screaming but was sobbing uncontrollably. Billy came back into the room with several agents and cut the ropes binding her hands and feet with a knife. Jeff kissed her on her forehead and stroked her hair. Her sobs were beginning to soften, but she still had her eyes pressed shut.

"It's over, Baby," he whispered as he put his face beside hers.

"Billy. I think you better come in here." One of the agents stuck his head around the door connecting the rooms. Billy went into the other room.

"Jeff," Billy said from the door. "If you can leave her, get in here quick."

"Sweetheart, I've got to go in the other room. These men here will protect you. Are you OK?" Cindy's eyes were still pressed shut, but she nodded. Jeff rose from the bed and went through the door.

In the next room, there were two bodies on the floor and one more in a chair. Blood was everywhere, and the smoke and smell of burnt gunpowder was strong. In the middle of the bathroom was a hole in the floor.

"They must have rented the room on the floor below," Billy said. "No telling how many escaped."

Jeff heard his name shouted from the hallway.

"Suzy!" he shouted.

With Billy right behind him, he bolted toward the elevator. The hall was full of men in suits, but Jeff didn't see Suzy. As Jeff turned the corner into the elevator alcove, the doors opened and Suzy stepped out.

"Where were you?" Jeff asked.

"One floor down—I just saw Celia run into an elevator going down."

"I'll be damned," said Billy. "All right, let's go!"

□□□□□

First Lieutenant John Frederick sat in the Tactical Control Officer's chair at the console of the Engagement Control Set of Bravo Battery, Fourth Battalion of the Forty-third Artillery Regiment (PATRIOT). He had assumed command of the Battery since the unsolved murder of Captain Maxwell. His palms were sweating as he ran through the checks required to ensure the system was at Battle Stations. The entire Battery had been on edge since the MPs had described Jerry Maxwell's crushed skull. The police thought that he had been mugged after wandering into an unfriendly section of Tel Aviv. That seemed strange, as it was out of character for their Captain. Lieutenant Frederick didn't want to think about all of that right now, and tried to keep his mind on his job.

They had received a message from Battalion Headquarters this afternoon to be on full alert for the entire evening. There was no indication of what they were to expect, but that didn't take much intelligence. They all knew there had been a lull in the SCUD firings and had read in the papers that Saddam Hussein might be preparing a major assault on Israel. There was no hard data to give this theory any credibility, so they had dismissed it until they received the alert. The soldiers figured that the brass had probably read the same papers, and now they were sitting here all night because a U.S. Cable News Services reporter had made up a theory to give himself a few more inches of print.

397

The PATRIOT system was operating smoothly. After the previous evening's missile failure, the entire crew had spent long hours going over every detail to determine the cause of the problem, but they had drawn a blank. Finally they had assumed that a malfunction on the missile had caused it to blow prematurely. "Shit happens," they said.

Lieutenant Frederick looked over the console and the radar display. Everything was ready.

□□□□□

Billy removed a radio from his belt.

"All units. All units. This is Pretty Boy. Code Bravo. Code Bravo. Female suspect fleeing premises. Five foot eight. One hundred twenty-five pounds. Looker. Black hair below the shoulders. Moving fast. Probably armed and dangerous. Top priority to apprehend. Repeat. Top priority to apprehend."

"She had on a red dress," Suzy said. Jeff felt the heat from the gun barrel as he stuffed it into his belt and followed Billy onto the elevator just as the doors were closing.

"All units. All units. Suspect is wearing red dress. Fire power which does not endanger civilians is authorized to stop."

"Go help Cindy," Jeff yelled to Suzy as the elevator door closed. He and Billy rode in silence, as the express elevator sped downward.

"I might not get a chance to say it later, so I'll say it now," Jeff said as the elevator approached the lobby. "Thanks, Billy."

"All in a day's work, buddy," Billy said. "It was quite a relief to know she's OK. By the way, you handled yourself real well back there. I guess some instincts don't go away."

"Yes, they do," Jeff said. "If that had been anybody else but Cindy in that room, I don't think I could have done it."

"Even me?" Billy said with a big smile. "You did it once before for me."

"That was a long time ago. I was younger then and probably not as smart."

The elevator door opened, and Billy and Jeff ran through the lobby of the hotel and out to the street. There were police everywhere managing the curious crowds of onlookers. Several agents approached Billy.

"No sign of her," one said. "We've got people everywhere, but nothing."

"She can't just disappear. Let's start a search of the hotel."

"Every street is blocked," the agent said. "There's a pedestrian walkway above the street, and we have people there, too. She's contained, but we haven't found her yet."

"Code Bravo, this is unit seven." It was the radio on Billy's belt.

"This is Pretty Boy. Go."

"We have a car approaching roadblock at high speed. It looks like it's not going to..." The transmission stopped.

Gunfire erupted from the north. Jeff looked in the direction of the noise, and when he looked back, Billy was gone. Jeff spotted him running to the car and ran after him. He got in the seat just as the car sped off in the direction of the gunfire. Jeff could hear the reports from Billy's radio that the car had broken through the roadblock and escaped.

"Lone occupant of the car was a female matching suspect's description," came from the radio.

"Where's the car now?" Billy asked.

"We don't know. Our car was destroyed as she broke through. We're on foot. Last saw the car moving north on West Peachtree."

"Roger," Billy said. "I'm in pursuit."

Jeff could hear other sirens behind them. There were two cars right behind and several more about a block back.

"Airborne Two, this is Pretty Boy," Billy said into the radio.

"This is Airborne Two. We have a potential. Matching vehicle moving west on Alexander and turning now onto the entrance ramp for the highway."

Billy slammed his foot on the brake and the car skidded to the left. He jammed his foot on the gas, and they shot through traffic again and slid into the intersection at the entrance ramp. The tires screamed as he forced the wheel to turn left. This time a wide turn sent the car partially into the north-south exit median. Jeff closed his eyes as dirt, rocks, and pieces of juniper bush flew up all around the car.

"Where in hell did you learn to drive?" Jeff asked. He grasped the handle above the door and tried to keep himself in the seat without much luck.

"Tank school, remember?" Billy grinned as he turned on the wipers to clear the dirt off the windshield.

"Pretty Boy, this is Airborne Two. You're doing good. She's about three miles ahead of you on 75. You'll need to be in the right-hand lane. There's some heavy traffic ahead. Be careful."

"Roger Airborne Two. Keep her in sight." Billy moved the car into the emergency lane on the right side of the interstate and pressed the accelerator. Jeff could only see the speedometer up to about eighty and the needle was out of his sight.

"You heard the man say to be careful, didn't you?"

"Yeah. See that place there?"

"What? What place?"

"Right there," Billy said. "That's a drive-in restaurant called the Varsity. They've sold more Cokes there than any other place in the world. I bet you didn't know that, did you?"

"Let me understand this," Jeff said. "You're driving this car over eighty in the emergency lane of an inner-city freeway at rush hour, and you want me to take in the local sights?"

"Well, hell, that's a pretty big deal. Of course, it helps to have the home of Coca- Cola next door. If you look out the back window, you can see the Coke Tower."

"I don't want to look, and I damn sure don't want you to look." Jeff sucked in a big breath as a vehicle pulled in front of them to the exit. Billy swerved to miss the car and then pressed the gas pedal to the floor again.

"Don't get all tense, buddy. This'll be a piece of cake. Trust me. You got any bullets left?"

"Yeah," Jeff said. "I only fired twice."

"Twice! Christ almighty. Only two shots. I take back what I said on the elevator."

"Hell, there was only one man in the room, and you shot him."

"Here, load this for me, would you?" Billy asked, handing Jeff his pistol and reaching into his jacket pocket for several magazines of ammunition.

Jeff ejected the clip from the pistol and inserted a fresh one. He handed the gun back to Billy, who put it into his shoulder holster, picked up the extra clips, and put them back in his jacket pocket.

"Pretty Boy, this is Airborne One. Suspect has exited at West Paces Ferry Road and is moving east. Her speed has slowed. It doesn't look like she knows you're following."

"Roger," Billy said into the radio. Jeff saw a sign for West Paces Ferry Road which said the exit was one mile ahead.

"Pretty Boy?" Jeff asked with an obvious tease in his voice. "Tell me about that."

"What's to explain? You don't think I'm pretty?" Billy asked.

The car was still in the emergency lane. Along this stretch of Interstate 75, there was a large concrete wall on the outside of the northbound lane, and it was so close Jeff could've reached out and touched it. The scream of the siren echoed from the wall and filled the car. Billy relaxed his foot on the accelerator and the car slowed slightly.

Billy pulled the wheel a little to the right to avoid a car moving toward the exit ramp. Jeff sucked in a breath as he saw how close they were to the wall.

Billy's foot slammed down on the brake pedal. They were approaching the ramp where Celia had exited, and a car had moved in front of them. Billy had one hand on the horn and the other on the wheel as he pulled it hard to the right. The fender hit the steel siderail and sparks flew. Once past the car, Billy pulled the wheel to the left and the car returned to the center of the exit ramp. There was a traffic light at the bottom of the ramp, and Billy blasted the horn in addition to the siren. Cars parted uncertainly in front of them as Billy maneuvered between the scattering vehicles.

They made a left and then a quick right through a parking lot. Another right out of the lot put them onto West Paces Ferry Road.

"Airborne, where is she?"

"It's hard to keep track of her because of all of the trees," crackled back the radio. "But she can't be too far ahead of you. Maybe a mile. Light blue car. I can't make out the type."

"I hope it's not a Ford," Billy said, turning off the siren.

"Why in God's name would you care what kind of car she has?" Jeff asked.

"Because once she sees us, she's going to try to get away. We're driving a Chevrolet, and everybody knows a Ford can beat a Chevy any day."

"You wouldn't want to make a little wager now, would you?"

"Don't tell me you're a Chevy man."

"I thought you'd remember that."

"Shit," Billy said.

"Does that mean our friendship's over?" Jeff asked.

"No, but it's definitely affected. I think I see her."

Jeff brought both of his hands to his head.

"You OK?" Billy asked.

"Yeah. I think the reality of the chase is catching up to me. Until now adrenaline kept me going. Now it just hit me that we're in a car about to engage a known foreign agent."

"Fun, huh?"

"Yeah. Real fun."

Billy felt inside his jacket and found his pistol. Jeff pulled his own from his belt, and then rolled down the window. The rush of cold January air instantly filled the car.

"Do you have a plan?" he asked Billy.

"No. If I can get beside her before she spots us, I..."

The blue car in front of them accelerated wildly and passed another car.

"Forget Plan A. She's spotted us," Jeff said.

"Great observation, but then you always did have a keen perception for the obvious," Billy said. "Hang on." The car accelerated.

"That's the Governor's Mansion on the left," Billy said as he struggled to keep the car on the road.

"For Chrissakes. Would you quit pretending you're a damned tour guide and just drive the car?" For the first time, Jeff noticed that they were in a very high-rent section of town, on a curving road with huge beautiful mansions and manicured lawns.

"I already told you not to get all tense," Billy said. They were gaining on the blue car, and Jeff could now see the driver's long black hair. The road narrowed. Jeff didn't know how they were going to get alongside her.

"See if you can hit a tire," Billy said.

Jeff aimed out the window. Between the icy wind and the bouncing of the car, the best he could do was point the pistol in the general direction of the tires and fire. He emptied the pistol with no luck.

"OK," Billy said. "Forget that. You're liable to hit somebody in the next county. I'm going to ram her." Jeff felt the car accelerate and braced himself. As they approached the car, he saw brake lights. Billy slammed the brakes as Celia skidded in a circle until the car was moving backwards. Smoke was billowing from her rear tires as she went by them in the opposite direction. Billy fired his pistol at the window as Jeff braced himself for the turn.

"This is going to be more difficult than I thought," Billy said. He had lost too much momentum to turn the car and had to stop and back up to turn around. By the time he did, they had lost sight of Celia, but Billy accelerated in the new direction.

"Isn't she heading back into the rest of your men?" Jeff asked.

"Yeah, but there's no telling how far back they are. They didn't learn to drive in tank school." Billy picked up the radio. "Code Bravo, Code Bravo. Vehicle has reversed directions and is now traveling west."

"Yeah," Jeff said. "We lost the rest of the vehicles when you started driving in the emergency lane."

"Airborne, this is Pretty Boy. Can you see her?"

"Negative, Pretty Boy. We can't see anything. Your backup is just exiting the interstate."

"Roger, Airborne. All units. All mobile units form a roadblock at the west end of the road."

The road ahead curved as it went up a hill. Just as they were about to crest the hill, they saw the blue car bearing down directly at them.

"Christ!" Billy yelled as he pulled the wheel hard to the right. The blue car turned with them, headed for a direct impact. Billy pulled harder right on the wheel, and they felt the tires leave the pavement. At the last moment, the blue car pulled away and struck them a glancing blow to their door. Jeff recognized Celia.

The side of the road sloped into a drainage area, and Billy struggled to get the car back onto the road as it bounced in the soggy turf. There was a small group of trees about a hundred yards ahead.

"We're not going to make it that way," Billy said as he cranked the wheel in the opposite direction. They turned to the right and slid onto the lush bermuda lawn. Billy slammed the accelerator, and the car went into a large sliding turn, the spinning tires spewing grass and mud as they tried to grip the lawn. He reached a gravel driveway, and it jumped forward as the tires found more solid footing.

"Clear on the right," Jeff yelled.

"I can't see to the left," Billy said as they approached the street.

"Me either," Jeff said, expecting Billy to slow. Instead, Billy pressed the accelerator harder and jerked the wheel to the left as the car jumped into the street. The spinning tires squealed as they hit the pavement, and the car leaped forward.

"She's got a pretty good jump on us, but I think we can still catch her," Billy said.

"What happened to your Ford theory?"

"Didn't you notice?" Billy asked.

"No. I'm sorry, but I didn't really have time. I was able to tell that there's no doubt it's Celia."

"Well, for your information, it was a goddamned Toyota. This'll be a picnic." They topped a hill and Jeff could feel the lightness in his stomach. He wasn't sure, but he thought they had been airborne for a moment. He saw another car ahead of them, but couldn't tell if it was Celia's. He didn't remember noticing if any other car had passed them while they were recovering from her attempt to run them off the road.

"That's her," Billy said.

"I hope you have a better plan this time."

"This time, she will go down. Trust me."

"That's what you said that night when..."

"I don't want to hear it," Billy said. Celia had caught up with some traffic and was about to pass. A car was coming from the other direction, and she pulled back into her lane.

"That poor sonofabitch in front of her doesn't know what's about to happen." Jeff watched as Celia moved directly ahead and rammed the car in front of her. The car spun to the left, and Celia edged by on the right. An oncoming car swerved to avoid the car she had pushed into the far lane, but it was too late, and they could feel the pressure from the crash.

The impact was far enough in front of them for Billy to find an opening on the road, and as their car sped past, Jeff heard and then felt the pressure from the explosion. He looked over his shoulder as they topped another hill, and all he could see was a large fireball.

"She may not be driving a Chevrolet," Billy said. "But I think she went to the basic Chevy driver's school. That was a hell of a move."

"Christ," Jeff said. "A few seconds earlier and that fireball would have gotten us."

"Reload," Billy said, and threw a magazine at Jeff. "This is actually going to be a whole lot harder than I thought."

"What now?" Jeff asked as he put the fresh magazine in his pistol.

"I don't know for sure, but if you get a shot at her, take it."

They had pulled within several car lengths of Celia and were keeping pace. The road straightened for several hundred yards.

"Here we go," Billy said. He pulled into the left lane and accelerated. When the front fender of their car got in front of her back fender, Billy pulled hard right. Celia had been ready and pulled right with him. She went off the road as Billy fell back. Her car swerved and then regained the road. Billy accelerated again and pulled directly behind her. He backed off a little, and then pressed his foot hard to the floor. Jeff braced himself for the hit.

Celia swerved wildly to the left just before their car hit hers. The impact sent her car careening to the left, but pushed the Chevrolet to the right. Jeff looked ahead and immediately saw her reasoning. A large group of live oak trees stood just off the right side of the road ahead. Billy noticed them at the same time and turned back to the left, but it was too late. The car skidded, and though Billy frantically turned the wheel in the opposite direction, their path to the trees could not be altered. The last thing they felt was the force of the collision.

□□□□□

Alleh was ready to turn on the fuel flow. All of the complex alignment procedures were complete, and the fueling was the last step before the missile was erected to its firing elevation. The survey crews had picked up their inertial instruments and optical devices and made the final settings for the inertial navigation system in the missile. He watched as they moved to the next firing location in their group. The vehicle with the American was still parked a short distance away, but he had seen no movement to indicate anyone was very interested. Alleh pulled the whistle from his pocket and gave three short blasts, which indicated to everyone around that he was about to begin the fueling process. Seeing no movement around the missile, he opened the valves to let the nitric acid flow through the hose.

He heard the vehicle before he saw it. He looked around toward the sound and saw the small truck approaching the American's location. The two men who got out of the back of the truck were clearly officers, but in the dark, he could not tell their rank. He moved to the front of the fueling truck so that he could still see the fuel hoses and also take in the activity around the two vehicles. The taller of the two officers opened the passenger door and the American got out and stood between them; Alleh could hear them talking. Another larger truck entered the firing area and six soldiers jumped down and moved toward the two officers and the American.

Alleh couldn't make out the conversation they were having, and he assumed they were speaking English, which he did not understand. The group seemed friendly at first, but the conversation gradually became more animated. The American began to wave his arms, and two of the soldiers behind him grabbed him as he struggled to get free. The taller officer, who wore a colonel's insignia, turned and walked to Alleh and asked him how much longer he would require before firing. He realized he had been paying so much attention to the activity around the American, he had forgotten to keep a close eye on the fueling process. He checked the gauges on the fuel truck and told the colonel that the fueling should be complete in a few more minutes. Lieutenant Ramin, Alleh's group supervisor, came around

406

the end of the fuel truck, and he and the colonel walked away from Alleh so that he couldn't hear their conversation.

Alleh turned off the valves to the fuel. He relieved the pressure on the hose and slowly turned the locking handle which held the hose in place. He breathed a sigh of relief as the hose came free without incident. He knew he was being watched by the colonel and the lieutenant, and was equally concerned that he gain their respect and that he not hurt himself as he was storing the fuel hose on the vehicle. He heard the colonel tell the small group of men to bring the American to the missile. The American was struggling violently and shouting words that Alleh could not understand.

When Alleh realized what was about to happen, he nearly sank to his knees with shock. He was mesmerized by the sight of the six soldiers lifting the screaming American onto the missile. The colonel saw him staring and barked at him to go about his business. Alleh quickly finished securing the hose in its compartment and went to the passenger's side of the cab where the controls for the elevation of the missile were located. Normally, this was the point where he and his lieutenant would go through the final checklist to ensure everything was ready and then they would erect the SCUD for firing. Lieutenant Ramin was not there. He waited.

In a few minutes, the colonel told Alleh to prepare the missile for firing. Alleh activated the lever which raised the missile. He could hear the American, now sobbing uncontrollably. When the indicator showed the missile was fully erected and locked, he walked around the vehicle to make the final inspection of the missile and launcher. It felt strange to do this without his lieutenant, but he knew he had to follow the colonel's orders.

The colonel asked him if all was ready, then told him to go with the others. The other operators had gathered behind the protection of a sand dune, and Alleh joined them. He heard the colonel shout something in English to the American, and then all was quiet.

When the first missile lifted from its launcher, the American began to scream. The missile ignited the powerful rocket motor and started its upward journey. They watched the missiles become small dots of light, and Alleh thought he could still hear the screams of the American soldier.

"Well," Lieutenant Ramin said, "I hope I don't die that way."

"You speak English, Lieutenant Ramin," one of the others said. "What did the colonel shout to him?"

"He said, 'Celia says to have a nice trip.'"

🔲🔲🔲🔲🔲

When Jeff regained consciousness, he could hear the sirens in the distance. The car was on its side and a large tree branch stuck through the windshield. He struggled to unbuckle his seatbelt and look across the seat at Billy, who hung limply in his own seatbelt. He was almost obscured by tree limbs, and Jeff couldn't seem him move.

Jeff heard steam rise from the engine and the cracking of metal cooling. He got his seatbelt loose, but his door was blocked. He called to Billy, but got no response. He heard helicopters and sirens approaching. He tried to get through the front windshield, but the tree limb blocked his way, so he crawled into the back seat and kicked the glass with his foot. It wouldn't give. He reached into the front seat and felt around until he found his pistol. Aiming it at the back glass, he covered his eyes and fired. The glass shattered, but remained in place. He kicked again and the shattered glass gave way. He continued kicking until he had an opening big enough to crawl through.

As he clambered out of the car, the police arrived with several unmarked cars. He crawled to the driver's side of the car and pulled on the handle, but the door was jammed.

"Let me help." One of the men from the unmarked cars had climbed onto the car with him. They pulled together and the door, with sounds of groaning metal, came open. The first thing Jeff saw was the bone of Billy's arm protruding at a grotesque angle.

"Why don't you let me get him out, General. Is he still alive?"

"I don't know," Jeff said. "Let's find that out first." He slid into the car, put his hand on the carotid artery on Billy's neck, and felt for the pulse. Nothing.

"I can't find a pulse, but it might just be his position." Jeff reached

408

around the other side of Billy's neck and probed with his fingers. "I've got it. There's a pulse."

"Make room." A group of uniformed medics had arrived. He slid to the ground.

"He's alive," Jeff said to the medic. "Pulse is rapid. Compound fracture of the left arm. Blood from his mouth. That's all I know." The team of three medics had already surrounded Billy. They cut the seatbelt away, and went to work trying to determine the extent of his injuries.

"Do you know what happened to the other car?" Jeff asked the agent.

"Over there," the agent said indicating with a jerk of his head. "Can't tell how badly she's hurt, but she's unconscious."

Two helicopters, marked with the medical red cross, landed on the lawn of a nearby house. He thought back to the night he and Billy had huddled waist deep in the corner of a rice paddy, waiting for the Medivac helicopter for himself.

"We're going to lift him out," the medic said. "Give us a hand when we lower him. Try to keep his back as straight as possible. We don't know if there are any spinal injuries, but we've put him on a backboard just in case."

Billy's head was restrained by a cervical collar as he was lifted from the vehicle. The splint on his left arm was taped to the backboard, but the bone still showed. The medics lowered him to Jeff and the agents, who placed him on a stretcher.

"What's your best guess?" Jeff asked the medic as he jumped down from the car.

"Don't really have one. He's breathing OK and that's a good sign as far as internal injuries go. It all depends on that and his neck and back." A third helicopter landed, but this one was smaller and had no special markings. Jeff watched it land and then saw Suzy as the door opened. She asked something of one of the uniformed policemen, and he pointed in Jeff's direction. Suzy looked his way, saw Jeff, and began to run toward him.

When she got to him, Jeff could see the tears on her face. She stopped just in front of him, and then flung herself into his arms.

"Billy's hurt bad," Jeff said.

She pulled away from him and looked to the medics who were wheeling the stretcher toward the helicopter.

"Is he going to be OK?"

"I don't know. They said we could ride in the helicopter with him. How's Cindy?"

"Pretty shaken up, but basically everything is surface. They've sedated her and are taking her to the hospital. What about Celia?"

"Over there," Jeff said with a nod of his head. "She doesn't appear to be hurt as badly as Billy, but she's still unconscious. They'll bring her on the other helicopter."

❑❑❑❑❑

"Targets!"

As the sharp call came from the young sergeant who was the shift Tactical Control Assistant sitting next to him, Lieutenant Frederick looked closely at the radar screen and saw the targets at the maximum range of the radar. He watched as the sergeant moved the crosshairs over the targets and clicked the hook button to designate them for display of information. The familiar small box came on the screen containing the pertinent data on the targets, and they watched the altitude and speed increase as the trace on the radar display moved steadily toward them. At about the same time they both began to recognize the pattern, the screen blinked and the target symbol turned to a small triangle and began to flash. Another flick of the screen and the target information box changed to display data for an incoming ballistic missile and showed the impact point. The lieutenant looked up at the sergeant sitting next to him, but the soldier's attention was riveted to the screen.

"Four targets. Splashdown shows target will be within our range within ninety seconds," the sergeant said.

Lieutenant Frederick felt the coolness of the sweat on his chest.

"I wish Captain Maxwell was here."

"It'll be fine, L-T. We know what we're doing here."

410

"I wasn't in the van for any of the other firings."

In addition to his other duties before he took command, Lieutenant Frederick had been the Maintenance Officer for the Battery's vehicles and generators, and that had been a full-time job since they had received the orders to move to Israel from Germany. He had spent some time at the console for drills, but there had never been a firing on his watch. A drop of perspiration fell from his finger to the console and he moved his hands to his legs to wipe the wetness on his fatigues.

"Four targets, time to first launch seventy-five seconds. More targets!"

The lieutenant looked at the radar screen and saw the new targets. They were coming from a slightly different location, but were on roughly the same path as the first group. No sooner had he seen these when a third set appeared farther to the south.

"Holy shit."

"Relax, Lieutenant. I don't think a lot of those are going to be in our sector," the Sergeant said.

"If they are, I hope this thing works."

"Not to worry, Lieutenant."

The sergeant studied the screen and the data on the readout.

"Time to first launch sixty seconds."

The screen flicked again, and the indicator on the lead targets changed to indicate that Bravo Battery had been designated to intercept. Lieutenant Frederick could hear the sirens outside the van, warning everyone in the area of the impending attack. All eyes in the van watched as the targets on the screen made their way steadily west.

"Time to first launch forty seconds. More targets."

New traces moving east toward one of the sets of targets proclaimed that the Israeli units had fired their PATRIOTs at the SCUDs.

"Time to first launch twenty seconds."

John Frederick wiped his hands on his legs again and leaned forward to get a closer look at the impact point the computer was predicting for their assigned group of SCUDs.

"Time to first launch ten seconds. Nine, eight…"

No one spoke as the countdown continued.

"Fire command, missile one."

The lieutenant watched the indicator for the fire command on the console and saw the red light appear under missile number three of launcher number four.

"Fire command, missile two."

They counted the missiles as the sergeant announced each of the fire commands. They heard the boom and roar of the launchings as the PATRIOT missiles started on their way toward the intercept. Eight missiles left in quick succession.

❑❑❑❑❑

Ahmad parked the car among the gathering crowd. He looked around enough to take in all the activity and then checked to make sure no one was watching him. He walked into the woods bordering the lawn of the stone mansion.

He could hear the activity behind him around the site of the crash, and could hear more sirens in the distance. He came out of the woods behind the building and started making his way toward the front yard. At the front edge of the house, he stopped to look around the corner and take in the situation.

"Hey, you," he heard behind him "What are you doing here?"

Ahmad put his hand in the pocket of his heavy jacket and turned his head to see a man who looked like he might be a gardener. He turned to face the man directly.

"Are you with the police?" the gardener asked. Ahmad could not understand the English, but he stood his ground and looked at the other man. There was a slight movement of the hand in his pocket.

The gardener started to move toward him, and there was a spit from Ahmad's pocket. The gardener looked surprised and he grabbed his shoulder. Another shot. This bullet found its mark and the gardener went down. Ahmad glanced toward the action on the front lawn, but nobody was looking in his direction. He moved to the gardener and dragged the body around the corner of the house behind a row of shrubs. He threw a

412

little pine straw over the corpse and turned back to the front of the building.

He saw the helicopters on the lawn with their blades turning slowly. He watched as Jeff and Suzy crawled into the helicopter nearest the street after the stretcher had been loaded, and then that helicopter rose and left. He saw the activity by the street as another stretcher was being prepared near Sharifa's car. The pilot of the second helicopter sat idly waiting for his passenger. In the seat next to the pilot was another man Ahmad assumed was a copilot or a medical technician. Ahmad approached from the opposite side, away from the activity, and neither man paid him any attention as he walked casually to the helicopter.

He ducked under the moving rotor and moved around to the large door open to the bay in the main body of the aircraft waiting to receive the stretcher. He jumped into the bay. The sound and vibration of the rotor was too loud for him to be heard, and the two men in front did not look around. Once inside, he knew he was right about the second man when he saw he was dressed in hospital greens. Ahmad moved to a position behind the two seats and removed the silenced pistol from his pocket. He pointed it at the head of the attendant and fired twice. The pilot swung toward Ahmad, who reached out and grabbed the flight helmet. The pilot was restrained by his flight harness, and Ahmad twisted the helmet back until the pilot's head was almost horizontal. He shoved the pistol in the gaping mouth and heard the hot metal hiss as it came in touch with saliva. The pilot's eyes were bulging and crossed as he looked at the gun in front of his face.

Ahmad put his finger over his mouth in the universal sign for quiet and moved on bended knees until he was between the two seats. With one hand outstretched to keep the pistol in the pilot's mouth, he worked the attendant's harness loose and pushed his body onto the floor in front of the seat. He duck-walked back to his shooting position and reached for a blanket lying on the floor of the transport bay. He shook the blanket with his free hand until it was unfolded and then moved back to the front between the seats and spread the blanket over the dead man.

The pilot followed all of Ahmad's movements with his head, the silencer of the pistol pressing painfully against the back of his mouth. With the attendant covered by the blanket, Ahmad again gave the sign for quiet. He slowly removed the pistol from the pilot's mouth and sat on the edge of the seat facing the terrified man. With the body on the floor, there was not enough room for him to put his feet in the front, so he sat with his knees pulled up facing the pilot. He held the pistol by his side away from the back of the helicopter.

He saw the pilot moving his hands. There was a button on the end of the shaft the pilot was holding. Ahmad raised the pistol toward the front of the compartment and pulled the trigger. It spit twice and smoke came from the radio. He surveyed the instrument panel and convinced himself there were no additional radios.

He looked toward the crash scene and saw the second stretcher being wheeled toward the helicopter. He was concerned that he would be expected to help load the stretcher, but remembered the attendant had been buckled to the seat. He waited.

No words were exchanged, and no one looked in his direction as the medics climbed aboard the helicopter to secure the stretcher. One medic jumped from the bay and closed the door. The second stayed on the aircraft, and Ahmad looked to the pilot, who was looking at him. The medic yelled something Ahmad did not understand, but he assumed it was the signal that they were ready. He motioned with his hand for the pilot to take off.

The pilot did things with the controls Ahmad was familiar with from his many rides on helicopters, and he felt the engines begin to turn faster. The machine shook until he thought it was going to come apart, and then lifted from the ground as Ahmad watched the pilot closely. The aircraft lifted over the mansion and turned to an easterly direction. Ahmad used his free hand and pointed in front of the pilot to a northerly course. When the pilot turned to start to protest, Ahmad raised the pistol. The pilot moved the controls and the helicopter turned to the north. Once the aircraft was high enough for him to get his bearings, Ahmad looked at the city until he was able to locate the direction to his target. He pointed and the pilot responded by turning the helicopter to a westerly course. Ahmad moved to his knees and started his duck walk toward the back of the helicopter.

414

The medic was doing something with the stretcher and looked up when he sensed Ahmad.

"Say, who are you?"

Ahmad didn't hesitate, and the first shot found its mark. The medic flopped onto the stretcher. Ahmad reached out with his left hand, pulled the medic's body from the stretcher, and moved closer to look down at his beloved Sharifa.

"Little Desert Flower," he said as he reached out to touch her cheek. She did not move as Ahmad looked around the bay and saw the medic's bag. He glanced over his shoulder at the pilot, reached for the bag, and dumped the contents onto the floor. He stirred through the assorted medicines and medical paraphernalia until he found what he needed.

He took one of the capsules in his fingers and turned back to Sharifa. He pressed the capsule until he felt it break and held it under her nose. In a moment, she began to stir. She looked at Ahmad, but showed no signs of recognition.

"Where am I?" she asked in English.

"It is I, little flower, Ahmad," he said. He began to unbuckle the straps holding her to the stretcher.

"Ahmad, where are we?" she said. Her voice was so weak Ahmad could barely hear her over the noise of the helicopter.

"We are in an aircraft," he said. "I'm going to take you home."

"Home," she said. "Really? We're going home?"

"Yes, but we have some work to do before we can get there. Are you going to be all right?"

"Yes, I think so. What has happened?"

"I was waiting for you at the airport. When you called me on your car phone, I came this way as you directed. Then there was a car wreck, and you have been injured. We are on a helicopter taking you to the hospital, but we are not going to the hospital. We are going to the airport."

"I'm beginning to remember."

"Are you hurt bad? Can you move when we get to the airport?"

"I think I am OK. Help me up." Ahmad helped her sit. Her eyes closed, and she reached to him for support.

"Just sit here until we get to the airport."

"No. I'm all right. Help me up the rest of the way."

The bay was high enough for her to stand with a small crouch, but Ahmad's height restricted him to his knees. She stood holding onto him for a moment until her head cleared. She looked in the direction of the pilot.

"He is not a friend," Ahmad said. "Can you give him directions to the airport?"

"Yes," she said. "Help me to the front of the plane."

Ahmad moved so she could get by him. He motioned her to the right and moved on his knees until he was directly behind the pilot. He raised the pistol until it touched the pilot's cheek. When the pilot looked toward them, Sharifa moved to the second seat and sat facing him.

"Please take us to Charlie Brown Airport," she said.

"I'm sorry, but I can't hear you because of the helmet."

"Take off his helmet," she said to Ahmad in Arabic.

Ahmad nodded and put the pistol beside him on the floor. He reached with both hands and grabbed the helmet and lifted. It wouldn't move, so Ahmad pulled harder. The pilot struggled and then motioned with his hands for Ahmad to stop. He took his hands from the controls, reached to his helmet and removed it. He turned to Sharifa.

"You won't get away with this," he said.

"Then that will be most unfortunate for you. Now take us to Charlie Brown Airport."

"This is a police medical helicopter. I am going to take it to the hospital."

Sharifa turned to Ahmad.

"Shoot him in the foot," she said in Arabic.

"Did you tell him what I said?" the pilot asked Sharifa. He heard the spit from the pistol and felt the impact on his foot. It took a moment before he realized what had happened.

"My God. He shot me!" the pilot screamed.

"Yes, and he will shoot you again if I ask him. And then again. Now you have a choice. You can take us to Charlie Brown Airport with only one hole in you, or you can take us with several. If it takes any more, the last one will be in your head when we land. Do you believe me?"

416

"Yes," the pilot said. "But I don't have a radio to call them and tell them we're going to land."

"What would you do if your radio was broken and you had to make an emergency landing?" she asked.

"There are procedures for that, but they are to be used only for emergencies."

"Trust me," she said. "For you this is an emergency of life and death proportions. If this helicopter does not land safely at Charlie Brown Airport, you will die."

The pilot moved the shaft in his hands, and the aircraft turned slightly, and began to descend.

"Understand that I landed at this airport yesterday, so I will recognize where we are. There is a private jet at the east end of the tie-down area. Land near it."

"The airport won't let us land a helicopter in the tie-down area," the pilot said. Sharifa turned to speak to Ahmad.

"No!" the pilot screamed. "Don't tell him again. I'll land anywhere you want."

"Good," she said. She leaned against the back of the seat and smiled at the pilot.

"You're a real piece of work, lady."

"Is the plane ready?" she asked Ahmad.

"Yes. I called them from the car."

When the helicopter touched down, Ahmad opened the main door to the back bay. He helped Sharifa to the ground and turned to the pilot.

"I hope you burn in..."

The bullet went in the pilot's mouth as he spoke. Ahmad jumped from the helicopter. Sharifa was already at the jet, going up the stairs to the open door. Ahmad could hear sirens and looked over his shoulder at the vehicles rushing in their direction. He ran up the ladder behind Sharifa.

The plane started moving as soon as Ahmad was inside.

"They're trying to raise us on the radio!" the pilot yelled at Sharifa. "They say we can't take off."

Sharifa waved her hand to indicate they were to go ahead. Ahmad reached behind the back seat of the plane and removed a long cylinder as he yelled to Sharifa to take cover. He flipped levers, extended the sight and moved to the door. The plane was picking up speed as the vehicles rushed toward them. Ahmad put the cylinder over his shoulder, aligned the sight on the front truck and pulled the trigger. The blast from the missile filled the small plane and the missile left a trail of smoke as it sped toward the truck. The driver must have seen what happened and swerved his vehicle to avoid the oncoming projectile, but the smoke trail of the missile showed the turn as it homed in on the heat of the engine.

Ahmad saw the explosion as he was pulling the door closed. The plane moved to the main section of runway and gained speed. Automatic fire extinguishers triggered by the flames of the missile back blast had filled the cabin with white powder. Ahmad moved to the window and saw that the other vehicles had stopped. He heard the pilot yell from the front and moved so that he could see through the windshield.

A fuel truck was moving in front of them at the end of the runway, in position to block their takeoff. They could see the driver of the truck running from the vehicle.

"Can you get it up in time?" Sharifa yelled at him. The pilot gave her a sideways glance, looked back at the runway and shook his head no.

Sharifa grabbed the pistol from Ahmad's hand and pressed it hard into the cheek of the pilot.

"Do it!" she yelled at him.

The pilot reached for the throttle controls and pushed them forward into the red.

"We aren't going to make it!" he shouted as the jet gained speed.

"Go to the other runway," Sharifa shouted back.

He pushed slightly on the control shaft between his legs, and the plane veered to the left. There was a narrow field of grass between the runway they were using and the next runway.

They felt the wheels leave the blacktop. At the center of the grass divider was a small ditch for water drainage. It was just wide enough to catch the front wheel of the plane. The landing gear gave when it hit the far side of the ditch, and the nose of the plane went down. The far side of the grass

418

was sloped upward toward the second runway, and the front of the plane bounced upward when it came in contact. The back wheels made contact with the runway and the pilot pulled the stick hard to the right.

Sharifa could feel the strong force of the plane's acceleration, and the nose stayed up as the plane sped down the runway. Near the end of the pavement, the pilot pulled back on the stick between his legs, and the nose lifted. There was a vibration as the pressure built on the back wheels, and then they were airborne. Sharifa yelled a whoop, pounded her hand on the pilot's back, then moved to the rear of the plane. Everything was charred from the back blast of the missile, but there was no fire. Ahmad had flopped into one of the seats, the white powder of the fire extinguishers covering him and sticking to the sweat soaking through his jacket.

She went to him and kissed him hard and long.

"You're wonderful," she said. "Now let's go home."

◻◻◻◻◻

The crew in the PATRIOT van collectively held their breath as the roar of the missiles continued. The roar trailed off into a silence as the missiles made their way toward the incoming SCUDs. Lieutenant Frederick listened as the sergeant announced all of the major events of the first missile and then grouped the events for the remaining flights.

"Ten seconds to intercept of first missile."

He could hear more launches from the other batteries and saw the traces of the PATRIOT missiles on the radar screen as they entered the battle. The screen was now cluttered with tracks all rushing to meet each other in the sky.

"Intercept."

John watched the screen for any indication of the kill, but could not tell anything. All of the missiles reached their targets and then there was quiet. There were no traces of the SCUDs on the screen. Surely that was a good sign.

"System indicates four solid kills."

There was a cheer in the van, and then they all settled around the screen to watch the other engagements in process.

Jeff was watching CNN in Billy's hospital room when the nurse stuck her head in the door.

"General Weyland, there's a phone call for you. You can get it down the hall at the nurses' station."

The nurse closed the door to Billy's room as she left. Jeff stood from his chair and moved to the door. He took one last look at Billy in the hospital bed before he went into the hallway. The prognosis was fairly good. There didn't seem to be any internal or spinal injuries. The broken arm, some broken ribs, and a major concussion. But all was going to be OK after some healing time. Jeff had come to Billy's room from Cindy's, where he had left Suzy. Cindy was still heavily sedated, but her physical injuries were minor. The doctor had said they would just have to wait and see if Cindy would have a problem adjusting mentally. He approached the nurses' station, and the nurse handed him the phone.

"General Weyland speaking."

"Sir, this is Colonel Sampson. I am with General Powell in the White House. If you are ready, the President would like to speak with you."

"Yes, I'm ready."

There was a pause and several clicks on the phone. Then he heard the familiar voice.

"How are you, General?" the President asked

"I'm fine, sir, but we've got some banged-up troops down here."

"I understand everyone is going to recover. I'm mighty pleased for them and grateful for Mr. Walker's contribution. I understand he had to go against city hall a little."

"Yes, sir," Jeff said. "But your call to his people cleared all that up. Thanks for that."

"No problem. Glad to do it. How's your daughter faring?"

"Physically, she's going to be fine, but we won't know for a while if there will be any emotional scars. She had a pretty scary time."

"I can only imagine what that must have been like. When she's able to travel, Barbara and I would like to have the two of you to the White

House for dinner."

"I know she'd appreciate that, Mr. President. And so would I."

"Have you heard the latest on our Miss Mitchell?"

"No, sir, I haven't. I've been back and forth between hospital rooms and spent a little time with the doctor myself. I really haven't heard anything since we got on the helicopter."

"You OK?"

"Yes, sir. Nothing a little Jack Daniel's and a hot bath won't cure."

"Well, I'm sorry to say it, but they got away. There was some confusion at the airport, and by the time anyone knew who to call, the plane had made it to the coast. We scrambled fighters from South Carolina and Florida, but they weren't able to locate the plane. They were tracked by various airport radars until they made it to the ocean, but then the pilot took it right down on the deck, and the radars lost them. By the time we got the fighters to the area, there was no sight of them."

"Not too many places they could go down there. Probably Cuba or South America."

"We'll probably never know. The fighters say they had the area going south pretty well covered. The only thing for sure is that they didn't come back into an airport in the States. They left the front landing gear splattered all over Charlie Brown, so they couldn't have landed anywhere in this country without causing a great deal of attention."

"If they could land at all."

"I also wanted you to know that the predicted major attack on Israel took place. Twenty-six SCUDs were fired and there was no serious damage to Israeli citizens. I have just gotten off the phone with Prime Minister Shamir and to say he is happy would be an understatement. The PATRIOTs performed flawlessly and intercepted all of the SCUDs they were assigned. You're to be congratulated. Because of what you have done for your country, the Allied coalition is solid, and we will win this war."

"Thank you, Mr. President."

"Thank you, General Weyland. You country owes you a debt which it can never repay."

421

military success--pentagon adv22 1-91
PATRIOT missiles successful; U.S. Navy downs Iraqi vessels
USWNS Military News
adv jan 19 1991 or thereafter

By GEORGE GROWSON

WASHINGTON—The Army announced today that overnight, U.S.
forces disabled an Iraqi patrol boat, a tanker, and a
hovercraft. Saudi forces engaged and shot down two Iraqi
jets. One of the largest amphibian rehearsals since the
Korean war is taking place in the Gulf at this time by U.S.
Marines. Also during last evening, the largest single SCUD
attack of the war was launched at Israel. It has been
assumed by the media that this was the major thrust Saddam
Hussein had been grouping his resources to execute. The
exact number of SCUDs launched by Iraq is not known, but
estimates are that as many as twenty missiles were fired at
a variety of targets within Israel, mostly in the vicinity
of Tel Aviv. According to the formal military briefing from
the Headquarters of the Allied Coalition, U.S. and Israeli-
manned PATRIOT missile sites successfully intercepted the
majority of the SCUDs fired, and those which were not
intercepted fell harmlessly on unpopulated areas.

SEVENTEEN

January 22, 1991

Air Corridor Juliet

Kingdom of Saudi Arabia

3:15 PM

"Eagle Flight Leader, this is Eagle Two, over."

"Go ahead, Eagle Two."

"Roger. I have positive indication of receipt of target frequency at code Bravo three two four. Bearing zero two seven. Range unknown."

"Roger Eagle Two. You have the lead. All other Eagles will follow."

The U.S. Air Force hunter-killer flight was made up of two F-4G Wild Weasel "hunter" and two F-16C "killer" aircrafts. The formation made a slight correction in their flight path as they turned to the bearing detected by Eagle Two. They had left King Abdul Aziz Royal Saudi Air Base in Dhahran with unusual orders to look for transmitters in Iraq within a given frequency range. The technicians at the base had worked through most of the night to recode the receivers and missiles on the airplanes to lock on the specific signal they were now seeking. The leader of Eagle flight, Captain Earnest Horn of the Fifty-Second Tactical Fighter Wing mobilized from Spangdalem Air Base, Germany, had asked what type of transmitter they were looking for. "Don't know" had been the answer. What did the transmitter look like? "Don't know" had been the answer again. Is there one or more than one? "Maybe" was the answer. The only definite information given was that when the green light on his hostile receiver box lit, the flight was to locate, engage and destroy the emitter which triggered it.

"Eagle Two, do you still have the signal?"

"Affirmative, Eagle Leader. I have the signal, and I am closing on target. Be advised this vector has us heading very close to prohibited bombing areas."

"Roger Eagle Two. Do you have range to target?" The Wild Weasel aircraft was the special air platform the Air Force used to seek out and destroy enemy radars and communication sites. With the latest state-of-the-art in electronic listening equipment, the Weasels could find such high-value targets as command and control centers, air defense sites, or any other location which required radio or radar systems to operate. They had first been used in Vietnam and, updated significantly, were still the Air Force's number one attack craft against any system emitting radio waves. The Weasel aircraft worked in pairs, which provided both air cover and additional firepower at the target area.

The electronic technician back at the base had told Captain Horn he wouldn't get a green light until he was within ten miles or so of his target. The receivers on the planes would only pick up the signals in the band of interest at longer ranges. Several types of emitters would be in the frequency range of interest, so they would just have to check each one they detected until they found the one that produced the green light.

"Eagle Leader, this is Eagle Two. I now have a range of five-five miles to target."

"Roger Eagle Two. We are in tow."

"Eagle Leader, this is Eagle Two. Be advised target range and bearing puts target inside prohibited bombing area number two seven."

"Roger Eagle Two, stand by."

Captain Horn flipped his radio frequency switch to allow him to talk to the tactical air control center in the underground bunker at Riyadh.

"Desert Control Three, this is Eagle Flight Leader."

"This is Desert Control Three. Go ahead Eagle."

"Roger, Control. I have a target on my indicators which is a possible for my mission. I do not, repeat, do not have a green confirmation as yet. Possible target location is within prohibited bomb zone two seven. I am requesting instructions."

"Roger, Eagle Leader, stand by."

Captain Horn was watching from the cockpit of his Phantom as they sped north through Iraq, flying close to the ground to avoid enemy radar. This seemed strange to Horn since most of the radars in Iraq had been shut down already. But tactics were tactics and theirs was to come in low, find and destroy the emitters, and then go high and get out quickly.

"Eagle Flight Leader, this is Desert Control Three."

"This is Eagle Flight Leader. Go ahead, Desert Control."

"Eagle Flight Leader, you are cleared to perform surgical strike of target within prohibited bomb zone two-seven. I repeat, you are cleared to perform surgical strike of target in prohibited bomb zone two-seven."

"Roger Control. Eagle Flight Leader requests confirmation of order by code, over."

"Roger Flight Leader. Stand by."

Captain Horn reached for the list in the sleeve of his flight jacket. He pulled out the list and clipped it on the board in his lap. The short list was covered in plastic and had the classified codes for the day.

"Eagle Flight Leader, this is Desert Control. I confirm order by code charley-charley-kilo, over."

Horn quickly checked his code list and noted that CCK was the correct code for enroute mission changes.

"Desert Control, I confirm code is charley-charley-kilo. Eagle Flight Leader en route to target. Out."

He switched the frequency back to his flight.

"Eagle Two, this is Eagle Flight Leader. We are confirmed to perform surgical strike on target in prohibited area two-seven."

"Eagle Flight Leader, this is Eagle Flight Two. How are we going to surgically strike something when we don't know what it is?"

"We'll just have to assume we'll be able to recognize it when we get there. Eagle Two, where do you show target now?"

"I have target on the nose, two-one miles."

"Roger. Eagle Flight, this is Eagle Flight Leader. We will slow our approach and let Eagle Two move ahead to locate and identify the target. We will come in behind Eagle Two after positive ID and description and perform surgical strike. HARM Missiles and two-zero-mike-mike. Eagle Flight acknowledge."

"Eagle Flight Leader, this is Eagle Two. I confirm surgical strike with HARM and two-zero-mike-mike."

"Eagle Flight Leader, this is Eagle Three. I confirm surgical strike with HARM and two-zero-mike-mike."

"Eagle Flight Leader, this is Eagle Four. I confirm surgical strike with HARM and two-zero-mike-mike."

"Eagle Three and Four, I am slowing to three-five-zero."

Captain Horn heard the clicks of the radios from the two other aircrafts as he watched Eagle Two move away from them to the north. They flew at reduced speed for several minutes, and he was just beginning to wonder if he would have to circle when the radio buzzed in his ear again.

"Eagle Flight Leader, this is Eagle Two. I have a green indication, and I have the target in sight. It's a long building lying from northeast to southwest. There's a cluster of six or so antennae at the north end. No personnel in sight. No signs of Anti Aircraft Artillery. I repeat, I have positive identification."

"Roger, Eagle Two. Eagle Flight, arm 'em up. Eagle Three, you're first. Left to right. Eagle Four, you work the antennae. Eagle Two, you're the lookout. Let's be careful."

The hunter-killer team went into a practiced formation for attack. They came in low, three abreast. About a mile before the target, they nosed up steeply, rolled over to get a good look at the target and turned to deliver their missiles and machine gun fire. As they swooped down on the target, each aircraft fired one High-Speed Anti-Radiation Missile, called a HARM, which homed in on the target's radio or radar transmissions. The other aircraft followed with twenty millimeter fire from the cannon located in the nose of the aircraft. On passing the target, they each nosed up and made an almost vertical climb and loop to make a quick damage assessment.

"Eagles Three and Four, make a second run down the long axis of the building. See if you can't get something in the front doors. Eagle Two, follow me for another HARM pass at the other transmitters."

"Roger. Eagle Flight Leader, be advised that I have lost my green indication."

"Roger, Eagle Two. So have I. My guess is we killed the transmitter."

"Or they shut it down."

"In that case, we'll make sure it doesn't come back up. Ready for the next pass?"

"Roger, ready."

"Here we go."

The four aircrafts continued to work the building until their load of ammunition was depleted. They executed a rendezvous above the target so the on-board cameras could make one last set of pictures for the bomb damage assessment crew and then headed south. Captain Horn switched the frequency on his radio once again.

"Desert Control Three, this is Eagle Flight Leader."

"This is Desert Control Three. Go ahead Eagle Flight Leader."

"Roger, Desert Control. Eagle Flight Leader reports mission accomplished."

"Roger, Eagle Flight Leader. You are cleared to return to base."

"Roger, Desert Control. Have a nice weekend."

January 22, 1991
Fairfax, Virginia
9:15 AM

The Ford sedan made its way down the quiet residential street as the two men inside looked at the houses, checking each one against the specific address they had been given. Apparently finding the right number, they pulled to the curb and got out of the car. From a distance, they looked like twins since they both were wearing dark gray flannel suits. They even had on matching hats and dark glasses. They walked to the door of the house and rang the bell, and after a short wait, the ring was answered by an attractive middle-aged lady.

"Mrs. Grant?"

"Yes."

"Ma'am, we need to speak to General Grant. Is he in?"

"Yes, but he's resting. He gave specific instructions that he didn't want to be disturbed. He's been working extremely long hours with the war, you know. Can you come back later?"

"No, ma'am, I'm afraid we can't. We really need to talk to him now."

"Well, maybe I can give him a message, and he can call you later," she said and started to push the door closed.

"No, ma'am, I'm afraid we'll have to insist." The man who had been doing the speaking looked at the other man and nodded. They both reached into their jacket pockets, removed their badges and displayed them to Mrs. Grant.

"Ma'am, I am Special Agent Al Forbes, and this is Agent Joe Ritch. We're from the Secret Service and are here on official business relating to the security of the United States. Now would you please get your husband for us?"

"Yes, of course." She looked nervously to the rear of the house and then back to the two men at her door. "I'll be just a minute. Would you like to come in?"

"No, ma'am. We'll wait right here."

She went toward the rear of the house while the two agents stood on the front stoop waiting for the General to come to the door. Neither of them had ever visited the home of a Lieutenant General before, nor had they ever arrested one.

Then they heard the scream. They ran into the house in the direction the General's wife had gone and followed the sound of the scream to what appeared to be the master bedroom. They ran across the room to the bathroom where Mrs. Grant stood in the doorway, still screaming. Al took her by her shoulders from behind as gently as he could and turned her away from the bathroom. Ritch went by him into the large master bath, his sidearm drawn and held high. In the tub was the large body of the General, fully dressed and covered with more blood than either of them had ever seen. On the side of the tub was an Army bayonet.

□□□□□

January 22, 1991
Mercy Hospital
Boston, Massachusetts
9:15 PM

Carol Layne looked up from her nurses' station to view the third floor hallway. It was a quiet night. Tuesday nights were always the quietest of the week, and she used the time to get caught up on the week's paperwork. She had just completed her rounds after coming on shift at seven o'clock, and unless something extraordinary happened, it would be uneventful until she was relieved the next morning. The night shift wasn't so bad. She only had to work three nights during the week, plus she made premium pay. The extra money really helped since her ex-husband had left the state and she hadn't been able to get alimony or child support payments. Her lawyers were working, but they were probably going to cost her more than she would ever collect.

A noise from down the hall made her look up to see a couple coming from the critical patient care wing of the ward. She glanced at them briefly to make sure neither of them were patients and went back to her work at the desk. She looked up to speak as they went by the desk, but they had turned toward the elevator and she couldn't see anything but their backs.

Fish waited until he heard the door closing before he turned around in the elevator to push the button for the lobby. When the elevator doors opened again, there was nothing but emptiness in the entire lobby. Even the Red Cross volunteer reception center was shut down, and no one was in the main lobby room as Sarah led him across the floor to the front door. He had been unconscious when they had brought him in through the emergency room, so he didn't know if the doors were automatic or not. There was a rubber mat in front of the doors, and the look of relief was clear on Fish's face as the doors swung open when Sarah stepped on the mat. That was the third and last hurdle he had been concerned about. His plan required getting dressed, making it past the nurses' station and out the front door.

As soon as they were outside the door, he leaned against one of the pillars of the portico. His face flowed with sweat, and he grimaced in pain as Sarah left him and went toward the parked cars. The coolness of the metal post felt good against his hot cheek. Lights came on in a station wagon in the parking lot, and he sighed audibly with relief as she pulled the car to a stop beside him. He waited for her to come around to him and help.

"In the back seat," he said.

She opened the back door and helped him to the car, and he made an audible grunt as he leaned forward to get into the opening.

"For once, I'm glad you talked me into buying a full-sized car instead of a compact or a van," he said as he fell into the seat. "I never would've made it into either of those."

"You're crazy," Sarah said. "Do you want to tell me what's going on?"

"No. Did you bring me the bag?"

"Yes. But what in the world are you wanting with that? What's so all fired important that you had to get out of a hospital bed to have it?"

"Where'd you put it?"

"On the front seat," she said. "Now are you going to tell me what's going on?"

"No. Do me a favor and move the bag here beside me." She did what he asked.

"Now, head for the White Horse Tavern," he said. "But stop a few blocks before you get there."

As Sarah drove the car, Fish unzipped the bag and fumbled with the contents until his fingers gripped a small wooden box. He pulled the box from the bag and placed it on his lap. He took a key ring from his jacket pocket and fumbled with the keys for a few minutes before selecting one. His hands felt the familiar key, which had been a constant reminder of the lock it fit for nearly twenty-five years. He put the key into the lock of the box and had to exert a little pressure to get it to turn. Every movement sent spasms of pain up his arm and shoulder, but he continued to work the key until the lock opened.

432

He opened the box, reached in and took out an object wrapped in an oiled cloth. The old oil had almost dried and made the cloth stick to the fingers and palms of his hands. He unwrapped the cloth to reveal a long-barreled thirty-eight caliber police special pistol with a matching silencer and a box of cartridges. He worked slowly and deliberately through the pain to attach the silencer to the pistol.

"I remember the day Cap'n Weyland gave this to me. We'd been with a Battalion of Mechanized Infantry on a routine mission to sweep through several fields where there were suspected Viet Cong hideaways, and we stumbled on a small group of soldiers in uniforms, which was very unusual that far south. After a gun battle, a dozen or so enemy soldiers ran into a small patch of woods. Our Dusters went in to flush them, and when that was done, we'd captured what turned out to be a North Vietnamese sapper team complete with explosives, long-range sniper rifles and this box. Cap'n Weyland gave it to me, and I've not opened it in over twenty years."

"What's in there?" she asked again, this time trying to look over the seat.

"Sarah, for God's sake, just drive the car."

"I still wish you'd tell me what's going on."

With the pistol assembled and loaded, he pushed the button to lower the window. Sarah had already arrived at the White Horse, and was stopped on the side of the road a few blocks away.

"Drive by slowly," he said. She started the car and did as he asked.

"Max, please," she begged. "Tell me what's going on. This is close to where they found you. Does this have to do with your beating? What are you doing back there?"

"Just drive. Do like I tell you, and everything will be all right."

She drove slowly by the popular night spot. Even on a Tuesday night, the parking lot was fairly crowded.

"I'm surprised there are this many people here," she said.

"Tuesday night," he said. "Lingerie modeling night. Big crowd of regulars from work."

A red import car parked by the curb caught Max's eye, and he looked at it closely as they went by.

"Go around the block and go back to the other side of the club. When we get to the other side, park in one of the spaces there. It'll be OK as long as you're in the car."

She did as he asked. When the car was stopped in a spot where they could see the door of the club, she turned off the engine.

"Keep the engine running," he said.

"Max…"

"Don't ask any more questions. Let's just wait here for awhile."

Thirty minutes passed.

Forty-five. Several people had left the club, but none seemed to interest Fish. Then a lone figure came out and headed in their direction, and Fish moved painfully on the seat and opened the door to get out.

"Max…"

"Just trust me and do what I ask, Sarah," Fish said. "Wait for me here. I just want to talk to him."

Fish moved as spryly as his body would allow in the direction of the oncoming man. They met near a grove of trees.

Doug Glover was visibly surprised as he recognized Fish.

"Max, they told us you were dead."

"I know what you thought. I need to talk to you." Fish pulled his hand from under his jacket and leveled the pistol at Doug's midsection. "Let's go over there."

Doug led the way in the direction Fish indicated into some large trees covering a small park. The dark was eerie as random streaks of light from the streetlights found their way through the canopy.

"Max, I can explain all of this."

"I'm not interested in your explanations. If you're a religious man, Doug Glover, say your prayers."

"Max. They made me do it. They…"

Fish was staring so hard into the eyes of the man in front of him that he saw the reflection of the flash from the pistol in their gleam as he heard the muffled report from the silencer. He watched as the eyes became grossly exaggerated and expanded, first reflecting surprise and then pain. Max pulled the trigger again and the light flashed two more times while the body was falling to the ground. He stumbled a little as

434

he turned and walked as fast as he could to the car. Sarah reached across the seat and opened the door for him, and he collapsed on the seat.

"Drive!" he shouted. "Fast and then slow. Go."

"Max." She didn't move. Both of her hands were on the steering wheel. She was looking straight ahead with tears streaking her cheeks, but she did not move.

"Sarah, if you fail us here, we're dead meat." Fish was gasping with pain and near collapse. "If we can make it to the first corner before anybody comes, we're safe. Drive, Sarah, drive!" he shouted again. He felt the car start to move and then accelerate down the street. He was turned on the seat so he could look out the back window to see the club.

"Turn right!" he shouted. She pulled on the wheel and turned the car. As they made the turn with tires squealing, he looked in the direction of the club. No one was on the street yet. He slumped on the seat.

"Slow down now, Sarah," he said. "And take me back to the hospital."

"Max, you shot a man."

"No, Sarah," he said. "That wasn't a man I shot. I'm not sure what it was, but it wasn't a man. He was responsible for soldiers of his own country being killed unnecessarily in combat, and no man would do that. Let me know when we're at the river bridge."

At the bridge, she stopped the car. He tried to sit up, but he couldn't.

"Sarah," he said. "You're going to have to do something I didn't want to have to ask you to do. Come around to my door."

Sobbing, she opened her door and came around to his side.

"Take it," he said, pushing the box toward her. "Take it all and throw it into the river."

"I can't," she said. "I can't touch that thing. It killed a man."

"The man it killed was a murderer. He watched them beat me and leave me for dead. He killed young Americans fighting for their country. Now take it and throw it in the river."

She reached into the car, took the pistol and the box and, in one motion, flung them over the railing of the bridge.

"The cartridges, too," he said.

She reached back into the car for the box of cartridges and flung them into the river without looking over her shoulder.

"Now drive me to the hospital."

The walk to his hospital room went uneventfully. Sarah helped him to the front door and into the elevator unnoticed. On his floor, he walked as straight as he could to his room. He went to the bed and collapsed. After a long while, he eased off the bed and began the process of getting himself and the room back in shape. He had just finished taking his clothes off, putting them in the floor of the closet and crawling back into the bed when the nurse came into the room. She put the thermometer in his mouth and began to take his blood pressure. She removed the thermometer and read it before putting it away.

"How are we feeling this evening, Mr. Fisher?" she asked.

"OK, I guess," Fish said. "I'm having a little pain. Do you think you could get me something?"

"Of course. Are you not having a good evening, then?" she asked.

"Oh, yes," Fish said with a smile, in spite of the pain it caused. "I'm having a very good evening. In fact, I'm feeling much better now, thank you."

January 22, 1991
Miami, Florida
10:30 AM

The yacht named "Majestic" slowly eased out of the Miami Municipal Marina and headed for deep water. She was a white 122-footer and the gleaming craft cut a wide path in the channel as she made her way through the south Florida boat traffic. Sharifa was in a lounge chair on the fantail, enjoying the sun. As the boat began to clear the traffic from Miami, she stood and removed the wraparound skirt and the light blouse. What was left was the bottom portion of a string bikini, and the warm south Florida sun felt good on her bare body. She picked up her empty drink glass and walked to the bar at other side of the fantail. The water of the Atlantic was

436

unusually calm, and the boat was smooth as it reached cruising speed. She mixed herself another drink, returned to the chaise and dozed in the warm sun as the big yacht made its way steadily south.

Ahmad came through the doors of the main cabin toward her, and if either of them was feeling self-conscious about her nakedness, they didn't show it.

"I came to fix you a drink, but I see you already have one."

"Just think, Ahmad. A few hours and we'll be in Cuba. A short flight from there to South America and then the flight that will take us home."

"Yes, it will be quite a homecoming."

"I wonder what has happened there. My mind is a jumble of the events of the last few days."

"As yet, we do not know. Maybe we will receive word soon."

Sharifa chuckled at some private thought.

"Yes?"

"I was thinking of the whimpering American General. The infidels are such fools to be tricked that way by a woman. It was so easy. I'm happy to be leaving this country and returning to my homeland and the man for whom we have accomplished our mission."

"Where did you leave the General?"

"I didn't. He left me, crying."

"It was quite a day."

"Yes, it was," she said, turning to look out at the sea. "I just wish we knew the outcome of our efforts."

"I must go below," Ahmad said as he left the rear of the boat.

Sharifa lay back on the chaise to get more sun on her body. She had just dozed off again when she heard someone and opened her eyes to see Ahmad looking down at her. In his huge hand was a folded piece of paper which he handed to her. She unfolded the message and saw that it was a telefax which she assumed the boat had received from Miami by cellular phone. She read the three short lines.

"The mission has failed. Code discovered and nullified. U.S. PATRIOT missiles successfully intercepted all special SCUDs." The yacht continued on its course out of the Miami harbor. Sharifa was quiet as she rose from the chair and stood by the rail and looked out to sea.

"How could it possibly have happened?" she said, looking back to the sea.

"I don't know," Ahmad said.

"It had to be connected somehow to Weyland. Damn that lousy Turk for missing the chance to put him out of the way. Maybe we can still recapture the initiative. At least we are going to have to try."

The boat pitched and then yawed as it slowed and began a right turn.

"I have a surprise for you," Ahmad said as he stood behind her.

As she turned, the door to the main cabin opened, and she saw Al Hamie coming onto the fantail. In panic, she looked over her shoulder but they were too far from the mainland for him to be recognized. Then she reached for her blouse to cover herself.

He chuckled at her awkwardness.

"I am embarrassed to be in your sight with so little clothing."

"I am sorry, little one," he said turning away from her as she buttoned her blouse. "I had hoped this would be a celebration for us."

"It appears I have failed you."

"No, you have not failed me," he said turning back to her and taking her in his arms, "any more than I have failed our people by choosing you."

"I am so ashamed," she said, her face down and her eyes staring at the teak decking of the fantail.

"Don't be," he said, reaching for her chin to raise her face to his. "You have nothing to be ashamed of. We have not failed. We have only not yet won. The Americans have saved themselves once again. But there will be another time." He reached out and kissed her, first on one cheek and then the other.

"I love you," she whispered.

"And I love you, little desert flower."

He turned and walked by Ahmad as he went in the door towards the main cabin. Sharifa turned her back to Ahmad and moved toward the lounge chair where the rest of her clothes still lay. She paused, removed the locket from around her neck, walked back to Ahmad and placed it in his hand and then walked to the rail, looking out at the sea again.

She stood by the rail and turned to look at Ahmad. Tears ran down her cheek as she looked deep into his eyes. Finally, he couldn't stand the look of her any more and he looked down at his clenched fist. She turned back to the rail and in one motion, she leaned forward and let herself roll over the edge and into the water.

Ahmad moved slowly to the rail and stood for a long while looking into the blue water. He watched the spot where he had seen her go under until he couldn't see it anymore. He looked into his hand at the small locket and closed his fist around it again, using the back of his hand to wipe the tears from his cheek. He waited there looking out at the sea until he no longer wept, and then walked toward the door of the main cabin.

□□□□□

January 24, 1991
American Airlines Flight 221
10:45 AM

Jeff leaned back in the airline seat and tried to stretch his cramped legs. He twisted in the seat again, trying to find a comfortable position.

"You OK?" Suzy asked from beside him, looking up from the magazine she was reading.

"Yeah. At least I will be after I've been out of this seat for a month or so."

"Anything interesting in the paper?"

"Not really. Some General stabbed himself in Washington, four million SCUDs were shot down over Israel by PATRIOTs, and the Knesset elected George Bush their new leader."

"Why so glum?"

"I just can't help but wonder what made General Grant throw it all away."

"You underestimated the power of a woman," she said with a smile.

"I did indeed. That woman, in particular. I guess the stakes were much higher than he realized when he made his pact with the devil."

"Aren't they always?"

"Yeah, I guess. Kinda makes you wonder what it's all about, doesn't it?"

"Well," she said, "cheer up. For the first time in a while, the future looks bright. Fish's recovery is progressing well and he'll soon be released from the hospital. Billy has been forgiven. Cindy is getting stronger every day. I've agreed to leave Washington and come to Alabama to marry you, and PATRIOT is shooting down SCUDs left and right in both Saudi Arabia and Israel. You've made a new agreement with the Star Wars group to use their technology for the next upgrade to PATRIOT. Hopefully, the war will soon be over and you can get back to your life as you knew it last year."

"Yeah. All's right with the world, that's for sure."

The plane landed and began the taxi to the new Huntsville International Airport. The flight attendant stood from her safety seat and reached for the intercom.

"Ladies and gentlemen, welcome to Huntsville, Alabama, home of the PATRIOT."

Yeah.